UNNATURAL CAUSES

Despite her passion to defend the underdog, determined London lawyer Geri Lander is forced to admit that Joanna Pascoe doesn't have much of a case. What happened to her husband is just another senseless tragedy. Then as she digs a little deeper Geri stumbles on a frightening discovery. Thomas Pascoe's death was not the result of food poisoning, but something far worse – a deadly bacterium, a so-called 'super-bug'.

Geri's fight for justice is thwarted at every turn, as it seems to be in everyone else's interest to cover up the truth. Meanwhile, more people are dying...

UNNATURAL CAUSES

UNNATURAL CAUSES

by

Janet Bettle

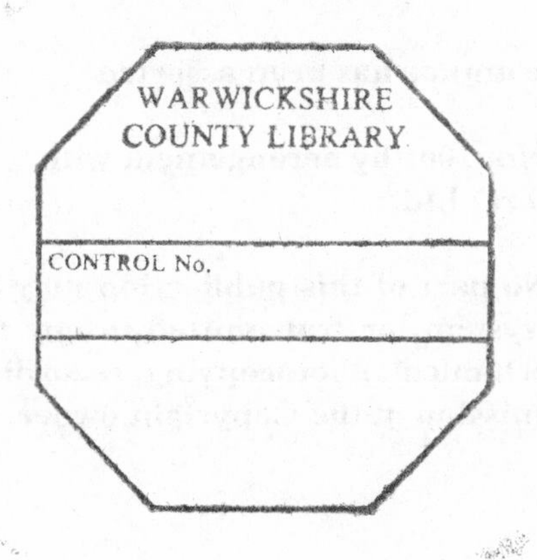

Magna Large Print Books
Long Preston, North Yorkshire,
BD23 4ND, England.

British Library Cataloguing in Publication Data.

Bettle, Janet
Unnatural causes.

A catalogue record of this book is available from the British Library

ISBN 0-7505-1656-9

First published in Great Britain in 1999
by Judy Piatkus (Publishers) Ltd.

Published in Large Print 2001 by arrangement with Judy Piatkus (Publishers) Ltd.

Magna Large Print is an imprint of Library Magna Books Ltd.

Printed and bound in Great Britain by
T.J. (International) Ltd., Cornwall, PL28 8RW

Author's Note

This is a work of fiction. In a work of this type, it is inevitable that there will be characters who are immoral, grasping and deeply unpleasant. All the characters in this book are products of my imagination. Reference to political offices and their occupants are made merely to provide a realistic setting for this novel. Names, characters, places and incidents are either the product of my imagination or used fictitiously. Should it transpire that despite my checking there are persons with similar or identical names or other characteristics to characters in this novel it must be emphasised that such resemblance is entirely coincidental and unintended.

There are quite a few Geris out there in the real legal world – female and male – prepared to risk everything to make sure that the boundaries are constantly being pushed. Without them, we would be nowhere. This book is dedicated to them all.

Thanks are due to my family – particularly Vernon who read the text through and helped enormously with the medical background; and to my sister Pat for encouragement.

Friends, too, deserve thanks – Pauline for her unfailing interest in the book; Helen and Lyndsay Cox for their great hospitality and invaluable help with some of the legal aspects.

Thank yous are also due to my agent, Carole, for taking the book on and for her suggestions. The various professionals who also advised must be acknowledged – thanks, all of you – you know who you are.

Preface

The autumn light insinuated its way through the white blinds and cast wavering orange strands on to the body. It was still warm as the two men set carefully about their task. They knew their business well and worked quickly and efficiently.

There was no heartbeat. Gloved hands felt for an absent pulse. A small beam of light was reflected back from unseeing eyes.

The room was silent, its windows permanently closed to the noise of the London streets below. The sounds from the rest of the building – the clatterings, bleeps and cries – were too remote to be heard, sealed off by two sets of doors and a long, bleak corridor. By the same token, the noises from inside the room – the shrieks of pain, sobs and prayers to God – had gone unheard outside its walls.

Eventually, the senior of the two men was satisfied and retreated to a corner to deal with the arrangements for disposal. The death, of course, had been no surprise and plans had already been put in hand for a swift, discreet disposal. Cremation, of necessity, and before nightfall at that.

The consultant struggled a little with the extra document, being unfamiliar with the questions it posed. The completed form was placed in the envelope which had been provided. He'd been told to keep it separate from the medical notes and on no account to allow it to be photocopied. It would be collected later that afternoon.

Their task was over. The doctors were relieved. Other hands would take over now. They could re-enter the land of the living.

Chapter One

It was deadlock.

Geri Lander looked at the faces around the polished maple table before she spoke. She had to sound as though she was in control. Any hint of self-doubt, and they'd close in on her. I've got fifty percent, she told herself. I only need Pete with me and the others can go to hell. She repeated the question, her voice low and tone even.

'Are you with me or not?'

The day had started with a high-pitched scream.

'Dad!'

It was enough to wake Geri, but without registering in her conscious mind. She lay for a moment, her body sprawled awkwardly in the double bed. It had taken her a long time to get to sleep and the bedding was in disarray, evidence of her desperate attempts to find a comfortable position.

'Dad, don't die! Stay here, I'm sorry...'

It was Rory. Real terror in his voice.

Geri raced along the landing to her son. She could see him in the gloom, sitting bolt upright in bed.

'Darling, I'm here ... it's only a dream ... it's Mum.'

She sat on the bed and drew him into her arms.

Tension seemed to drain out of him and he started to shake.

'Mum, it was so bad.'

She spoke softly to him.

'I know.'

'No. It was the same, but his eyes were open. He was looking at me and it was *my fault.*'

'Rory, it's all right. It wasn't anyone's fault.'

'But he seemed to be saying something... I couldn't hear him, but I knew what he meant...'

She held him even closer.

'It was a dream, Rory. Sometimes strange things happen in them, but they're not true.'

He started to sob.

'Mum, I'm frightened.'

She moved under his duvet.

'I'm here now. Let's snuggle up.'

Rory nodded tearfully and lay down again. She turned towards him, chin on his tousled hair, arms around his back, and held him tight, willing his demons to depart. Gradually the sobs subsided and he found his way back to sleep. Geri lay beside him, listening as his breathing became steadier.

She couldn't sleep now. It was uncomfortable, wedged on the edge of the single bed. She couldn't turn over for fear of waking her son. And last night's disquieting thoughts had returned.

The elation of a big win. Five hundred thousand pounds after a two-week hearing. It had been a record amount for post-traumatic shock. She had destroyed the company witnesses in cross-examination, eliminated any case they might have had. That felt good.

But with thoughts of the case came the toe-curling memory of what had happened afterwards. She ought to get in touch with him, apologise. It was hardly his fault that he looked as he did, after all.

She finally crept back into her own bed at five-thirty, and slept for two and a half hours. The next thing she heard was the sound of her son padding downstairs. Geri listened carefully, out of habit. At eleven, he was no more likely to tumble than she was.

'Christ! It's gone eight!'

She must have slept right through the alarm clock.

'Rory, can you get dressed – RIGHT AWAY. I mean it, we're really late.'

She heard him retracing his footsteps and flung open the door of her wardrobe. Not the sensible suit again. Two weeks of that was enough for anyone. Her eyes settled on the dark green micro mini. It could go with a roll neck jumper and the burgundy jacket.

Geri dressed quickly, stretching her long legs down the opaque tights. Her comfortable, clumpy shoes were just too tempting. She wasn't in Court today. It would be a quiet day spent catching up with the backlog. So what if she didn't look like a proper solicitor once in a while? The clothes looked good on her anyhow. At a shade under six foot tall and reed thin, anything did.

'Mum, you're in the paper again!'

Rory must be downstairs already.

'Coming.'

He was in the kitchen, sitting at the scrubbed oak table. Geri threw bread in the toaster and searched for the marmalade while he read to her.

'"Colin Evans, a Derbyshire teacher, won record damages yesterday at the High Court..."' He paused as something else caught his eye. 'Oh, look, Mum, there's a side bit all about you.'

He started reading the profile. God, she'd had no idea they were doing that.

'"Geri Lander, 35, took over the high-profile law firm set up by her late husband, Simon Lander, after his..."'

She breathed in sharply. Not now, not like this. *Please.*

'"...death in 1996. Since then..."'

She could breathe again.

'"...she has made sure that the practice remains at the cutting edge of legal reform. The Islington-based firm has been involved with landmark decisions on safety issues. Friends point to Ms Lander's remarkable touch for finding winning cases.

'"One said yesterday: 'Geri simply has a nose for success ... she can spot the case which will lead to a change in the law and won't give up until she gets her way.'"'

Geri smiled to herself. Couldn't have been one of her partners. They'd wanted her to settle a year ago for a third of the damages that were eventually awarded. They would use phrases like 'obsessive', 'flogs moribund horses', and 'won't take a realistic view'.

She put toast and marmalade in front of her son. She'd skip breakfast herself and get a

Danish at eleven.

'Here, quick as you can, gorgeous. And don't take this newspaper stuff too seriously, Rory. It's just a journalist trying to liven things up a little. It's the Judges that change things, not people like me.'

Finally ready, they set out through the Islington streets in her battered Renault. As they turned on to the Essex Road and the inevitable traffic jam, Geri turned and smiled at her son.

'Thanks for getting yourself up so quickly, Rory. I must have slept through the alarm.'

He grinned at her.

'No worries, Mum.'

He was so like his father. At times she would watch him quietly, noting the expressions, the gestures. It was mesmerising. But, like her, he carried a terrible burden.

As they pulled away into the maze of streets near Rory's school, his good mood seemed to ebb away. She parked the car nearly beside the entrance, and he turned towards her.

'Er, Mum, I didn't like to mention it earlier but I'm not feeling too good. And it's getting worse.'

'You seem all right to me.'

Geri hated these moments. Rory had got himself up, eaten his breakfast, collected his books, all without complaint. Was he brewing something or did his illness have more to do with neglected homework? Or was it the nightmare and he didn't want to mention it?

'I've got stomach ache. It started after breakfast and got worse in the car.'

She looked at him closely. She just had to get to

work today. She'd been out of the office for two weeks. It would be chaos until she got on top of things again. But if he really was ill...

'I don't think you're too bad, Rory. Just go in and see how it goes. The school will always ring me if they think you're not well.'

She wanted to cross her fingers as she said it. Geri Lander had been known to reduce a company hatchet man to tears in the witness box. Each of her partners could recall ferocious outbursts from her which had left them reeling. Geri was no soft touch.

But for some reason she lived in dread of the silent disapproval of Rory's teachers. They must think she was failing him somehow: working all hours, sending an eclectic variety of after-school carers to pick him up. And there had been the business of her husband's death...

Well, they'd have to carry on disapproving. There was nothing she could do about it.

Except hope that Rory was OK. Anxiously, she looked at him again. He certainly looked healthy. Impulsively, she reached over and kissed him on the nose.

'Mum!'

He looked around to make sure none of his friends had seen her. Satisfied that they were undetected, he grinned at her and undid his seatbelt.

'Ingrid will pick you up, Rory. I'll be back as soon as I can.'

He nodded and got out of the car. She watched him scan the groups meandering up to the school gate. Seeing someone he knew, he moved off towards the entrance and was soon out of sight.

Geri started the car and pulled away towards the main road. Senior partnership in the firm definitely had its advantages. She could drop her son off at school every morning and arrive at the office at 9.20 without fear of censure. At least, not to her face.

After a brief crawl through the traffic on Upper Street, Geri reached the offices of Lander Ross & Co. She parked the car in her usual space at the side of the entrance. The building had been a gentleman's townhouse once, and still boasted original fireplaces and an interior they were forbidden to change. Not that Simon had been one for decoration, anyhow – the magnolia emulsion that he and Geri had applied six years previously during a quiet weekend was still there, albeit rather tattily in places.

In any event, no one expected a radical Islington firm to emanate the designer lawyer chic of the City firms less than a mile away. It suited Geri rather well to work in this old building where everyone had their own room and the windows still opened. She had no desire to work in an anonymous subdivision of some law factory, in which every office was designed to fit in with the corporate ethos. She was perfectly comfortable in her rather shabby and inefficiently large room with her Van Gogh prints.

As Geri walked into the reception area, she smiled at Tracey, the newest recruit to the firm. Tracey grinned back. The good thing about Mrs Lander was that you never knew what to expect. That outfit!

'Welcome back, Mrs Lander.'

Tracey was beaming and Geri returned the greeting.

'Hello, nice to see you again. But it's only been two weeks in the Strand, Tracey.'

'Even so, it hasn't been the same... Jackie will tell you about it, I expect.'

Geri frowned but decided not to take it any further. She walked towards her office, just along the corridor from reception. There was an overpowering aroma wafting from it. Going into the room, she was almost engulfed by the most enormous bouquet that she had ever seen. Carnations, lilies, orchids, arranged artfully in the West End and delivered that morning by taxi. The stems of the flowers had been wrapped up in a vast bag of water which made the arrangement so heavy it needed a shot putter to carry it.

Rooting through the undergrowth, she found a note from Mindaction, the group that had funded yesterday's case.

'For our biggest gun,' it said. Then, in smaller writing, 'Simon would have been proud of you.'

It made her sit down rather suddenly. Looking out of her office window on to the tiny paved garden at the back of the building, Geri tried to concentrate on something, anything, which would hold back the images of him. Strangely, it was at moments like this that she missed him the most. When times were bad she could focus on the work to be done and the lessons to be learned; but now, when she had achieved something, she needed him more than anything in the world.

Men.

Oh, God, she thought. I can't bring myself to ring Tony.

She had gone to bed with him for the simple reason that he looked like Simon. She hadn't told him, but it had been the first time since the death. They had been spending the odd evening together, nothing more. But last night, the need to recapture something of her old life had overwhelmed her and they had returned to his Highgate flat.

But he wasn't Simon. Everything was different and the most stupid thing of all was that they had got to the point of no return before she had realised, come to her senses. She had lain there, embarrassed, wondering how to get out without hurting him. For it wasn't Tony's fault that he looked like her late husband. And he was a good man.

It should have been special – the moment when she started to pick up the threads of normal life. But instead the memory of it just made her cringe. She had faked her responses, made her excuses and left for home. He must have known, been as embarrassed as her about it.

'Welcome back!'

It was Jackie, her secretary, bright and cheerful as always. Just what Geri needed to shake her back into today.

'There's rather a lot I need to go through with you, but first we'd better find a home for these,' said Jackie, moving towards the flowers.

Geri nodded. 'Let's put them in reception. But hang on, they weigh a ton – let me take one side and you go for the other.'

The secretary nodded and the two women carefully manoeuvred their way out of the office, Jackie moving backwards through the open door. From somewhere behind the foliage, she tried to run through the day ahead with Geri.

'There's been a partners' meeting called – there's an agenda on your desk. They brought it forward so I've rearranged a few of your other appointments.'

'Thanks, Jackie.'

'And I've left ... oh, bugger ... no, it's OK.'

Her foot had caught on a pile of filing left outside the door.

'Here we are – over on the table, I think,' puffed Geri.

The women gratefully laid down the flowers on the circular table in the centre of reception and made their way back to Geri's room.

'There's a pile of messages – I've divided them into congratulations for the Evans case, requests for interviews and information, firm business and messages on other cases. Don't forget the Mitchell trial next week – I take it you're not instructing counsel?'

Jackie Wilberforce was one of the old school of secretaries. She used to work for Simon, but had stayed with the firm after his death. Fiercely loyal, she was a godsend to Geri. She typed like a whirlwind, and organised the office with consummate efficiency. Most important of all, she had staying power.

Many didn't. Geri would never forget the time they had taken on a secretary who had been working for the firm on the other side of an enormous factory accident claim. They were relying upon a star witness. Or at least, had been doing until the secretary let slip to Geri that the man had secretly decamped to Uruguay eighteen months ago without leaving a forwarding address. Departing staff could carry dangerous secrets with them.

'Jackie – Tracey said something about some problems when I was away. Has something happened?'

There was a brief pause.

'In a word, yes. Last week Mr Davies and Mr Warburton sent round a memo saying there would be no summer bonus this year.'

'They what?'

'They said that the firm couldn't afford it.'

Geri stood up.

'That's outrageous. I'm going to see them right away. Jackie – I had no idea.'

'Well, the meeting's in twenty minutes – it might be an idea to save it until then. But the staff aren't too happy. They've always had a holiday bonus, ever since ... well, you know.'

Yes, Geri knew. Ever since Simon had been alive. And she wasn't going to be the one who ended that tradition. Staff at Lander Ross were hard-working and good at their jobs. They deserved an extra couple of hundred pounds to spend on their summer holidays. And it was a firm tradition. What the hell were her bloody partners doing stopping it while she was away?

As Jackie left, Geri sat at her desk and ran her eye quickly over the neatly arranged messages.

She would have to ignore the media requests – they would come back if they really wanted her. There was an agenda for the partners' meeting. She looked at it quickly and groaned: firm finances, state of partnership accounts, recapitalisation options. The last thing she needed with her backlog of work was yet another argument about money.

There was a financial report attached to the agenda. No point in trawling through that until she had more time. If there was a problem, they would just have to meet the bonus payments, even if it meant the partners reducing their drawings for a while.

Looking down the cases, notes and memos, there were three offers of settlement on other matters. One, from a top notch firm noted for its aggressive defence tactics, insisted that the offer be accepted or rejected by 3 p.m. that afternoon, after which it would be withdrawn.

Bloody cheek, she thought to herself. If they want to settle, they can wait until tomorrow.

Geri was still flaming about the bonuses. How dare they make an announcement like that when she was away? Talk about mice playing while the cat was on a two-week trial!

She marched along the narrow passageway to the boardroom, in good time for the meeting. For once she was first in the room, and was just about to start examining the accounts when one of her partners walked in.

Roger Warburton was the partner in charge of commercial work. He was also responsible for the collation of financial information. Now in his mid-forties, he had failed to make it to partnership in a famous City firm and had been forced to seek alternative employment when he was thirty-two. A large, ponderous man, finding himself in the altogether more informal environment of Lander Ross & Co. had not caused him to change his formal dress of black jacket, stripy trousers and fob watch. It was as if he was trying to make it clear that his natural home was still the square mile rather than N1.

Geri let him sit down and then gave him both barrels.

'Roger, what the fuck are you doing telling the staff they can't have their bonuses this summer? Didn't you think to discuss it with me first?'

He took a deep breath under the onslaught.

'Geri, unless we do something quickly, we won't be able to pay their wages, let alone a bonus.'

'What?'

'Look at the overdraft. One hundred thousand limit and we're up to ninety-eight. We can't meet the wage bill next week.'

Horrified, Geri turned to the accounts. As she read, the two remaining partners came into the boardroom.

Cefan Davies was first. Plump, with fashion victim glasses and an irritating Welsh accent, he dealt with conveyancing.

'Ah, the mountain comes to Mohammed,' he sneered.

Geri ignored him and concentrated on the accounts. Behind Davies came Pete Sinowski, the quietly efficient but painfully shy solicitor who ran the private client department.

Geri looked up.

'Now you're all here, I want to know who the hell has been taking decisions about staff bonuses?'

They looked rather shame-faced. Like a row of guilty schoolboys, they stared glassy-eyed at her. Suddenly, Geri realised how Margaret Thatcher must have felt running her Cabinet. Perhaps she should have worn the suit after all.

'Well?'

'We can't afford it,' said Roger.

'So why did nobody discuss this with me?'

'We had to take urgent steps, Geri. This is a crisis. I did try to ring you at home last night, but the babysitter said you were out with someone. That you were going to be out until very late.'

Geri reddened visibly at Roger's words but still managed to glare at him.

'There are all sorts of ways round this difficulty. Cutting bonuses is not one of them and I'm not going to agree to it. You can't tell me you only made this decision last night – I'm furious that nobody contacted me about this last week. It's inexcusable.'

Cefan Davies took up the attack in his sing-song voice.

'There are four partners, you know. If you're away, we can hardly let the firm grind to a halt.'

'I'm the senior fucking partner! You do not make major decisions without me. I own fifty percent of this firm, in case you've forgotten.'

Geri knew perfectly well what they were thinking. Only because you inherited it from your bloody husband. Otherwise, you'd be the junior partner which quite frankly is where you belong. At least then we could get you to make the coffee at the meetings. And do the minutes.

'But, Geri,' protested Roger, 'a decision had to be taken. We can review it now, but you've got to bear in mind what I'm saying about the state of our finances.'

'First of all I want an apology.'

Geri was at her most insistent. They all knew she would be quite impossible until she got what she wanted.

'I'm sorry,' mumbled Roger, eyes fixed on the table.

'Cefan?'

'I'm not the slightest bit sorry.'

He stared back at her, aggression in every line of his body. For seconds, they met each other's eyes, neither backing down.

It took Pete Sinowski to calm the situation.

'Look, this is getting us nowhere. Let's look at the money side of things properly.'

Roger took up the lead, relieved.

'I've got last month's income details.'

He circulated the month's accounts. Geri made sure that Cefan looked down before she did and studied the breakdown showing the income each partner had brought in.

'Geri, look at these figures,' said Roger. 'We just haven't had enough money coming in since the start of the year. This month is the worst, but in line with the general trend.'

He turned to the print out.

'My profit income was ten thousand, as you'll

see.' Roger was visibly proud. One of his small management buy outs had gone through, creating a good month's figures for him. 'Cefan brought in four thousand.'

The Welshman was quick in his own defence.

'Of course, we're between rushes – we've received the Christmas completion monies and we're waiting for the Easter work to start paying. I'm forecasting about twenty transactions next month – we've a lot going through. Quite a few remortgages in the pipeline, too.'

Roger pressed on, impassively.

'Pete brought in four thousand as well.'

Pete Sinowski had been brought in to run the private client department three years ago. Efficient, pleasant and affable, he had been Geri's main source of support in the firm since Simon's death. Private client – drafting wills, organising probate and generally picking up the odd areas of practice that no one else covered – was a steady but traditionally low earner in the firm. This month, he had brought in the same as Cefan Davies.

Lander Ross was a partnership. Geri had inherited Simon's share, and as a result was the senior partner with fifty percent of the equity. Roger and Cefan had twenty percent each and Pete the remaining ten percent. Of late, they had been arguing about one subject only: money. Like many firms, once the solicitors had bought in to the partnership, they could take out a share of the profits equivalent to their proportion of the business.

Roger looked at Geri She knew that this was

going to be painful

'Geri has brought in one thousand, eight hundred pounds.'

Which was less than she was drawing each month, let alone meeting the cost of her secretary and running the building.

Cefan Davies was smiling to himself. His figures may have been bad but Geri's were appalling. There was no way round it. She was on the defensive now.

'Yes, it has been a bad month. But we need to remember that my legal aid litigation is never going to make the profits the commercial department will. There's been no real increase in legal aid rates for six years, and the income criteria are so strict that you virtually have to be on benefits to qualify now. And once they stop legal aid altogether for injury claims...'

'But this is a business, Geri. We can't afford to subsidise your good causes forever.' Cefan's refrain was as familiar as it was annoying. She glared at him.

'Perhaps you should remember why this firm was set up. Lander Ross existed long before you joined, Cefan. Simon set it up to take on some of the hopeless cases. He made a fuss for people who otherwise didn't get noticed. Every now and then he would win a big one and the money would come in.'

Cefan remained unconvinced.

'Frankly, Geri, *you're* drawing money that *we're* making for the firm. You've got to start pulling your weight. When did money last come in in a big way from litigation?'

'There was the Abrahams medical negligence case. No one thought we'd win that. We did and brought in fifty thousand. And, of course, we'll get paid for the Evans case now that's been heard. I take it you've seen the papers this morning?'

She was rather put out that no one had congratulated her yet.

'Geri.'

It was Roger who took up the attack now.

'The Abrahams case was eighteen months ago. Since then you've not brought in more than seven thousand in any one month. You won't get the payout from Evans for a few months yet and we've got to get through the next few weeks. It's no good just having a big payday every couple of years – we need to be looking at the steady earners.'

Wounded, she turned on him.

'But the whole idea is that we work across the broad spectrum. There are times when the commercial work subsidises litigation. And, remember, it's the litigation work we're famous for – that's what brings in the clients. That's our profile. Without it we'd be no different from every other law firm outside the City.'

She looked around the table. They really didn't get it. Simon had spent the last year of his life dealing with this nonsense daily from Roger and Cefan. She would never forgive them for that.

'I really am starting to get a little hacked off with these complaints – you all knew when you joined us that we're a special type of firm. We're radical. We campaign. And if your work subsidises the litigation cases, that's the way it has to be. You were glad enough to get your jobs at the time, I seem to remember.'

Cefan's voice was becoming higher. It did that when he was angry.

'You've peddled that excuse for years. But you've got to look at the bottom line, Geri. A few years ago, you could take on the long shots because the unions or the legal aid fund would pay you even if you lost. But you've got to accept that it's not like that any more. The unions send their work to Shaner's and you can forget legal aid now. You don't get paid at all on the conditional fee work when you lose. You're living in the past, Geri.'

Roger was nodding.

She took her time. I must not get hysterical, she told herself. When she spoke, her voice was slow and deliberate.

'I am not going to turn this firm into some ordinary high street outlet. My husband...' she paused, and looked hard at each one of her partners. None of them met her gaze. '...set this firm up to carry out a particular role. If you are not prepared to continue his work, then so far as I'm concerned, you can all just piss off now.'

There was silence.

Pete spoke finally. His tone was gentle, almost conciliatory.

'Geri, we all understand that. And I certainly want the firm to keep on campaigning. But we do need to stop losing money.'

'Then we get some costs in. We all leave this meeting and go through our files this morning with an eye to some interim billing. And I've got the trial in Mitchell next week. If we win, we're on a conditional fee so we'll be able to get an extra percentage. I think we're looking at profit costs of well over fifteen on that.'

Geri tried to draw them together. She needed to tackle her backlog of work, not sit arguing all morning.

'For now I'll talk to the bank and extend the overdraft. Then we need to review the position generally, and tell the staff we're trying to find a way of honouring the summer bonus scheme.'

Cefan was looking thunderous, Roger less than impressed. Geri carried on.

'In the meantime, we'll meet again in a week to review how much we've billed. We can get over this hump. It's just cash flow. Are we agreed?'

'No,' said Cefan. His jaw was clenched. He really could look very unattractive when he was spoiling for a fight, she thought.

'What?'

'No. We are not going to pay the bonuses. And we need to make a decision on litigation today. We've got to do something for once.'

Geri went crimson.

'What are you suggesting?'

'That we drop your conditional fee work and move away from personal injury litigation.'

Her jaw was almost clenched, it was so tense.

'No. Absolutely not.'

'Then, Geri, we have to have a vote on it.'

She glared at him. So it was going to be a showdown.

'OK. Let's take it one by one. We tell the staff

we will try to pay their bonus. And I continue my personal injury work.'

Cefan wasn't to be outdone. He looked directly at her.

'And I move that we continue to cancel the bonus. And you start to accept all types of litigation with a view to reducing your dependence on personal injury claims.'

Roger slowly, carefully, indicated that in the circumstances, and with much regret, he would have to vote for Cefan's proposal. They had forty percent between them. Pete Sinowski had the remaining ten.

'So, are you with me?'

Geri had to repeat the question. It was almost comical, the way Pete was squirming. She wondered what pressure Cefan and Roger had put on him before the meeting. While she'd been away doing the trial.

Finally, he spoke. His voice was hesitant, uncomfortable.

'I don't think we should say anything about the staff bonuses – it's almost worse to raise hopes if we can't honour them. So I'm against you on that. But I'm with you, Geri, for the moment on the litigation work. Personal injury work is what this firm is famous for. But we do need to review it, try and find a way to improve the income.'

She had expected a tantrum from Cefan. A slamming down of papers, possibly a walking out of the meeting. But he simply smiled to himself. Roger Warburton, strangely, looked much more concerned than his co-conspirator.

Geri decided to wind things up before they got any worse.

'Well, on that note, we'll adjourn. I'll call a meeting after I've spoken to the bank.'

The other partners nodded. Cefan and Roger left the room together.

While the meeting was in full flow, a lady in that nebulous phase of life between middle age and the onset of early dotage entered the Lander Ross reception area. Immaculately dressed in a grey Eastex suit and pink silk blouse, she presented herself to Tracey.

'I would like to see Mrs Lander, please.'

Tracey took in the cut-glass accent and the hair permed in a style which she had only ever seen before on the Queen's Christmas broadcast. She was duly impressed.

'I'm afraid she's in a meeting. Could I make an appointment for you?'

'No, thank you. I'll wait.'

Tracey did not know how to deal with this. Clients did not wait in reception without an appointment. For a start, it stopped her gossiping on the phone to her circle of friends, and, worse, it made her worry about whether she should make conversation or dispense coffee and bonhomie. Such topics had not been part of her NVQ. Unsure what to do, she flannelled.

'I'm sorry but I don't know when she's likely to be free.'

'Then I'll wait.' The curt repetition was softened by a charming smile, but even Tracey, not normally the most perceptive of receptionists, realised there was absolutely no point in arguing.

'May I ask what it's about?'

'You may. At this stage, I think you should simply let Mrs Lander know that I have come about a suspicious death.'

Tracey tried to sound completely unfazed. A keen participant with her boyfriend Keith in murder mystery weekends, she was rapidly coming to view this new client as a cross between Margaret Rutherford and Miss Marple. The reference to a death made this impression complete. Nodding sagely, as though she dealt with this type of situation on an hourly basis, she completely forgot to take down Joanna Pascoe's name.

Chapter Two

At first, Charlie Jacobs didn't realise he was going to die.

Mr Grimwood had asked him to start clearing out the old feed from number one silo before the new consignment was off loaded. Charlie didn't like the idea, but Mr Grimwood was the boss. Even so, empty silos gave him the creeps. The vastness, the strange echoes that reverberated off the walls, the feeling that he was in the bowels of some metallic monster.

But orders were orders, so in he went, down the long ladder, mobile phone rammed into his trouser pocket. Down he climbed, out of the late-spring sunshine and into the dark clanging tomb. He walked forward and bent towards a small pile of old grain, hoping that for once there would be no rats to jump out at him. He hated rats, loathed them, but in farming they were a fact of life.

Something clattered behind him. Startled, he turned. Someone was pulling the ladder up.

He turned on his heel and rushed back, jumping at it, but it was way out of reach. There was nothing to panic about, he told himself. Somebody probably needed it to go down another silo.

He didn't want to hang around, though. Not in this place, with no means of escape. 'Help!' he called into the gloom. His voice sounded reedy, pathetic in the vast emptiness. Nobody would hear him anyhow. His voice would have to travel fifty feet up, out and down again to anyone passing by.

As he listened to his shouts echo around the silo, the mobile phone rang from his pocket. Charlie looked heavenwards. Of course, he had only to ring out for help. Lucky Mr Grimwood had made him take the phone.

Relieved, a smile on his lips, he pressed a button. Before he could speak, he heard the voice of his boss.

'Charlie...'

'Mr Grimwood – lucky you rang. Someone seems to have taken the ladder and I'm still...'

'I want to know about David Vane, Charlie.'

He felt the first cold stab of realisation gripping at his bowels. Play for time, he told himself.

There had to be a way out of this.

'Who, Mr Grimwood?'

'Don't fuck me about, Charlie. I found his letter to you this morning.'

'But I don't know him ... there was some letter asking about supplies.'

'Shall I read the letter to you again, Charlie? It says, "Further to our telephone discussion, perhaps we could arrange to discuss matters further". Think about it, Charlie, I know you've been talking. You just tell me what you said.'

He was silent, his pulse racing. He needed time to think, work out what it was safe to say to Mr Grimwood. Calm down, think, take your time...

He heard the sound of an engine running outside the wall of the silo. Then a creaking, monotonous whine.

The conveyor belt! It had to be. Carrying a steady load of grain from the pile outside the silo. It would make its way steadily up the side until it reached the top.

Charlie looked up. As he did so, the grain started to tip over the uppermost edge and fall down to the silo floor. He moved to the edge, away from the pile that was already starting to form. As he stood, rats appeared from the shadows, making their way to the new food.

Charlie spoke into the phone. He babbled, words falling over themselves as he bargained for his life.

'Mr Grimwood, he just rang, honest. I said I didn't know but that if he could write, I'd pass it on to you.'

'If you'd passed it on to me, I might just have

believed you, Charlie. But you didn't. So I don't.'

That was the point at which Charlie Jacobs wet himself.

'Please, Mr Grimwood, I didn't know what to say...'

Even at the edge of the silo, the grain was gathering around his knees now. He could hear little, just the dreadful grinding and the steady hiss as the grain hit the pile and spread itself. He'd heard about how grain behaved – there were tales that it was like a liquid, flowing gently but inexorably into any space. He waited. There had to be a way out of this.

The dust swirled around him, making him cough. His eyes started to stream. The grain was up to his hips now, and Charlie realised he could no longer move his legs. They were trapped, immobile against the vast weight pressing against them. He was rooted to this spot, stuck at the bottom of a fifty-foot grave with several hundred tons of grain waiting to entomb him.

'Charlie...'

He spoke quickly into the phone.

'Mr Grimwood, for God's sake, let me out! I'm sorry. I'll tell you everything. This man rang, asked about some permits for antibiotics and I said I'd check – he tricked me into saying that we had sold some, Mr Grimwood – honest. When I realised, I told him it had been a one-off. He doesn't know anything more, I swear it.'

Grimwood heard the panic in his voice and smiled to himself. It sounded as though Jacobs was telling the truth, he thought. Lucky he'd been able to nip things in the bud. But his employee had been very stupid indeed. He knew too much and had too little sense to keep quiet. From now on, Benny Grimwood would be operating alone.

Grimwood reached for the conveyor controls and turned them up. He needed to move quickly now, finish the man off before he got any ideas about calling the emergency services. He'd keep him talking for a bit.

'Charlie, I want to know exactly what you said.'

In response he heard screams, pleas for him to stop the belt, to let him out, for God's sake.

Then, suddenly, the screams turned to groans. The grain would be pressing against Charlie's chest now, making it impossible for him to shout. In a minute or two he would be unable to breathe. The grain would suffocate him slowly, pushing out the air as it flowed into his body.

And there Charlie Jacobs would stay for the time being, incarcerated in number one silo, well away from anyone who might care to hear his secrets.

Benny Grimwood turned off the phone.

Dr David Vane knew that he was meant to be undertaking scientific research, but the conditions he had witnessed had pushed him right over the edge.

'This is a total disgrace. Who the hell is your vet?'

His brown hair flopped over his face as he shouted. His height and broad build – he had earned a blue as a winger in the Cambridge rugby squad – allowed him to tower over the portly, tweed-jacketed farmer.

'This is my farm. You've no right to talk to me like this...'

'I bloody well have! I am a Ministry vet and what you're doing here breaches every regulation I can think of. Look at the state of the place! What the hell do you think you're doing?'

Some of the farm hands were nearby, pretending to be busy but rather enjoying the encounter. David had already toured the barn behind them. The door was still open and the shrieks of twenty thousand chickens poured out of the building. David had walked up and down the passageways, seeing the tiny cages, each crammed with five hens. There wasn't enough room for the birds to walk or even stretch their wings. Deprived of their usual activities of dust bathing, scratching the ground and nest building, they stood listlessly, sometimes rubbing bloody and raw skins against the wire edges of their cages.

Most of them had been debeaked – their upper beaks chopped off to prevent them from trying to eat each other. Despite this, David noticed several corpses, propped up by other hens in the cage, their bodies carelessly left until someone bothered to remove them. At the corner of the building was a stinking pile of dead hens in varying stages of decay. Simply slung on to the heap, they had been left to putrefy in the warm spring sunshine. Getting as close as he could bear, David had seen amongst the bodies large numbers of chicks – no doubt the male offspring, useless to the industry and which had been thrown live on to the heap to join the bodies there.

The farmer's face was becoming redder by the second.

'I'll not have this – I'll be asking you to leave my land.'

'Ask what you bloody well want. If you chuck me off, I'll be back with the police.'

'You have absolutely no right to come here and...'

'You have absolutely no right to run a farm like this. Look – your chickens are crammed up so tight they can't even shit without hitting each other. You've stacked their cages up so high the ones at the bottom are getting no proper light. Your stock is filthy and infested with three types of parasite that I can see and probably several more I can't. When was your last inspection?'

'Fourteen months ago.'

'And you've probably changed your stock completely since then. What do you do with the carcasses? You don't find buyers for them whole, I take it.'

'Perfectly good pie manufacturers, a few ready meals people.'

David wasn't surprised. Since he had started this job, he had given up meat unless he knew its source.

'Well, I'll need to take some bloods. I want twenty samples. Shall we get on with it?'

The farmer stood open-mouthed as David strode back into the barn. He really hadn't expected this at all.

David had the equipment in his briefcase.

Twenty syringes and phials. Quickly and skilfully, he took the samples, labelled them and stacked them neatly in the case. The farmer stood awkwardly by. He was sure that the civil servant didn't have the power to do this, but God knew what would happen if he complained about it.

'Now I'd like to take a look at your feeding arrangements.'

The farmer looked startled.

'I thought you were here to look at the books?'

He was definitely not enjoying this. He'd thought the visit to his Sussex farm had been something to do with set aside payments.

'I'm not a fucking librarian. I don't want your books. Where are the feedbags?'

David knew he was going too far, but with a bit of luck no one would believe the farmer if he complained.

He was shown the plastic bags of animal feed. Beside them was a scoop. He looked at it carefully, dusting some of the white powder off the edge.

'Adding a little something, are we?'

The farmer said nothing. David looked at the cupboard behind him.

'Open that, please.'

The farmer protested.

'You have no right...'

'Then I'll open it myself.'

Farms like this wouldn't be organised enough to have a locked cupboard. It duly opened, and David saw the tins for which he was hunting. Several different varieties. One of particular interest.

'Just for when they get ill, you know.'

'Then what's it doing on the feed scoop? You're probably giving it out twice daily. That's a criminal offence.'

The farmer, blinking rapidly and wondering whether his pacemaker would cope, didn't know that David was bluffing. He wasn't interested in trying to have him prosecuted. The farmer was supremely unaware that his farm was the forty-fifth and last in David's survey – the results of which would turn out to be so important they would be on the desk of the Minister of Agriculture by the following week. But David Vane wasn't going to go without giving this fat and ignorant farmer the fright of his life.

'Do you realise what you're doing? You chuck a bit of that antibiotic into the feed and think you're keeping the stock healthy, don't you? Have you any idea how dangerous that really is?'

There was a glimmer of understanding in the farmer's eyes now.

'But the new stuff kills everything...'

'And what are you going to do when it doesn't? When there's nothing left?'

'How do you mean?'

'That drug is the last resort. There *are no more* antibiotics. Once your birds develop bugs which are resistant to it, there will be nothing anyone can do.'

'Surely there's always something?'

'No. There are only so many types you can use. The reason I'm so mad is that this stuff shouldn't be available to you. It's been kept back so you people couldn't bugger up the last defence we had. I bet you didn't get it from a vet.'

David had nothing but contempt for the farmer. Let him stew for a bit.

'I'll be reporting back. You may need to see a lawyer. Quickly.'

With a bit of luck, he'd go along and get screwed for a few hundred taking advice he wouldn't actually need from some fat and clueless solicitor.

David walked across the filthy farmyard. He had never become accustomed to factory farms. Even those that were run in accordance with regulations produced a combined assault upon his senses which left him reeling. It was the sounds that were the worst. Used as a boy to the gentle cluckings of his mother's hens in the back garden, he found it almost impossible to believe that the constant shrieks coming from the barn were from the same species. There was nothing gentle about the sound. It was hard, loud – the sort of noise which rang in his ears long after he had left the scene.

He left the farm in his green MGF. Pointing it back towards London, he started to calm down a little. People never expected civil servants to have tempers, but he saw no reason to keep calm when faced with unacceptable practices. He had come to the service wanting to change things for the better. He'd actually done so, in many respects, advising on hygiene and farming practices. At thirty-nine, he probably knew more than any other person in Britain about how foodstuffs are manufactured. Yet he was happy to remain within the anonymity of the civil service. Of course, he could have made his fortune feeding media scare stories about where meat comes from and what is done to it – he had plenty to tell and his rugged good looks would be a dream come true for any commissioning editor.

But David Vane had long ago made the decision that if he was going to change things, he would need to go about matters in a scientific, rational way. So, quietly, efficiently, and for a salary less than most of his contemporaries', he was making substantial inroads into long-established abuses.

His temper and lack of tact were, however, quite legendary. He got away with this at work because he was brilliant at his job. The Ministry knew they would never find a replacement with David's ability to identify a problem and come up with a practical solution. So they put up with the irate calls from offended farmers. Since his promotion, he had learned to rein himself in a little when he was dealing with the politicians, but it was never easy.

David knew, as he drove back that afternoon, that the farmers were only part of the problem. They were subject to market economics. Except that the market was no longer a quaint square at the heart of a pretty town, but a hellish place dominated by the purchasing powers of the big five supermarkets.

The supermarkets wanted their eggs and meat cheap, so the manufacturers had to keep the costs down. So the farmers borrowed to invest in large-scale battery developments, which could halve the price of production. Once the investment was made, they had to make profits large enough to live on and pay back their loans. The competition was extreme, and every economy had to be made. In a sense, it wasn't really the fault of the farmers. But as soon as one found a way to cut corners, the others would follow suit; and the search would be on for a new way of knocking a few pence off the price of a box of eggs. A penny off could mean the difference between a large order and no business at all.

As a result, the birds had been squeezed together and stuck into stinking huts for the entirety of their lives. David had often been told that they knew no better. How could they miss the pleasures of picking around on the outside if they – and their parents before them – had never known life outside the battery house? Chickens were not the brightest of beasts, after all. Yet, he could never quite rid himself of the image of his mother's hens and the thought of the miserable specimens on the battery farm made him uncomfortable. He knew that most people wouldn't dream of picking up an egg from a battery cage and asking to buy it – but once it had been put into a clean box and presented appealingly at the local superstore, they were only too happy to scan the surrounding shelves for the lowest price that week.

But he wasn't there to think about animal welfare, there were plenty of bodies better placed than he to do that. What really worried him was the health risk – not to the chickens, but to every single member of the population. And the Minister for once was going to have to do something.

He reached the M25 junction at 4.30 p.m. and decided to make for home and draft the report on the word processor in his study. He always worked best in his East Anglian cottage, despite the frequent breaks to contemplate the view leading down to the river at the bottom of his garden. He'd work from home tomorrow, telephone the office first and then leave the ansaphone on. One of the few advantages of Liz's leaving with the children was that no one expected him to be sociable any more. He could buy in some take-aways and work as long as he pleased – get the report absolutely perfect.

After all, his discovery was going to change the face of British food production.

Chapter Three

'Geri, it's Nigel Jenner from Pratt Rose.'

'Thanks, Jackie, put him through.'

Just what she needed, the prat from Pratt's. She'd been trying to get hold of the bank manager ever since the meeting but he was on a course and there was nobody available to make a decision as to whether she could pay the staff next week. Geri wanted to scream. Instead, Nigel had chosen that moment to ring. Typical. Absolutely bloody typical.

Geri was still seething from the partners' meeting. Nigel had better be a bit more sensible than usual. His firm worked exclusively on insurance cases, defending claims against large companies. He fought hard. His clients loved him because he told them he never stopped trying, but he cost them thousands. He'd only ever settle at the last possible moment, when it had become clear he was going to lose and when nobody was too interested in negotiation.

The good defence lawyers, Geri knew, made their decision early and made it well. If it was a good Plaintiff case, they would pay some money into Court pretty damn quick. Then the Plaintiff would run the case at a costs risk – if he got less, he would have to pay the insurers' costs as well as his own. There was nothing like it for encouraging early settlement.

But Nigel rarely did that. He would spin things out until the trial date was set. Then he'd try and make an offer.

'Geri, good to talk to you.'

'Thank you, Nigel. What are you going to do me for?' She was not averse to using a little charm at times.

'Wallington. According to my diary, there's a hearing next month.'

'Yes, I'm just getting the bundles ready, actually.'

Just to let him know she was spending time on the case. The costs are going up by the minute, Nigel, better make me an offer.

'Yes, I'm just reviewing. And I ought to mention we've got a video you might like to see...'

Oh, bugger.

Derek Wallington had suffered a back injury at

work five years previously. He had tried every treatment offered, but nothing had helped. He was in constant pain and had never gone back to work. The only problem was, nobody could say exactly what the matter was with him. Nigel was arguing that he was perfectly fine and was just putting on a show for the Court. Standard defence, malingering. Sometimes it worked a treat.

It was important not to sound worried.

'When did you get it?'

They had to produce it to her promptly. A few years back, the Defence were able to ambush the Plaintiff at trial. Tell him nothing in advance. It was only when he got into Court and saw TV monitors all over the place that he realised.

'Only last month.'

'Then I'd better see a copy.'

Geri thought Derek Wallington was genuine, but you never really knew for sure. And it was amazing what videos could show.

Insurers loved to use them. They would get a trained investigator to video the Plaintiff doing all sorts of things which the Plaintiff swore were quite impossible after his accident. Sometimes, it did real damage. More often than not, though, the videos were rather dull and simply showed a rather grainy image of someone pushing a trolley around Tesco's. It wasn't unknown for Nigel to try to negotiate with the threat of an unseen video hanging over his opponent. But you never knew.

'How much are you seeking, anyhow, Geri?'

So that was it. There was nothing in the video.

He wouldn't want to negotiate if there was. Not before she'd seen it, anyhow.

'The specials, with interest, come to just over sixty.'

Special damages were the out-of-pocket expenses – loss of earnings, cost of travel to the doctor and so on. She continued quickly. The specials had been added up fairly creatively and she didn't want to talk about them in too much detail. Let him pick it up. It was his job, after all.

'Generals, I'd say, are around eighteen. It was a pretty nasty injury – permanent problems.'

General damages are there to compensate the Plaintiff for the pain and difficulties caused by his injury. The worse the injury, the higher the award. The level of generals could only be set by looking at previous cases where similar injuries had occurred, and by looking at the Judicial Studies Board Guidelines.

'Eighteen? Come on, Geri, that's right up in the next bracket – we're looking at thirteen, max.'

'No. These are permanent problems.'

'But he's fifty-five, for heaven's sake. No spring chicken.'

Geri always despised this line of reasoning. The older the Plaintiff, the less likely he was to be too put out by pain and injuries. The old were used to suffering. And they wouldn't have to suffer for long.

'You know my views on that argument, Nigel,' she said, willing herself to smile down the line. 'And anyhow,' she continued, 'are you about to make an offer or are we just arguing for fun?'

He laughed. He liked negotiating with Geri.

She could charm the pants off the entire department, he always said.

'Look, we can go to fifty all in.'

'Sorry, Nigel. I'd be embarrassed even to tell my client about that offer.'

'Well, all right. Look, let's not muck around. My file limit on this is fifty-five. And there is the video.'

You wouldn't be so keen to settle if there was anything worth seeing on it, thought Geri. And she never believed all that stuff about file limits. He would boast to the insurers he had secured a marvellous victory even if she got every penny she was asking for.

'Nigel, look, I know you're doing your best, but I'm not going to be able to recommend that to Mr Wallington. Anything over seventy-six – and my costs, of course – and I could try and talk him round. But he's really looking at seventy-eight.'

There was a pause. This was a recognised point in the elaborate dance of settlement negotiations. The first real feedback from the Plaintiff. It set the upper parameter.

Nigel paused just a little too long.

'Well, I'm just off to a meeting, Nigel. I really do have to fly. As we're so far apart on quantum, shall we just leave things as they are?' Geri asked sweetly.

'Er, no. Look, last offer. We'll pay it in tomorrow if you refuse. Seventy.'

'Make it seventy-five and I'll recommend it to my client.'

'Geri, do you want this written in blood? How much more can I give?'

'Seventy-five, plus costs, and that's another trial you don't have to prepare for, Nigel.'

The trial was set for the summer. Just when Nigel would be on a reduced staff because of the holidays. He might even have his own plans to be away in July.

He gave in.

'OK. Done. I'll get a letter off. You recommend it to your client. If you accept, let me know within a week, OK?'

'Fine, Nigel. I'll get back as soon as I can.'

Geri put the phone down with a grin. She'd get some costs in on that one at least. Lucky they'd been doing the bundles – they could charge several hours for that. Mr Wallington would be delighted. Things were definitely looking up.

She phoned her secretary.

'Jackie, we've had a good offer on Wallington. I told the client we'd probably get sixty-eight and the offer's seventy-five. Could you do him a quick letter? Just the usual – that I recommend he takes it, and could he let me know in writing and give me a ring if there are any queries?'

'Sure.'

Jackie had a standard form letter on the WP for these occasions.

'And, Jackie, we've decided to have a run of interim billing. Could you get a print out from accounts of the current state of play on my active files? May as well sort out the costs of Wallington at the same time so we can get an all in settlement.'

'Yes, I'll come down and get the file myself. In the meantime, Tracey popped up a few moments ago to say that she had a new client for you. There's some woman in reception who won't go away. She says it's about a suspicious death.'

'What?'

'Like I said. Mind you, it might be Tracey getting a bit carried away.'

'For God's sake, what is she doing? I've got to get the bundles together for Mitchell next week – the Judge will kill me if I'm late filing them – and I haven't got through the in tray yet ... I simply can't see her.'

'Well, leave the bundles to me – I've got the files up here anyhow. See this lady, pop her into touch and then you can get on with the other stuff. Tracey said it was impossible to get rid of her, and it did sound quite interesting about the death.'

With rather bad grace, Geri agreed and walked quickly into reception. Approaching from behind Tracey's desk, she saw the new client sitting rigidly to attention in one of the chairs, eyes fixed directly ahead. Mentally Geri allowed herself twenty minutes – get the client in, listen, tell her she needed more information and would she please make an appointment by phoning Jackie. Definitely not Tracey.

'Good morning. I'm Geri Lander.'

Much, much later, Geri would cast her mind back to the first time she met Joanna Pascoe. At that stage, of course, she had no idea whatsoever of the effect that this new client was going to have on every aspect of her life. She certainly seemed an unusual person to come seeking the services of a radical law firm, but then it took all types.

She was smart, certainly; probably in her fifties; definitely upper-middle-class. Geri noted the immaculately coiffed hair and the perfectly applied make-up. The voice was cultured, but brisk and to the point.

'Joanna Pascoe. I'm so pleased you could see me today.'

Geri led Mrs Pascoe into her room and they both sat down. The older woman moved a black patent handbag from the crook of her elbow and took something out before setting the bag on the floor beside her feet.

Geri started the interview.

'I must apologise for the mess. I've just finished a rather long trial and am in the process...'

Joanna's manicured hand regally dismissed all further apologies.

'Please don't worry. The trial, I suppose, was that of Evans?'

'Why, yes.'

'I've been following it with some interest. Quite a victory, one could say.'

'We do what we can. Do you have a legal background?'

'Not really. I sat as a Magistrate for some years, but handing out penalty points for speeding offences is hardly the same. No, I came to see you because I need your help.'

'I see.'

'It's about my husband. Or late husband, I should say.'

Mrs Pascoe looked steadily at Geri, holding her gaze. Geri opened her blue notebook and took up a pen.

'I suppose you want the details first? His name was Thomas Pascoe, age fifty-four, occupation General Practitioner. He died in St Thomas's hospital on October the fifteenth last, from multiple organ failure.'

Geri was writing furiously. Most clients took fifteen minutes to give this much information. At least this one seemed reasonably clued up.

'The reason I've come to see you is that I'm convinced I haven't been told the whole story.'

'What do you mean – some mistake at the hospital, medical negligence?' Mrs Pascoe smiled briefly at Geri and continued. She would tell her story properly, efficiently, but most definitely in her own way.

'Not at all. My husband ate some chicken when I was out one evening and his infection started with that. He wasn't too bad to start with – he had rather a fever, a bad stomach-ache, was a bit confused. He stayed off work for a week. Then he got worse. Vomiting ... er...'

'Yes, I understand. What happened next?' Geri spared the other woman further embarrassment.

'The problem was, the illness wouldn't go away. The tummy upset seemed to get worse and worse, and he became covered with red blotches. That's when they put him into hospital. They assigned him a room on his own and put him on their most heavy duty antibiotics.'

'And?'

'And nothing. Whatever he had was resistant to everything. Completely untreatable. And nobody has ever explained why. He had some new sort of infection which just couldn't be treated.'

'Where did you get the meat?'

Joanna looked faintly embarrassed.

'I'm not sure. We tended to shop at the same supermarket, but not always, and I didn't think to keep the till receipt at the time.'

She continued, watching Geri steadily.

'I know that it sounds hopeless at the moment, but since Tom's death I've been rooting through his medical journals, trying to find out more about these new bugs – superbugs, they call them – that don't seem to respond to treatment. There are actually quite a lot. What I would like you to do – if you would be prepared to – would be to read what I have found and let me know whether you think there is any possibility of bringing a claim?'

Oh, dear, thought Geri. I'd better bring her down gently.

'But what would you be seeking? We'd have to value his life to you – how much money he brought in, that sort of thing – and not everyone wants to think in those terms. And I've got to say that unless we can prove where the meat came from and what the matter was with it...'

Joanna Pascoe shook her head.

'I know what you're saying. But before you make up your mind, I'm going to ask you to look at this.'

She took a video tape from her lap and placed it carefully on the desk. It must have been in her handbag when she came in.

'When my husband was in hospital – before it got really bad – he asked me to film him with our camcorder.'

She paused.

'Please watch it. You'll understand then why I want you to become involved. Try and help me find the answers to what went on. I can't really describe what it was like when he was dying. He was shut away at the top of the hospital – nobody saw him apart from a couple of staff. It was awful.'

It was the first time she'd faltered during the entire interview. Her modulated tones wavered just a little, and she looked away from Geri. Quickly, though, she recovered her composure.

'One of Tom's partners – Dougal Baines – has helped me with some of the research. He's sure that something strange was going on.'

She carried on, seeing the doubtful expression on Geri's face.

'Look, I know you must meet more than your fair share of people with chips on their shoulders. But believe me, I've looked into all this as much as I can and I'm sure there's something rotten in the system. I just can't pinpoint exactly what it is. Tom wanted me to try and find out. Please, just watch the video. It will make sense then.'

Geri certainly did spend much of her time telling clients not to launch into doomed proceedings. Well, she reasoned, if this one wanted to pay her to watch a home video, she was hardly going to object. Not on her profit figures.

And anyhow, there was something about all this that was starting to make the hairs on the back of her neck tingle. That was a sign to her that here was something worth looking into. Healthy men should not be dying from food poisoning.

Was there a new bug around which defied all attempts at treatment? Even if there wasn't, some explanation was needed from the hospital at least. Perhaps they'd fouled up on the quiet. Something to look into, certainly.

Geri smiled confidently at her new client. A good settlement on Wallington and a new case. Looked as though it would be privately funded, too. Apart from that spat in the meeting, today was turning out rather well after all.

'I'd love to look into this further – and please let me have copies of what you've found so far. I'll have a look at the tape, of course.'

She hesitated.

'I'm afraid I will have to seek some money on account. Or would you like some advice on how to make a legal aid application?'

Joanna Pascoe looked faintly embarrassed.

'No, I don't think I qualify for legal aid – who does these days? Perhaps if I wrote a cheque ... would five hundred be adequate for the time being?'

Geri was delighted.

'Yes, that would be an excellent start. I'll not charge you for this interview, of course, but I'll have to start the meter running once I begin to dig a little into the background. I'll send you bills at monthly intervals and transfer the billed amount over from my client account as the costs arise. There will be a letter sent out to you confirming all the details.'

'Yes ... of course.'

It was the first time, apart from talking about

Tom's death, that Joanna had not seemed completely in control of the situation. Geri wondered if there was more that she needed to know about her, but decided to leave it for the time being.

Joanna wrote a cheque – Coutts, Geri noticed – and passed it over before getting up to leave the office.

'I'll pop round with the material I've collected when I have a moment,' she promised as she left reception, swiftly and elegantly, leaving a faint waft of Dior in her wake.

Geri returned to her room, and rapidly dictated some file-opening instructions to Jackie. As she finished, her phone rang.

'Tracey told me you'd finished your appointment.'

'Sorry, Jackie, I forgot to let you know.'

'Don't worry. It's just I've had Clements on the line, reminding us that they want a response to their offer on the Winbly case by 3 p.m. I've told them you can't possibly get back to them until tomorrow and that we'll fax them by 5 p.m. then.'

'Thanks, Jackie.'

'No problem, but someone called Ingrid rang – said she's meant to be picking Rory up from school and can't make it because her kitchen's flooded and she's got to wait for the repair man.'

Damn! Not again. The after-school carer had agreed to pick Rory up from school and take him home in return for a vast fee last month and this was the fourth time she had failed Geri. Rory was eleven and probably old enough now to be trusted to make his way home, but she had long ago sworn that he would never return to an empty house. She felt bad enough not being there for him at the end of school – the least she could do was make sure that someone else was. But Ingrid, despite her inflated wages, was no more reliable than any of the others. And on a day like this, when Geri was snowed under ... she wanted to scream.

'Oh, Christ. Well, thanks for sorting out Clements and getting the extension. I'll go and pick him up – take some files home.'

'If you want to dash off at three, I'll bring the post down to you early and the urgent files to take with you. In the meantime, I've done the bundles in Mitchell – if you'll check them, I'll get a trainee to take them over to the Court.'

'You're wonderful.'

'Yes, I know, but it doesn't hurt to be told it again!'

It was always a complete nightmare returning from a long and difficult case. Geri loved appearing in Court and was good at it. But she understood only too well why most solicitors are happy to use barristers for their Court work. Litigation demands constant activity from a solicitor – moving the case along, collecting the evidence, getting a hearing date, negotiating with the other side. Everything has to be done to a deadline. When she was out of the office on her trials for days on end, Geri's other cases would stop in their tracks, and she would return to a pile of unattended files and unanswered telephone calls.

As if that wasn't enough, she also had to run the firm – the overdraft had sneaked up whilst she had been away on the Evans case. She knew that if she'd been in the office, looking at the daily accounts, she could have taken action sooner and gone on to the offensive with Roger and Cefan.

For the next two hours, she worked her way through the neglected piles of work, dictating quickly into her machine until she had filled three tapes. Jackie came down with the post at 2.45.

'I have to say, I'm glad you're disappearing early – I can't fit any more typing in my room. If you want to go, Tracey's nipped out to the kitchen so no one will know anything about it.'

Geri sneaked out of the door, feeling for all the world like a truanting school girl. She might be the senior partner but the last thing she needed was grumbling that she didn't put the hours in. If anyone did see her, with her pile of papers she could have been off on business anyhow.

The scene at the Bury St Edmunds farm could have come straight from hell. Grimwood had been telephoned that morning by the farmer, and had agreed to come straight down.

He knew what was happening as soon as he got out of his car. The stench of death was all-permeating, working its way from the barn, through the yard and out to the car park. He followed the smell, trying not to retch as it grew stronger.

Taking a deep breath, he went into the gloom of the barn. Gordon Bell, the owner of the farm, saw him and beckoned him over. Breathing tentatively, Grimwood stepped forward.

In front of him was a long row of cages, stretching the length of the barn. In the box in front of him, one chicken stood listlessly. Its feathers had fallen out and there were pustulating sores on its body. Its head drooped on to a thin chest. The other six birds in its cage were dead, their bodies littering the tiny space. The remaining specimen stood on two of the bodies. As Grimwood watched, it too fell, lying awkwardly across the other corpses.

He scanned the other cages in the row. They were full of dead or dying birds, in their hundreds. Two farm hands were at the far end of the row, emptying cages. With gloved hands, they took the bodies out of the cages and slung them carelessly into a black refuse sack.

Grimwood couldn't stand the smell any longer. He turned and ran for the door. He just made it into the open air, where he was thoroughly and copiously sick.

'You see now why I wanted you to take a look for yourself,' said Gordon Bell.

'But I don't understand – perinycin should stop this happening.'

Grimwood was at a loss, for once.

'Well, I gave it to them as routine. When the first infections started, I doubled the dose, then trebled it. That was four days ago. Now...' Bell waved a hand sadly towards the barn.

'I'll talk to my supplier – perhaps there's something they can do, a new drug. There must be something.'

'Too bloody late, isn't it?' said the farmer, bitterly. 'Nothing's going to save my stock. I'm fucking ruined, and it's your bloody fault.'

'Now hang on...'

'No, you listen to me for once. You said this stuff was a miracle, would wipe out any infections and keep them healthy. And you said it would make them grow better. Well, it did for a few months, but look at them now.'

Grimwood looked away.

'You wanted the stuff. Perhaps you weren't giving it out right.'

'Don't give me that! I've half a mind to report you...'

'Making your own noose, that'd be. You know it's against the law to use perinycin without a vet's permission.'

'I don't particularly care any more.'

Grimwood turned to face the farmer.

'It'd just be your word against mine.' His face took on a new look, menace flashing from his dark eyes. 'And if there was any trouble, I'd come looking for you. Or rather, looking for those pretty daughters of yours. It would be such a shame if they were to be involved in any sort of accident.'

There was fear in the farmer's face now. He'd heard the tales about Grimwood's past.

'All right. But I'm having nothing more to do with you, Grimwood. I'll burn my stock and sell up. I'm out of farming from now on.'

Probably for the best, thought Grimwood, nodding slowly.

Geri got to the gates of Rory's school at 3.20. As she waited, a steady stream of pupils left. At the back, alone, walked her son. Seeing him looking around for Ingrid, she climbed out of the car and shouted to him. Some boys walking on the other side of the road sniggered. One of them made a comment which Geri couldn't hear.

Rory walked over to her rather sheepishly. She grinned at him.

'Hi! Ingrid had some crisis so I knocked off early. How are you feeling?'

'All right, I suppose.'

He got into the car, and placed his bag on his knees. Geri noticed some scuff marks on the elbows of his blazer.

'What happened to you?' she asked.

'Nothing. I played football at break – must have got some dust on it.'

She was about to ask more, but he pushed on, changing the subject.

'Mum, we got to use the microscopes today in biology. I saw a cell from my mouth – it was amazing.'

By the time they reached home, Rory had told her about most of his day. Over supper in front of the TV, she told him about hers. It was a regular routine between them.

She didn't mention the partners' meeting, but told him all about her new client.

'Do any of your textbooks talk about food poisoning?'

'There's a bit about bacteria replicating – we did that today when we looked at cell changes. Sometimes they can change when they multiply.'

'What makes them change?'

'In biology today, Mr Kennedy said that they change to adapt to the world around them and make the best of it. Those that change in the best way continue the species. He gave us a diagram of a body – our cells fight the bacteria but the bugs adapt to get round the defences.'

'How?'

Rory looked embarrassed.

'Actually, I didn't quite understand that bit. Why do you want to know?'

'Well, this lady who came to see me – her husband had food poisoning and whatever he'd got wouldn't respond to drugs. He became terribly ill – eventually died from it.'

Rory looked at her thoughtfully as he finished his food.

'You ought to post a query on the internet. Someone will be able to tell you.'

Geri sighed. Not the internet again. He spent half his life on it already.

'No, really, Mum, the discussion groups are brilliant. I got my physics homework done by a man in Baltimore last week.'

He was already climbing the stairs before she could respond.

Up in his bedroom, Rory's PC churned into life as he went on line. With worrying skill, he posted a query with a medical discussion group.

'I want to know how bacteria can become immune to antibiotics. Are there any bacteria which are immune to all drugs?'

He signed off and sent the message to the group.

'What happens now?' asked Geri, amazed by the ease of the process.

'We look tomorrow. If someone answers, they'll either e-mail us direct or post a reply to the group. Can I watch *EastEnders*?'

She smiled at him. A favour for a favour, after all.

'OK, but only if I can have a look at your biology textbook.'

She took him off to bed at nine, tucking him in and leaving a light kiss on his cheek. He smiled sleepily at her.

'See you in the morning, Mum.'

'Night, night, darling. No dreams tonight.'

'OK.'

It was a ritual played out since a few weeks after Simon's death. It didn't always work. Rory had heard the ambulance siren, had come downstairs to find a group of men clustered around his father, trying to bring life back into his body. He had sat there for some minutes, absorbing the scene before Geri had seen him, cowering behind the banister.

Since then he had re-lived that night many a time in his dreams. Always he would wake up, screaming, 'Dad, don't die!'

He'd been told that heart attacks strike people sometimes without warning, that there was little anyone could do, that it was no one's fault. But deep in his subconscious images and thoughts whirled ceaselessly.

Geri watched him fall asleep, chest rising slowly under the Spiderman duvet cover. He'd had it for so many years the pattern was almost washed out, but he insisted on keeping it.

She hoped desperately that the dreams would stop soon. Telling him what had really happened would surely undermine what healing there had been.

Leaving his room soundlessly, she returned to her seat in the living room and opened his textbook. Never much of a star at biology at school, this time she was going to have to understand cell division and replication if she was going to have a hope of researching the case properly. Geri shook off her shoes, opened the book and started to read.

It had been one hell of a day. She had started it off feeling tired after the trial and the party. Then the row with bloody Cefan and that solid trawl through her caseload. And the money situation. She had a nasty feeling that particular problem wasn't going to go away. And something was up with Rory. Goodness knew how she was going to tackle that.

She was exhausted. Totally shattered. It was something she lived with constantly. Desperately, she forced herself to keep her eyes on the text of Rory's book. She woke with a start fifty minutes later.

She had never been too good at science at school. The only and unexpected child of two school teachers, she had shone from the start in the arts, but failed dismally at maths and science. At University, they'd told her she was an inductive reasoner. She found the answer first, and worked back from it. Deductive reasoners worked in the opposite, logical order.

Inductive reasoners make good lawyers. They can work backwards from the desired result – success for their client – to the facts at the core of the dispute. Then they can take the Judge along the reverse path with them.

The only trouble was, Geri had to understand and take in vast amounts of information. For Mr Evans, she'd had to take on board research exploring the psychiatric effects of witnessing dreadful events and the various mechanisms for the development of clinical depression. In the past, she'd had to understand subjects ranging from the mechanics of locking mechanisms on certain types of doors to the way in which laser beams work. She had to understand the problem before she could show the failures to deal with it. So far she had always managed. Sometimes it took time, but with the aid of some late-night reading sessions, she had got there in the end.

The cat nap had helped. This time, she could follow the book. It was after all aimed at eleven-year-olds and was fairly easy going. Geri understood the basic principles of bacteriology after an hour.

The tape which Joanna Pascoe had given her was still in her handbag. She may as well take a look now. She checked that Rory was still asleep before putting it into the video recorder and switching it on.

At first it seemed like a typical home video – a slightly shaky start, and a blurred figure in front of the lens. Then the auto-focus cut in and she saw a middle-aged man. The most striking thing about him was his extreme thinness. He had obviously been considerably larger in the recent past, because his skin seemed to hang in folds, all elasticity gone.

He looked directly into the lens. She had one of her medical witnesses use a phrase once – IDL. In the brutally casual medical way, it stood for Imminent Death Look. Tom Pascoe had that written all over him.

He was pale – almost transparently so. The darkness of his eyebrows and eyelashes stood out strangely against his white skin. Even his lips were white. The sheets and counterpane on his bed were white too, and he seemed almost to merge into them.

His eyes were focused beyond the camera. And he was angry, his mouth set in a grim line. He spoke slowly, but the fury was clearly there. He was in simple surroundings – a small, white world made up of a bed, a cabinet and a drip pumping fluids into his left arm.

'I'm Tom Pascoe, a General Practitioner from North London. Three days ago I was told that I was dying from a multi-resistant organism. I have asked my wife to film me.' His voice was slow, each word delivered only after visible effort. The camera closed in a little. 'I don't know who will see this. I have asked Joanna to take it to a good solicitor, someone who will fight hard for me. But I have no idea who you are, whether you are male or female, or how old you are. So I must guess.'

Despite the warmth of the early-summer night, Geri shivered. This man was speaking to her from beyond the grave. It was most unnerving.

'By the time you watch this, I will be dead. I don't want to die. Five weeks ago, I was fit and well, working full-time. One night, I ate a meal of chicken which gave me a stomach upset. I felt unwell, and then became a little feverish. Eventually, I was admitted to this hospital. At first they had no idea what was happening to me. Then these started to develop.'

Slowly, he moved his pyjama jacket up over his stomach. The camera focused on pink lesions on his skin. Then he slowly covered his stomach again and moved so that he was sitting upright. 'I am in considerable pain from my stomach. This is because I have an intestinal haemorrhage. I also have an infection in my heart which means I am constantly out of breath. That is why I am speaking slowly now.'

He stopped for a few moments. He was sitting on the bed. His weight seemed to make no imprint on the bed clothes. It was as though he were a ghost already.

'I am going to die. The bacteria have spread into my blood. If I survive the intestinal bleeding, the superbug will spread throughout my body. My liver will fail first, probably, then my pancreas. I may well get meningitis. I will probably lose consciousness at that point.'

Clearly in pain, he gazed towards the camera.

'I have lost five stone in five weeks. I cannot eat or drink. Because there are no antibiotics to treat me, I am a huge risk to the hospital. I am barrier nursed, which means that those who come into this room do so only with face masks and gowns on. They change clothes completely before they see anyone else. I am not allowed to touch anyone, even my wife, in case I pass the illness on.'

He was clearly starting to tire. Each word was a struggle. Geri felt embarrassed to be watching someone staring into the abyss, in such pain. She wanted to recoil, make some excuse.

'I am waiting to die. I cannot leave this room, which I hate. I will never feel fresh air on my face again. I will never so much as hold hands with a human being again. I must just lie here, monitor my own pain, and wait until I lose consciousness and finally die. In the meantime, I sit here and watch the ceiling. Planning this video has at least given me a day's worth of productive thought.'

He was staring intently into the camera. Geri felt a chill run through her spine. She didn't want to watch the video, but she couldn't stop either.

'I have never been so angry about anything in my whole life. Whatever was in that chicken is killing me – and killing me in a way that is utterly grotesque. I ask whoever is watching – I beg you, in fact – to find out what the hell happened to me.'

The lens lingered on him for a few moments longer. He seemed to be considering whether to add something more, then shook his head and grunted. The image faded suddenly and the screen went blank.

Geri carried on looking at the TV, too shocked to move. His haggard face seemed etched on to her eyes. When she tried shutting them, it was still there. His voice reverberated around her head. The anger had been almost palpable. Coming from one so clearly ill, its power was extraordinary. Geri sat in silence for many minutes, her mind a blank save for the images she had just seen.

The sound of the grandfather clock chiming midnight finally shook her into movement. She needed sleep desperately after last night. Carefully, she replaced the video in its envelope. She wondered if Joanna had seen it since his death. Somehow, she suspected not.

She checked Rory before she turned in. He was sleeping well. In the corner of his room, his computer sat silently. Its internet message had already been picked up in thirty different locations over the world. By dawn, it would be in hundreds.

Chapter Four

Lunch at Le Gastronome is always a deeply civilised affair.

The restaurant's proprietor propounds the French philosophy that only barbarians rush such a meal. It is, after all, the watershed of the day, and should be celebrated as such. And if the Minister for Agriculture wanted to take a few hours to sample some of the best of his country's produce, then he was only doing his job properly.

'May I first congratulate you, Mr Moncrieff, on your choice of venue.' Gerald, the NFU rep, puffed plumply. He loved these lunches and lied most convincingly to his accounts people about how effective they were in influencing the Minister.

'Thank you.' Callum Moncrieff's Scottish burr was at its most pronounced when he was trying to charm.

And being charming came naturally when you had spent fifteen years making the transition from student to member of Her Majesty's Government. The splendid and relaxed ambience helped to create a mood of goodwill towards the world. Even, in fact, towards Gerald, who was usually particularly irritating.

Callum looked in delight at the plate of *roulade de saumon* in front of him. Brought fresh from a lake not far from his home, the fish was quite delicious. Callum ate it all, pausing only to take sips of the mineral water – French, *naturellement* – provided at the table. He knew that there would be a soft sell at some point, and prided himself on always keeping a clear head. He would enjoy the meal, but stay in control.

Callum was good at retaining charge of a situation. All that was required was a little preparation, that was all. The third of six children born to a Calvinist minister and his wife, he had learned some important political lessons very early on. He could get what he wanted, quietly and effectively, by laying the ground first. Never one for tantrums as a child, one of his earliest successes had been his campaign to acquire his older brother's bike. Callum had been six at the time. Donald, at nine, was his parents' first child, and had always had the best of everything. There was no money for Callum to have a bike, so, every week or so, a fault would appear in Donald's. A puncture, perhaps, or a gear linkage failure. Then the handlebars became wobbly. Donald had started to become a little worried. Whenever he used his bike, something went wrong.

In their room one night, Callum had struck the killer blow.

'Perhaps it just wasn't built very well – too much seems to fail. The only thing left is the brakes. What if they went? You've got to be able to trust the bike if you're out on it. You know what McKilley's hill is like in the wet.'

Donald had stopped riding his bike. When his mother noticed, Callum suggested that he wouldn't mind taking it apart and mending it if he could use it. After all, he wouldn't be going as far as Donald, being younger.

Donald and his mother agreed, and Callum had his bike. Naturally, it never went wrong again.

From Callum's point of view, it had been an ideal campaign – nobody was even aware what had happened and his prize had been obtained through agreement. It was the end game which excited him the most – setting up the pieces carefully so that the conclusion was inevitable.

The Moncrieffs' third child had grown into a devastating force. Good-looking to the point of sinfulness, his father had always thought. Tall, angular, with soft dark hair softening the slight cragginess of his jaw and cheek bones, he had the talent, essential in any politician, of remembering the name of every person he met (a card index compiled nightly helped him with this). When he stooped slightly to look into someone's face as they were talking, they would feel that Callum would listen to them alone all day.

Of course, this was particularly effective with women. Callum had lost his virginity to a farmer's daughter in a barn at the age of fifteen. Twenty years later he still became turned on by the smell of straw. He had progressed through many girlfriends and was currently enjoying simultaneous relationships with a twenty-two-year-old political researcher in London and his political agent in Scotland.

The soft sell came with the main course.

'Ah, *poulet aux poires*.'

Quite an unusual combination, but it really did go down rather well. It would have been even better with a bottle of Chablis but such was life.

'Minister, there may be a move from the EC soon about high-intensity farming.'

The use of the title didn't flatter Callum at all. He was so used to hearing his father thus addressed that the term conjured up a rather dour old man rather than a key member of Her Majesty's Government.

'Ah,' he responded. 'Well, as you know, I always make a practice of listening to all points of view.'

'Very wise, if I may say so. Rather than bore you now, we've prepared a few facts and figures about British farming. It might supplement some of the information you're allowed by your civil servants. Could also let you see some of the problems with the Food Safety people.'

'What problems?'

Gerald sighed.

'Oh, Minister, I don't want to ruin your lunch. But I'll send you the resumé. I should say that the farming community is under some pressure at the moment – particularly the high-intensity businesses. We really are facing difficult times. After BSE, food production has never quite recovered. Bankruptcies are at the most horrendous level. Even union income has gone right down – so many farmers out of business.'

Not enough to stop them paying for a meal like this, thought Callum to himself

'Well, thank you, Gerald. If you could send your resumé, I will of course read it urgently. I take it you don't want dessert?'

Gerald, who wanted nothing more at that moment than a large helping of *profiteroles aux chocolat et framboise,* felt obliged to agree sadly. Callum loved to torment him in this way.

Moncrieff drove himself back to London. He always enjoyed the rare privacy of a decent run along fast roads with the Mozart Clarinet Concerto swirling its way around the Jaguar. He'd drop in a reference to Le Gastronome when he next saw his parents. His father would be bound to disapprove. He had never wanted his son to go south to a life of gluttony and sin. Well, Callum had certainly enjoyed the gluttony and was looking forward to some sin later.

As he drove, he thought through his strategy. The reshuffle couldn't be more than six months away and he was going to have to play things carefully in Cabinet. The PM was strong at the moment, but things could change quickly. Overall, it was in his interests to play along. Get a reputation as a safe pair of hands. Establish his party base, move up the Cabinet a little (he had no intention of lingering in Agriculture too long) and wait for his chance. He was the youngest man in the Cabinet, and could take his time.

One hand on the driving wheel, he extended the other to the mobile phone, safely plugged into its station. The call was answered before the ringing tone had sounded.

'Katrina, I want to work at home tonight.'

He smiled to himself. She'd understand.

'Of course, Minister. Do you need some files brought to you?'

'I think I might. Shall we say, nine o'clock?'

That way, he wouldn't have to feed her. They could get straight down to business. Good old Katrina. Never let him down. Great body, too.

Benny Grimwood had to type the two warnings himself. It would have been impossible otherwise. It took some time, his stubby index finger pausing over each key. He used the old manual typewriter, not trusting the computer with its word processor. Someone might be able to date what he was doing. At least with the manual machine, he was safe from that. He had used carbon paper to make copies. Charlie, said the warnings, must stop going into the silo unaccompanied or his employment would be terminated.

Grimwood looked at the calendar in front of the desk and double checked the dates he'd typed in. Yes, Charlie had been at work on both of them, one two weeks ago, the second three.

He took the originals to the metal sink in the office and struck a match. The flimsy paper burned quickly, edges blackening and turning in on themselves. Soon, the two warnings were cinders, flushed down the plughole by Grimwood. The two copies were filed carefully in the staff folder, ready for inspection when the time was right.

Grimwood had already phoned the police, and told them that he was concerned that his employee had not turned up for work. He had tried his home, he told them. Charlie lived alone, and he was worried about him. He might be overreacting but the man had never missed a day before. The officer promised to send a car round to Charlie's cottage as soon as he could and said he was sure it would be nothing too serious. He wished all employers could be as caring, he told Grimwood.

Benny Grimwood knew he should never have trusted Charlie Jacobs. He did better on his own, always had. In the Paras, they'd always told him he needed to work more with others. Teamwork and all that. It had made him want to throw up. That's why the Army had got rid of him in the end. Brilliant soldier, they'd said – he knew, he'd seen some of his file. But they'd made him see a shrink and the fool had said he had a personality disorder. Just because he didn't go running to others whenever he needed help, the stupid berk had thought there was something wrong with him.

Well, it was the Army's loss. He'd been ready to leave anyhow. His brother had been killed in a car crash five years ago and someone had to run the agricultural supplies business. Father had been past it and Benny could finally show the old man what he was made of. So he had taken over the business, trying to learn as he went.

Only, it had started to go wrong very quickly. Somehow, he just couldn't get on with the regulars. Jerry, his brother, had been blessed with an easygoing charm. Benny just couldn't work the same way and one by one, the customers had deserted.

Some of those who had stayed had tried to pull a few stunts over payment. Benny had put a stop to that with a few well-publicised incidents, but these hadn't exactly helped his reputation. He'd got his money all right, but the remaining customers had deserted in terrified droves.

His break had come with a visit from an old Army contact two years previously. He had some mates in France apparently who could get hold of some medicines that were banned in the UK. Wonderful stuff, not harmful. And if Benny wanted to sell them on quietly, he'd make a mint. The farmers were crying out for them.

He'd gone for it. He'd had little choice really, not with the business in the state it was. And it had worked like a dream. The farmers buying the drugs didn't want chat or easy charm. They just wanted the goods. Payment was all in cash, too.

Father had been impressed with the upturn in

business. Benny had taken care of him well, providing everything an elderly man could want. He had died in comfort, heartbroken over the loss of his first son, but surprised and delighted with the success of his second.

Benny Grimwood looked upwards and watched a fly buzzing around the light bulb. This David Vane might know rather too much. It might be an idea to stop supplying for a few months and lie low for a bit. There were no drugs on the premises at the moment, so there was no evidence. The farmers wouldn't dare say anything – they'd be putting themselves in the dock. Bell would keep quiet.

Thinking about Bell, there must have been something wrong with the last consignment. He would have to have a word with his supplier next time they met.

Geri needed some new cases. That was the only way to generate some more income. As a result, she threw herself into the interview with a Mrs Coverdale with such determination that the older woman was quite convinced she had the claim of the century. Pleased with the sympathetic reception, she droned on endlessly. By 2.45 Geri realised that unless she took urgent action, she would be trapped for the rest of the day.

She tried to give the usual clues but Mrs Coverdale spoke on. And on.

'Yes, well, I'll write to them, of course.'

Geri tried shutting her notebook with an air of finality.

'Make sure you mention the stereo at all hours.

And as for their children – never out of the garden, shrieking. I was only saying to my son Kevin...'

'Yes, Mrs Coverdale. Now, unless there's anything more...'

'Well, there is. He's out all day and I know they're claiming dole. I think we ought to tell them that we know what they're up to.'

'I don't think that will really help, honestly. Let's just stick to what we can prove – the noise nuisance.'

Geri knew what would finally get rid of the woman.

'Now, I think we've taken up just over the hour, so shall we call it seventy-five pounds? Perhaps, if I can have one hundred and fifty on account, that will allow me to draft the letter.'

It never failed, and never ceased to amaze Geri that while one half of the population was terrified that they would be charged merely for going in to make a solicitor's appointment, the rest assumed they would never have to pay a penny. Mrs Coverdale clearly fell into the latter category.

'I'm sure you understand that my firm cannot undertake work on your behalf without a deposit in our client account. Of course, we'll only charge you as we do the work. The money will be safe in a special account for you, and will be transferred as we bill. Is that satisfactory?'

Mrs Coverdale gaped like a rather plump goldfish.

'I didn't think to bring my chequebook, actually.'

'Well, if you could just pop the cheque to me,

I'll draft the letter and have it ready to send out just as soon as the payment is made,' said Geri sweetly. And looked pointedly at the clock.

'Yes, well, I'll be off now,' said Mrs Coverdale, wondering if it wouldn't be more sensible (and certainly cheaper) simply to send young Kevin round with the Rottweiler.

As soon as Mrs Coverdale had gone, Geri threw her most urgent files into her large briefcase. She'd been trying to ring Ingrid for most of the morning, but there had been no answer. Probably got a better offer and not answering the phone. Once again, she was going to have to leave the office early. She couldn't take the chance that Ingrid would let her down again. Hurrying now, she made for the door.

As she passed quickly through reception, she saw Joanna Pascoe, sitting primly by the entrance. Tracey looked at her employer and paled.

'I'm ever so sorry, I forgot to tell you – Mrs Pascoe's here to see you.'

Conscious that she could hardly tell her off in front of the client, Geri delivered what she hoped was a thousand-watt glare at Tracey before making her way over to Joanna Pascoe. She had thought of little else but Tom Pascoe since she woke up and wanted the case badly. But she needed time to get herself organised before she could throw herself into it properly.

'Mrs Lander ... I hope you don't mind, but I've brought the material which I've found...'

With horror, Geri saw that Joanna was gesticulating towards a pile of papers and magazines standing three foot high on the floor beside her.

'...and I wondered if now would be a good moment to go through them? Your PA,' she smiled at Tracey, who blushed, 'was saying that you've no more appointments this afternoon.'

Geri wanted to scream. Not now, when she was trying to make a discreet exit! For Christ's sake; she thought. How can you walk in on a busy solicitor and tell her to start ploughing her way through a stack of journals on a Wednesday afternoon? Did it really look as if she had nothing else to do? This was a big claim. It needed proper consideration, time to reflect and obtain the evidence. She didn't need to be hassled like this.

Geri opened her mouth to speak then looked more closely at Joanna's face.

The older woman looked completely exhausted. Her impeccable make-up failed to disguise the dark shadows under her eyes, and the wrinkles around her mouth seemed deeper somehow. The hair which yesterday had seemed almost to be cemented into place was today slightly wispy, straggling around the edges of her face.

And Geri couldn't get it out of her mind that Joanna had been there when her husband had spoken to camera. She would have been with him in those last days when it had got even worse.

'Mrs Pascoe, this is excellent but I'm afraid I'm in rather a hurry...'

'Oh, I'm so sorry, I did try to check that I wouldn't be inconveniencing you.'

'No, it's not work. I've got to pick my son up – I've been let down by my after-school carer.' Geri was speaking quietly, trying not to let Tracey overhear, or else it would be around the firm in twenty minutes flat.

'Well, I must let you dash. Perhaps if I made an appointment?'

Joanna moved towards the pile, and stooped to pick some of the papers up.

At that moment, Geri realised she must have carried the whole lot in herself. It would have taken the best part of the afternoon – no wonder she looked so tired.

'How did you get those here?'

'On the bus, of course. I don't drive.'

The tired smile made Geri feel suddenly terribly guilty. She sent up a silent prayer of thanks that she had not snapped at Joanna.

'Well, I can't have you carrying them back ... perhaps if you'd like to leave them in my room?'

Joanna Pascoe looked perplexed.

'Well, you see, the problem is, I do need to explain them to you. They'll make no sense otherwise. It's clippings from journals mostly, and I have no copies...'

Geri had nine minutes to get to the school gates. The urgency found its way into her voice. 'I know! Pop them into my car, and explain the sequence to me – perhaps I can drop you off somewhere?'

'That would be most agreeable. Where do we go?'

Joanna's court shoes clicked around to the back of the office where she gratefully unloaded the files into the boot of the Renault. Geri couldn't help but smile at the sight of her new client as she installed herself carefully in the front seat. She looked as though she should be making polite conversation in South Kensington over petits fours rather than staring down at the rubbish littering Geri's car. There was hardly room for the poor woman's feet amongst discarded sweet wrappings, some ancient press reports and, worst of all, a less than savoury rugby boot of Rory's. Joanna, though, made herself comfortable and didn't even look too put out when Geri jumped a red light on the City Road. They got to the school gate just two minutes late. Rory, waiting by the wall, walked up to the car.

Joanna was already climbing out.

'Young man, I must be in your seat.'

Rory was amazed. He had little recent experience of anyone over forty.

'No, er, well, don't worry, I'll go in the back.'

'How kind! Then let me stand back while you get in.'

Geri tried to offer an explanation.

'Rory, this is Mrs Pascoe.'

'Joanna, please.'

'Joanna, who came to see me yesterday. I'm trying to help her look into a claim.'

Rory had already worked out the connection.

'Are you the lady with the dead husband? I mean... Oh, Christ, sorry,' he finished sheepishly.

Joanna smiled gently.

'Don't worry. Yes, I am. I was just dropping off some materials to your mother who is kindly taking them home.'

'I was going to check my e-mail for you tonight.'

'Your what mail?'

'E-mail. Mum and I put a query on the internet about your ... er ... dead husband.'

'Late husband, Rory,' muttered Geri.

'Er, yeah. Anyhow, I was going to check it when we get in.'

'That would be wonderful. You'll have to show me how it works.'

'Yes, sure,' said Rory before Geri could remind Joanna that she was dropping her off.

They arrived outside the house, finding, for once, a parking space opposite the front door.

'What a charming place,' said Joanna. Rory stood by as she climbed daintily out, and followed her automatically to the boot.

'Perhaps,' she smiled at him, 'you'd like to help us?'

'Sure.' He grinned back. Geri, who waged an ongoing and only partially successful campaign to persuade her son to carry in the shopping each week, could only gaze in respect at the older woman.

After two trips each, the papers were stacked neatly in the living room.

'Mum, I'm starving.'

'I'm not surprised, young man, after all that work.'

Geri remembered the empty larder. She'd meant to do the shopping on the way home.

She opened the fridge door.

'Sorry, I didn't get round to the shopping. No biscuits ... crisps gone ... fruit out unless you want a black banana?'

'What *have* we got?'

‘Two eggs, some old jam…’

‘Do you have margarine and flour?’ asked Joanna, suddenly.

‘I think so,’ replied Rory.

‘Then let me make you a cake.’

‘A cake? Mrs Pascoe … Joanna … we haven’t really time. I’ve got to get changed, help sort Rory out…’

‘Well, if you do that, I guarantee to have some jam cake ready for you in six minutes. Just show me where the bowl and whisk are first.’

Geri found the long-neglected utensils and left Joanna in the kitchen before going upstairs to change into her non-work clothes. She reasoned that if Joanna was not behaving like a client, she need not act like a solicitor. As she descended the stairs, she smelt the unmistakable aroma of fresh cake, and walking into the kitchen, saw Rory, tucking into some jam squares.

‘It’s delicious, Mum – do you want some?’

Geri hadn’t eaten cake in years. She took a slice.

‘You’re right, it is good,’ she laughed, enjoying the vanilla and jam sweetness. Joanna looked delighted.

‘It’s a bit of a cheat really. I used the microwave – the cakes taste much better somehow and only take three minutes.’

Rory helped himself to another slice.

‘Can I go upstairs and check the e-mails?’

‘OK,’ said Geri.

As he disappeared upstairs, the two women moved into the front room and Joanna knelt down delicately in front of the pile.

Geri sat on the other side of the papers, perched on the edge of her chair.

'Joanna, I watched the video last night. It ... it's very powerful. I know what you mean now about wanting to make a fuss.'

Joanna turned to her.

'Then you must understand why I'm doing this?'

'I do,' said Geri simply.

'I hope it didn't seem too strange, but it was just important to him – well both of us, really – that someone saw what it was like.' Joanna swallowed hard and turned to the papers before continuing.

'I'm afraid there's rather a lot to read. The first document – here at the top – is a list of what I've found. Most of it is from Tom's old journals – they were clearing out his surgery and I put them all in the spare room. I've tried to dig out everything I could find on bacteria. Lucky I kept them really.

'The starting point, though, is this. It's a photocopy from his microbiology textbook and explains how bacteria work. And this...' she produced some more pages with a flourish '...is the basic theory on antibiotic resistance. The main thing to bear in mind is that the bugs can adapt to drugs over time and become immune to them. Tom had some sort of multi-resistant infection, and I want to find out what he got it from.'

'Where do you think he caught it?'

'Well, you'll see that there's quite a few articles on how bugs can become resistant to drugs. The latest material seems to be saying that the infections can even cross the species barrier.'

Geri watched her carefully.

'The only explanation which makes any sense to me is that the chicken that he ate that night had a multi-resistant bug, and that Tom caught it.'

The hairs on the back of Geri's neck were tingling again. If she could show that Tom Pascoe had been killed through eating infected meat, the claim could be enormous. But proving it was going to be almost impossible.

'We need to get more information from the hospital. Results of stool samples, the exact bug involved, their investigations and reports ... but we need to show that this could have been avoided. We're going to have to show that this meat shouldn't have entered the food chain. But unless we know where you got it from, we're going to have problems.'

'Mum, Joanna – there's an e-mail!'

They heard Rory's feet clump along the landing, and hurried upstairs to him.

'Come quickly.' He ushered them into his bedroom and gestured towards the screen of his PC. 'It's from a Professor Lebrun in Cambridge. He says he can tell you about antibiotic resistance, but not over the internet. He's given a phone number.'

'Let me write it down, I've got a pen downstairs...' fussed Joanna.

'No need.' He pressed the P button and the message was churned out of the printer. Geri took it.

'I'll put it with the papers. Rory, can you do your homework while I start reading what Joanna has brought? We can get a take-away later.'

Joanna intervened.

'Do say no if you'd rather not, but I love to cook and I noticed that you had some pasta and tuna in the kitchen. If you're busy, I could easily make something for you both...'

Geri was about to refuse politely, but Rory spoke first.

'Brilliant – thanks, Jo.'

Geri winced at the shortening. Joanna looked quite pleased.

'Well, I'll go to the kitchen and leave you both to it. It should take about an hour.'

Leaving Rory in his room, Geri returned to the living room and started to scan Joanna's papers. She must have found everything that was ever printed in the *British Medical Journal* about antibiotics. At the bottom of the pile were the most recent articles, those arguing that superbugs could leap the barrier between species – the barrier that was once thought to provide an impenetrable defence to the transmission of illnesses. Belief in the species barrier had held up BSE research for years.

As Geri read, she made notes in margins. As always, she forced herself to suspend judgment until she had read everything. She would keep an open mind, allow ideas, possibilities to hover.

As the hour drew to a close, the smell of cooking from the kitchen was just too tempting. She entered the room, and found that Rory had brought his homework down to the kitchen table and was sitting, entranced, as Joanna told him of her own schooldays.

'We had prep every night until eight. We used to sit in a hall to do it, and if we daydreamed, the teacher would rap our knuckles ... then we'd get an hour to read until lights out at nine.'

'When could you watch TV?'

'No TVs in Norfolk where I went to school. We used to read – rubbish, mainly – and talk. Anyhow,' she smiled at Geri, 'supper's ready.'

Joanna placed the full saucepan on the heat mat, and dispensed food until two plates were full with tuna and spaghetti.

'I hope you don't mind, but a little basil does help. I found some in one of the cupboards.'

Geri grinned back.

'No, of course not. I was just thinking, we ought to celebrate – I've got a bottle of Côtes du Rhone somewhere. You will stay, won't you?'

'Oh, no, I just thought I'd cook you a little something as a thank you for saving me from having to lug the papers back home...'

'No, you must – there's far too much for us anyhow.'

'Yeah, stay, Jo – you can tell me more about school. What were the bedrooms like?'

'Well, if I'm outvoted...' Joanna sat at the table while Geri opened the wine and Rory fetched another plate.

Two hours later, the wine was gone, the food eaten, the plates cleared away and the three of them were still sitting at the table. Geri hadn't laughed so much since Simon had been alive.

Rory had sat in fascinated awe, listening to tales of bearded gym mistresses, posture training and elocution. They had each tried walking with books on their heads – Geri with conspicuous lack of success. Rory had delivered the latest in-jokes to shrieks of laughter from both women and was trying to teach them the nuances of rugby positions.

'So, you see, the backs are actually the forwards, and the forwards are at the back. It's all quite sensible really.'

Joanna looked totally bemused. Her hair had loosened itself, curling around her face. She was slightly flushed – almost girlish.

'Clear as mud. Anyhow, I really ought to be on my way. It really has been lovely. Thank you so much for letting me stay.'

'No, thank you for cooking such a fantastic meal,' said Geri.

'Much better than a take-away,' added Rory.

'Well, thank you – but I must dash now.'

'Let me give you a lift,' offered Geri.

'No, I wouldn't hear of it. I can catch a bus from the Essex Road.'

'Not after dark. It's pretty dangerous out there, you know.'

'I have caught buses all over London at night. Nobody would dare mug me,' protested Joanna, getting up from the table.

She continued to refuse a lift, but finally allowed Geri to ring a safe minicab firm for her. As they waited, Joanna suddenly cursed.

'Damn ... oh, excuse me.' She giggled. The wine must have got to her. 'I meant to put in another article that one of Tom's partners found recently. It's still at the surgery – I forgot to pick it up.'

'Just pop it round. I've got enough reading anyhow to keep me going,' replied Geri.

The minicab arrived and Joanna left, waving through the window as she was driven away.

The house seemed rather quiet without her.

'She was all right,' said Rory, yawning.

'Yes, I know what you mean. Rory, I'm going to have to make a start on those papers she brought – do you think you could put yourself to bed tonight?'

He nodded and walked upstairs. Then he returned.

'Forgot to give you a kiss. I love you, Mum.'

He kissed her gently on the cheek before turning away, embarrassed, and hurtling up the stairs.

'I love you too,' she called after him.

Geri sat down close to the pile of papers and started at the top. She suddenly felt rather lonely. After that disastrous night, she hadn't rung Tony. He'd kept away, too. No doubt he realised it hadn't worked.

She knew that she was stuck, trying to press the rewind button on her life. She'd loved Simon desperately. The only sort of men who attracted her nowadays looked like him. But they never *were* him. The trouble was, she didn't want anyone else. She knew all the arguments – she was only in her mid-thirties, he had been gone two years, she was too young to sink into permanent widowhood. But until she fancied someone, nothing would change.

With an effort, she pulled herself back to her work. It had to be done now. She needed desperately to sleep, but the next day at work was already full.

By 2 a.m. she knew how bacteria could acquire resistance to antibiotics. As the clock struck 3 she finally reached the bottom of the pile and had covered six pages of her notebook with comments and queries. She could finally go to bed.

There was one big problem. Perhaps the most basic question for any litigator. Whose fault had it been? Even as Geri tried to sleep, she did not stop work as her mind continued to race. There had to be an answer. Someone to shoulder responsibility for Tom Pascoe's death.

Deep in her subconscious, a thought was forming. It was throwing ideas into her conscious mind which seemed to be random and disconnected. It was only when she had found the link that the answer would be clear.

Chapter Five

As Geri finally found sleep, the man who could have answered all her questions was just about to get up. David Vane loved the early morning. The sixteenth-century smallholder who had built the cottage in which he lived had arranged for it to face east, into the rising sun, so that the first shards of light fell into his living room, and above it the main bedroom.

The light fell across David, waking him gently. He started for a moment and then lay back, savouring the thought that he was working at home today and did not have to rush for the 7.20 to Liverpool Street. As he lay, he remembered his dream, tried to fall back asleep and re-enter it. Liz had been walking by the mill, Tom and Benjamin walking between them, hands held. She had turned to him, smiling, about to burst into laughter.

But it was no good. He was awake for the day. The only way he would see the boys was by looking at the silver-framed photograph at the side of the bed. It had been a typical playgroup portrait – the two boys sitting on a church hall table, smiling abstractedly towards the camera. Tom, at four, had been holding Ben safely, looking calmly out; the two-year-old was looking slightly quizzical, perhaps wondering why he was sitting on a table facing a bright light and an unfamiliar photographer.

David found it difficult to look at the picture. He always did. He had seen nothing of them for eighteen months and was unlikely to meet them for a long, long time. He knew little about them now – his memories must be out of date. Tom would be at school; Ben would be talking properly. Liz had written a few times, no doubt out of duty. Then the letters had shortened, become less frequent, and had finally stopped. There had been nothing he could do, stuck on the other side of the world.

David moved across the floorboards towards

the chest of drawers. The bedroom took up the roof space of the cottage and he could only stand straight in the middle of the room. The light brown beams stretched upwards, across to the central beam. Thick enough to have come from the Armada, he had been told – but then so had every other large beam in England.

The staircase wound its way around the back of the fireplace. David had never bothered to put in a banister rail, even when his wife had nagged him. Now there seemed little point. He used his hand to steady himself, feeling the bristles from the horse hair mixed into the fabric of the building. Once downstairs, he walked through the sitting room and into the large kitchen which dominated the cottage. Away from the morning light it was colder here – it would warm up once the night storage heater had dispersed a little more heat.

Plugging in the kettle, he looked through the large leaded window on to the garden. It had been a wasteland when he had bought the cottage ten years ago. David had levelled the soil over the course of a winter, building up the boggy area at the back until it became fertile again. Then he had dug the borders and worked the soil, filling it with compost until it supported a herbaceous border that flowered for ten months of the year. Immediately outside the window was the herb garden that he had created three years previously: sage, parsley, dill, chives – all growing neatly and divided between tiny cobblestone borders.

He needed a weekend in the garden. The

ground elder was starting to show itself and he had to get a grip on it before it covered the border. But the report had to be finished first. Yesterday he had set out the research methodology and results. Today, he was going to finish the vital section – the recommendations. By tomorrow the report would be on the Minister's desk with a polite note suggesting that he might like to consider it over the weekend.

He took the coffee into the small study and turned on the PC. He had planned the report with considerable care. It would have to be perfect. Any inconsistencies or ambiguities and the Minister would be able to wriggle out of any action. The conclusion would have to be utterly inescapable, so clear that Moncrieff would have no option but to do as he recommended. He wouldn't want to. He would struggle, look for alternatives, an easy way out.

Scientifically, the report was a breakthrough. Salmonella TO2. A brand, spanking new organism. But this was not a new arrival to be welcomed. It came laced with the potential to wreak complete havoc.

And, politically, it was going to be a bombshell.

It seemed to Geri that she had only just dropped off to sleep when the alarm clock stirred her into her weekday morning routine: harry Rory out of bed, feed him, drop him at school and fight through the traffic to the office. He had wandered through the school gate, bag slung over his shoulder, his face a picture in resignation.

She was greeted at the office by the sight of four

tottering piles of letters to sign. There must have been over a hundred. Even Jackie couldn't have done them before five – she must have stayed late again. Mechanically, Geri signed her way through each pile, popping each completed letter into the out tray for posting.

There was also a print out of work in progress on her most active files, so that she could dictate some interim bills. As ever, this was a haphazard process. In theory, it was just a case of working out how much time she had spent on the case, and attaching her usual hourly rate. But it was rarely that simple. What if the file had become temporarily lost in the temp's nonsensical system and took an hour to find? What if Geri had been in and out of the office and had wasted time re-reading what she had looked at three hours earlier? What if there was a point of law which she had to research and which she knew she should have had at her fingertips before she took on the case?

And then there were the problems which came from knowing the clients. The elderly ladies who paid from the grandchildren's present funds; the unemployed who needed the damages cheque to get decent treatment so they could work again; even the unions – she dare not charge too aggressively the few that had stayed after Simon's death. Geri worked her way through the pile and by 11 o'clock had billed two thousand pounds.

It was a start, she knew, but no more than that. And she still had to ring the bank about the overdraft. Please God let someone who could do something be there today.

The commercial manager was icily polite. He had never approved of them anyhow, just taken their filthy money.

'Mr Rogers, we need to arrange some temporary finance to get us over a ... er ... hump in our billing.'

'Yes, Mrs Lander, I was looking at your account earlier this morning. You are about to go over your overdraft limit and your pay day is imminent.'

Yes, yes, she wanted to say, I wouldn't be ringing you if everything was just fine. Instead, she kept quiet.

'I am becoming a little concerned at the state of the account, Mrs Lander... I think that some changes may be required.'

'Well, of course, but we need to consider matters fully. I was planning to carry out a business plan review,' countered Geri.

'A very good idea. Perhaps a management consultant would be of assistance? We can help with that.'

Sure you can, thought Geri. A kickback from the proceeds and a few free drinks at the next Lodge meeting.

'Well, perhaps if I could consult my partners? We're thinking of some changes, but in the meantime...'

'You'd like an extension on the overdraft?'

'Well, yes. Please.' Somehow, she never could regard overdrafts with approval. To Geri, they were a sign of indebtedness, of failure to cope, rather than an essential element in the financing of most businesses in the country. Probably an excess of lower-middle-class values. The aristocracy never seemed frightened of vast debts.

'If I mark you up to one hundred and ten thousand for a month, with a meeting before the expiration...'

'Thank you.'

'Usual terms, four percent over base and one percent arrangement fee.'

That would be over a thousand pounds just for the bloody telephone conversation. And they thought lawyers charged too much.

'But that's extortionate!' Geri protested.

'Standard rate for the product. In any event,' he went on cheerfully, 'I don't have the authority to negotiate anything different.'

Geri wondered how an overdraft could possibly be regarded as a product.

'Well, I suppose I'll have to accept, then.'

'Fine, I'll mark you down, and contact you in a fortnight to arrange a meeting.'

As Geri hung up, she remembered Rory's internet query. Undoing her handbag, she fished out the details of who to contact.

A Cambridge number. She rang.

'Porters Lodge, Trinity Hall.'

'Professor Lebrun, please.'

A voice came on to the line. She had expected to hear elderly, academic tones. Instead, he sounded young, definitely of her generation.

'Hi, Dermot Lebrun here.'

It was difficult not to smile in response. He sounded fun, distinctly unstuffy.

'My name's Geri Lander. I'm telephoning after you left a message on the internet...' Geri briefly explained about Joanna's husband.

She had long ago come to the view that there are three sorts of expert witness. First, there are those who regard all Court work as an unnecessary intrusion and refuse all requests to get involved in legal claims. It is not such an unreasonable stance given the demands of solicitors for last-minute reports and the constant requests to explain, expand upon or even change sections of evidence. Worst of all there is the worry that at some point he could find himself alone in the witness box, being made to look a complete fool by a man in a wig. It was no surprise, all things considered, that many experts looked on legal work with some distaste.

Geri knew that in a case like Joanna's – one at the cutting edge of scientific research – she would have very few experts to choose from. She hoped like hell that this Dermot Lebrun was going to help.

But she didn't want him to be at the other end of the expert witness spectrum: the professionals who regard their real skill as standing up in a witness box and supporting a given point of view. They may have impeccable experience and qualifications, but these are the experts who, for a necessarily generous fee, regard themselves as being involved in a case to help prove a point. They enjoy the cut and thrust of the Courtroom, give as good as they get to the opposition and will support the case of their paymaster to the point of professional ridicule. They can be readily identified – their first question on being contacted by solicitors will relate to the level of their fees; and all communications thereafter will be accompanied by a polite request for payment.

Please let him fall into the third group, she thought – the experts who look upon Court work as a duty to be carried out and balanced with their real professional interests. Rather quaintly, in the view of the professional witnesses, they stick firmly to the traditional view that the expert is there not to take sides, but to assist the Court. If current research goes against the cause of their side, they will spill the beans. By the same token, if there is a fair point to be made, they will research the night away without charge to find the necessary academic papers.

'Do you have the hospital records?'

'I'm just in the process of getting them,' replied Geri.

'So we know it started as food poisoning, probably from chicken. And we know that the organism concerned was multi-resistant. Hmmm.'

Geri was about to start apologising, to say that she knew it was little to go on, but could he possibly...

'Could you nip up to Cambridge one day?'

'Why, yes.'

'It's just that it would be much easier if I could take you through the research on this – there's rather a lot involved.'

Geri thought of the mountain of papers already sitting in her living room. This was the point at which she was going to have to warn Joanna about costs. Once she had to start travelling, talking to experts in firm time, the billing would have to escalate.

'Yes, of course. Perhaps next week?'

They made the arrangements and Geri hung up and noted her diary. She had just finished dictating a letter to the hospital to get Tom Pascoe's notes when the door opened.

Gloria Aitken was truly vast. Given, of necessity, to wearing dresses that were the cathedrals of the tent world, she seemed almost to flow into Geri's room and sat, unbidden, in front of the desk.

'I've come to see you about getting some extra staff,' she announced.

Gloria presided over the secretaries at Lander Ross and was their unofficial union spokeswoman. Fast, efficient and possessed of negotiating brilliance, she had been Cefan Davies's secretary since he'd joined the firm. Her room was situated next to his at the top of the stairs above reception – an ideal spot from which to monitor comings and goings. Her door was never closed and, over the years, Gloria's office had become something of a drop-in venue for anyone with a grouse or a piece of choice gossip.

Gloria had taken up causes and pursued them to some effect against the partners. Even in the most politically correct practices, with above average salaries and profit sharing, staff problems still arose.

Today, though, Gloria was her own representative.

'Mr Davies,' she was always formal when referring to her principal, 'has been asking rather a lot of me lately.'

Geri was perplexed.

'Erm, how?'

'He is arranging remortgages for several clients – three in particular. He suggested that they might like to rearrange their finances and get a lower interest rate deal.'

'Fairly standard practice, surely?'

Geri was inwardly applauding Cefan. This was a standard way to drum up some conveyancing work in a quiet period – when the lenders had less business, they often dropped their rates. This encouraged existing borrowers to remortgage and provided some welcome work for conveyancing solicitors. Surely Gloria couldn't object to that?

'Yes, it is standard, but he is making so many enquiries and applications, Mrs Lander. There must be nearly twenty. I have to say, it's easy for Mr Davies just to tell me to apply to all these lenders, but I'm left filling out all the forms. They're a nightmare to do on the WP – each one takes ages and I'm getting behind.'

'Have you spoken to Mr Davies about this?'

'Yes, I have, but he just tells me that he's shopping around for the best deal.'

Geri knew very well that form filling is the least popular task of the legal secretary. It is fiddly, time-consuming and fundamentally boring. It is also perceived as being low-skill and she was not surprised at Gloria's next request.

'It's taking up so much time that I'm not able to keep up with the other work. What I think is that we need an extra secretary to deal with the applications so that I can keep my head above water.'

Not on our cash flow, thought Geri to herself.

She smiled at the secretary. She'd have to exercise some tact here.

'I see the difficulty, and I know how hard you work, Gloria ... but I'll need to find out more about this. I'll have a word with Mr Davies about the extra work, and have a chat with you after that.'

Gloria seemed satisfied.

'Thank you, Mrs Lander. In the meantime, if I find it a little too much, I'll just take a short break.'

Geri was wise to this.

'I'd rather you reported it direct to Mr Davies if you find it too much in the meantime.'

Let him deal with it.

'Certainly.'

As the secretary left, Geri looked at her appointments diary. She had three meetings with clients – these were due to start at 1 p.m. and carry on at hourly intervals until 4 o'clock. Then she would have to sign off her post. In the meantime, she would need to field around twenty phone calls – from clients, opposing solicitors and Courts – all of which would require the digging out of the relevant file, a response and a file note or letter.

And she still had to start preparing the Mitchell case for trial. It was in for hearing next week. The legal arguments would need two days' work to research and get ready for the Court. And then she needed to start the financial review for the bank ... she wondered at times what Gloria really had to complain about. At least she could go home and switch off for the evening. Geri's evenings had tended of late to be a continuation of what she was doing in the office all day.

Thinking about Gloria, she knew she would forget to speak to Cefan if she left it any longer. No time like the present, she thought to herself, as she made her way up the staircase to his room.

He was just coming out of, his office, carrying a sheaf of papers.

'Geri, I was coming to see you.'

'Well, shall we have a chat in your room, since I'm here?' She smiled, trying to be pleasant.

'Of course.' He led the way back in and sat at the desk. Cefan Davies had always been a great believer in office psychology. The furniture was solid but contemporary – everything giving off a subtle message that this was a man who was up to date and go ahead, but trustworthy and dependable. Lots of wood, but some garish prints. A year planner supplied by a computer manufacturer, looking satisfyingly full. Two telephones and a personal fax in the corner.

Geri sat opposite him in the leather-upholstered chair. It squeaked disconcertingly whenever she shifted her position.

'Geri, before I forget or lose these papers...' He passed them over the desk to her. Geri saw the heading on the first sheet. Something to do with Islington Council.

'I've managed to get hold of a local population study. Did you know that the borough has one of the highest percentages of single parent families in London?'

For the second time that day, Geri was perplexed. Cefan had never expressed an interest in social patterns before.

'Well, I suppose it's no surprise, really.'

'Have you ever thought, Geri, whether the needs of these parents are being met?'

She realised with dreadful certainty what this was leading to and countered quickly.

'They're being met by specialist family law solicitors.'

'We could meet them better.'

'No, Cefan. We are not a family law firm. We were not set up to do that work. I do some other areas of litigation, but family law is a vast area. It has its own specialists – there is no way I plan on joining them.'

'But think, Geri – you know perfectly well that you need more clients. If you're not getting them in the personal injury work, then the obvious answer is to expand into the family side of things. You'll be meeting a real need. You're not saying that a single mother who needs some money from her ex-boyfriend is less worthy than one of your union clients, are you?'

'No, I'm not. You know that perfectly well.' She rose to the bait.

'Well then,' he allowed himself a satisfied smile, 'you'd be meeting a real need. And what's more, most of the work is done on legal aid, so you'll not have all the problems with losing conditional fee cases. No one minds if you lose on the legal aid – well, no one except the legal aid fund.'

'But you're not hearing me, Cefan. I'm not a

family lawyer. You'd have as much of a clue as I would on how to fight an ancillary relief application...'

Tactless. She'd forgotten that he'd walked out on his wife and three children three years ago and had been fighting off her lawyers ever since. Damn!

He looked suitably wounded and her point was lost.

'Now, Geri, we're talking about litigation here. All I'm saying is that if you took the trouble to move into family work – everyone has to learn new skills at times – you might be able to turn your profitability around. We've got to move with the times, meet the needs of our community.'

Geri had been trying very hard but this was too much. She saw red. Cefan had fought these little battles, one after the other, when Simon had been in charge. She'd never forgive him for that. He may have driven her husband to the pits of despair, but he wasn't going to succeed with her. If this was his latest little campaign, she was going to have to nip it in the bud.

She stood up. Instinctively, he moved back. Good.

Her voice, when she spoke, was low, cold and furious.

'Cefan, listen to this and shut up for once in your life. I am not going to do family cases – repeat N-O-T. If you're so keen on the idea, put yourself on a family law course. You're shitty enough to enjoy making money out of matrimonial disasters. Just don't try me on it any more. Understand?'

She glared at him. As he opened his mouth to respond, the office tannoy crackled into life.

'Phone call for Mrs Lander, please.'

'I've got to go.' As Geri left, she realised she'd completely forgotten to mention Gloria. She'd have to tackle him again about that one.

She raced down the stairs to her office and picked up the phone.

'Geri, it's Ingrid. Said she couldn't wait for you to ring back,' said Jackie.

'Hello, Ingrid. Geri here.'

The voice of the after-school carer sounded guilty.

'Hello, Mrs L. Sorry to get you out of your meeting, but I've had a few family difficulties and I'm going to have to stop picking Rory up. Sorry, but you know how it is...'

Geri's pulse was still racing after the encounter with Cefan.

'Ingrid, this isn't on. I've been paying you well over the odds and I need someone reliable'

'Well, thing is, I can't do it any more. Got to go – sorry.'

The voice tailed off and the phone was hung up.

Damn! Geri could have kicked herself. It was all bloody Cefan's fault. She shouldn't have been so heavy with Ingrid. A bit more tact and she might have stayed on for a while.

Geri looked at her appointments diary and wailed inwardly. When Rory had been a baby, she had read endless books debating the comparative merits of nannies, nurseries and childminders, agonising over which to use. But none of the books had told her that arranging good child care to cover the after-school period was a hundred times more difficult. No nanny or nursery wanted a child for only two or three hours a day; childminders had their own children to deal with then and after-school clubs were worryingly like detention. Why did the English education system insist on sending children home at 3.20 when most working parents clock off at 5.30?

Jackie came into the room.

'Trouble again?'

Geri nodded.

'I'll cancel the last appointment – Mrs Jarvis can wait a few days. I'll bring the post early and you can slip away again.'

At moments like this Jackie came into her own, but Geri knew that short-term fixes were not going to be enough.

'Thanks, I'll get through the first two. And I'll try the agency straight away.'

As Jackie left, Geri rang, to get the usual response – no they couldn't supply anyone today, but would ring her back with some suggestions tomorrow. Geri knew what that meant. They'd scrape the barrel for the carers everyone else rejected. It simply wasn't fair to Rory to subject him to this. She put her head in her hands. Something was going to have to change.

'There must have been something wrong with that last lot. I've had a farmer lose all his stock – the perinycin had no effect at all.'

Grimwood was sitting in the roadside cafe, a mug of tea in his hands. Frankie Stiles looked quizzical. He'd been in the Army with Benny, but had been dishonourably discharged when he'd been caught supplying cannabis to the squaddies.

He'd carried on the business after he left, and had built up a nice little line in supplies. Enough to buy him a neo-Georgian mansion in Chingford and a rather impressive motor boat in which he made regular forays to the continent. And, like every good businessman, he was always looking to expand.

He'd hit upon the perinycin run from one of his contacts. The profits looked good, and the stuff came in along his usual supply routes – students who would carry it through customs for a few hundred, bent port officials and the odd lorry driver desperate for some hard cash. So far it had been a raging success. But he knew that it had a limited shelf life.

'There's a chance some illnesses might become resistant to it, Benny.'

'How do you mean?'

'Well, if it's given out too much, the bugs change themselves and get immune.'

'So what do the farmers do then?'

Stiles smiled thinly.

'That's their problem. Perhaps there'll be another antibiotic invented, perhaps not. But,' he sat back and steepled his hands thoughtfully, 'it does mean that we'll need to work out how we're going to play this.'

Grimwood nodded.

'You mean, how much we can get before we shut up shop and scarper?'

'Yes.'

The two men paused a while and thought through the options. Stiles spoke first.

'I think we need to stop supplying for a while – get the farmers worried and push the price up.'

'And then we do one last deal?' replied Grimwood.

'Correction. One last *big* deal.'

Benny Grimwood allowed himself a brief smile.

'One last fucking *enormous* deal.'

Chapter Six

Geri had raced through the afternoon appointments and had driven like fury but she was still late. Rory was waiting outside the gate, alone, staring into the gutter.

She parked in front of him and he grinned. He looked so like Simon.

''Lo, Mum. Another crisis?'

As he got into the car, she noticed red rims around his eyes.

'Rory, what's up?'

'Nothing.'

It was said too quickly, too determinedly, to be the truth. He looked straight ahead of him, face set in a slight frown.

'Tell me,' Geri asked, gently.

'I said, nothing.' His voice wobbled slightly.

She drove off, crashing the gears. They sat in awkward silence for the journey.

Once home, Rory scurried upstairs, pleading homework. Geri decided to start preparing the Mitchell case, but her mind kept returning to her son. She wondered whether to follow him upstairs or let him be alone for a while. With a start, she realised it had been just like this in the last months with Simon. She had never known when to pursue him, insist he talked, and when to leave him be.

There was a sharp tap at the door.

Joanna stood on the step, smiling brightly. She was neatly turned out in a tweed suit and brown coat. Her hair was back to its tidy state.

'Hello, glad you're back ... I've got those extra papers I mentioned last night – and thank you for such a pleasant evening.'

Geri returned the smile.

'Come in. And thank you for cooking last night – it was lovely.'

They sat at the kitchen table. Geri's papers from the Mitchell case were spread out in front of them.

'Joanna, I've dealt with that internet reply – it's from a Cambridge professor who sounded quite interested. I've arranged to go and see him next week.'

'Excellent. Thank you, Geri.'

'But, look, I really need to talk to you about money.'

A frown stole across Joanna's features. Geri continued, gently.

'It's never pleasant to speak about costs, but I've got to warn you that suing people isn't cheap. At the moment we've got some good material, but we've no idea what your chances of success are. The professor will have to charge, and so shall I for taking half a day to go and see him. Joanna, I don't want to get you into deep waters, financially, without warning you first.'

'Yes, I understand.'

There was a pause, and Joanna sighed.

'I suppose I ought to tell you now, really, rather than later. I'm not terribly well off ... well, actually, I don't have enough money to bring this claim.'

Geri sat silent, watching her carefully. She'd been tactless enough earlier with Ingrid. When in doubt, keep your trap shut, she told herself.

'Tom and I never had children. We saved a little, but lived well – holidays, clothes – and then he got involved with a Lloyds syndicate and lost everything. They're still after us. I'm paying a little every month from some insurance money that I got when he died. I've got the house but the mortgage is enormous, and there's a holiday cottage in Devon with negative equity. The insurance keeps me afloat, but with the Lloyds repayments, there's no slack in the system at all.'

'How about bank accounts?'

'There's just one. Coutts – memories of better days, I suppose. The five hundred I gave you was all there was in it.'

Geri felt awful.

'Joanna, I'm sorry – I didn't realise.'

'No, you have to charge – you can't work for free. It's just...'

She struggled to continue.

'You know from the video that Tom never knew

exactly what killed him. He wanted so much for someone to make a fuss on his behalf He wanted me to go to the law, get questions asked ... but I just can't risk any more money.'

Her voice was suddenly old and quavering. She was a woman with a fierce loyalty to her late husband, but not enough cash.

'Joanna, there *is* a way. I can take cases on a conditional fee basis. If you lose, you don't pay anything. If you win, you pay extra. That could be the answer.'

'But it's like you said earlier – we don't yet know if the claim has a chance. I can't ask you to spend hours wading through the papers for nothing.'

This was the moment Geri could have backed out, let things lie. As it was, she took a decision that would change everything.

'I'm quite prepared to do it. In fact, I want to make a fuss. After that video, Joanna ... well...'

Joanna turned towards her. Her eyes had gone rather red.

'Geri, thank you. You'll never know how grateful I am. But I've got to make some contribution towards all this. Look, hear me out on this – I know you need help picking Rory up. I rang the office and managed to get your secretary to tell me what had happened this afternoon...'

Geri could imagine even Jackie giving way under Joanna's insistent probing.

'...so I wondered, could I do that for you? At least for the time being. It will make me feel that I'm helping in some way. And God knows, I have nothing else to do in the afternoons.'

Geri thought through the offer. If the agency had sent someone like Joanna along, she'd have jumped at her in a shot. But she was still a client, and Geri knew she should never get too involved or she'd lose her professionalism. But professionalism wouldn't pick her son up from school and cook his tea!

'That would be wonderful – but let's just try it for a week or so,' she said carefully.

'Done! Now, I've got to dash off – bridge night, you see. But I'll be there for Rory tomorrow. 3.20, isn't it? OK!'

After Joanna had gone, armed with details of where to find the school, Geri climbed the stairs to Rory's room. At the front of the house, it overlooked the quiet residential street. This was Islington, but too far east to be trendy. The roads were long and straight, populated by a few rising stars on their way to grander addresses, some long-term residents and a clutch of students.

Rory was sitting at his computer.

'Look, Mum – I'm at the Natural History Museum. There's this thing about identifying some skeleton on Bodmin Moor – have a look.'

'Perhaps later, Rory. I came to ask what you'd like for tea?'

Over supper, she told him about the suggestion and asked him if he'd mind Joanna picking him up.

'No, it'd be brilliant, Mum. Much better than Ingrid, anyhow.'

The cottage was dark by the time David Vane had finished his report. The only light came from the screen of his word processor. As always, he'd worked with total concentration, forgetting coffee, lunch, tea. He'd even ignored a distressingly full bladder.

But the report was ready. He clicked on the 'save' icon and copied the file on to disc. He'd print it out at the Ministry tomorrow and walk it round to the Minister himself. He didn't want any excuses about not receiving it. He would have a word with the permanent secretary – make sure it was in the red box for the weekend. Then he'd get himself booked in for a briefing meeting on Monday morning.

The Minister would only take risks if pressurised. David was going to have to exert that pressure.

He sat back and considered tactics.

The next day, as David Vane started to print off his report in Whitehall, Geri decided to have another go at tackling Cefan Davies. She could then get down to preparing the Mitchell trial. The hearing was starring to loom over her. She had two working days and a weekend to get ready for it. She needed a clear run.

Geri knocked at his door and entered as soon as she heard him respond. She needed to get in quick, raise the problem with Gloria first and not allow him to knock her off course with ridiculous ideas about becoming a divorce lawyer. And she must not lose her rag. Not this time.

'Cefan, I've been having a word with Gloria,' she started.

'I see.'

He was frowning at her. He never made it easy for her to talk.

'She's been telling me she needs an assistant as she's rather snowed under with mortgage applications. I said I'd have a chat with you.'

He looked irritated. Keep calm, Geri told herself.

'Don't know why she's gone crying to you. She hasn't mentioned it to me.'

'Well, she said she had. But never mind that. Is there actually a problem? She's a pretty good secretary after all, and I think we ought to listen to what she has to say.'

Geri was trying to be fair, but he was having none of it. 'Curmudgeonly' was a word which was made for him, she decided.

'No, she's just bleating. I have been doing some remortgage work, and she just gets fed up with having to form fill. But, quite frankly, it's got to be done.'

'Cefan, she did mention a lot of applications were being made.'

There was no point in another argument. Let him see the problem, perhaps agree to ease off a little or change the time constraints on the work. She loathed the man, but they were partners. They had to work together.

His eyes seemed blank behind the irritating little glasses. But his face reddened and his mouth set into a pugilistic grimace.

'What the fuck is this? I'm looking around, trying to get the best deal for my clients. The market's changing so quickly at the moment, you don't know which lender has the lowest rates until you get a written offer. So I'm casting their nets wide. With the best will in the world, I don't think even Gloria can start telling me how best to serve our clients!'

The phone rang. He picked it up without even acknowledging Geri.

'Philip ... yes, thanks for coming back. Just a few details on the valuations ... hang on a moment.'

He looked at Geri. 'Look this is going to take some time. I'll get back to you.'

Bloody hell, she thought. You're in the middle of explaining a problem to your senior partner, not lecturing the office junior. The least you can do is carry on talking to me and ring him back later.

But this wasn't the time for another out and out confrontation with Cefan. Bloody impossible with him on the phone anyhow. She left. He made no apology and offered no polite end to the conversation. He just dismissed her.

Geri was finally able to start on her financial review, and spent an hour analysing the firm's sources of income. She managed to reply to all her messages, and settled a claim for a figure that was twice what the client was expecting. At midday there was an appointment with a new client, a Mrs Edith Berryfield. She turned out to be a former secretary, a small lady in her sixties with hair in a greying bun and a nervous manner.

'And I was just coming out of the manager's office when I fell ... you see, there was no lighting over the staircase. I'd been on to him to buy some new light bulbs for months, but nobody did anything. So I fell right down and broke my hip.'

'Have you been back to work since?'

'No. They retired me on health grounds. There were no pensions for the female staff until recently, so I didn't make any contributions. I managed to save a little so I don't get benefits.'

The claim sounded like a winner. The name of the company was vaguely familiar to Geri: Garside Communications.

'Why did you come to us, Mrs Berryfield?' she asked, playing for time while trying to recall why she had heard of the company.

'Well, Mr Lander acted for me some time ago. I, er, had a few problems with my health and they sectioned me – put me in a mental hospital. Mr Lander helped get me out. And then, I think someone else from your firm did some work for the company and they were very impressed.'

Geri's heart sank. A conflict of interest.

'Ah. Well, Mrs Berryfield, if both you and the company have been clients, we wouldn't be able to act for both sides. I would need to talk to my partners about whether we can take on your case.'

The woman seemed deflated.

'Oh. Well, perhaps I ought just to leave it?'

Leave a claim that sounded like a dead cert? She must be joking!

'No, you shouldn't. Look ... I'll have a word with my partners. I really would like to act for you but it may mean asking the company to use alternative solicitors. I'll do my best.'

Geri smiled at Mrs Berryfield. The firm couldn't act for both parties to a dispute. It would have to choose which to represent and which to send elsewhere. Lander Ross had always had a policy of sticking with the Plaintiff. It was that type of firm, after all. And Mrs Berryfield had been a client long before Garside came knocking on the door. All the same, she'd have to mention it to Roger at the next meeting.

Mrs Berryfield coughed gently.

'As I said, I've got some small savings put by and the Citizens Advice Bureau told me I won't qualify for legal aid. They told me to ask if you did cases on a no win, no fee basis?'

'Yes, I do.'

After she had signed off her post, Geri put all her calls through to Jackie and went into the firm's library. The room, just along from hers at the back of the building and also overlooking the tiny garden, was empty.

The tools of the lawyer's trade are books. Textbooks, commentaries, working party documents – but most of all law reports. These are case summaries, reproducing the words of the Judges who determine the important issues of the day – interpreting Acts of Parliament or even making completely new law. Judges must give reasoned decisions, and, in an important case, these can be many pages long.

The law library at Lander Ross was good. Simon had always reasoned that if you wanted to change the law, you had to understand it properly first. As a result, a selection of different reports was ranged around the shelves – the All England reports, in their distinctive blue and gold binding; the Personal Injury and Quantum reports, in their bright yellow; and the relatively dowdy black Weekly Law Reports. It was an expensive library to run. The reports were constantly updated at vast cost and the textbooks were all latest edition. But that was how it had to be. One day, perhaps, they could afford to subscribe to the CD Rom versions of the publications. But it would take more than a run of interim billing to pay for such a big step. And Geri loved the musty atmosphere and quietness of the library. The dull whir of a computer would be quite out of place.

Run-of-the-mill litigation lawyers think of the law as providing a set of rules to determine issues between parties. Great lawyers – and Geri was becoming one – regard the law as a flexible tool, there to be shaped and adapted to support their causes. This process was not easy. Geri would often read late into the night, looking up every case in which a judgment might assist her. Sometimes it was no more than a throw-away line, but the thrill of finding something – anything – that would provide a basis for a new development in the law was like nothing else. She was not alone in this. Many of the greatest Judges in the land forged their reputation at the Bar by constantly pushing at the boundaries of the law.

The Mitchell case was on for its liability trial on Tuesday. Geri needed to find and photocopy all the case reports which she needed so that she could take them home over the weekend and start preparing her arguments. Stewart Mitchell was an eighteen-year-old who had enormous problems. He had been sent to a boarding school by his parents where he had got into the habit of taking large quantities of drugs. Soon, he had developed a range of psychiatric illnesses, all of which could have been drug-related. Whenever he came back from hospital, however, he went straight back to drug taking at school. He had stayed there until sixteen, at which point he left and had drifted into petty offending, alcohol and drug abuse.

Geri was trying, on behalf of Stewart Mitchell, to sue the school for failing to deal with his drug taking. She was arguing that they should have known what was going on, and that had they dealt with the problem sooner, Stewart wouldn't have ended up in such a mess.

Geri had agreed that there should be a split trial. In any action for personal injuries, there are two basic issues to be decided. The first is whether he or she wins their claim; the second is how much money they should be awarded. In most cases, the two points are decided at the same hearing; but sometimes, when the question of liability is complicated, there will be an earlier hearing to look at liability alone.

As she studied the reports, Geri started to build up a pile of those she wanted to photocopy. In a larger firm, someone would have done this for her, but at Lander Ross late on a Friday afternoon it was down to her. Unlike some of her brethren in the profession, she had a good working knowledge of the office photocopier and all its foibles. From time to time, she wondered how Joanna was coping with Rory.

She worked steadily, noting the points which she could use to draw her argument together.

This was the part of the job that she loved: constructing an argument from bits and pieces of judgments delivered over the years. This was how the law progressed, developed, adapted to the demands of the age. But it needed people like Geri to work it gently into a different shape.

By 5.45 she had prepared all that she needed. Taking a few textbooks from the shelves, she set off for home, setting the burglar alarm in the empty building and signing herself out.

It was actually rather nice to come back to a house with lights on. As she opened the door, she smelt the unmistakable aroma of curry – her favourite supper. In the kitchen, Rory was doing some homework while Joanna sat, pen in hand, reading what looked like a scientific paper. Everything was quiet.

'Hi, Mum.' Rory grinned.

Joanna looked up and smiled too.

'How did it go?' asked Geri.

'Fine,' they both said at once.

Joanna laughed.

'We found each other at the gate, and popped into Safeway on the way back. Rory said you both like curry on a Friday, so I thought I'd help out.'

'Joanna, you shouldn't!'

'Well, it must be awful to come in at six and then have to start cooking.'

'Will you stay for supper, Jo?' asked Rory.

'I'd love to, but I've got to be off. Rory, if I dish it up, do you want to change so you don't get the food all over your uniform?'

As he clambered upstairs, Joanna took her coat

off the peg and turned towards Geri.

'I thought I ought to mention – he was a little quiet when I picked him up, and there was a shoe print on his blazer. I pretended I hadn't noticed.'

Geri sighed.

'Oh, dear. I'm sure something's going on, but I can't get him to talk.'

Joanna sighed as she put one arm into her coat.

'It's the timing that matters. He'll talk when he's ready ... but listen to me, lecturing away when I've no experience of children at all!'

She sounded a little wistful.

'There's another article on antibiotic abuse, by the way – it's on the kitchen table. Rory downloaded it from his internet thing this afternoon. Quite useful, actually. I've also been to the Newspaper Reference Library at Colindale this morning – brought back copies of a few press cuttings.'

She pointed to a pile of papers. Geri, who used Nexus Lexis to track down newspaper articles, tactfully kept quiet.

Joanna left happily, with promises to pick up Rory on Monday. The chicken balti which she had made was quite delicious.

Rory, though, was quiet. Usually, he chattered away at supper time, particularly at the end of the week. But tonight, he ate a few mouthfuls of food, then pushed the rest around his plate.

Geri tried to probe gently.

'Is everything all right at school?'

'Yes.'

'I don't mean just lessons, but outside.'

His lip started to tremble and he looked away.

Quickly, she put down her plate and moved towards him.

'Mum...'

Geri put her arms around him just as the tears came. She could feel his sobs as he shook against her.

'Come on,' she said gently, 'let's try and sort it all out.'

He sat down and stared bleakly in front of him.

'There's two boys – older than me.'

He paused.

'It's all right, Rory, you can tell me.'

'They started picking on me in the playground...'

He sniffed loudly.

'It was after I got the prize for maths. They said I was a creep.'

He couldn't meet her eyes.

'Then they said I only got it because my dad was dead and everyone felt sorry for me,' he sobbed. 'And they put notes in my jacket, saying they were going to get me.'

At last he turned towards her.

'But they didn't do anything. They just kept on shouting names, you know.'

'What did they call you?'

He frowned.

'Er ... I can't remember ... but then I tried to get back at them, but they're bigger and there was a fight.'

At least he was talking. She knew he wasn't telling her everything, but it was a start.

'But, Mum, please don't talk to the school.'

'I could tell Mrs Davidson – there are ways of

sorting these boys out.'

Geri could certainly think of a few.

'No, honestly, Mum – she already knows, I'm sure, and it will just make things worse if she tells them off. They tried to do something when Martin Jenkins got hit all the time last term and he just has to stay in all the time now. If I keep my head down, they'll pick on someone else next term.'

He had a point. The summer holidays weren't too far away. Perhaps the whole thing would die down before the autumn.

'Rory, I'll do whatever you want – but only if you talk to me about it. I want to know what's happening, and I promise I won't talk to anyone unless you agree.'

He nodded tearfully at her.

That night, the nightmare came back. Geri was with him for two hours, holding him as he trembled, too terrified to close his eyes again. In the end, he could only sleep if she put the spare bed in his room and promised to stay there all night. As she lay, she could hear him moving fitfully, turning over and over.

This was when she hated being a widow. She could cope with most things, but the responsibility for her troubled child lay on her shoulders alone. In the dark of the night, she just didn't know if she was up to the task.

Rory had never asked her if Simon had killed himself. She wondered sometimes why he didn't suspect. He was younger then – just nine – perhaps he hadn't really taken on board the depression, the arguments and the drinking.

Perhaps he suspected, but didn't want to know.

She held him tight and thought back to that terrible night, the TV blaring out some dreadful movie as she found Simon downstairs, the empty jar of sleeping tablets to one side and the whisky to the other.

She couldn't possibly tell Rory yet. If he didn't want to hear, it would push him over the edge. The one thing he knew was that he was loved – had been loved – by both his parents. If he doubted that, he would have nothing.

Chapter Seven

'For God's sake, I've got to have some perinycin!'

The farmer had driven twenty miles to speak to Grimwood personally.

'I'm sorry, I just can't get it at the moment ... there's some clampdown.'

Barry Jackson, the farmer, paused for a moment.

Grimwood noticed the pause.

'Have you been visited by anyone official?'

'There was some bloke having a nose round. Didn't find anything – I keep the stuff well away from the feed.'

'What did he ask you?'

'Nothing much. Gave me a lecture about antibiotics. Never had to run a chicken farm himself, no doubt. Anyhow, I just nodded in the right places, said I'd never dream of doing anything in that direction myself, and off he went.'

The farmer continued, warming to his theme.

'But they'll never do anything about the perinycin. It's an open secret. They know what's going on and don't want to stop it. They know there'll be a crisis if they do.'

Grimwood frowned.

'That's as maybe, but I can't afford to take the risk. And I can't get the stuff anyhow at the moment.'

'But my stock are going down with something – I've lost over fifty chickens this week.'

'Look, if I had some, you could take it now. But I can't help you.'

'I'll pay double, treble. How much do you want for it?'

Grimwood shook his head.

'No. Best thing you can do is slaughter the lot of them before they all go down with it, and get rid of the meat pretty damn quick.'

'No other bloody option, have I?'

'As soon as I've got something, I'll let you know.'

'Perhaps I'll have to go elsewhere.'

'Best of luck to you, if you do.'

He watched as Barry Jackson manoeuvred his Range Rover out of the entrance. It was difficult not to smile. The strategy was working like a dream. His phone was constantly ringing with farmers desperate for perinycin. They were all willing to pay silly money.

Soon they could go into supply mode again. Then they would make the final deal.

It was Saturday. Rory had asked, rather sheepishly over breakfast, if they could go to West Tilbury. They hadn't been for a while and he often needed to go when things were difficult, so Geri agreed readily. She quite liked the place too.

Geri and Rory drove out of Islington and found their way to Grays. Before long, they were rounding the bends by the great sweeps of the Thames. The great hill rose to their left and they climbed it along the quiet lane. At the top, they parked and made their way around the church-cum-house into the graveyard.

It always took Geri a while to orientate herself. The graves were not, by and large, well kept and the grass grew high. After ten minutes they found the two stones, George and Mary Lander of this parish, departed in 1974 and 1975 respectively.

Simon's mother and father had been born in the same village, gone to school together and married at eighteen. They had worked all their lives together and when her husband had left this world Mary had followed within the year out of sheer loneliness.

Further down the hill were the previous generation. Emma Lander, gone in the 1950s. Her husband James lay in a military cemetery in Northern France.

They sat at the top of the hill and gazed down at the river, far below. Simon had not wanted a burial here. An atheist in life, he didn't want the church in death. But his roots had been here, in this Essex soil, and generations of his family lay here in eternal proof.

After that, they walked quietly down the road, past the listed pub and to the front of the old post office. It had long ago been converted into a private house.

'I can remember your dad telling me about the building,' said Geri.

'What did he say?'

'If you look at the side, there's a window – that was his room when he was growing up. Your dad used to say that there were big jars of sweets for sale in the post office part. He used to nip in there when your grandparents were asleep and take them ... no wonder he always had such a sweet tooth.'

Rory looked at her carefully.

'It's good having a past, isn't it? I mean, knowing where you're from, where people lived ... do I sound stupid?'

She thought about it. Her own parents had been neatly cremated in an anonymous crematorium in West London. There was nothing to mark their passing.

'No, it's not stupid, I think it's very true ... but you have to look to the future, too, Rory. The past isn't everything.'

She wondered even as she said it whether she really believed that. She looked around her – the beauty of the village had been preserved by the local council, but few young families could afford to move in any more. The village shop had closed many years ago and the church had been sold off for housing. Yet it was special.

Afterwards they drove back to Islington. Rory

seemed a little easier and watched TV while she worked on the Mitchell case. As ever, Geri wrote her opening speech out in longhand, setting out a précis of the evidence and law, telling the Judge what a strong claim it was. She wouldn't use her long note, but she had a recurring fear that she would dry up and forget what she wanted to say. This scrawled page was her escape route.

Then she moved on to the law. The cases were neatly photocopied, but she needed to work out how to take the Judge through them. It was always difficult, trying to find an interesting way of distilling all the reasoning into principles which you could apply to the case. The best lawyers made it into a fascinating voyage of logic. Most made it deeply tedious.

At 9, she tucked Rory into bed. She was almost ready for the trial.

David Vane had spent a satisfying weekend in the garden. The ground elder was now out of the soil and in the compost bin. He had, with extraordinary care and delicacy for such a large man, planted out the small seedlings which he had been raising on the kitchen window sill. He had cleared the overgrowth of weed from the pond and cut back the bulrushes at its margins.

The Monday train had been on time and he had been able to run through his report before his appointment with the Minister. He would have no problems with explaining the science to Callum Moncrieff – the Minister's intelligence was accepted even by the Civil Service mandarins who on the whole regarded politicians as rather dim party apparatchiks. The difficult point was going to be getting him to agree to the right response.

David had insisted on this morning appointment and the diary secretary had grudgingly agreed. Now he was seated opposite the Minister, who was sitting back in an overstuffed chair, listening carefully. His dark eyes studied David intently as he fired off the occasional sharp question.

'Minister, you'll have seen from my report that the real problem lies with the farms. They are operating on the black market and we have very little control over the situation.'

'How many human cases have there been?'

'Twenty notified.'

The Minister stared at him.

'But there is no proven link between carcass and human illness?'

'Well, you've had the hospital notification forms which I sent on...'

Moncrieff waved his hand dismissively.

'No, I mean outside evidence proving a link?'

'Not as such, Minister, but...'

'Has anyone lodged a legal claim?'

David was becoming angry.

'With respect, Minister, I'm not here to advise about the law. We need to stop this situation from getting out of hand, and you'll see my recommendations in the report.'

'Yes. Somewhat radical, you might say.'

'But it's the only way. The lesson we learned from BSE is the necessity of taking decisive action. This is what we've got to do here.'

'Well, thank you, David, for doing all this work. I shall need some time to consider your report. I'll get my secretary to arrange another meeting as soon as I am in a position to take it further.'

He's not bloody well going to do anything! thought David.

Callum Moncrieff stared straight at him.

'Minister, people are going to die if this is not brought under control. You are going to have to act now. If this worsens, it will soon be uncontrollable...'

'Dr Vane ... David ... I *am* concerned, I *will* be taking action, but this does have ramifications. I won't be rushed into anything, you understand?'

David Vane didn't let his gaze waver. I'm not going to give way. I'm going to make it impossible for you to do nothing, he thought.

The Minister got the message.

'I'll give this top priority and come back to you urgently.'

'Yes, Minister.'

Monday morning is a bad time to have a partners' meeting. Tempers are at their worst, pressure mounting after the weekend. This meeting was going very badly indeed. Geri had announced her review of income and expenditure to a less than ecstatic response. Now she had to deal with the Garside claim.

'There's something further I should mention. I've had a meeting with a new client – Mrs Edith Berryfield. She's got a reasonable claim in negligence against one of Roger's clients, Garside Communications. I think we may need to tell

Garside and ask them to seek alternative representation.'

Roger looked peeved.

'But, Geri, they're potentially an extremely important part of the practice. Mr Garside is a personal friend of mine and we billed over twenty thousand from them last year.'

'Are you acting for them on anything at the moment?'

'Not as such, but I'm sure they'll be coming back in the reasonably near future.'

'Sorry, Roger, but we can't represent both ... you know the policy we've always followed when this happens.'

'Where is this policy written down?'

Trust Cefan to put a spanner firmly into the works.

'It's not written down, but we all know that this is the way we have operated in the past. Something has to take precedence, and we're a litigation firm after all.'

'But we're a business. Businesses don't send their best clients away. Not businesses that are going to continue, anyhow.'

'Cefan, we have to stick to our policy, even if short-term...'

'Short-term, my arse! The only policy that makes any sense, short-term or long-term, is to stick with our profitable clients,' he growled.

'We can't throw away twenty thousand pounds worth of business for a one off piece of litigation,' added Roger.

Geri tried to keep calm. There had never been any question about this in the past. Lander Ross kept its litigation clients.

'What would you be looking at in profit costs for a claim of this type? Two thousand if it settles? This company is a regular client – we could even defend it in this claim if we told this woman where to go. How can you chuck away ten times as much – recurring – for a one off fraction? It just makes no sense at all.' Cefan was firmly on the attack now.

Geri looked uncomfortable. He worked out why in an instant.

'You're not planning to take this claim on a conditional fee, are you?'

'Well, as a matter of fact, I am.'

Geri's three partners breathed out simultaneously. Even Pete looked worried. She decided to keep very quiet about Mrs Berryfield's stay in the psychiatric hospital.

Roger glared at her.

'Well, really, Geri, this is just beyond the pale. First you want to make a decision that is quite clearly commercially disastrous and turn away a potentially important client. Now it turns out you might not even be paid at all by the client you want to keep instead.'

'What percentage of new litigation clients are being taken on on a conditional fee basis?' asked Cefan.

Geri thought of Joanna. She was now on conditional fee, as was Mrs Berryfield.

'It varies. There have been some lately, but...'

Roger was icy.

'May I suggest we agree that any new proposals for conditional fee clients be put before a partners' meeting for approval? This does seem to be getting out of hand.'

Geri needed to finalise her preparations for the Mitchell case. She had only one working day left to do so and did not want to spend it in interminable argument with her partners. Suddenly, she saw a way through the meeting.

'I am prepared to seek approval for all new conditional fee cases – provided you agree today to dropping Garside and letting me take on Mrs Berryfield.'

There was a pause. Roger looked at Cefan.

Pete chose his moment well.

'I would be prepared to accept that, Geri.'

Geri and Pete had the majority share. They would win this one.

Roger accepted defeat with little grace.

'Well, in that case, I'll have to go along with it. But it's commercial suicide in my view, and I want that noted in the minutes. And, in future, my agreement to dropping any more clients should not be assumed.

'I have to say, Geri, I am extremely worried by the direction in which you are taking this firm. I have reviewed litigation profits for the last three years, and you can't be permitted to ignore the downward trend. I think that your business review should look carefully at moving into different areas – mainstream profit-orientated litigation.'

'You mean, family law?'

He'd obviously been speaking to Cefan recently.

'Amongst other things, yes.'

'And are you going to do this work, Roger?'
He looked quite horrified at the idea.
'Of course not. You're the litigator...'
He didn't dare add that she was a woman and that women should do family law. But she knew he was thinking it.
When Geri replied, her tone was glacial.
'Well, as I've already explained to Cefan, I'm not a family lawyer and I have no intention of becoming one. And I have a trial tomorrow for which I need to prepare now, so unless there are any other matters, I suggest we end this meeting.'
Geri knew that she was starting to sound tetchy but she simply had no time to argue further. It was all very well fighting her corner in these meetings, but it was the bottom line that was clearly going to count. That meant winning cases. Lots of them.

Chapter Eight

Tuesday started in a rush. Geri slept through her alarm clock and was woken by Rory twenty minutes before school started. Horrified, she had missed breakfast and driven frantically to school as he munched some toast in the car. They chatted as she raced through the morning traffic.
'How did it go yesterday with Joanna?'
Geri had worked late, putting the final touches to the Mitchell submissions. She had got home at eight, in time for homework and bed.

'It's OK.'

'Good – I'm glad. It's only a short-term thing, though – I'm waiting for the agency to find someone new to pick you up.'

'Couldn't Joanna carry on?'

'The trouble is, she's a client, Rory. It makes it awkward ... you know. We don't know where we stand with each other.'

'But Dad used to get clients to do all sorts of things – there was Gordon who did the windows, and then there was the man who sorted out the garden...'

'Yes, but...' she wove into a bus lane, watching carefully for police cars '...I'm just not comfortable with the idea,' she finished.

'Why does the work thing always have to come first, Mum?'

She saw the orange stripes in the mirror and pulled back out, stopping a Mercedes in its tracks.

Rory had a point. And he had struck at her most vulnerable area.

'I'll have a think about it. Now, do you want me to talk to Mrs Davidson about ... well, about the other boys?'

'No. Please, Mum, don't. It wasn't too bad yesterday. Just let me keep out of their way.'

He looked frightened and she cursed herself for raising the subject. Like Joanna said, she should have waited for the right time.

Fifty minutes later, Geri was in the robing room of the County Court. Her opponent, a barrister from specialist Chambers in the Temple, was already wigged and robed.

'Pleased to meet you. I'm Piers Ablett.'

Geri was able to get ready quickly. Solicitors don't wear wigs in Court and the black robe which they wear is much less ornate than the barrister equivalent. The barrister robe has a discreet pouch fitted on to the back. Centuries ago, the idea had been that the grateful client could shovel payment into the pouch without the barrister ever having to come face to face with something as vulgar as cash. Solicitors, though, were considered to be less bashful about payment and perfectly able to dirty their hands with money. As a result, their robes have no pouch.

'I've got photocopies of the cases I'll be referring to.' Geri handed her copies to Piers Ablett and received his in return. They contained no surprises. She already knew how he'd be putting his argument.

Stewart Mitchell was waiting for her in the interview area. He was a bundle of nerves. As soon as she entered the tiny room, Geri was hit by the stench of stale alcohol and body odour.

'I can't go through with this,' he hissed.

His hands were trembling as he spoke.

'Don't worry – you're not on trial for anything. You're just here to tell the Judge about what happened.'

'No, I just can't. I was on a bender, last night. I can't think, you know...'

Oh, Christ. The trouble with acting for the disadvantaged was that they made bloody awful witnesses most of the time. Stewart looked awful. He had obviously tried to shave, and his face was pitted with razor cuts. God only knew what the

Judge would make of him.

'You know how I get, Geri ... I'm going to get the shakes as soon as anyone asks me anything.'

'Calm down, Stewart. Look, we've filed a statement in the Court from you. I don't need to ask you anything more, so it'll be really quick. Believe me.'

'But what about the other side? They'll crucify me.'

'No, they won't. It's mainly a question of law, rather than them not accepting what you say. Just stick with it, Stewart. We've come so far, let's give it our best today.'

He sat thinking.

'All right. But I've had enough of this. No more after today, OK?'

'Let's worry about that later.'

She didn't dare tell him that if he won today, the other side were bound to appeal.

She slipped out of the room to check the listing. Judge Ludgate. He was a regular at the Court and Geri had appeared in front of him often. He would be fair, but would find it difficult to find a way through the authorities against the Plaintiff.

Geri looked with disappointment at the cases ahead of her in the list. County Courts have to deal with a considerable amount of urgent work and that morning, Geri saw that there were two injunction applications in front of her. This was no surprise – they were probably applications from battered wives seeking urgent protection. But she needed to get Stewart on the witness stand as soon as possible, before his nerve went completely.

Geri went back to the interview room and waited with him. It was over an hour before they were called on, and her client was becoming more agitated as the minutes ticked by. She longed to be able to sit quietly in the robing room and put the finishing touches to her case, but she was needed by Stewart. Left to his own devices he would have done a runner ages ago.

Finally, they were on. His Honour sat across the modern courtroom, smiling benignly down at them. He was in his late-sixties, a rather rotund man with white wavy hair.

Geri, as Plaintiff's lawyer, opened the case. There was a set formula.

'May it please Your Honour, I appear on behalf of the Plaintiff in this matter. My learned friend Mr Ablett appears on behalf of the Defence.'

Geri was rarely referred to as a 'learned friend' by her opponents. By tradition, barristers refer to each other as 'learned'. As a solicitor, despite a First from Oxford, Geri was merely 'my friend' – a subtle put down which made it quite clear she was from the junior side of the profession. Some members of the Bar regard this as a ridiculous distinction and ignore it completely, but they are very much in the minority.

Geri gave a brief history of the case to the Judge, explaining to him that this was a hearing on liability only.

The school had long ago stopped trying to justify the actions of its staff in not dealing with Stewart's obvious drug problem. This was a sensible move as it would allow the Judge to focus on their defence. This caused real problems for Geri. Stewart Mitchell was a mess. But how could she prove that this was the school's fault? He might have ended up in such a state with the best of care. Some people were just born losers, after all.

Stewart would have to give evidence. Because of the concessions that the school had made, it would be cut right down. She filed a statement on his behalf, setting out the link between the drug taking and his ongoing problems.

'And with that in mind, I'll call the Plaintiff.'

Stewart shuffled into the witness box. He could barely read the oath, printed on white card and held in front of him by an usher.

Geri went through his name and address, and he confirmed that his statement was true. This avoided the need to trawl through the history of what had happened. It was all in the statement, which had been compiled by her months ago. Goodness knows, poor Stewart would never have remembered what to have said if the statement hadn't been there.

There was no point in asking him anything more. He'd only get muddled and go off at a tangent. 'Thank you, Mr Mitchell. If you'd like to stay there a moment, you may be asked some more questions by my learned friend.'

Piers Ablett took his time getting to his feet. A frown worked his way across his features, as though he'd only just considered the evidence and a thought had suddenly occurred to him. The thought had in fact crossed his mind eighteen months previously when he'd discussed tactics with the Defence team.

'Mr Mitchell,' he smiled quite charmingly at the Plaintiff, who, bemused, smiled back, 'could you just tell me a little about your parents? Do you still see them?'

'No.'

'They're divorced, I believe?'

'Yes.'

'Your mother's had a few psychiatric problems, hasn't she?'

'Erm, yes ... but I'm not sure...'

Piers Ablett turned his face away from the witness, but continued to question him. This is a standard tactic, guaranteed to annoy people. Frightened that they are being ignored, they talk. Too much.

'She spent some time in a psychiatric hospital, didn't she?' Piers Ablett continued to look away into the middle distance.

'Well, she did ... she got a bit out of order when she found out about me going to prison...'

Piers Ablett paused and looked at the Judge.

'Mr Mitchell, are you aware that mental illness can run in families?'

'I dunno. You tell me.'

'It does, Mr Mitchell. And are you seriously suggesting that if you'd gone to any other school, you'd never have taken anything at all? Seriously?'

Stewart looked desperately across the room at Geri. He was starting to get flustered. She avoided his gaze. Any suggestion that she was helping her client with his answers would be fatal.

'Well, are you going to answer?'

'Don't know, really.'

'And you've served three sentences of imprisonment – they can't have helped you very much.'

All of a sudden, the barrister was sympathetic and polite again. Stewart, desperate for a break, was unable to see the yawning trap.

He relaxed. Bad move.

'You're telling me! The first one, the detention... God you've no idea...'

And he was off. Telling the Court all about the iniquities of the juvenile detention system. 'It really screws you up, you know? Kids like me just needed a bit of help and all we got was a load of stuff ... and the drugs that are there! God, I never had LSD before I got into the system. And ... well, I made a few contacts there, like – know what I mean?'

'And did you take LSD at school?'

'No, cannabis, a bit of speed...'

All of a sudden Stewart seemed to realise that he'd not helped his case too much and belatedly shut up.

It was one o'clock. Ablett looked meaningfully at the clock.

'Your Honour. I don't know if this is a convenient moment?'

In other words, lunchtime. The Judge beamed at him for his kind consideration for the judicial hunger pangs.

'Yes, of course, Mr Ablett. Shall we say two o'clock?'

He looked rather severely at Stewart.

'Now, you are giving your evidence, young

man, and must not talk to anyone about the case over the lunchtime adjournment. Do you understand?'

'Er, yes,' lied Stewart.

Geri groaned inwardly. She'd buy him a sandwich and sit with him. He deserved it, after all, and she could keep an eye on him.

She took him to a small cafe near the Court and bought him a bacon roll.

'Am I doing all right then?' he asked.

'Look, Stewart, one of the rules I've got to stick with is that we're not allowed to talk about your evidence over the break.'

He grinned at her.

'Well, I'll not be telling.'

She sighed. It was tempting. All the work she'd done on the case, and he was losing it with every word he spoke. The worst thing was he'd never know it.

She shook her head and spoke gently but firmly.

'Sorry, Stewart. I'm not allowed to tell you what to say – it's called coaching a witness. And once you've started giving evidence, I can't even tell you how you're doing. That's just how it is.'

He looked at her for a moment and then started to chew on the roll. As he lifted it, she saw how badly his hands were trembling. It really wasn't fair. He was a mess, and it was the school's fault.

He stood up.

'Is there a toilet round here?'

She pointed towards the gents at the back of the cafe and he shuffled towards it.

While he was gone, she sipped at her tea and looked out over the gingham curtains to the street beyond. It was cloudy now and passers by had buttoned up their coats.

Stewart returned and took up the attack on his roll again. His hands no longer trembled. He'd been shooting up in the toilet, she knew it instinctively. Geri just wasn't in his scheme of things any more. He gazed at the wall behind her, eyes following goodness knew what patterns dancing wildly in his brain.

'I think we'd better get back to Court, Stewart.'

They were back on at 2 o'clock. Geri took him to the witness box and resumed her place at the front of the Court before the Judge entered.

She would have to re-examine. She was allowed to go over anything raised in the cross-examination once more. But it was a high-risk strategy. Funny how they didn't write books about how to extract evidence from a client who was high as a kite.

She'd been surprised that the school hadn't tried to strike her case out before it even got this far. There was some law to support them in saying that there was no claim in such a situation. Now she knew why they'd agreed to a trial. They knew they'd do better when the evidence was heard. In other words, they knew that Stewart would contribute to his own defeat.

'Mr Mitchell, one of the matters that His Honour will be considering is the cause of your problems. What do you have to say about that?'

Stewart didn't take the cue. He looked puzzled. Christ, he was going to say he didn't know. Geri spoke just before he did. She had to.

'Would you say that it was your introduction to drugs at the school...'

Piers Ablett was on his feet before she'd finished the sentence. He didn't have to protest. Judge Ludgate was in before him.

'Mrs Lander, you will be perfectly well aware that that was a leading question.'

Of course she was aware of it. You can't prompt your own witness with questions like that. But it had stopped Stewart putting an end to his case there and then.

'Your Honour, I accept the point and will not re-examine further. That is the evidence which I will call.'

Piers Ablett was calling no evidence and started his submissions immediately. He was good, making his points swiftly and effectively. Geri knew that Judge Ludgate was with him. He was nodding as the advocate spoke, and carefully noting the arguments as they were made.

Geri was able to speak last, as the Plaintiff's lawyer. Judge Ludgate smiled pleasantly as she spoke, and listened carefully to her complex arguments. As she ended her speech, though, he put down his pen and spoke.

'Mrs Lander, your comments on the law are as interesting and well researched as ever. But how do you propose I should deal with the fact that your client didn't seem to have any idea what caused him to come off the rails?'

'Your Honour is quite entitled to look at all the circumstances of the case and draw an inference.'

'Well, that's all very well, but it's for the Plaintiff to prove his case and this one seems to accept that his problem came from all sorts of sources. There has to be a limit to causation after all.'

Geri tried to persuade him that Stewart Mitchell was hardly in a position to know what day of the week it was, let alone how his problems had come about, but she knew she had lost. The judgment against her client came as no surprise.

It was 6 o'clock before they were finished. Stewart had not wanted to talk afterwards and Geri returned to a deserted office. Automatically, she signed off her post for Jackie and read through the day's messages.

Afterwards she sat quietly in the empty office. Simon had always told her to look for the lesson in defeat. What could she have done to improve matters? In the States, she could have coached Stewart remorselessly through all the anticipated questions. Here, though, coaching was forbidden. In any event, she had never dreamed that he would have been so diffident about what had caused his problems.

She looked at the computer print out on the file. All the work had been recorded, in units of six minutes. There were an awful lot of them.

She had just lost over twenty thousand pounds for the firm. Or rather, Stewart had just lost it for her. Under their conditional fee agreement, the firm would get nothing. If you counted the loss of Garside, she had cost the firm forty thousand pounds in the course of one day. No wonder her partners were fed up. So much for her campaign on her profit figures.

Geri drove home, thankful that the traffic was running reasonably freely. The only lesson she could draw from the case was that she should never have taken it on. The legal aid board said she hadn't a chance and wouldn't finance it, so why had she gambled the firm's time on it?

As Geri drove, the old fear came back. It always stalked her at moments like this. That she wasn't actually that bright, just hard-working. That when it really came down to it, she wasn't a good lawyer. That, although she hid it well, she was lacking.

Rory and Joanna were in the sitting room, watching TV.

'Sorry I'm late,' mumbled Geri.

'Don't worry. We've left some lasagne and salad... I'll just sort it out. I take it things didn't go too well? Rory told me that you had a big trial on today.'

Fortified by the meal and a cheap bottle of wine, Geri told Joanna about the case.

'The problem is, I'm on my own in the litigation department. When Simon was around, I could bounce ideas off him. Now, I've only got my own judgment and I'm not sure it's that good. I should never have brought this case. Sorry, Joanna, I shouldn't be telling you this. If you want to go to another solicitor, I won't take offence.'

Joanna bristled.

'Don't be ridiculous! If you're trying to push at the boundaries, you're going to fail sometimes. By rights, you should fail far more often than you do.'

The older woman became thoughtful.

'I often think that what really holds us women back is that we're so frightened of making fools of ourselves.'

'How do you mean?'

'Well, look at me, for instance. I didn't go to University because no girls I knew did and I was worried I'd seem strange. I nursed for a while because that was what seemed to be expected. I married and didn't work because of what people would think. When I was older, I was out of date in nursing but didn't retrain because I thought that people would think I was past it and I wouldn't get any jobs. If I'd just gone ahead and not bothered what anyone thought, things could have been so different.'

'That's all very well, but I still got it wrong,' protested Geri.

'You made an attempt and your client didn't come up with the goods. Typical man if I may say so!'

Geri laughed.

'But, Geri – as you get older and battier like me, you don't care what people think any more. It's so liberating, I wish I'd felt like this years ago. Trust in yourself – you have to. The only other alternative is not to do anything, which is far worse than making the odd mistake.'

'Joanna?'

'Yes?'

'Do you really mean all this or is it a pep talk?'

'I do mean it – it's only lately I've thought it all through myself. You know, it's since Tom died that I've really started to do what I want. It sounds dreadful, and I miss him more than anything. But I feel that I'm doing something now, not just marking time anymore. I've learned so much – the reading, the science. And I like helping out with Rory. I'm actually doing something useful for once.'

Geri thought of her talk with her son that morning and made a decision.

'Would you like to pick him up long-term? I won't be offended if you'd rather not.'

'I'd love to.'

'And I'm going to start paying you.'

'Don't be ridiculous – I'm doing it in return for your taking on the case.'

Thank God, she thought, she'd agreed the conditional fee arrangement before the last partners' meeting. She'd never have got their approval on this one now.

Geri grinned.

'OK. But the moment the case finishes, payment starts.'

'Done!'

Chapter Nine

'Minister, this will bankrupt me. It will bankrupt every high-intensity chicken farmer in the country.'

Charles Aiden-Davies was quite pale. The shock of what he had just been told had had an immediate effect.

Callum was concerned. Not about Aiden-Davies's overdraft, but about the political fall out.

The farmer and lobbyist was fast recovering himself.

'Stock replacement would be quite impossible. We'd have to buy in from the continent – and there would be no guarantee that we'd even solve the problem. All you'd do is bankrupt that sector of the farming economy for nothing.'

'We could devise a compensation scheme,' murmured Callum.

'That might pay for the new birds, but what about the time delay? The overdraft interest would continue, and there'd be no income for months. It's quite impossible.'

'But we have got to deal with this,' insisted the Minister.

'Yes, I accept that. But remember BSE? The damage that did to the beef industry was quite dreadful. The volume of stock you're looking at now is just enormous. Quite frankly, our farming industry will never recover.'

Aiden-Davies paused.

'It will, of course, leave you very exposed, Minister.'

The thought had already occurred to Callum. Very quickly after reading the report, in fact.

'There must be a ... lower key ... way of dealing with this. Assurances from the industry, phasing out, price adjustments.'

Callum needed six months. Six months, and he'd be elsewhere – hopefully. Trade and Industry if the PM's hints could be believed. He'd never get it if this blew up in the meantime.

Aiden-Davies's words made far more sense, but once that blasted report went on the record he'd be vulnerable forever. Overruling clear advice from his in-house experts was a dangerous business.

Still, the news could be contained for the moment. No one had got it into their heads to bring a claim over any of these deaths. There just wasn't the information available to them. The legal threat, if it came, would be from a group action – families and solicitors joining together to try and find an answer. He would get plenty of warning of that: notices in the legal journals, letters in the press. And it would be months before anything really got going.

No, he was OK. He just needed to sit tight and keep his nerve.

'Where am I taking the grain from, Mr Grimwood?'

Bill Fosdike had bought a hundred tons for selling on. He was ready to load his truck and moving towards the silos.

Benny Grimwood had never much liked Bill Fosdike. The man never paid on time for his grain, and always wanted too much of a discount. Grimwood knew it was vital that he carried on business as usual. Charlie's body would remain in number one silo until the grain was removed or the smell became too much.

'Take it from number one,' he called.

Fosdike nodded and reversed the lorry towards the silo. Grimwood left him to it.

He walked through to the office and shut the

door. He had a good view of the yard. The two part-time labourers he employed were cleaning one of the empty silos and Fosdike would be busy for a while.

Quickly he dialled the number Stiles had given him. As expected, an answering machine cut in. He left the agreed message. No name or other details. Just a quick suggestion it might be time for a drink together.

It was time to open up supplies again. Grimwood had worked out what sort of profit they could make and could resist it no longer.

Geri had an hour in the office before she was due to start for Cambridge. It was as good a time as any to tackle Gloria.

'I've had a word with Mr Davies. He's trying to shop around for the best deals and realises what a strain it is on you.'

Gloria snorted dismissively.

'You realise. He doesn't.'

'But anyhow, once this glut has gone through, the work should calm down a bit. All I can ask, Gloria, is that you bear with it for a while.'

She looked uncertain.

'I have to say, it seems a real waste of effort. It's all with the same surveyor – that one he's always lunching with – and he's quite impossible to deal with.'

'Bear with it, Gloria. Let me know in a fortnight if it's still too busy and I'll see what I can do then.'

Satisfied, at least for the moment, Gloria nodded.

Geri had always loved Cambridge. Used to the urban splendour of Oxford, she had found the quieter beauty of Cambridge entrancing on her first visit there as a student.

The city had very happy memories for her, for it was at a conference in Jesus College that she and Simon had become lovers. They had sat together as delegates from the firm, both aware of the electricity that crackled between them. Each had been too shy, too nervous to make the first move. Fortified by a drink too many at the end of conference dinner, they had walked along the Backs that warm night, exchanging words, thoughts and dreams. It had been only when the misty July dawn started to break that they had returned to Geri's room and made love for the first time.

She had avoided Cambridge since his death. It would hurt, she knew. As she negotiated the one-way system she resolved to keep a firm grip on herself. She would keep away from the river, meet the professor and get back to her car as quickly as she could.

Dermot Lebrun had suggested they meet at his rooms in Trinity Hall. Nestling between the shopping streets and the river, the stunningly beautiful but tiny college has produced a disproportionate number of top thinkers.

He opened the door quickly, beaming a greeting.

'Ms Lander, I'm Dermot Lebrun. Thank you for coming to see me.'

Geri smiled a greeting. Lebrun was enormous,

filling the doorframe with his bulk. He didn't seem fat, just large and muscular. He looked to be around forty, with neatly cropped thick dark hair. He was wearing a black sweatshirt emblazoned with the Trinity Hall Boat Club logo, Levi 501s and some trainers. Geri felt distinctly overdressed in her dark blue trouser suit.

He motioned her towards a table neatly set out with a china tea pot and matching service. The dons might change, but the rituals never did.

'I hope you enjoy Darjeeling? There are a few ginger biscuits, if I can tempt you.'

Her room at Jesus that night had been rather like this. Large, oak-panelled, looking over the quad through mullioned windows. A sofa, some chairs around the electric fire mounted in the old chimney piece. The bedroom at the back, leading off the sitting room. Only they had never made it to the bedroom... Christ, she would have to drag herself back to the present, and fast.

'Thank you, Professor. As you might recall, I'm trying to find out about superbugs.'

Quickly, efficiently, she told him what she knew. At the end, he nodded.

'So really, what I need to know is ... could Tom Pascoe have caught a superbug from eating chicken?'

The professor breathed out heavily. He was sitting in one of the chairs, his frame far too large for it.

'Yes. He could. But proving that is going to be impossible.'

'OK. Let's try that in stages. How could he have caught the superbug from meat?'

'Realistically, there are two ways. Indirect and direct. First, he could have caught an ordinary bug from the chicken – say salmonella. Once he had gone into hospital, he might have been exposed to other micro-organisms. There is research which proves that some bugs – the ones that tend to lurk in every hospital and which are often antibiotic-resistant – can transfer their immunity to new bugs.'

Geri wrote furiously in her notebook. She had a tape recorder running as well, but needed to write down the main points to make sure she understood them. She always found it easier to make the logical connections when things were written out.

'So what we have,' she tried to summarise, 'is bug A, caught from the chicken. This meets superbug already in the hospital. The superbug transfers its resistance to bug A?'

'Yes, in a nutshell.'

'So then it would be the hospital's fault, exposing him to the superbug?'

Lebrun frowned.

'It's not as easy as that. You'll always get superbugs in hospitals – there's no way round it. They have all the ingredients there: rapid throughput of unwell people, high usage of antibiotics, a warm environment. The bugs get exposed to the antibiotics and have time to build up their immunity. The existence of superbugs doesn't necessarily mean the hospital is at fault.'

Geri pondered a while.

'You mentioned two ways in which Tom might have got the superbug.'

'Yes. The second is that the chicken itself was infected with a superbug and he caught it directly from the meat. My own view is that it's possible for interspecies transfer of bacteria to happen. And we do know that intensive farming carries a risk of superbug development.'

Geri sat up, startled.

'Why?'

'Again, the same risk factors as hospital. High throughput of carriers, ill health – the animals are often unwell as the conditions are fairly appalling – and high usage of antibiotics.'

'Why antibiotics?'

'Factory farmers run a constant risk of infection running through their stock. When chickens are kept so close together, an ordinary illness can run riot. So they tend to give antibiotics routinely to stop anything developing in the first place. They also help the stock grow quicker.'

'I never knew that.'

'Oh, yes – in the US, getting on for fifty percent of all antibiotics manufactured go into animal foodstuffs.'

Geri was flabbergasted.

'How long has this been going on for?'

'Years.'

'So how come we aren't seeing more problems with superbugs in meat?'

'Vets are careful about what they prescribe. They try to make sure that the bugs don't have regular exposure to all the antibiotics.'

'But I know from Tom's wife they tried all sorts of antibiotics and they had no effect in his case.'

Dermot Lebrun took a sip of tea.

'I've suspected for some time that farmers are getting hold of some last resort antibiotics. As their own stock has developed resistance to the antibiotics which they can use, the temptation must be to get hold of more effective drugs. Perinycin can be got on the black market, without the involvement of a vet.'

Geri paused to write again.

'So if a farmer is giving this stuff to his chickens, they might start to carry a superbug which is resistant to everything?'

'Yes. And then you've got a real problem on your hands.'

'What would happen?'

Lebrun put down his teacup, placing it neatly in the middle of the saucer.

'On the assumption that someone picks up the bug from the meat – say, for the sake of argument, he doesn't cook it through properly – he'd experience symptoms. Perhaps gut rot, sickness. The exact form of these would depend on the nature of the superbug. Then the bug would start to take over his body. The blood would pick it up and carry it to all of his major organs. As they became infected, they would start to fail and he would die. It'd be a slow, pretty horrible death.'

Geri thought of the video.

'And there would be nothing anyone could do?'

'Not a thing. Just wait for him to die. Barrier nursing, keep him away from other patients in case he passed on the infection.'

'How could we show that's what happened to Tom?'

'Like I said, it's going to be impossible. There have been a few cases of slaughterhouse workers getting multi-resistant bugs and the suspicion is they caught them from the carcasses. But no one has managed to prove the link. At the moment, it's purely theoretical.'

'Would the Ministry of Agriculture know about farmers using last resort drugs?'

'Well, they should do, but they're hardly going to admit it, are they?'

'If you had to choose which was the most likely way for Tom to have got the superbug, would you have said it was by coming into contact with a hospital bug or by the chicken itself being infected?'

Dermot Lebrun considered the options.

'I would have to go for the carcass being infected. From what you've said, he was pretty ill before he even went to hospital. Normally, you'd expect someone who was fit to get over a food poisoning type bug and not need admission. The fact that he was already ill with the same sort of symptoms before he went in implies to me he'd already got the superbug by that stage.'

Geri was nodding. It made sense.

'But look,' he continued, 'there's a real danger here. If my theory gets out but is wrong – and if the media get hold of this – there could be a real fiasco. What we need is an inquiry into the situation rather than a scare story.'

Geri heard the college clock chiming 1 o'clock. The professor shifted in his chair.

'Look, I'm terribly sorry, but I need to grab some lunch as I'm lecturing at two. Perhaps you'd like to join me?'

He was rather good-looking and probably excellent company, but suddenly the last thing Geri felt like doing was eating. She shook her head.

'That's very kind, but I should get back. Thank you so much for seeing me today, it's been very helpful. If I send you a formal letter, perhaps you could prepare the report and let me know what your fees are?'

He waved one hand gently.

'I'd be delighted to – I'll write it up as soon as I can. Will you get details from the hospital – his notes and so on?'

'Yes. I'll get on to them this afternoon.'

Geri left the college deep in thought. If the professor was right, this was a time bomb. There *must* be a way of proving the link.

She was so distracted that she turned left instead of right down the side of the college and suddenly found herself on a bridge. She stood at its highest point and looked down the river. It was the first really warm day of summer and some students were punting underneath her, the dappled water reflecting back a thousand images of the scene above. If she stood on tiptoe, she could just see the end of the Master's garden at Trinity Hall. It led gracefully down to the river, set out to lawn but with a glorious flower border down one side.

Simon was with her. Right there, at her side. Some deep-seated vestige of rationality stopped her from turning to face him. But he was there. She could feel the gentle breeze dividing as it moved around him. And she could sense his smell – that peculiar combination of lemon and something very slightly spicy.

He was speaking to her. It felt like speech at the time, certainly. But she'd never be able to recall the exact words, which would puzzle her for years to come. She got the gist, though. There's something in it. Go in, make a fuss, cause a stink. There was something worth going after. A smile broke across her face. She needed so much to see him, touch him. He hadn't gone after all. Finally, she turned towards him.

But there was nothing, of course. She was on her own, just a silly woman with far too vivid an imagination. The tears came then, along with the memories. Two lives, intertwined just as their bodies had been that first night. Together at work and at home. The arrival of Rory, the three of them on holiday in Provence. The big cases, the successes, the expansion of the firm.

Then his depression, the days when nothing would lift his spirits. The pills, the counselling, the tension in their home. And finally, brutally, finding him that night.

Geri tasted the salt of her tears as she stood on the bridge. Facing away from passers by, nobody could see her. A few moments to get a grip on herself and she'd be fine.

'Are you all right, Mrs Lander?'

Dermot Lebrun was next to her, frowning slightly.

'Oh, yes, er, something in my eye, I think.'

'Happens now and then,' he replied. 'Now look, I've got some sandwiches – how about sharing them with me?'

'Oh, I couldn't possibly...'

'Please, I've bought far too many. You'll be helping me out, really.'

He held up a large brown bag which seemed to be bursting at the seams.

In spite of herself, Geri laughed.

'OK, if you put it like that.'

He grinned at her. When he did that, he looked oddly cherubic. They walked together back to the college entrance, through the quad, up some steps and on to a paved area. There were some benches right beside the river and they sat down, hearing an occasional light swish as a punt made its way along its watery path.

'Now, I have cream cheese, salmon, bacon and brie and, er, Marmite.'

'Cream cheese, if I may.'

They sat in silence, watching the punts floating by. Geri, facing the river, couldn't look at his face without twisting her head. She allowed herself a brief glimpse of Lebrun's left hand, though. It was large, tanned a very dark brown, and the skin looked hard. There was a surprisingly slim wrist, and a few dark hairs could be seen making an escape bid under the cuff of his sweatshirt. Simon had had fair-skinned, small hands – no larger than her own, really. Their softness had betrayed his lifestyle. Lebrun must live rather differently.

A few minutes later, he spoke again, his voice gentle, with the softest Irish lilt.

'Now, if you don't mind my asking, what was really the matter back there?'

Geri blushed. He didn't look away.

'It's just ... well, look, it's to do with my husband. Late husband.'
'I'm sorry.'
'I just had this feeling, you know...' She struggled for a moment. How could she tell him without sounding deranged?
'That he was with you?'
She looked at him suddenly, surprised.
'Well, yes, sort of I know it's silly but...'
'It's not silly at all. Who's to say it doesn't happen?'
'But you're a scientist. Logical and looking for proof in everything, surely?'
He grinned and turned to face the river, stretching out his legs languidly.
'So, let's think about it logically then. We can only prove someone's existence by the effect they have on the rest of us – we see them, hear them, feel them.'
'And I did all of those.'
'Ergo, he does exist. It may be that he's not in the form that you and I are in. But that doesn't mean he's gone completely.'
He looked at her intently, piercing blue eyes sympathetic. For a moment their eyes met. Geri looked away first.
'Now, how about some afters?'
Dermot rummaged around in the bag and extracted two chocolate muffins. Geri laughed and waved her hand.
'No, thanks, I really can't.'
'OK.'
He nodded and started to munch his way through one.

'If you're wondering, I had rowing training this morning. It's the fellow's team – we may be getting on a bit, but we keep on trying. But it does give me something of an appetite. Sorry if it's like sitting with a refuse disposal unit.'

'No, I'm just enjoying being here. It must be the most wonderful place to live.'

He smiled.

'Not bad, I have to say.'

They heard the college clock chime 2 o'clock.

'Damn! Got a tutorial to give.'

He stood up. Geri smiled at him.

'Yes, I'd better get back to London. Thanks ... for everything, Dermot.'

'No worries. I'll get on to the report as soon as I can.'

She watched as he strode quickly back towards the college. It would be difficult to imagine anyone more different from Simon. Large, athletic, ate like a horse. Fastidious Simon would have been horrified. Or would he? Lebrun had a sensitive side to him. Perhaps they were not so different now that she thought about it.

As she drove back down the M11, Geri thought through what he had said about the antibiotics: the Ministry of Agriculture would know all about antibiotic abuse, but they'd never admit it. But if no one tried to stir things up, nothing would happen. The trouble was, she needed more evidence before she could even think about launching a claim. And all the evidence was held, if it existed at all, by the Ministry. She needed a way into the charmed circle.

Geri stopped at the office to sign her post and

dictate a formal letter of instruction to Dermot Lebrun. The hospital notes had arrived yesterday and she asked Jackie to include them in the instructions for the professor.

Geri left the tape for Jackie to transcribe and slipped a blank one into her dictating machine. She stopped for a few moments to get a form for Joanna to sign, then went into the library. The large green book which she was seeking was in its usual place. Carefully, for it was heavy, she took it from the shelf

It was 5 o'clock when she got home. Rory was upstairs at his PC, Joanna stirring something on the cooker.

Geri told the older woman about her meeting with Lebrun.

'So the problem is, we need evidence – hard evidence, not just theory.'

'Is there a way of getting what we need from the Ministry?' asked Joanna. 'You know, freedom of information, public records, that sort of thing?'

'It won't be in the public domain for some time. My guess is that the Ministry will keep quiet anyhow. But there is something called pre-action discovery.'

'What's that?'

'Sometimes, before you start a claim, you can force a potential Defendant to give you information.'

Geri opened the book which she had brought back from the office library.

'This is the County Court Practice. It's called the "Green Book" for short, and it sets out the procedure for bringing County Court claims.'

She flipped through the pages.

'Here it is. Section 52 (2) of the County Courts Act 1984: "the Court shall have power to order anyone who is likely to be a party to proceedings to disclose documents which are relevant to the claim before the proceedings start".'

Joanna was delighted.

'So let's do it!'

Geri laughed.

'Well, hang on a bit. It's not that straight-forward. The Courts are careful about all this, and there is a public interest defence. They can refuse to give us the information if it goes against good government.'

Geri thought for a few moments.

'But we haven't really any option if we want to get the information. Let's stick our necks out a bit. Even if we don't get it, we'll have caused a stir in the Ministry. And the beauty of starting off in the County Court is that the press won't know anything about it. I want us to get as many facts right as we can before this becomes common knowledge. We can always transfer to the High Court if we want publicity later on.'

Joanna was jubilant.

'Wonderful. How long will it take?'

'If I draft the application tonight, we can issue it tomorrow and serve it. The Court will slot it in when they've got a three-hour space free. And I'll need you to sign this so we can get Tom's medical notes.' She passed the consent form to Joanna.

Geri settled down at the table and drafted the documents whilst Joanna finished making supper. After half an hour or so, Rory drifted downstairs and started to help with the vegetables. Geri worked on, eager to finalise the paperwork before she got cold feet over the whole idea. The application itself was easy – she was simply seeking all documents detailing the use of antibiotics, including perinycin, in the British chicken industry.

She then had to draft an affidavit in support. This was a formal document setting out why she was making the application. She had to show why she was seeking the documents, and what relevance they might have to any future proceedings. It would have to be enough to persuade the District Judge at least to look sympathetically on the application and listen to her oral argument properly. After three goes, she was satisfied, and put the tape in her handbag for Jackie to type up in the morning.

'Let's celebrate.' Joanna smiled. 'This is a momentous – er – moment!'

They opened a bottle of wine. Rory poured some Coke into his glass.

'Is this all because of the professor?'

'Yes, it is – we'd never have found him without your internet!' Geri grinned.

He beamed back at her.

'Told you so.'

'To creating a stir ... good luck to us!' said Joanna, raising her glass.

'Good luck to us indeed,' murmured Geri.

The wine had boosted her spirits. Bringing a new claim was always exciting for her. But this time – if the professor's hunch was right – she was on to something enormous.

She had to have those documents. There had to be something, somewhere. She would have to pray that the Judge would agree with her.

Chapter Ten

The application and affidavit were ready by the time the Court office opened at 10 a.m. Geri took it directly to the issue desk. The staff, who knew and liked her, found a slot the following week which had come up following the settlement of a matrimonial finance dispute. Geri faxed the documents to the Ministry as soon as she returned to the office. As she reached her room, she found Gloria sitting opposite her desk. She was in tears.

'Gloria, whatever is it?'

'I've been sacked.'

'What? But why? What's been going on?'

'I stayed late to get through those bloody application forms. I needed the phone number of a client, so I went to get it from Mr Davies's room. He came in and hit the roof. Said I shouldn't bugger around in his room. This morning, he said I was sacked.'

Geri was horrified. Gloria was one of their best secretaries. What was Cefan doing?

'Gloria, go home for the moment. I'm going to see Cefan and I'll ring you later. I'm sorry – I had no idea.'

As Gloria sniffed her way through reception to the obvious astonishment of Tracey, Geri raced up the staircase to Cefan's room. She didn't bother to knock.

'I've just been talking to Gloria.'

'Do come in, Geri,' he answered sarcastically.

'What's going on?'

'What's going on is that I found her in my room at eight o'clock last night. Going through my papers.'

'Did you ask her what she was doing?'

'No, it was perfectly obvious. I don't trust her, frankly. And what's more, I'm fed up with her. Ugly, moaning, fat ... so I sacked her.'

'She's one of our best secretaries.'

'Not to me, she isn't. Ugly as sin. Arse like a fucking two-ton truck.'

Geri knew he was goading her. She tried to reason with him.

'Cefan, you can't act like this...'

'I bloody well can! Are you trying to force me to have a secretary I can't stand?'

He really was like a two year old. Petulant, sulky, spoiling for a fight.

'We can't just sack a perfectly competent secretary. Quite apart from anything else, she can go straight to an industrial tribunal.'

'Would that upset you? To have your precious little ideologically sound firm exposed in public?'

'Look, Cefan, I'm the senior partner. If you had a problem with Gloria, you should have mentioned it to me.'

He glared at her.

'I disagree.'

This was outright hostility.

'And I've already been on to the agency about her replacement.'

'Cefan, I'm going to have to offer her her job back here. We can't afford another secretary.'

'Well, that's rich coming from you! You chuck out a good client, then you lose your precious conditional fee case – how much have you cost us this week, eh?'

There was no point in talking to him when he was like this. In any event, Geri wanted to kick him in the groin, if truth be told.

'I'm not going to discuss this further. I'm going to contact Gloria and offer her her job back. Your conduct is going on the agenda for the next partners' meeting.'

She turned on her heel and left him to it.

Cefan smiled to himself. That would give her something to think about. He needed to keep her busy for the time being.

Geri's faxed application had gone to the senior lawyers in the Ministry and from there straight to the Minister's desk. Callum Moncrieff saw it after he had returned from a Cabinet committee. Immediately, he summoned Geoffrey Atwell, the brightest legal adviser in the department.

The right-hand drawer of Moncrieff's desk was locked. In it lay David Vane's report. Only he and David had seen it so far. He had explained some of the recommendations to Charles Aiden-Davies, but the lobbyist would keep quiet. Vane was another matter. Moncrieff had already taken the precaution of having the scientist's personal file brought up to him.

There was little ammunition in the first section. No mistresses or drug habits. No predilection for hanging around gay bars. This appeared to be an intelligent man, separated from his wife, who retreated to his garden at weekends.

The security investigator had noted that David had gone to Court once, wanting his children to live with him. He had lost. The wife had gone to New Zealand with them.

Callum smiled. He had found his way in.

Geoffrey Atwell knocked at the door and came in.

'Are you aware of this?' growled Callum, gesturing towards the Court papers.

'Yes. I made the decision they should come straight to you.'

'Has the Court power to order us to disclose these documents? Surely the government can't be subject to this or every tin pot Court would be faxing us every day?'

'I've been checking that, Minister. Under the Act – the County Court Act 1984 – the Crown can be ordered to produce documents.'

'So how do we defend ourselves? We can't agree to send out government papers to anyone who wants them – it's outrageous!'

Geoffrey Atwell smiled weakly.

'There are two defences, Minister. The first is that this is a fishing expedition.'

'What?'

'Fishing expedition. In other words, there's no real case, they're just trawling for information without really knowing what they want. There's got to be some meat to the allegations, if you'll excuse the pun.'

Atwell made a mental note not to try a joke again. The Minister obviously wasn't in the mood.

'And secondly there's a public interest defence – that any material should be held back because good government requires it.'

Callum glowered.

'The problem with that, presumably, is that we'd need to say what we had and explain why it's not in the public interest to disclose it.'

'Quite,' agreed the lawyer. Fat lot of good he was. He wanted a way out of this, not a nodding donkey.

'Right, Atwell. It's a point of principle then. We have nothing to disclose and if we did would refuse anyhow.'

'Yes, Minister.'

'And we're having the best QC around to say this to the Court.'

'Minister, I'll phone around and book a senior man, but may I say ... in the County Court, it's relatively rare for a senior member of the Bar...'

'Bugger that. We're going to send out our message loud and clear. No fucking about with our records!'

'Quite, Minister.'

'Geoffrey, are these hearings in public?'

'No, Minister, they're held in the District Judge's chambers. No Press.'

'Well, let's be thankful for small mercies, then.'

David Vane was next to be summoned to the Minister's office.

'David, I'm afraid some lawyers want to get involved with the antibiotic situation.'

There was a flicker. Definitely something there.

'I'm rather worried that we as a Department are going to have to act defensively if the lawyers get in on the act.'

'I'm not quite with you,' replied the scientist cautiously.

'Well, as you know, I'm keen to take action with you on dealing with antibiotic abuse. I've already started to warn some of the industry's leaders of what we'll be recommending soon so that they can begin to consider their methods. But, quite frankly, if the lawyers start getting on the gravy train, we'll be forced to postpone making radical changes until they leave us alone. It could be seen as an admission of liability, you see.'

David saw.

Callum Moncrieff decided to press the point.

'I've always felt that lawyers are the chief threat to reform. They don't actually want the system to change, you see.'

Definitely interest there.

'They want the problems to be perpetuated, so that they can make a fuss and bring their claims. That's all that motivates them – money.'

David was nodding. Thank God, he was going to come on board.

'Minister, I agree about that. But we really do need to implement my recommendations.'

Moncrieff wasn't going to get off the hook by blaming his problems on lawyers.

Callum nodded vigorously.

'Absolutely, David. I can tell you now I plan to bring them in. But we cannot do so while this litigation is threatened.'

He showed David the faxed application. David read it quickly, and looked at him.

'They want our documents. Does this cover my report?'

'Yes,' Callum answered, 'and if they get their hands on that, the lawyers will have a field day. They'll launch their litigation on the back of it and you and I will be unable even to make a start on sorting out the industry. Goodness only knows what might happen if the delay's substantial – it could run to years.'

David looked directly at him.

'Are you trying to say that I should destroy my report?'

'No, not at all.'

Callum could be very emollient at times.

'What I propose is a way forward for both of us. If you were to redate the report, say to this time next month, we could then argue that it didn't exist at the time of the application. You can then produce it next month, when hopefully the lawyers have moved on to grasses greener, and then we can look at implementation.'

Callum smiled at him and delivered the clincher.

'And I can say at this stage that if you agree with me on the way forward today, I'll be proposing that you be promoted and given responsibility for putting your recommendations into immediate effect. You'll be answerable to me only and have direct access.'

'When you say access...' started David.

'I mean, there will be no political interference from me,' replied Callum. There won't be, he thought to himself, because I'll be safe in Trade and Industry, with a bit of luck.

'If we can move this on together, David, I'll be asking you to attend a consultation with the QC we're instructing on the application. Our legal team may need a statement from you.'

'How long do I have to decide?'

'Until four this afternoon. The hearing's next Tuesday.'

David returned to his office, took his phone off the hook and started to think. He tried to work logically through the arguments. He was being asked to tell a lie. They wanted him to say that a document which he had prepared – one he had been working on for months – simply didn't exist. What's more, they wanted him to give evidence to a Court on oath that the document didn't exist. But on the other hand, the report would resurface in a month's time. It would be no different, save that it would have a changed date on it. And Callum had a point about lawyers. David thought about the battle over his boys. He could see now that it had been hopeless from the start. Liz had always cared for them. She was a good mother, loved them and was available to look after them. He could only offer a nanny and his presence at weekends and most nights after 8 o'clock if the trains were running to time.

He hadn't stood a chance. But his solicitor had

told him to fight on and the barrister had agreed with him. Of course they had, at nearly two hundred pounds an hour! When he had lost, David had paid them off in dignified silence and resolved never to get involved in litigation again.

If there was litigation over antibiotics, he knew his plans would be stalled. He wouldn't be able to change a thing until the immediate threat was over. And that could take months, years even.

Liz had always told him that he was too much of an idealist. The Court Welfare Officer in the family proceedings had given it as her opinion that he was unrealistic. That had stung. David wondered if he was just being unrealistic now.

He looked out of the window. He knew that his recommendations would work. They would save lives. He was being given the power to put them into practice, without political interference. A legal case would stop all that.

Put like that, his decision was obvious. He found the disc containing the report, inserted it into the WP and found the date in the heading. Then he pressed the delete key.

He prayed he was doing the right thing.

Chapter Eleven

Geri had finally cleared her backlog by the end of the week. On the Sunday, while Rory was at a birthday party, she had gone to see Gloria at her home.

It was an immaculately kept flat in Delancey Street, Camden, not far from Regents Park. The walls were covered with abstract paintings. Thick double glazing insulated the rooms from the street noise and the atmosphere was one of light and calm.

'Where did the paintings come from, Gloria?'

'My son did them. His father left when he was a baby. I had to start work pretty quickly – that's when I joined the firm.'

'What's he doing now?'

'He's in advertising. Doing OK, actually. These were done when he was at the Royal College of Art.'

Geri cleared her throat.

'Look, Gloria, I've come to say that I'm sorry about what happened this week. I've spoken to Cefan. I can offer you another job at the firm, working with Pete Sinowski.'

Gloria smiled at her.

'No, it's OK. I've been putting a bit away. I'd like to move on, travel a little. I've been taking Urdu lessons for a few years – perhaps this is the right moment to go to India. I've wanted to do it all my life.'

Geri was astounded. Gloria saw her expression and smiled.

'I think it's time to try something different. I've got to say, if it wasn't for you, Geri, I'd be straight off to the industrial tribunal. Cefan treated me very badly and I'd have no problems nailing him to the floor. But you've been very good to me, and Simon was a gem. So don't worry, I'm not going to do anything which would damage you.'

Gloria frowned.

'And, in any case, I wasn't telling you the whole truth. I *was* snooping just a little in his room that evening.'

'What?'

'Geri, there may be nothing in this, but I'm afraid something dodgy is going on. Mr Davies is so – so uptight at the moment. And I don't trust that surveyor, either.'

'What are you saying, Gloria?'

'I can't say anything more – I didn't find anything. But I'd look into it, if I were you.'

Geri had spent the rest of the day thinking about Gloria's words. Finally, at 7 in the evening, she rang Cefan's home number. She felt distinctly foolish as the ringing tone sounded. What would she say?

She was actually relieved when no one answered. She could tackle him at work to-morrow.

Geri arrived in a rush on Monday morning. She needed to prepare for the pre-action discovery hearing the next day, and stopped first in the library, where she took out the textbooks they had on County Court procedure.

Her post was ready in her room, opened and placed in separate piles by Jackie. On top of the middle pile was a bulky document, attached to a letter. It was Lebrun's report. Geri scanned it quickly. He'd had the hospital notes for only a few days – he must really have pulled out all the stops.

Tom Pascoe had died from a multi-resistant

organism, commonly known as a superbug. The illness had come on after eating chicken, so it would be reasonable, in the absence of any other explanation, to assume it had started as simple food poisoning. The most likely explanation was that the chicken he had been eating was also infected with a superbug.

A long section of the report set out the role of the Ministry in preventing superbugs from developing. Dermot Lebrun had carefully described the powers of the Ministry, and the concerns that had been voiced about stock consuming large amounts of antibiotics.

It was a superb report. Geri turned to the covering letter. He hoped the report would meet with her approval and would she like to phone on receipt? Geri phoned the college immediately, but he was 'on the river', according to the Porters Lodge.

Geri put the phone down, disappointed. She'd been thinking about Dermot quite a bit. Still, she could try later. She paused a moment, considering what to do next.

I'd better talk to Cefan about those mortgages before I get stuck into this, she thought to herself.

His room was empty. In Gloria's room, a young secretary sat idle, polishing her fingernails.

'I'm Geri Lander. Do you know where Mr Davies is?'

'No, I'm only starting today. I was told to turn up, but no one seems to be expecting me. I haven't a clue what I'm meant to be doing. There've been phone calls from a couple of clients, but I don't even know where the files are.'

'Well, you hang on here, and I'll try to get hold of him.'

Geri tried a number from the phone on the desk. No answer. Something was starting to feel terribly wrong.

'He's not at home. Perhaps he's just a little late this...'

The tannoy burst into life. Phone call for Mrs Lander.

Geri phoned the switchboard.

Mrs Davidson, Rory's form teacher, came on the line.

'Mrs Lander, I'm afraid that we've had a bit of an incident here.'

Geri's heart plummeted. Rory!

'Some of the older boys have had rather a go at him. He's not seriously harmed, but he's taken rather a pasting and needs to go home.'

Geri dropped the phone and stumbled down the stairs. Jackie wasn't in her room. No time to search and tell her she was going. She'd ring from home.

She raced to the school and made straight for the headmistress's office.

'He's just being tidied up a bit, Mrs Lander,' said Mrs Smithers, as though he was a messy piece of baggage someone had left behind. Geri was about to explode but the headmistress carried on. 'Before he comes, I ought to mention that we've been trying to monitor the situation for some time. He does seem to attract the bullies and his form mistress wonders if it is to do with low self-esteem. We can refer him to the borough psychology service – they can do wonders...'

Geri was in a haze. She just wanted her son.

'In the meantime, keep him home for a while if you want – let the heat go out of the situation.'

There was a knock at the door and Rory was brought in. His right eye was red and swollen; he had a badly cut lip and a cut on his forehead.

'Mum.'

Geri hugged him.

'What did they do?'

'I couldn't get away, Mum, I did try...'

'Rory, it's not your fault. These boys need sorting out.'

She raised her voice and glared at the two teachers in the room. She wanted to ask them, why didn't you do anything? Why subject my son to this? At least they had the grace to look embarrassed. Probably terrified she'd start a lawsuit.

Not trusting herself to speak, she took him from the room and drove home as quickly as she could. He sobbed quietly to himself, wincing occasionally as salt tears rolled into the cuts.

Once home, she took him into the kitchen where she tried to get him to talk.

'Tell me about it, Rory. I need to know so that I can help.'

'No. They just got me, that's all.'

'Please, Rory.'

'Mum, I don't want to talk about it. Not now.'

Better not push it.

He sat quietly while Geri rang Jackie. No appointments had been booked in, and the secretary would be able to hold the fort.

She sat down beside her son again. Gently, she

asked, 'Do you want to do something or shall we stay in?'

'Can we go to Dad's tree?'

By lunchtime, they were in the garden of remembrance, sitting opposite a Japanese acer. Underneath it was a plaque, telling anyone who might care to read it that it had been planted in memory of Simon Lander, solicitor and legal reformer.

Both had cried endlessly. Now they sat, holding hands. Neither of them spoke.

They stayed for nearly two hours before walking home through the city streets. It was early-June and the hanging baskets and window displays were starting to come out. Geri had never realised before how strange they looked – little miniature bundles of the cottage garden stuck outside the urban façades.

It was 3.30 by the time they got home. Rory had started to talk, just a little.

'You can't help me. No one can.'

'Please let me try, Rory. Why are they picking on you?'

'Because I'm useless at everything.'

'But you're not!' Geri thought of the glowing reports from the school.

'Yes, I am...'

The phone rang. She wanted to ignore it, but he stopped talking, waiting for her to pick it up.

She snatched the receiver, snapped her name into it.

It was Jackie.

'Geri, I've been trying to get you since lunchtime. I know this is a terrible time to ring, but you've got to know. Something awful has happened.'

Jackie was right. It was awful.

Cefan had disappeared, along with his surveyor. Two and a half million pounds of client money had gone with him.

It had taken them most of the day to find the files and get into his computer. No wonder he had sacked Gloria. Roger and Pete eventually put the pieces together. Cefan certainly had been remortgaging with a vengeance. To several different lenders at a time, in fact – all happily unaware of the others. Each had forwarded a cheque made payable to the firm, completely unaware that five other lenders also thought they were exclusively lending on the security of the building.

The cheques had been paid into the firm during the course of last week and the money had immediately gone out to a numbered account in Liechtenstein. The lenders were no doubt anticipating their charge certificates, which Cefan had promised would be in the post shortly. But they would never get them.

In other words, he had carried out the classic mortgage fraud.

Geri sat down, unable to speak for the moment. Thoughts raced randomly around her brain. She had not the faintest idea what to do.

Rory looked at her, concerned.

'Mum, what is it?'

'Something terrible at work.'

His face clouded.

'No, Rory, really bad. I think the firm may be in real trouble.'

The phone rang again. She picked it up on the first ring.

'It's Pete. You've heard, I take it?'

'Yes.'

'I think that we have to tell the Law Society first.'

Of course. The Law Society compensated those who lost out through mortgage fraud. They operated an insurance fund into which all firms had to pay a levy. Geri had always resented it, wondering why she had to pay for the frauds of the crooked firms. Now her practice was one of them. They would be reported to the Office for the Supervision of Solicitors.

'Yes. Pete, can you contact them?'

'It's – let's see – four-thirty. I'll get on to it straightaway. I'll give them your home number. They'll probably ring you to confirm. They'll investigate, you know. Are you in tomorrow?'

With horror, Geri remembered the pre-action discovery hearing. The books were still on her desk. She'd not even started to prepare for it.

'Yes, but I'm in Court in the morning.'

She rang off and the doorbell sounded. Geri felt like screaming. What else was going to happen today? Rory went to answer it.

'Jo!'

'My word, whatever happened to you?'

Joanna walked through to the kitchen. She looked worried and out of breath.

'I'm so sorry – I couldn't find Rory at the school gate. I thought he'd wandered off home without me... But what's been going on?'

Geri suddenly realised, no one had thought to tell Joanna that Rory was at home. She must have been worried sick.

Geri told her about what had happened to Rory. Then she continued, 'Joanna, I don't know how to break this to you. I can't believe it myself yet. I've just found out that one of my partners has carried out a mortgage fraud. I had no idea ... anyhow, the firm is going to be investigated. I may be stopped from practising, I don't know at the moment.'

Joanna sat down, shocked.

'But why would they stop you working if it was another solicitor?'

'I'm the senior partner. I should have realised what was going on.'

'But surely they can't expect you to keep tabs on everyone else? That's ridiculous.'

Joanna paused. 'Are you going to go back in? I can look after Rory if you need to.'

Geri didn't know. Her son needed her. She had to be there.

But she had to get ready for the hearing. She'd requested it, after all – she could hardly back out of it on the day. And she'd be crucified by the Ministry lawyer if she didn't know her stuff.

She found the answer.

'I'll stay home until he goes to bed. Then, if you could babysit, I'll go in. Stay the night if you'd like to, Joanna – the spare room's made up.'

'That would be very kind.'

Joanna was recovering her composure. Thank goodness something was getting back to normal.

'And I'll stay on tomorrow – look after Rory while you're at the hearing.'

Joanna had planned to be there herself. As the potential Plaintiff, she was allowed to. It must have cost her a lot to make such an offer.

'Thanks, Joanna.'

Geri sat with Rory, who watched TV quietly. By 8, he was exhausted. Gently, she put him to bed. When he was finally asleep, she kissed him and slipped out of the house.

The office was deserted. Geri signed herself in and made her way into her room. She started to read the textbooks left open from that morning on her desk. She couldn't concentrate. Cefan Davies had managed to destroy everything she and Simon had worked for. The firm would no longer be remembered as solicitors who changed the law; rather they would go down in history as perpetrators of one of England's largest mortgage frauds.

She knew that she should have realised what was going on. The more she thought about it, the more clues she realised she'd missed. The multiple applications. The use of one surveyor. Cefan's tetchiness. Gloria's sacking and her words of just the previous day. It all added up to such an obvious answer, and she had missed it completely. If the Office for the Supervision of Solicitors decided that she was guilty through ignorance, she'd be barred from practice.

It was eerily quiet in the office. The sounds of daytime life – doors opening and closing, printers whirring, fax machine grinding – were all absent.

Geri shivered. She'd come out in her casual

clothes, without a jacket. It was colder now. She heard a shriek from the street outside and hoped that this wouldn't be yet another night when the office was burgled.

Pull yourself together, she told herself. If you sit here and act like the world's biggest neurotic you'll not stand a chance tomorrow. Joanna deserves better. Geri noticed an old coat hanging from the hook on the back of the door. She must have left it there last autumn – probably worn it into the office in the morning, but forgotten to put it on when she left. Well, she was grateful for it now, she thought, as she slipped it over her shoulders.

Best start with the cases on discovery, she decided. She started to read, a lonely figure huddled in the coat for warmth. By 2 a.m. the last of the street noise had gone and she was no longer afraid. She'd read through the cases and could make a start on the photocopying. She'd use the new machine at the top of the stairs. Usually there was a queue for it – there had to be some advantage to being at work in the early hours. She logged the number of copies taken so that she could charge them to the file.

By 3.30, she had her raw materials. All that was left was to mould them into an argument. She'd spend the next hour preparing her speech, then type out a skeleton argument. Funny how the printed word carried so much more clout these days.

By 6 o'clock in the morning, she was ready. She wanted to sleep, but the thought of Rory waking up and finding her not at home forced her to the car. She was back in time to get him up and organise breakfast. All she'd missed had been a night's rest.

By 9, she had returned to the office, ready to do battle before the District Judge. If she lost, there would be no documents. Without any documents, there would be no claim.

Benny Grimwood had asked to speak to the police. The time was right for Charlie to be found. The weather was getting hotter and the day before he was convinced he had detected the first hint of a smell from number one silo.

Two officers appeared first thing in the morning. DC Morris, who was clearly in charge, rated the disappearance of Charlie Jacobs as a fairly low priority. Sometimes, people did just go. Without family demanding to know what had happened, there was little incentive to dig too deep.

DC Morris listened to Grimwood whilst his assistant, PC Wilson, simply looked bored.

'I know you're busy people, but I had to warn Charlie a couple of times about getting into the silo without permission...'

'I know it might seem an over-reaction, but perhaps it might be worth going through the silos?'

DC Morris didn't look too thrilled at the prospect.

'What makes you think he might be in there?'

'Nothing as such, officer. It's just ... well, I've been worried about him. It's been nagging at me a bit, and I just thought – no stone unturned, that sort of thing.' Grimwood hesitated for effect. 'And it may just be me, but I thought there was a funny smell yesterday.'

DC Morris breathed out heavily.

'So what you want us to do is move several hundred tons of animal feed from the silo?'

'Well, I can't really see any way around it.'

'What sort of smell did you mean just now?'

'I don't exactly know – just strange. Let's go over there and try now.'

The officer followed him sceptically. There was a light breeze around the yard and the heat had yet to get up. The two men stood for a moment, sniffled ostentatiously. Grimwood watched the senior officer carefully. As he positioned himself downwind of number one silo, his expression changed from one of bored politeness to rather intense interest.

'I think we'd better empty the silo,' said DC Morris.

Chapter Twelve

Geri sat at the large maple table in the robing room, checking that her photocopied authorities were in order. There was nothing more distracting than trying to refer the Judge to a page number only to find his copies didn't tally with your own.

She checked her appearance in the robing room mirror. She wasn't at her best. Her hair needed a wash and was hanging like a wet

Monday. There were grey rings under her eyes and her skin seemed sallow. Still, her suit seemed to look OK. She adjusted a blue chiffon scarf around the top of her jacket to try and divert attention away from her face.

She returned to the table and carefully placed the photocopies of the cases she wanted to use in three piles. There was one for her, easily recognisable by the scribbles and notes all over the script, and pristine copies for the Judge and her opponent.

Suddenly, the door crashed open. In marched a small procession, headed by a rotund male of around fifty. He was followed by a younger man, tall, thin and elegantly camp, who was holding a cigarette in his right hand. Behind them both trooped a younger woman, smartly turned out in a blonde chignon and dark Jaeger suit.

The younger man delved into his jacket pocket and produced the most ornate cigarette lighter Geri had ever seen. He moved the cigarette to his lips and produced a flame. She decided to assert herself.

'Terribly sorry, but the Court is fairly strict about not smoking.'

The man ignored her completely.

She raised her voice.

'It's no smoking.'

He looked surprised, as though he hadn't noticed her in the room. Probably hadn't.

'I take it you don't mind...' He tried to smile, but it didn't really work.

'I'm afraid I do.'

'Hmmph.'

He sat down in the chair, wincing as the air was pushed noisily from a hole in the side padding. The older man took some spectacles from a case and polished them vigorously. He put them on and looked at Geri.

'Are you in the case of Pascoe, by any chance?'

'Yes, I am. I'm Geri Lander.'

His courtesy was elaborate.

'Who is your counsel? I have some authorities for him.'

The double assumption never ceased to annoy Geri. First, that she would use a barrister. Secondly, that the barrister would be male.

'I'm Mrs Pascoe's solicitor. I'm doing the application myself'

He broke into a broad smile.

'My dear girl, you should have said so earlier.'

No bloody chance to, thought Geri.

'May I introduce myself? My name is Gordon Hodder. This is my junior, James D'Arby Colinder.'

The younger man smiled weakly at her from his seat.

Hodder didn't bother to introduce the woman.

'And this is?' asked Geri, smiling pleasantly.

Gordon Hodder looked momentarily at a loss. He clearly hadn't a clue what her name was. She put him out of his misery.

'I'm Angela Simons, solicitor at the Ministry.'

'Now, before you ladies get down to small talk, I have a few cases for you,' said Gordon Hodder.

Geri could have hit him. Instead she continued to smile sweetly. Sometimes it was quite helpful to play the useless female. And anyhow, what the hell was the Ministry doing sending a QC to the County Court? Something had to be up.

Barristers can be divided into two groups. The vast majority are juniors for all of their careers while a few high flyers are selected to become Queen's Counsel. They are the top specialists, able to command enormous fees, and usually demand the services of a junior barrister to assist them. Geri knew all about Gordon Hodder. He was a top personal injury specialist and had represented the government on several big cases. If they were keen to have a heavy hitter it was no surprise they were using him.

But in the County Court? The application was being dealt with by a District Judge – the most junior rank of the judiciary. QCs simply didn't appear in places like this.

He produced a bundle of sheets of paper.

'My authorities. And a skeleton argument.'

Geri ran her eye down the lines. Nothing surprising. He was sticking to the usual defences – first, there was nothing worth seeing; second, that it was not in the public interest to disclose what they did have.

At the end of the bundle was a copy of an affidavit. Geri looked at the name on the first line of text. It had been sworn by a David Vane, MRCVS, PhD. She scanned the rest of the document. It stated that the Ministry had not, at that time, obtained any information about perinycin use in livestock.

'We haven't been served with a copy of this,' protested Geri. 'It should have been with us days ago.'

'Well, you can apply to adjourn if you wish.'

It was a standard Defence tactic. Turn up with late information. The Plaintiff would want to get things moving, would try to avoid having to wait for another hearing.

'Is he here, this David Vane?' demanded Geri.

'He's been delayed on the train but he's on his way,' replied the QC.

'Then I'd like him called, please. By the way, these are my authorities.'

She put his copies on the desk and left the robing room. Denise, the Court usher was in her usual seat in the public waiting room. The other seats were empty. Dr Vane had obviously not yet arrived.

'Hello, Denise. Who have we got?' asked Geri.

'Judge Butcher today. He's come over for a few days from his usual stamping ground.'

Geri smiled broadly. At least something was going right. Henry Butcher was a gem of a District Judge. He usually sat in the Midlands, but had family in Canonbury and liked to sit in Geri's Court when the regular Judges were on holiday. He had been appointed early, at the age of forty-five, and had been sitting for nearly twenty years. He had long grown sick of the law, and detested lengthy legal argument. He prided himself on looking for justice and to hell with what the cases actually said. He'd also held something of a torch for Geri for years. There were advantages to being known in a Court after all.

Swiftly, she made a decision on tactics. She needn't have stayed up all night after all. Sod's law really. If she'd taken a chance and just gone to bed, she'd have ended up with a Judge who wanted to know every last thing about the law on discovery.

'We're ready when the Judge is,' she told Denise.

They were called in quickly after that. Gordon Hodder looked most uncomfortable in the Judge's room. District Judges rarely sit in proper Courtrooms. They tend to work in large offices, with a table in front of them at which the advocates sit. No one stands, except witnesses who are taking the oath, and the proceedings are kept as informal as possible. Definitely not the sort of thing QCs are used to.

'May it please you, sir, I appear on behalf of the applicant, and my learned friend Mr Hodder, QC appears on behalf of the Respondent. He is assisted by Mr D'Arby Colinder.'

The District Judge looked bemused. Looking at the two men, he smiled. He hadn't had a QC in his room for fourteen years. And the swine had obviously been having a go at poor Mrs Lander, judging by the state of her.

'Welcome to the Court, everybody. Yes, Mrs Lander?'

Geri made her application in seven minutes flat. She told the Judge that her client was the widow of a man who had died from a superbug, and that a number of experts (one was a number, after all) had indicated to her that there were wider concerns about antibiotic use in livestock. She needed to establish the state of knowledge of the Ministry of the problem before she could properly advise her client, and could she have the order as sought, please?

Geri abandoned the legal argument completely. That would only obscure the simplicity of her request.

'Thank you, Mrs Lander. Well, I have to say, it all sounds perfectly sensible to me.'

Gordon Hodder stood up.

'Mr Hodder, we don't stand on ceremony in this Court.' The Judge was starting to enjoy this.

'No, sir. Sir, I wonder if I might start with the case of...'

Hodder was completely flummoxed. He'd thought he would be responding to Geri's cases. She'd given him nothing to reply to. Nothing other than common sense, and he'd always had problems with that.

'...ah, yes, in...'

'Mr Hodder,' Judge Butcher's eyes were merry, 'you may have noted that Mrs Lander did not trouble the Court with authorities. I really would be far better assisted if you could make any replies which you think appropriate to her submissions.'

The QC swiftly recovered his composure.

'Of course, sir. There is a simple answer in fact. The Ministry has not formulated a view on the use of antibiotics in livestock. I wonder if I could take you to the affidavit of Dr Vane. Sir, I ought to mention he has been delayed en route. He's on a train from Manningtree, in Essex.'

The Judge smiled.

'I know that fine well – complete nightmare. Don't worry, he can come straight in as soon as he arrives. Home of the Witchfinder General, that town. Matthew Hopkins?'

The QC clearly didn't have a clue. The Judge rolled his eyes and turned to the affidavit.

'Sworn today, I see.'

'Yes, sir.'

'When did you provide a copy for Mrs Lander?'

'Erm – today, sir.'

'So, Mr Hodder, you're expecting to proceed today on the basis of a document which should have been served last week?'

'Well, sir, Mrs Lander has kindly indicated to me that she makes no objection...'

'Sir, I'm quite happy to go ahead. I've read the affidavit. I shall need Dr Vane to be called, though.'

The Judge smiled at her.

'Very reasonable, Mrs Lander.'

The usher tapped at the door.

'Dr Vane is here, sir.'

'Excellent timing, if I may say so. Show him in, please.'

Dr Vane was led in by Denise. Good-looking and slightly nervous, thought Geri. Definitely worth prodding a bit in cross-examination.

'In that case, I'll proceed straight to Dr Vane's evidence,' said Hodder.

The Ministry solicitor put down her pen, taking a brief break from her scribbling. James D'Arby Colinder had done nothing throughout the brief exchange. It wasn't a bad way to earn a brief fee.

David was aware as he was shown to his chair that he was being scrutinised by five pairs of eyes, It made him most uncomfortable.

He was sworn in, and the QC asked the usual questions. His name, his qualifications, the fact that he had sworn the affidavit. These formalities always have to be gone through and help a witness to get used to giving his evidence.

Then it was Geri's turn.

She tried to be polite to experts, as a rule. The Court tended to respect them and there was a risk of losing the sympathy of the Judge if she didn't tug a forelock or two.

'Dr Vane, can you tell us exactly what information the Ministry has on antibiotic use in livestock?'

David paused to consider.

'We have details of permitted drugs, dosage recommendations, efficiency trials.'

He looked at her steadily. Everyone was writing down what he said. Five copies of his words. He would have to be careful.

'What about antibiotic abuse?'

'If you mean using such drugs in such a way that resistance can be built up, the research, I understand, has been medical rather than veterinary.'

'Are you familiar with the drug perinycin?'

'Yes, I am.' This was where it was going to get tricky.

'Are you familiar with any work that has been carried out to establish the use of perinycin in livestock?'

Familiar with? I've done the bloody work, he thought to himself.

David looked at the faces in front of him. It wasn't too late to tell them, say that the affidavit was wrong, he was terribly sorry.

He took a deep breath and hoped to hell that he wasn't making a dreadful mistake.

'The Ministry does not have any such work at this time.'

His voice was firm. But he'd hesitated. Geri had noticed it. So had the Judge.

'But are you familiar with any such work?'

Christ! They'd said he'd only be asked if the Ministry had anything. And they hadn't – not yet. This was going a stage further. Still, in for a penny.

'No, I am not familiar with any such work. None has been brought to my attention and I in turn have not passed any information on to the Ministry.'

Geri stopped questioning.

He was off the hook.

No, he wasn't. She'd thought of something else.

'You said a moment ago that the Ministry doesn't have any work relating to perinycin use *at this time*. Are you anticipating that there may be some work in the future?'

Christ, that was difficult to answer. His report would be produced at some stage. He decided to hedge.

'It is a situation which one might want to review in the future – particularly, if I may say so, in the light of the concerns which you have made out. If you'd come to us first instead of launching into this...'

'Dr Vane, if you could just confine yourself to answering the questions. We're not interested in polemics here.'

Geri grinned at the Judge's intervention and decided to stop there, while things were looking good.

Gordon Hodder was carrying on with his submissions. He'd obviously got the most enormous brief fee and felt that he had to speak for as long as possible to justify it. His voice was too loud for the room and seemed to be echoing through Geri's head. She was tired and losing the train of what he was saying. It just seemed to be the same old thing.

We know nothing. Hear no evil, see no evil, speak no evil.

He finally finished just before lunchtime. Geri summed up her case as she'd opened it, telling the Judge that they ought to have the opportunity to check what the Ministry had on perinycin. It was a simple request, simply put.

The District Judge adjourned to 2 p.m. to prepare his decision. Geri needed some fresh air. She left the building for the shopping arcade a few blocks away and went to Marks and Spencer for some sandwiches.

David Vane, the witness, had clearly had the same idea. She saw him hovering at the display before choosing some cream cheese and celery in granary bread. Perhaps he was a vegetarian. He was next but one to her. There was no one around. She could easily take him to one side, ask him what he really knew. That pause as he spoke ... she'd had a feeling that he knew more than he had said.

But it's a dangerous business approaching witnesses. It can so easily lead to a charge of intimidation. So Geri turned away and left the store. She sat on the seat near a fountain outside and ate her lunch. She thought of Rory and Joanna and punched her home number into her mobile phone.

Joanna answered.

'How's Rory?' asked Geri.

'He's OK. Quiet, not doing much, but OK. How about you?'

'We've had the argument, just waiting for the judgment. Fingers crossed. I'll call you as soon as I know.'

She pressed the hang up button and walked back to the Court building. The Judge was ready for them promptly at 2 p.m.

District Judge Butcher had forgotten most of the law he ever knew. One matter he had not forgotten, though, was how to wrap up his judgments so that they couldn't be appealed. He knew that all he had to do was listen politely, consider all the points made, apply any legal tests which were required and come to a conclusion. So that was what he did that afternoon. After an hour, he had judicially disposed of the Ministry's arguments, and had ordered that Geri be granted copies of all the documents which she had sought.

Gordon Hodder was furious. He had never been gracious in defeat.

'The application has been so vaguely worded, sir, that we don't know what documents are covered by it.'

'In that case, I would be happy to attend at the

Ministry to conduct my own assessment of their documents, sir. Given that it now seems to be conceded there are some papers to see,' replied Geri sweetly.

Even better. She could dig out everything they had.

'So be it. Sounds very sensible to me. Thank you, Mrs Lander.' The Judge smiled.

Geri waited for the Order to be typed and walked back to the office. It was 3.30 and she was exhausted. All she wanted to do was sleep. She went straight to the fax machine, kept in an alcove just off reception. She smiled as she pressed in the numbers and sent off the Order. This would give them something to think about.

Still grinning, she marched into her room.

Someone else was in her chair. A man in his thirties, by the look of him, speaking into his dictating machine. In front of him lay one of her files, open.

'What the hell is going on?'

'Ah. Mrs Lander, I presume.' He smiled at his own witticism.

Geri was unimpressed.

'Yes, I bloody well am. Can you tell me what you think you're doing?'

'Certainly can. The Office for the Supervision of Solicitors has intervened in your firm. They've asked us to take over your caseload while they investigate. I'm just reviewing your files.'

'And where are you from – the Law Society?'

'No, I'm Jeremy Gilbert from Winchell Robins.'

Damn! Apart from Shaner's, their biggest competitors.

'But you can't just come in here and take away all my clients...'

His smile was as broad as it was insincere.

'I suggest you check with the Law Society. Firms that relieve their clients of millions of pounds tend to find themselves in trouble. We've been asked to run your cases while you're being investigated. It's called an intervention.'

'But they're prize clients for you...'

'Well then, you shouldn't have made it necessary for the intervention to happen. The clients will be asked if they consent. But don't argue with me. Take it up with the Office for the Supervision of Solicitors if you're so pissed off.'

He looked back at the file. She was clearly being dismissed. From her own room in her own firm.

Geri stalked off down the corridor towards Jackie's room. A note had been left on her desk.

'Sorry, Geri. The police told me I had to go home – if you need me, call me there.'

The police? Was she going to be arrested? Well, they'd find her soon enough. In the meantime, she'd better sort out this intervention business.

Geri phoned the Law Society. They put her through to the Office for the Supervision of Solicitors.

'Yes, Mrs Lander. In the light of the scale of the fraud, we had no other option. We have to intervene. We did phone earlier, but you were at Court and we spoke to Mr Warburton instead.'

'But you've just put all my files in the hands of one of my main competitors! He'll simply take my clients away.'

'The work had to go to specialist firms. It's inevitable they will be competitors. And your clients will be asked for their consent and be kept in the picture.'

Geri looked up at the ceiling.

'How long will this go on for?'

'Until the disciplinary proceedings are dealt with.'

'Which means?'

'Mrs Lander, you really need to speak with your partners about this. We've called for your accounts and understand that they will be with us by the end of the week. If they confirm that a fraud has been carried out, it is very likely your practising certificate will be revoked.'

Geri thought her heart was going to stop.

'You mean, I won't be able to work any longer?'

'Yes. Well, not as a solicitor, anyhow.'

'But you don't understand...'

'Mrs Lander, I'm not going to argue with you. We'll make our decision when we've investigated properly. Until then, we have to protect the public.'

Geri hung up. So now the public had to be protected from her. She sat at Jackie's desk. The Order might as well not have been made. It was no good having it if the firm would no longer be in existence. No other solicitor would fight Joanna's case on a conditional fee.

The tannoy sounded.

'Phone call for Mrs Lander...'

Geri picked up Jackie's phone.

It was Roger.

'Geri, couldn't find you.'

'That's because there's some creep from Winchell Robins in my room.'

'Ah, yes. I wanted to warn you. The Law Society has intervened. I've sent off the daily and weekly accounts for the last six months to them.'

'Thank you, Roger.'

'Geri?'

'Yes?'

'It's not looking good.'

'I know, I've just been speaking to the Law Society. We may be struck off.'

'And I've got to tell you that there are two police officers in the building. They've just finished interviewing me and want to see you next. They're in the boardroom now.'

'I'll be straight over.'

Geri walked into the large room. A rather pleasant-looking man was sitting at the end of the table. Mid-fifties by the look of him, slim, well dressed, with a pink tie. He seemed rather urbane for a policeman.

Beside him sat a younger man. Thirty something, stockily built in a Mr Harry suit which was creased at the back. He had short, dark hair and, by the look of him, far too much attitude.

They had some files open in front of them and looked up as Geri entered.

She introduced herself. Better try and be pleasant. She needed them on her side.

'I'm so sorry I wasn't here earlier – I was in Court. I didn't expect such a quick response to our – er – difficulties.'

The older man smiled in response.

‘No, well, we always try to carry out our investigations as quickly as we can. Particularly in a situation where the amount involved is so large.’

Geri breathed in sharply.

‘I am Detective Sergeant Edgar, and I have overall control of this investigation. This is Detective Constable Lambert, who is assisting me.’

The younger man grunted and glared at Geri.

DS Edgar set out the parameters. They were looking into the dealings of the firm to establish the extent of the fraud, he said, with particular reference to whether charges would lie against all four partners. He would need to carry out a formal interview later, under caution.

‘Obviously, at the moment, I need to get the full picture of what’s happening. I’ll need full access to all files.’

‘Of course.’

‘And your bank accounts – personal as well as practice.’

‘Yes. I’ll sign whatever’s needed for you to get access to those.’

‘There is one matter we need to ask you about now.’ This was DC Lambert. He reminded her, in a strange way, of Cefan. That pugilistic look. He’s already made up his mind, Geri thought.

‘Please do.’

She was so tired. She was going to nod off. The room was hazy, spinning gently.

‘I’ve seen the log of office users yesterday. Do you agree that you came into the office last night?’

'Why, yes, I needed to prepare for today.'

'At nine?'

'Yes – I came in late.'

'And do you agree that you stayed all night, and left this morning before the staff arrived?'

What was he implying? DS Edgar was quiet, listening carefully to her response. He seemed to be leaving the questioning to his assistant for the moment.

'Yes – it was an important case and I hadn't had time to prepare yesterday.'

'Where did you go during the night here?'

'My room, the library. The photocopier.'

'Do you mean the photocopier at the top of the stairs?'

'Yes.'

'That's outside Mr Davies's room, I believe.'

They'd obviously had a look round already. Probably seen the log.

'Well, it is, but I didn't go in, if that's what you're asking.'

'Are you sure?'

'Absolutely.'

'Could anyone verify that?'

Geri snapped.

'Of course not. Do you imagine we have staff hanging around at three in the morning just to see where I might go?'

He looked mortally offended. Damn! She needed them on her side.

'Look, I'm sorry. It's just that I didn't have any sleep last night, as you'll know. I'm very tired and need to get home.'

Surely they couldn't be thinking she'd been

destroying evidence? She'd hardly have signed herself in and filled out the photocopy log if she'd wanted to keep it quiet. Or did they think it was some complicated double bluff? She didn't know what to think any more.

'Of course, Mrs Lander. We'll leave it there for the moment, then.'

She didn't feel up to arguing. She had felt so good at 3.30 that afternoon. Now she just had the most awful feeling that everything had started to come tumbling down.

The silo was almost empty now. The augur had been running for some time, gently moving the grain downwards and out through the bottom. As the level had gone down, the smell had worsened in the heat of the summer day. It was a strange smell, sweet and rotten at the same time.

Benny stood back, allowing the police to deal with the discovery. Two more had turned up in a Range Rover, summoned by DC Morris. When the last of the grain had been extracted, Grimwood motioned towards a long metal ladder lying in the yard.

The officers looked at the youngest of the foursome, who reluctantly nodded and carried the ladder out. Carefully he placed it alongside the silo and climbed to the platform at the top.

'I think you'd better come up,' he shouted to his colleagues.

It had been quite a struggle to get the body out. In an advanced state of putrefaction, they had had to place what remained on a stretcher and winch it up to the top. Then they'd had to turn everything around and gently wind it down to the ground.

Grimwood had looked briefly at it. The torso was a gaping hole, most of the organs shredded by the rats. Some weevils had infiltrated the flesh and were crawling everywhere, making the corpse look as though it was teeming with movement.

The head was the worst. The grain had found its way into the mouth, ears and nostrils and had forged a path right down. The result was an obscenely swollen face, puffed up by the grain and the decomposition gases.

Even Grimwood had been shocked. He had always killed quickly, and had never had to stay around to view the body. This was something different.

The officers, more used to dealing with domestic disputes and drunks on a Saturday night, were also shocked. The body was gingerly placed to one side for the paramedics to take away. There would be a post mortem as soon as the pathologist could get to the mortuary. Everyone tried to look away from the mortal remains of Charlie Jacobs.

DC Morris cleared his throat.

'Mr Grimwood – you said something about some warnings?'

Benny started.

'Oh, yes. Sorry, officer, I'd forgotten ... please bear with me, I don't feel too good at the moment... Yes, if you'd like to come with me.'

He took the officer up to the office and went

through the filing cabinet.

'Have a look in there,' he said, offering Charlie Jacobs's file to the officer. 'I don't think I can bear to go through it myself at the moment.'

'No, I quite understand, Mr Grimwood,' soothed DC Morris. Quickly, he leafed through the file, extracting the two copy warnings.

'Well, this does tally with the information you gave us. I wonder if I can take the file away?'

Grimwood waved his hand dismissively.

'Yes, of course.'

The officer left the room quietly. Must have been an awful experience for Mr Grimwood. Still, these things did happen. What could you do with staff who ignored warnings, though? He'd better get on to the Health and Safety Executive, although this had all clearly happened some time ago. Hopefully, they'd just have a quick look around and come to the obvious conclusion.

Chapter Thirteen

Dermot Lebrun rose at five to get a couple of hours on the river before breakfast. He loved the early training sessions with the rest of the crew. With hardly anyone else up, they had the river to themselves and had worked hard.

He loved rowing, had taken it up as an undergraduate. It was the ultimate team sport to him. The eight rowers had to work in perfect balance and harmony. If one of them was out of rhythm, they all suffered. So they had to work as one, their lungs gasping and their muscles screaming as they powered the boat down the river.

That morning had been particularly beautiful. The sun was up, but not hot enough yet to permeate the gentle mist lying above the meadows. There was no wind, and the water dappled the languid reflection of the boat as gently it made its way along.

They had pushed themselves hard and he had worked up quite an appetite. After the session, Dermot went to the senior common room for breakfast. There, over his bacon and eggs, he started to read a copy of the *Guardian*. On the third page, his eye was drawn to a photograph of Geri.

'Mortgage fraud at leading solicitors' read the headline.

He stopped eating and read quickly down the page. It was impossible.

He'd thought a lot about Geri since they'd met. Indeed, he'd rather neglected some of his other work to do that report for her as soon as possible. There was something deeply attractive about her, he'd decided. Not just her looks. No, they were fantastic enough but he could see beyond that. It was more to do with an underlying vulnerability. He didn't dare analyse it too carefully. Sir Galahads, he knew, were distinctly out of fashion these days. All he knew was that he hadn't felt like this for an awfully long time.

He'd had little to do with women since Marie had left. Startling really, how easily he had adjusted. Mind you, Cambridge was the perfect environment for a celibate. There was a long tradition of brilliant academics who had dedicated their lives to their work, without the distractions of a family. Nobody regarded him as odd in dividing his time between his work and the river – indeed, there were many who lived similarly.

The difference was, he hadn't particularly planned that things should turn out like this. Marie had always seemed so independent, lecturing him at length about marriage being institutionalised slavery. He'd leafed through enough of the feminist magazines she left around the place to come to the conclusion that she'd regard a proposal as a terrible insult. So he'd kept quiet, agreeing with her that modern living meant allowing partners to keep their separate identities. Pity, really, because there had been a time when he'd wanted nothing more than to marry her and settle down into peaceful domesticity.

Then Marie had been offered a wonderful job at Princeton. She had wanted it so much, but he knew he could never live in the States. He was too firmly rooted in Cambridge. Besides, she needed to pursue her own way in life, she told him. With frequent visits and e-mails, they had an ideal opportunity to combine a modern relationship with professional success. This was the way of the future, she had said.

He'd agreed reluctantly. Within six months, she had married her Head of Department at Princeton. The last he'd heard, she had given up work altogether to look after her growing brood of children.

He'd not set out to avoid women after that; it

was just that nice ones didn't seem to come his way any more. The only single ones he ever seemed to meet were his students and the fear of being branded an aging Lothario put paid to pursuing that option. The thought of getting involved in singles clubs or agencies appalled him. Besides, he wasn't unhappy as he was. The only cloud on his romantic horizon was his mother, still in County Clare, who had taken to sending him resumés of each single girl she met. He was the only unmarried child from her seven, and it was clearly starting to get to her.

She'd adore Geri, he found himself thinking. They were two of a type – tenacious, bossy and intelligent.

He turned back to the newspaper. Surely Geri couldn't have done this thing? The report was reasonably full. A male partner, it said, had apparently decamped with the money, leaving the remaining three to pick up the pieces. So she hadn't done anything, he thought. All this would knock her for six, poor woman. He knew she'd left a message and he hadn't got back to her. He better give her a ring quickly, before she got the wrong idea.

Jackie phoned down.

'Professor Lebrun, Geri.'

She grabbed the receiver.

'Hi, Dermot.'

'Geri, good to hear you. I'm, er, sorry about all this hassle you're getting. Are you still going to be doing the superbug case?'

Geri smiled.

'At the moment. God knows what will happen, but I'll keep on until I'm stopped. It's pretty appalling here. But the good news is that we've got our Order for discovery – we're going to be able to look at the Ministry's documents, see what we can find.'

'That's brilliant.'

He paused a moment.

'Could I help? I mean, you may want somebody to assist with looking...'

'If you could, Dermot, it would be wonderful.'

'OK, all hands to the pump then. Just let me know when you get the date. And Geri?'

'Yes?'

'Don't let the bastards get you down.'

She grinned into the phone.

'Thanks, Dermot.'

She hung up and the phone went again immediately. It was Jackie once more.

'I've got the bank on the line. Do you want to call them back?'

'No, I'll deal with it now.' Better get it over with, thought Geri.

'Sebastian Rogers here. Mrs Lander, I've noticed from the press this morning that you've been having a few problems.'

'Well, yes, Mr Rogers, but please let me assure you that the losses to clients will be reimbursed by the Law Society scheme – we shouldn't be having to meet them ourselves.'

He wasn't having any of that.

'That may be so, but we are rather concerned about the effect of the publicity. As you'll be aware, we've already been rather worried about the financial health of the firm.'

Worried about the bank's money, more like, thought Geri.

'It's too early to gauge the effect. In fact, one of my clients was only this morning telling me it would make no difference to her loyalty to the firm.'

Joanna had said as much over breakfast when she'd arrived to look after Rory.

'I'm afraid that's not going to be enough. No, Mrs Lander, I think we're going to have to look at refinancing.'

'What do you mean?' An awful feeling of dread was creeping over her.

'We will have to consider calling in the overdraft.'

'But you can't!'

'You'll see from the agreement that we can call in the finance on demand.'

'But that's crazy! We'd never repay it just like that – we need to keep on running the firm and maintaining the cash flow.'

Mr Rogers sighed down the phone.

'I'm afraid that there does come a point where we do, as lenders, have to take positive action.' He had obviously said this many times before.

'But that's not positive – it's wiping us out as a firm! And you'd lose the money you'd already got in the business.'

'I think you'll find that the four partners are all jointly and severally liable for the debt, Mrs Lander. As I understand the three that remain do have sufficient assets to meet the overdraft as it stands.'

'But only by selling our houses!'

'Sometimes that is the sacrifice that needs to be made.'

Geri thought of her house. The thought of its going to pay off the bank was unbearable. She gripped the phone and pleaded for time.

'I'm just about to go into a partners' meeting, Mr Rogers. Could we discuss your concerns and then arrange a meeting with you?'

He answered shortly,

'Yes. At ten tomorrow.'

There was silence in the boardroom as Geri entered. The emptiness of Cefan's seat seemed to cast an atmosphere of quiet despair.

'Pete, Roger, I think we need to consider the way forward very carefully. I've just been speaking to the bank. They want to call in the overdraft.'

She'd never noticed before but Pete bit his nails. They were right down to the quick, reddened and ugly.

Roger replied first.

'I suppose we need to think about assets. If it came down to it, how much could we raise?'

'I have my house,' said Geri.

'I remortgaged last year,' said Pete. 'Only a few thousand equity.'

'I lost rather a lot on some investments,' said Roger gloomily.

'You've got a house in Hertfordshire,' pointed out Geri.

'It's my wife's.'

She started to hear alarm bells in her head.

'So are you both saying you have no real assets?'

'Yes,' they replied in unison.

They were jointly and severally liable for the overdraft. That meant that each of them was responsible for the whole debt. Since she was the only one with any capital, the bank would expect her to pay it all. She could seek recompense from Pete and Roger, but if they had no money, she would get nowhere.

She could lose everything.

Roger spoke again.

'Look, we've got to stay positive. I've just had a big cheque in from one of my companies – thirty thousand. That's going into the office account today. We've billed twenty thousand between us to help the cash flow and let's not forget the equity in the building – there's an awful lot of lease left.'

Geri nodded.

'I've arranged to see the bank tomorrow. Could we prepare some figures? Show them we're about to receive some cash and that they should give us some time? If we can all go, perhaps we can put up a good fight.'

'Yes,' said Roger. 'I'll see what I can do. If the worst comes to the worst, we can always sell the business. Someone will want to take it over. If there's anything left after this bloody intervention.'

'Geri,' asked Pete, 'how far on are you in the antibiotic case? That could be a real money spinner – couldn't you raise an interim bill on that? Jackie said you'd had a good result in a hearing on it yesterday.'

Geri looked sheepish.

'Well, actually, I'm doing it on conditional fee.'

'What?' Both men were horrified.

'It was the only way. The client turned out not to be as well off as she looked. Honestly, it's a brilliant case, and if we win the fee will be enormous...'

'But, Geri,' protested Roger, 'you quite clearly agreed you would seek our approval *before* you took on any more conditional fee work.'

'But I'd already taken it on by the time I agreed that.'

'How long before?' Even Pete, normally her staunchest supporter, looked angry.

'I don't know exactly. One or two days...' She crossed her fingers beneath the table.

'I have to say, I would have thought it only fair to mention that case to us at the time.' Roger was getting pompous.

'Look, I'm sorry. I had no idea this was going to happen. It is a good case, honestly.'

She realised she was starting to sound desperate.

'Anyhow, if you could get the interim billing figures, Roger, I'll go and start to prepare something for the bank tomorrow. Can you ring me at home? The police want me off the stage as much as possible.'

Roger agreed and they ended the meeting.

Geri returned to her room to sign her post. As she sat at her desk, she thought about Roger's words. They could sell the firm. The name wouldn't be worth much, not after what had happened, but there was value to the lease, bought at a knockdown price in the recession of the 1970s. And there was the interim billing and work in progress. They might just be able to pay off the overdraft from the proceeds.

Simon's death had meant that the mortgage on her house had been paid off. She had some small savings. Selling the firm would mean she could look after Rory, perhaps move to a smaller place. She didn't need all this worry.

She shook her head suddenly. She couldn't believe she was thinking like this. Not when she had fought for two years to keep the firm loyal to Simon's ideals. She couldn't just give up now.

As Geri thought through the options, Jackie came in and coughed lightly to get her attention.

'Geri, we're all a bit worried about the situation. There are so many rumours.'

Geri looked up at her. She owed Jackie a lot.

'No one knows what's happening at the moment, Jackie. I've got to say, it may well get difficult. We're going to lose a lot of work through what Cefan did.'

'I don't know if it will help, but if there's anything the staff can do – taking a wage cut for a while, working part-time – we would like to do our best.'

Geri was deeply touched. This was a secretary who could walk into a better paid job in a City firm next week if she chose.

'Jackie, you don't know how grateful I am ... what I'm going to do is let the dust settle a bit for the moment, and then decide what to do.'

Jackie paused for a moment.

'You won't know how I started work here – Simon always said he would never mention it.'

'No, I don't know.'

'I'd been fired by another firm. One of the partners was touching me up and I complained. They sacked me. I came to see Simon and he brought a claim for me – it was years back now, before all this sexual harassment thing took off. Well, I had no money, so he said I could work for him. We agreed that he'd take some money out of my wages for the costs, but he never did. *And* he won the case and got me damages. And, Geri, he wouldn't take a penny – just said it was worth it to have me as his secretary. I was just so grateful to him – he was a wonderful man.'

'Yes, he was,' said Geri softly.

'It would be such a pity if the firm went – we all care so much about it.'

Jackie seemed close to tears. She put down her files and left quietly.

As Geri tried to plan her encounter with the bank the next day, Jackie hurried back to her own room, closed her door and rang Directory Enquiries.

'Office for the Supervision of Solicitors, please.'

She pressed in the number and was put through to a rather harassed-sounding woman. Quickly, Jackie explained why she was ringing.

'I know this is a little unusual, but I have been working with Mrs Lander for years, and her late husband before that. She really had no idea that this mortgage fraud was going on – she's the most honest person you'll ever come across.'

There was a pause as she listened to the voice at the other end of the line.

'Testimonials? Well, yes, I could speak to those who know her – can you give me an address and reference number?'

Jackie wrote down the details, thanked the woman and hung up.

She thought for a moment. Geri always said that you needed to work out your strategy first. The authorities had to know what people thought of Geri. Awkward, intransigent, self-opinionated, most definitely. But never, absolutely never, dishonest.

Gloria had to be the first stop. If she could provide a statement, setting out how Cefan had kept his fraud secret, the authorities would be bound to be impressed. If even his secretary didn't know what was going on, how could Geri?

And then, surely, some of the clients could help? Jackie knew that Geri would never allow her to approach them for testimonials. She was there to help them, not the other way round, would be her attitude. They could speak volumes in her support. But Geri always talked about confidentiality. She couldn't tell people she was even acting for someone without their consent.

But there was no harm in asking them to agree, and suggesting they might like to write a letter to the authorities. Former clients might be able to help too – those for whom Geri had fought and won good awards – surely they'd be prepared to write supporting her?

Jackie scanned through the names on the client

list on the computer and selected thirty. She'd need to visit them quietly, explain the situation and leave them with the address. She'd have to ask them not to mention it to Geri or her boss would stop it immediately. Clever she certainly was. But sometimes, she had no sense at all. Particularly where her own interests were concerned.

Jackie Wilberforce was going to have to do battle for her.

Geri arrived home to find Joanna cleaning the kitchen floor. The older woman looked sombre.

'Joanna, it's important you hear this from me first. The Law Society will want another firm to handle your case while they investigate me.'

'But I don't want another firm.'

'That's not the issue...'

'It most certainly is, Geri! I have asked you to present this case. You have agreed. If anyone tries to tell me they have the power to interfere with that – without any findings against you – well, I just won't agree and that's that.'

Joanna sat down at the kitchen table.

'In fact, I'm going to write to the Law Society and tell them so right now. It's despicable.'

Geri went up to Rory's room and sat on his bed. He was at his desk, reading a natural history magazine.

'How did it go, Mum?'

'Not too well. I think we may have to put an end to the firm.'

'But you can't do that – Dad would hate it.'

'But I could spend more time with you.'

'Yes, but it's just not like that. You're at the firm. That's what you do.'

'What do you want? I mean, if we forget what I've always done, and think about what you really want.'

He looked thoughtful.

'I don't know.'

'Rory, sometimes we do need to change things, move on a little. We don't have to put up with things forever.'

'I just wish Dad was here,' he blurted out.

Geri's voice was soft.

'I know. So do I.'

'The boys at school – they keep saying that I'm useless, spastic, stupid...'

'But that's just nonsense! You're the most special person in the world to me.'

'Am I?'

He actually looked surprised. She'd thought it was obvious.

'Of course you are.'

'But that's only because Dad died?'

'No. Rory, you've got to understand – I love you and Dad loved you. And I'm worried that I'm not with you enough, that I'm away at work too much.'

'So you are saying you'd actually give up work for me?'

'Yes, I would.'

'But what about the firm?'

'I don't know. Like I said, things move on. Sometimes you have to change, not do something just because you've always done it.'

'But I'd still have to go to school. You'd just be

at home doing nothing.'

He had a point.

'Rory, it's been bad for both of us. I've been trying to keep the firm like it was – like Dad had set it up ... but I just don't know any more. You're more important to me than the business.'

'But what would you do?'

'Rory, all I'm saying is that I'm going to think about everything. At the moment, I don't really know what will happen, but we're going to be together on this. Perhaps we should go away, think a bit, just the two of us.'

He smiled.

'That would be good.'

Stiles had finally got back to Grimwood. He'd been abroad for a while and they'd had to wait. Now they were back in a different cafe – the last thing they wanted was to become regulars anywhere. So they sat in the back, tea and sandwiches in front of them.

'The time's right now,' said Grimwood.

Stiles nodded slowly.

'You're in the best position to judge that. How much will it go for?'

'I think we can safely bet on three times the usual.'

'Volume?'

Grimwood smiled to himself as the other man barked out his queries. Stiles disguised it better with his apparent bonhomie, but when it got serious they were two of a kind.

'As much as you can get. This is going to have to be the big one.'

'OK, I can get a thousand tons. But it will have to come through gradually, along my usual routes.'

Grimwood frowned.

'No other way, Benny. Anything else will be too risky.'

'How long then?'

'I can bring the stuff up to you every fortnight throughout the summer. Should be able to finish delivery by the end of September.'

'OK. In the meantime, I'll keep pushing the price up.'

Stiles picked up his cup and looked over the rim at him.

'Benny, I'll need some of the money up front for this size of consignment.'

Damn! Usually Stiles trusted him to pay from the proceeds. This time was clearly going to be on different terms.

'How much?'

'Two hundred grand.'

Grimwood let out a small breath.

'Take it or leave it, Benny. I can't order that amount without paying for it up front.'

Stiles took a sip from his cup, and replaced it carefully in the saucer.

Grimwood's mind was working hard. If he could get three times the usual price, he was looking at a total profit of seven hundred and fifty grand. Three-quarters of a million. On that, he could leave England and settle down in his place in the sun. If he had to take a bit of a risk to do it, then that's how it was.

He had the remains of his father's legacy, and a

little in the bank.

'OK, but I'm at my limit. No stunts about needing more money at the last minute.'

Stiles looked him in the eye.

'No stunts, Benny. Not with you.'

Chapter Fourteen

Geoffrey Atwell sat back in his chair. It had been an horrendous few hours. He had brought the fax up to Moncrieff at 5 p.m. yesterday. He'd already heard the news: Angela Simons, the junior solicitor he had sent, had phoned it through. He'd delayed telling Moncrieff until the Order appeared, though.

The Minister had looked at the document briefly. His expression was thunderous.

'Get Hodder.'

He almost spat the words out.

Atwell looked nervous.

'That may well be difficult. He's probably not contactable at the moment. And he'll be in Court tomorrow, I would imagine. Perhaps if I arrange another consultation reasonably soon?'

'Get him here for ten tomorrow or he's sacked.'

'Minister, with respect, that's rarely a wise move. Sacking your QC sends out very bad signals to the opposition. And, it has to be said, there's none better than Hodder, even if he wasn't successful today.'

Moncrieff growled his response.

‘Then just make sure he’s fucking well here tomorrow!’

So Geoffrey Atwell spent most of the evening on the phone to Hodder’s clerk. Luckily, he was most accommodating. Mr Hodder had been due to appear in the High Court, but the case had settled and his junior could deal with it instead. Anything to oblige. And of course the QC would come to the Ministry. No need for the Minister to have to come to Chambers. Of course, there would be the fee to consider...

And this morning, by the look of it, Moncrieff had calmed down a little. But not much. Hodder made the first move. This was his consultation, after all.

‘Minister, I’m grateful for your time. I felt that this would be a good moment to discuss tactics.’

‘Later,’ growled Moncrieff. ‘First, what the hell is this?’

He was holding the faxed copy of the Order for discovery.

‘I want an explanation, Hodder.’

‘I did my best, Minister...’

‘Obviously not fucking good enough then, was it?’

He glared at the QC, who avoided eye contact.

‘You were sent to that Court to do a job. You failed. Can you give me one good reason why you should continue to act in this?’

The only one that Hodder could think of was the five thousand pounds his clerk had agreed with Atwell for yesterday’s hearing. This bollocking today was going to be worth another thousand, his clerk had told him. Well, he could bear it on those terms.

'At the end of the day, it's down to the Judge.'

'Judge, my arse! You're a QC after all. Appearing in a Court presided over by some small-time Judge and a girl solicitor – are you saying she got the better of you?'

Hodder was struggling.

'Well?'

'No, but you just never can tell in litigation...'

He smiled. But it was weak, and he knew it. He tried to change the subject.

'Have you heard about the difficulties at Mrs Lander's firm?'

'Yes, I have. Will that put an end to this ridiculous business?'

'Maybe. There has to be a chance they'll fold. But I don't think we should get too excited about that – if it happens quickly, the Pascoe woman will probably just take her case on to someone else. Now, if we can get to the stage where Mrs Lander has seen the documents and ruled the case out – then we might find that no other firm will take it on. I've had a word with my clerk – she's known as the sort who won't drop a case unless it's an absolute no-hoper.'

The Minister thought over the QC's words.

'So what we really need to do is convince this woman that there is no case?'

'Yes.'

'What do you suggest?'

'Well,' the QC raised an eyebrow, 'your instructions are quite clear that there is no case and that your Department has no knowledge of perinycin abuse.'

Hodder was extremely careful how he put this type of question. Like most barristers, he would never ask his client to tell him the truth. That was far too dangerous. It was almost asking for trouble. It was much more sensible simply to ask for the client's instructions – to ask him what he wanted the Court to be told.

Moncrieff nodded firmly.

'Yes, those are my instructions.'

'In that case, we have to keep uppermost in our minds the fact that we need to convince this woman as quickly as possible she will find nothing.'

'How do we do that?'

'She needs to be given the impression that nothing is being hidden from her. And we need to put her in the frame of mind where she will be reluctant to do any more work on the case.'

D'Arby Colinder made his first contribution to the consultation.

'I wonder if a paper chase might be a good idea?'

The Minister raised his eyebrows.

The junior carried on.

'In a case of this type, it can be useful to disclose a vast number of documents – completely inundate the other side with material which is useless to their case.'

Hodder took up the theme.

'Every solicitor will expect to find some leads. It's suspicious if there's nothing at all. But sometimes one can be quite frank about the leads and provide reams of material for the other side to pursue. Believe me, Minister, if all that material is produced and considered, and the leads go nowhere, most solicitors will develop a real reluctance to carry out any more work on the case.'

Moncrieff steepled his hands together.

'Is there not a risk that if vast amounts of information are collected and produced, then our opponents might not ask why we didn't seem to have processed the documents and perhaps made a substantive report dealing with the situation?'

Hodder nodded, slowly.

'Yes, that could be so,' he conceded.

'What if a report were to be made available?'

'Well, we would have to state why we didn't disclose it at the hearing. Dr Vane did give his evidence...'

'No, Mr Hodder, there was nothing at that point...'

He was quick to smooth things over.

'But it might well be that Dr Vane will want to consider the materials and prepare some recommendations. Would he need to disclose that?'

'If it were produced before the documents were examined, yes. If it came into existence afterwards – well, there's been a recent case which says that we ought now to disclose right up to the point of evidence being given at a hearing.'

D'Arby Colinder looked thoughtful.

'Of course, we'd have to bear in mind what the report said. If it didn't help the Plaintiff, early disclosure would not harm us one bit.'

Callum Moncrieff was warming to the man.

Geri, Joanna and Rory were having lunch in the kitchen.

'If you want a break, why don't you have my cottage in Devon for a few days? There's no one booked in it until August.'

Rory looked at his mother pleadingly.

Joanna carried on.

'It's really rather nice – it's on a farm, next to the farmhouse. Lots of animals, very quiet. Mortgaged to the hilt and a bit more, of course.'

'It sounds wonderful, but I think that the police will want me around in case they have more questions.'

Sooner or later Geri knew there was going to be a very long interview. More like an inquisition. She was not looking forward to it. She had already let them have the run of the office and access to her bank and building society accounts. At least they would be able to see that she had not received any money from the fraud. Quite the contrary. If the firm folded, she could be ruined.

'But after?' Rory looked at her, beseechingly.

The idea of a break away from everything was very tempting. Why not?

She smiled. 'Yes.'

'And there was a message for you to ring Roger,' said Joanna. 'He said he's got some figures for you.'

After the consultation had finished, Callum Moncrieff summoned David.

The Minister was at his most charming.

'Thank you for popping up. I just wanted to say

well done about the hearing.' David felt distinctly uncomfortable about the hearing and didn't want to dwell on it. This was written all over his face and it encouraged Callum enormously.

'I also need to mention a few more developments.'

'Really?'

'You may be aware that the firm that's creating all the problems is now having some difficulties of its own.'

David hadn't seen the newspapers.

'It seems that one of Mrs Lander's partners has made off with rather a lot of somebody else's money. I'm afraid that our suspicions about the firm were quite right.'

David smiled weakly.

'Anyhow, I've been discussing the situation with our legal advisers. It seems that if Mrs Lander goes down the pan, so to speak, the case may be taken on by other solicitors.'

David grimaced.

'Are you trying to tell me that things are going to be delayed – that I shouldn't be preparing my new report?'

'Not at all, David. All I want to do is decide with you which way things can be progressed most effectively.'

Callum moved from behind the desk and motioned David to one of the comfortable chairs on the other side of the room. He sat down with a show of informality.

'David, I'll be straightforward. This case can go all sorts of ways at the moment. If new solicitors are involved, there's going to be a delay of several months while they come on stream. That will mean we can't start the implementation process as quickly as we'd both like.'

'Yes, I see that.'

'On the other hand, if Mrs Lander stays involved in the matter long enough to form the conclusion that the case is a no-hoper – well, then we could dispose of it very quickly indeed and move on to dealing with your proposals.'

'Yes, but I can't make up her mind for her.'

'That may not be so. We're going to stick to the letter of the Court Order and disclose absolutely everything which might be of relevance to the claim. Everything except, well...'

'Yes. I see.'

'Now, what might be helpful would be if there was some sort of, shall we say, interim report from you, carried out before the information is disclosed.'

'But that would say just what the original said.'

'With respect, David, a scientist can change his mind, can't he? There's been many a situation where the problem has only been appreciated after the interim report was prepared.'

'What are you asking, Minister?'

Callum Moncrieff took his time, looking directly at David.

'I want you to prepare an interim report which concludes that there is no problem with perinycin abuse in British farming. You can always correct the situation in your final report.'

David was appalled.

'But I couldn't possibly do that! I can't just write something which I think is rubbish – something which is directly contrary to everything I've been warning you about.'

'If that's really how you feel then you should stick to the original plan and move straight on to the full report in due course – but you will have to understand that if that happens, the case may well continue and delays occur.'

Callum looked directly at David.

'My priority is to sort this problem out, and I don't want to see delays. Sometimes, one has to be a little ... flexible ... about matters if one wants to achieve a particular result. David, if you can think of any other way round the problem, I'll gladly listen. I just need to get things into position so that you can go into action.'

His gaze had not wavered for a moment.

'Believe me, I feel as strongly as you do about this situation.'

That, at least, was true. He wanted out of the Ministry of Agriculture more than anything else in the world at the moment.

David Vane paused for a moment. Good. He was taking the bait.

'Look, I need to have a think about this, Minister.'

'By all means, David. Remember, we're working together on this. Call me any time.'

David went back to his office. He was rapidly starting to feel hemmed in. If he blew the whistle, he'd lose his job and his reputation. None of the other scientists in the department would be able to sort out the antibiotic problem and the Minister would probably do nothing. So he could rule that one out.

He could stick to his original plan and simply redate his report. But what if the solicitors went out of business and a new firm took over? It could be months before he could do anything. He would have to wait until they abandoned the case before he could produce the final report or else it would have to be produced to them.

So far, there had been only sporadic outbreaks of the superbug, but sooner or later there was going to be a large-scale problem. All that was needed was for a food handler to go down with it.

The other option was to do what the Minister said. Prepare an interim report to kill the case off. Then get down to business. He would be lying and he would be prostituting his scientific integrity in the short term, at least, but hadn't he done that already? On oath, in a Courtroom, before five witnesses. What they said about little lies leading to big ones was right after all.

He stopped all phone calls and locked his door. The original report was in his right-hand drawer, locked safely away. He could reproduce much of it. The pages relating to the scientific background, research methods, and aims could all be copied easily into the new document. Reading it through once more, the only information which showed the extent of the problem was his own research – those farm visits. And, to be fair, not all of them had turned up perinycin abuse. It would be perfectly possible temporarily to delete the reference to the problem farms, and report only on the innocent ones. He could always 'discover' the wrongdoers in time for the final report.

David sighed. He could see no real option other than to go along with Callum Moncrieff. Not while the lawyers were involved, anyway. Whatever else, he knew that they wouldn't sort out the problem. And only he could stop them making it considerably worse.

Once again, David got his report up on screen. This time, instead of just deleting the date, he copied the file. The previous research could stand. He got to the section dealing with his farm visits and started to delete some of the entries. Then he deleted the conclusions and rewrote the final section.

By 5 p.m. he had finished, tired and short-tempered by now. He scanned the new document quickly. Checking that the Minister was available, he walked it round to the office.

Moncrieff was all smiles.

'David, this is really going to help us. Would you like to start drawing up your plans for the implementation process first? As soon as this case is out of the way, we can get going and it always pays to be ready.'

Of course, once the case foundered, he wouldn't have to tell Vane immediately. Every passing day took him closer to the safe haven of another Department. He really must insist on an urgent meeting with the Prime Minister.

David was delighted.

'Yes. I'll start drafting some timetables. It will be a large-scale exercise... Minister, may I suggest one thing?'

'Yes, of course.'

'Now I've done the report, can we move this case on quickly? Get them round to look at the documents urgently so we don't lose any more time?'

'Good idea. David, can I arrange a meeting between you and the junior barrister in the case? He's offered his assistance in preparing the documentation, and has some very helpful ideas about how we can stop this litigation in its tracks. I'll get Atwell to arrange something urgently. Can you do it tomorrow?'

David nodded.

'Good. Then I'll tell Mrs Lander to pay us a visit in two days' time.'

Benny Grimwood put the last thirty thousand into the safe and locked it carefully. He was ready for the first consignment.

He'd also made some enquiries about Spanish properties. There was nothing tying him to England any more, not now Father had gone. He missed the old man still. Mother had been a complete tart who'd decamped when he was six. But Father, well, he was the only person on this earth Benny had loved.

At least he'd gone to his rest thinking that his son was a success. But now, the family house was empty and forlorn. It was time to go.

Chapter Fifteen

Geri arrived at her office early that Thursday morning. She was greeted by the Ministry fax, inviting her to come and inspect their papers the following day. The legal department were short-staffed, it said, and sorry about the short notice.

Geri rang Joanna.

'Can we make it tomorrow at the Ministry? I may need help going through the information.'

'Certainly,' said Joanna. 'And Rory can come too.'

Geri was about to protest, but stopped. He was eleven, after all, and could be trusted to be sensible. He couldn't go to school for the moment. He might well be very useful, and it would help him stop brooding.

'OK.'

Tentatively, Geri rang Dermot Lebrun.

'Hi, Geri. Any news?'

She smiled into the receiver, absurdly pleased to hear his voice again.

'Dermot, I've just heard from the Ministry that we can inspect their files tomorrow – is that out of the question for you?'

'As it happens, it's fine. I've got a meeting at the Natural History Museum at six that evening, so I'm coming down to London anyhow. I've a lecture to do here at ten, and after that I can be with you. What time do you want me?'

She could have kissed him. But for the fact that she was on the phone to him, she probably would have.

'As soon as you can get there.'

There was a telephone message asking her to ring DS Edgar.

'Thank you, Mrs Lander, I was just trying to arrange an interview under caution. I'm a little busy myself next week – how about Monday week at ten a.m.?'

She smiled. Nobody seemed to want her around next week. If she could get the Ministry visit over with tomorrow, she and Rory would be free to go on holiday. Today was going to work out.

The remaining three partners of Lander Ross & Co travelled together to the bank. Roger had spent most of the previous day preparing a report outlining the firm's precarious finances. The figures didn't stand up to close inspection. The worst howler was including in sums owed to the firm the charges made to Cefan's defrauded banks. Somehow, they felt it unlikely they would see *that* money.

On the face of it, though, the report made encouraging reading. Staff wages had been paid and the interim billing figures looked good. They were solvent, once you counted in the value of the lease and the distinctly shrunken goodwill.

They were shown into Mr Rogers's office. It was a modern building, all arches and smoked glass. Geri hated it. The walls seemed to amplify rather than reduce sound and the room was too small for the four of them to sit in comfortably. Instead, they were huddled around Mr Rogers's desk.

Geri spoke first.

'Thank you for seeing us, Mr Rogers. We've carried out a review of the firm's finances, and the position is actually rather encouraging.'

She looked to Roger who handed around copies of his report. The bank manager looked, hawk-like, at the billing figures. He was a tiny man, with a fussy manner and a nervous tic. His room was far too tidy. Geri decided she disliked him even more in the flesh.

'How much of this do you expect to see?'

'There's usually eight percent wastage.' This was the figure for clients who didn't pay and could not be pursued for the money. Sometimes, the debt was so small it wasn't worth chasing; on other occasions the client was too broke for them to sue.

'And when do you expect to see the money you've billed?'

'We allow twenty-eight days for payment.'

'Is that realistic?'

'Well, I'd say three months to see the majority of that sum,' admitted Roger.

'What about outgoings?'

Roger had prepared a spreadsheet setting out the monthly expenses – staff, rates, heating, lighting, stationery.

Mr Rogers didn't look impressed.

'On these figures, you might make a small inroad into the overdraft, but there's no radical improvement forecast. There's also a risk that things might get considerably worse.'

'What we've all got to bear in mind,' said Geri sharply, 'is that if we shut up shop tomorrow, we'll see nothing for the billing run. Nobody will bother to pay us if we're six feet under.'

Mr Rogers nodded slowly and allowed his face to display a cadaverous smile.

'But that's your problem, with the greatest respect. And I understand that you're not in a position to bill for the immediate future as your work is being dealt with by another firm. All you're asking for is a favour so that your liabilities can be paid from the firm rather than your personal money.' Geri decided to call on history.

'This firm has been clients of your bank since it started up. We've been good customers. Are you really saying that this relationship counts for nothing?'

Mr Rogers picked up the spreadsheet and turned it face down in front of him.

'I'm willing to recommend that we grant a three-month delay before we call in the loan, subject to two conditions.'

Geri looked at him.

'First, we will require weekly breakdowns of profit and loss. If you start to stray away from these recommendations, we may need to review the situation.'

'And second?'

'We would require a charge over your house, Mrs Lander.'

Geri breathed in sharply.

'But why? On these figures, we'll be able to pay

you from the income – that's the whole point of waiting.'

'It's a question of risk. If we're going to give you the benefit of time, we will need a fall back position in case these figures aren't achieved.'

'But it's my *home*.'

'Sorry, Mrs Lander, but the bank would expect me to cover its risks. We cannot grant a delay period unless we have some security.'

Geri thought quickly. If they called in the overdraft now, she would end up paying it herself. That would mean selling the house to raise the money. If she allowed them to have a charge and got some time in return, she might eventually save the roof over her head. There was no choice. 'Very well, I agree.'

David had prepared a list for the paper chase. He started from his interim report, and had set out all the research papers included in it. Then he had carried out a literature search, until the list contained vast reams of information. Much of it – the majority, in fact – would be completely irrelevant to the claim. That didn't matter. What was important was that the other side gained the impression that the Ministry was bending over backwards to supply everything.

As Geri agreed to sign away her home, David was seated in the Ministry library, checking the papers for disclosure. He would pass on his list to the solicitor. It contained no details of what was in the reports – just date and journal references. She would no doubt start at the beginning, The most boring stuff had therefore been placed there. Last but one, at number one hundred and twenty-nine, was the new interim report.

The documents, in frustratingly muddled order, were placed in the noisiest room in the Ministry, right beside the cafeteria. There they would wait until the inspection the next day.

David returned to his office. He'd neglected his in tray for the last few days and it was looming large. He set to it, keen to get organised.

Halfway down the pile were slip numbers 21 and 22. Different hospitals – one in the North West, one in the Midlands. Two more superbug deaths. He called up the graph on his PC – one document that certainly had not been added to the pile for disclosure. He had noted that there was no even distribution of superbug deaths. They would occur in small groups, peak, and then ebb to nothing for a few months.

David had expected this. Each was a mini-outbreak – probably infected carcasses from the same stock reaching the food markets. The trend, he knew, would probably be towards bigger outbreaks. All that was needed was for infection to be passed on by the slaughterhouse men or the butchers.

Then the big outbreak would occur.

He shivered in his air-conditioned room. Once the infection got hold, it would rampage through the population. It would be impossible to isolate so many patients, and cross-infection would be inevitable.

It would be a disaster on an unprecedented scale. Every disease-forecast model which he had used had come up with the same answer.

Predicted deaths of over a million.

He had to stop it before things got to that stage.

Jackie, too, was working to a list. She had covered numbers one to twenty-six, visiting several in the evenings and a few in her lunch hours. Quickly, she had explained what was needed, and provided the address to write to. Every single one had agreed readily.

'But not a word to Mrs Lander, please – she'd kill me if she knew I was doing this. And, please, can you write quickly if you're going to? It's really important.'

Chapter Sixteen

Rory had been delighted at the prospect of helping with the documents. The three of them had travelled to the Ministry in high spirits.

The Ministry lawyer had looked perplexed as he had shown them into the tiny room, packed to the ceiling with papers. It was certainly unlike any litigation team he had ever seen – a rather glamorous solicitor, an older woman in a somewhat lurid cerise suit and a boy wearing trainers and jeans. He waved them into the room.

'Take as long as you need. Photocopier is down the stairs and eight doors to the left. Keep a note of how many you take – we'll trust you to pay at the end.'

They didn't know where to start. On the table

in the middle of the room was a typed list, headed 'Documents the production of which is not objected to'.

It started with an article in *Nature*, dealing with the acquisition of resistance. The list continued, all the way down to number 130.

'I know what they're doing,' said Geri, 'it's a standard tactic. They've provided so much stuff that we're meant to give up and go home. The answer is to work out how we're going to deal with it and work methodically.'

'It may mean they've got something to hide,' said Joanna, excited.

'What I suggest is that Rory makes sure we work down the list and finds each report. You and I, Joanna, scan them. If it looks useful, we put it in a pile for the Professor this afternoon. Make sure you tick each report as we get it, Rory.'

'Sure. Right. I need *Nature*.'

He looked around him.

'Where is it?'

Geri laughed.

'They have to show us their documents. They don't have to organise them for us.' He started to look through the piles.

'Got it. Right, Mum, off you go. Now, what do I get for Jo...'

He was actually rather good at it, climbing up and down the shelves and rooting out the articles as they appeared in the list. An adult would have tired before lunchtime, but Rory was still going strong, ticking off each entry as he deposited it before Geri or Joanna.

They were finding it less easy. By about 11 a.m.

the cafeteria was starting to get busy and the swing doors crashed irritatingly into the wall of their room. It was a frequent interruption, but sufficiently irregular to catch them all by surprise. Then they would wait for the next one, not quite knowing when it would happen. It was extremely wearing.

By midday, Geri called a temporary halt to discuss progress.

'Found anything, Joanna?'

'To be honest, nothing more than I already had. There's a few *BMJ* entries that looked hopeful for a moment, but the research that they quote has nothing on perinycin.'

'No, it's the same for me. It's meticulous, though – all the footnoted research has been dug out for us.'

They searched on. As time went by, they became less fussy about what material would be retained for the Professor and his pile grew a little. Shortly before two, Geri went out to get lunch. She brought back rolls for all of them, with an extra for Lebrun in case he hadn't eaten yet.

He arrived at 2.30, looking quite dapper in a bright blue suit and yellow tie. He was apologetic about it.

'I'm actually presenting a paper tonight, so I had to dress up a bit ... girlfriend chose it for me. Sorry I'm so late – bloody trains were an hour behind.'

Damn! He was spoken for. Lebrun was actually goodlooking, in a completely different way from Simon. Perhaps she was starting to move on after all? Geri found the thought rather cheering.

'We've got a pile of papers for you, Dermot. Nothing earth-shattering at the moment, but we're still looking.'

He sat at the table, reading swiftly through the papers. They carried on checking the material which Rory was digging out.

At 4 p.m. they stopped for a break.

'I don't want to sound too gloomy but there's nothing new here,' said Lebrun. 'All of this is stuff which you could get through any literature search in a good science library.'

'Is there anything in the idea that with all this information, they should have processed it into some sort of report?'

'That could well be the case – let's keep our eyes open for something along those lines.'

It was almost the last document. Simply referred to as Vane, IP, July 1996.

'I've got it!' shrieked Rory. 'Right up on the top shelf. IP stands for internal papers.'

He threw it down from the stepladder on to the table. Geri picked it up.

'Interim report into the use of perinycin in UK farming stock. Author, Dr. D. Vane,' read Joanna.

'But he gave evidence at the hearing. Said he didn't know of a report,' said Geri. 'He must have been lying! We've found it ... let me look.'

She grabbed the paper and turned to the first page. It was dated two days ago.

'Done after the hearing, so technically he could say that he hadn't prepared it at the time. He did say that there might be future work.'

Geri broke her self-imposed rule and turned

first to the conclusions. She couldn't bear to wait.

She couldn't believe it.

'"No reason to believe that perinycin is being used ... checks not revealed any abuse ... unless a link is established, no reason to implement any new practices..."'

They were sunk. Not just holed, sunk. The Ministry had inspected and found nothing.

Without a word, Geri passed the document over to Dermot Lebrun. The room was silent, apart from the crashing of that bloody door.

Geri couldn't bring herself to speak. She looked at Joanna and shook her head. They sat silently while he scanned the document.

'Oh, dear,' he said at the end.

Geri photocopied the report and put it in her bag. She'd brought a big one in case there were lots of documents. Instead, it hung limply from her shoulder.

'I'm starving – have you eaten?'

Dermot Lebrun had appeared behind her.

'We had a sandwich at lunch,' muttered Geri. 'There's a spare one for you somewhere...'

'Well, how about I buy you all something?'

Joanna turned to face him.

'I think that's a wonderful idea, Dermot – but not for me, thanks all the same. You go, Geri, and I'll take Rory home.'

'But...'

Before she could finish, Rory spoke up quickly.

'No, you go, Mum. Joanna and I'll be fine.'

Dermot and Geri took the tube around to South Kensington. He waved a special pass at the door to the museum and was ushered in. The cafeteria was still open and morosely they shared a macaroni cheese.

Lebrun had been silent on the tube and during the walk through the underpass. Geri hadn't felt much like talking either. Now, though, he looked up from his plate and paused for a moment before speaking.

'It was too squeaky clean, Geri. There's been a cover up.'

She looked sadly back at him.

'But how do I prove it?'

He thought a while.

'Ultimately, it'll prove itself. Look around you ... Darwin had to wait his time. He was ridiculed, but now he's an icon of his age. You just can't hide the truth.'

'That's all very well, but where does it leave the claim?'

'It's going to be a case of re-reading everything you've got. Go through that report at the end. Look for any logical inconsistencies. There's bound to be something.'

She looked up at the domed roof, then across at him. He grinned back, crinkles appearing around his eyes. Shame about the girlfriend.

'Thanks, Dermot – it was good of you to come. Can you let us know how much we owe you?'

'Sure, sometime. Let's leave it a while, see how the claim pans out.'

'Look, I'd better leave you to your talk.'

Geri stood. He seemed to be about to say something, the fingers of one hand suddenly lifting as though he was about to make a gesture.

Then a waitress came along to clear the table and the moment was lost.

'Yeah. See you soon, Geri.'

That evening, Joanna was philosophical about the day's efforts.

'You tried, Geri. We all did. But if the evidence isn't there, we're only prolonging the agony.'

Geri yawned, tried to hide it.

'And you look absolutely shattered. All that hassle with the firm, and then this. I'm sorry.'

Geri managed a smile.

'It's not your fault. I'm just sure there's something going on, but it's so difficult to get any evidence. Every time I thought I was on to something today, it slipped away – like sand in my fingers.'

'Why don't you get away for that break? Take the report, leave the firm to it and get some sleep?'

Joanna sounded brisk and reassuring.

Rory was looking hopeful again. Geri grinned at them both. She needed to escape, too.

'OK, we leave at nine tomorrow, Rory.'

'Ye-es!' He clapped his hands then threw his arms around them both. Joanna dug a large key out of her handbag.

'I'll just write some directions ... could you give me a ring when you get there? I'll worry until I know you've arrived safely.'

Chapter Seventeen

They had started promptly at nine, setting off from Islington with the Renault boot crammed full of holiday impedimenta. Rory had been trusted with the directions, which he had placed carefully in the glove box.

'I can't think when we last had a holiday,' said Geri. A sunny mood was overtaking her with every mile she put between herself and the offices of Lander Ross & Co.

'Can't remember myself,' laughed Rory.

They had stopped to fill up with petrol on the M3 and had then headed off down the A303. Geri wasn't used to the route and had imagined it would be a dual carriageway. Some parts were, but others seemed to wind their way around most of the villages in southern England. They didn't mind, though. They were in no hurry and the countryside was glorious.

'Mum, look!' shouted Rory.

They were travelling down a long hill at some speed and his sudden shout almost jolted her off the road. She recovered and saw to her right the grey rocks of Stonehenge. They stood, fenced off from the world, bleakly on their grassy base. How on earth had those enormous stones got there?

They stopped for lunch at a pub near Yeovil. Rory negotiated his way through a vast plate of ham and chips, while Geri chose a cheese ploughman's. Replete, they carried on their route. Even the Renault seemed to be enjoying a decent run, although Geri had been careful to make sure that she had her AA membership card with her.

Finally, they were in Devon and Rory dug out the directions.

'Take the next turnoff. We're nearly there, Mum.'

She found the exit and sped up the hill. Before long, the slip road became a tiny country lane. The hedgerows must have been ten foot high, and there was no room to pass oncoming vehicles. Used to white lines and several lanes of traffic, Geri prayed that nothing was coming the other way.

They turned into an even smaller lane. She drove at ten miles an hour. They opened the car windows and smelt the flowers from the road-side.

'Here! On the right – gate's open.'

They pulled on to the farm track and after a hundred yards or so, found the cottage. It was quite stunning. It sat next to the long house of the farmer, facing the farmyard. It was on the crest of a gentle hill which rolled down to a fast-running stream coming directly off the moor.

The farmer was ready for them.

'Mrs Pascoe called me – said you'd be coming. I've put some milk and bread in the fridge for you.'

They opened the door. It was an upside down cottage – the two bedrooms and bathroom were on the ground floor. Stairs in the middle led up to the living area – a huge open-plan space, with the kitchen on one side, and a sitting area on the other.

'It must have been a barn,' said Geri. 'Look at the ceilings.'

'And what about that view!' replied Rory.

It looked down over the fields to the stream. She could see some sheep and lambs in the nearest meadow, and donkeys in the farther field. After the stream the land rolled upwards to the next farm.

There was a note from the farmer, telling them the names of the sheep and saying that they could walk wherever they wanted, provided they shut gates behind them. And avoided the geese, who could be a bit touchy. If they wanted to feed the pigs, they particularly liked half an apple each.

They spent the first day on the moor, driving up to Princetown and looking at the grey walls of Dartmoor prison. Then they drove off, looking for the ponies who wandered free. It was stunning scenery. Simon would have loved it.

They left their troubles behind them. Neither wanted to talk about home. Each just wanted to have a break. So they travelled. They saw the genteel delights of Dartmouth and the precipices of Kingswear. They escaped Brixham with relief and took a day trip to Exeter.

They went to bed early every night, exhausted. Rory had not a single bad dream.

Joanna, too, had a short break while Geri and Rory were away. She had an old school friend who lived in Stratford upon Avon and was delighted to have her to stay for a few days.

It was rather handy for Leamington Spa, the base for the office for the Supervision of Solicitors. She'd telephoned in advance and insisted, politely as ever, that somebody take the time to listen to her comments about Mrs Lander. She would need an hour, she'd told them. In the end, they'd agreed to see her.

'What shall we do for our last day?' asked Geri towards the end of the holiday.

Rory had found an Ordnance Survey map in a pile of tourist information near the pot-bellied stove. He studied it for a while and pointed to an area on the moor in which the contour lines were so close as to be virtually indistinguishable.

'There's a dam and a reservoir up here. We can park there,' he pointed to a sign, 'and then follow the footpath up to the top.'

They had set off with packed lunches and rucksacks purchased in Totnes earlier in the week. The footpath followed the bed of a stream – a typical Dartmoor river which burbled over large slabs of granite and tumbled down mini-waterfalls. It was flat for a while, and then passed the ruins of what must have been a grand old house.

After that, the route started to climb until they were walking up the side of a tor. As they got higher, they started to find isolated scree from the granite tops and the soil became thinner. Finally, they were above the tree line and could hear the sound of rushing water. It became louder as they continued.

Rounding a bend, they could see the dam, water pouring over the edge and down a hundred feet to the bottom.

'Nearly there, Mum.' Rory grinned, scrambling up the final ascent.

They finally reached the top twenty minutes later, passing the dam and catching their breath at the sheer beauty of the reservoir behind. They found a spot near the side where they could sit on a slab of granite. A heat haze hung over the water making the surface shimmer. Sheep grazed peacefully around them.

They opened their rucksacks. Sandwiches, crisps and Coke for each of them.

As Geri munched her way through her lunch, she made her decision. It was funny. You could agonise over something, see both sides of the coin forever. But if you went away, had some time to think, it was really rather easy. Obvious even. She'd been too close to it all. Had been unable to stop and think about what was important.

'Rory, when all this trouble with the firm is over, I'm going to change jobs. Give up the firm.'

He looked at her closely.

'Are you sure?'

'Yes.'

'But, Mum – what about ... you know.'

'Dad?'

'Yes.'

'Rory, I've been trying to keep things going for him, but it's not working. You're far more important – and we both have to move on from it all.'

She took a deep breath.

'I want to tell you something. It may upset you, but I think you should know.'

'Tell me.'

'Your dad had become very down – he was having all sorts of trouble at the firm. He was on pills from the doctors but they didn't work... He killed himself.'

Rory blinked slowly, keeping his eyes on the water. The tors were reflected on the shimmering surface and they both watched, entranced. Finally, he spoke.

'So when I saw him that night – he'd done it in the living room?'

'Rory, we'll never know if it was an accident or if he meant to. He had the pills and some whisky – he may not have known what he was doing. But, yes, he'd stayed downstairs after I'd gone to bed. I've cursed myself so many times for not going and checking on him but, you know...'

'You'd had an argument, hadn't you?'

'Yes.'

'I heard you. That night, I mean.'

She looked at him, astonished.

'The living room is below my room, isn't it? I heard you shouting at each other. You wanted to stop work, he said you couldn't afford it...'

'Rory, I never knew.'

'I thought he'd had a heart attack after it.'

Geri took his hand and looked deep into his eyes.

'You mean, for these past two years you thought...'

'I thought he'd got so worked up that ... you know.' He looked embarrassed, sheepish even.

'But then at school one of the boys said he'd killed himself. Said he'd done it because I was so useless. So the way I was thinking was, whatever happened, it was all my fault.'

'But, Rory...'

'If you wanted to stop working because of me it was my fault. And if I was ... well, if it was like they said at school, that was my fault, too.'

Geri wanted to kick herself. Why hadn't she taken a few moments to think about it from his perspective?

'I got it so wrong, Rory. I didn't tell you what happened – I couldn't really handle it myself. But you must understand, it *wasn't* your fault. Dad was ill, on medicine. He had problems at work, with money. He loved you more than anything in the world.'

'Then how come he killed himself?'

There it was. The obvious question, brutal in its simplicity.

Geri paused a moment and then shook her head.

'Sometimes there's things you just can't answer. He was ill. The world he was living in wasn't real any more. We'll never understand what was going on in his mind, Rory.'

He looked back up at her, his eyes red.

'But we've got to move on, Rory. I carried on working because Simon wanted me to do so. And he'd cared so much about the firm, his work, his campaigning. But all the time, I just wanted to throw it in and spend time with you. That's what I should have done.'

She moved towards him, held him.

'He loved you more than anything in the world, Rory. And I do.'

He smiled through the tears that had started to fall. Geri spoke on, gently.

'Let's decide gradually what we'll do. I need to look around, think a bit. That may take a few months, but I'm not going to be too busy in the meantime. I'll have to do something for work – we'll need the money – but I want something that fits around your school better. If it comes down to it, I'll just not work for a while.'

He turned to her again.

'Mum, I feel so different now. It's been brilliant to be away like this.'

Simultaneously, they thought of Joanna.

'What about the case?' he asked.

'I'm going to look at that report one last time tonight. Either we chuck it in or I'll make it my swansong.'

They laughed and set off down the hillside. It was quicker going downhill and they were back in the cottage in time for a special last tea.

After Rory had settled, exhausted, Geri sat alone for a while. It was difficult to throw herself back into work, especially now she had decided to leave the firm. Dermot had told her to look at it again, find the little nugget of truth escaping from the cover up. And she owed it to Joanna. Somehow, she couldn't get that video out of her mind. Whatever she did in the future – even if she never went near a law Court again – she would never completely forget Tom Pascoe's image, speaking to her from beyond the grave. She would read the report carefully, and make a final decision. That much, at least, was owed to him.

It was a hot evening. All the windows in the cottage were open as wide as they could go, and the sounds of the farm drifted in as she read. It was strangely soothing.

She concentrated on the farm visits. Dr Vane must have carried them out before the hearing, but had kept quiet about them. That was all very well, but it didn't provide hard evidence for a claim. He had visited twenty-nine farms, and found nothing apparently. Not a shred of evidence of perinycin abuse.

There were some graphs in one of the appendices, setting out each farm, stock levels, acreage and antibiotic usage. Geri allowed her eye to wander over them. They wouldn't take the argument any further.

Then she saw it.

The penultimate graph, plotting feed patterns and intensity levels.

The farm numbers were out of synch. The previous graphs ran from 1 to 29. In this one, the numbers went up to 45, and there were gaps between them. She counted the number of farms. Still on 29.

This report had been produced *after* the hearing! They could have held it back as it hadn't been written at the time of the Court order. It had been produced *for* them. To knock the case into touch.

She thought on. Dr Vane had done the farm visits. He had kept quiet about them at the hearing. What if he had found something? What if he had looked at 45 or more farms and only found 29 to be using antibiotics properly?

That would mean he had found perinycin on at least 16 of them. Around thirty-five percent. That really would be a problem.

The hairs on the back of her neck were tingling again. It wasn't enough to win the case – far from it. But as Geri sat in the cottage, she realised that the Ministry was trying to hide something. She'd never get the information she needed by going back to the District Judge. They'd just say it had been a typing error.

She had not really expected to find anything on this final scrutiny of the report. But as she stared at the page, cold fury overtook her. The Ministry had set her up. A scientist had deliberately falsified his research to get the government out of a hole.

Bastards!

Quickly she rang Directory Enquiries and got Trinity Hall. Professor Lebrun was in his rooms, they were just putting her through...

'Dermot, listen, we've got them!'

Breathlessly, she explained.

Suddenly it occurred to her that this might not be a good moment.

'I've just rung without thinking. Are you ... er...'

She started to blush.

'Is this a bad moment?'

'Not at all. I was just getting ready for bed, actually.'

'I didn't realise you lived in the college – I thought I'd have to beg for a home number.'

'No, us single types tend to live in. But it's

brilliant news, Geri. Where do we go from here?'

Geri couldn't help herself wondering about the single type comment. A suit was such a personal thing – she'd assumed his girlfriend would be living with him at least. Enough, she thought to herself sharply. There's a job to be done here and going all doe-eyed about my star witness isn't going to help.

'I think we issue proceedings and let the shit hit the fan. But I'll sleep on it.'

'Let me know, won't you?'

'Of course. I'll be hammering on your door for a new report after this, Dermot.'

'With pleasure. But I'm off to Geneva for a conference tomorrow – perhaps we could meet when I get back?'

'Yes. Have a good time.' She paused. 'I'll look forward to next time.'

'So will I, Geri.'

She hung up, the warmth of his voice echoing in her head, and turned back to the report. Before she had hesitated, worried about causing a food scare without any real evidence. But now she was sure that there was something. She might be wrong, but she had never been more convinced of anything in her life. There was just – only just – enough here to take things a step further. But once the claim got into a Public Court, goodness knew what information might come to light. She had to do it.

Buoyed up, Geri took a pen and paper and began to draft the pleading. She'd start it in the County Court again, then transfer it to the High Court. That way, if they tried to pull any procedural stunts, she'd be in front of Judges who liked her.

Pleadings are normally drafted by barristers. Geri was reasonably good at preparing her own. In any event, another lawyer might pour cold water on the whole idea. Quickly, she set out the case in the quaint terminology of the Court. The Ministry had been negligent, she said, in failing to prevent perinycin being used in livestock when it knew or ought to have known that it was so used. And it was negligent in failing properly to monitor perinycin use. That should flush out Dr Vane and his real survey. The Ministry had failed to act upon expressed concerns in the specialist press that antibiotic abuse was occurring.

As always, when she set the claim out on paper, she felt more optimistic about its chances. There was evidence to support what she was arguing. And there was some evidence to undermine what the Ministry would say in reply.

It took over an hour to finalise the allegations of negligence. Then she had to set out why Tom had died.

'Damn!'

She would need a medical report showing the link between his death and perinycin abuse. It would have to come from a doctor of medicine – Dermot Lebrun wouldn't do. His evidence was going to be crucial at the trial, but the County Court Rules made it imperative at this stage to have a medical report.

Damn, damn, damn!

Geri eased herself up from the armchair and stretched. She moved towards the phone, standing on the windowsill overlooking the farmyard, and dialled Joanna's number. It was answered on the second ring.

'Joanna, we've got them!'

'What?'

Briefly, she explained about the mis-numberings.

'It must mean he visited other farms and decided to delete them from his report. It's the only explanation I can think of.'

'But, Geri, surely we wouldn't win the case just on that?'

'No, but it's enough to get us into Court. We can ask Dr Vane in front of all the newspapers whether he visited other farms and what he found. Who knows? With the publicity, someone may come forward ... at the very least it will cause one hell of a fuss.'

Joanna's voice was incredulous.

'Are we going to do it?'

'Yes. I've drafted most of the pleading. There's just one problem. The rules say there's got to be a medical report substantiating the claim. We're going to use Dermot Lebrun as our expert on perinycin abuse, but we've got to have someone medically qualified to back us.'

'What about Dougal Baines?'

'Who?'

'Tom's old partner. He's the one who helped me so much earlier, before I met you. He's still practising – he'd help us.'

'That would be brilliant. Can you get on to him tonight?'

Geri went through what was needed and left it

in Joanna's willing hands.

It was 3 o'clock in the morning before she got to bed. She had fiddled around with the pleading, checked and amended it again. Finally she was happy with it. She folded the paper and placed it carefully in her handbag.

Before she drifted off to sleep, she realised she was happy. Happier than she'd been for a long time. She knew she should be worried. She was being investigated, her firm was going down the plughole and she had just launched into litigation which could make her look the legal twit of the year. But she didn't mind, not now. She was sticking her neck out, but it would be worse to keep quiet just so that no one criticised her.

And she was going to start to live as she wanted. She would love Simon forever, but he had finally become part of her past, rather than her justification for the present.

If she was struck off, she'd just have to find something else to do. Something would emerge. She knew that she was honest, after all. And for the time being, she was in business and had work to do.

Chapter Eighteen

Grimwood had laid off the remains of his staff in readiness for the first consignment. When he'd taken the business over there had been six. Now, though, he was down to two part-timers only.

They'd had to go. Hiding such a large quantity of antibiotics from them would have been quite impossible. Before he'd used rooms in the house, but that was out of the question now. So, he'd summoned them, given them a fortnight's pay and told them to go immediately.

He worked the combination on the safe and looked at the money. Two hundred thousand pounds. He'd been buzzing around like a blue-arsed fly to liberate it from various accounts. It had been a bit of a struggle. But it was there, neatly stacked up and bound for a new home.

The telephone rang.

'How much is chicken feed at the moment?'

It was Stiles, using their pre-arranged code. If Benny told him he'd had a new delivery, Stiles was to keep away until the coast was clear.

'I've just got some old stuff left, if you'd like to pop round.'

Half an hour later, the truck appeared at the end of the drive. As expected, Stiles himself was at the wheel. He'd even got hold of an old grain lorry so nobody would think it suspicious. Together, they unloaded it, working silently. Grimwood nodded when the task was over, and gestured to Stiles to follow him to the office. There, he undid the safe and handed the contents over.

'Ta,' said Stiles. 'I don't need to count this lot.'

Grimwood smiled briefly.

'See you in two weeks, then.'

'Yes.'

On the Friday of Geri's holiday, David Vane had

taken Callum Moncrieff through the costings. 'One of the problems, of course, will be ensuring that the recommendations are complied with,' said the Minister.

'Yes. The problem will be that we need total compliance. We only need a small percentage to be missed and the whole thing could just start up all over again.'

'Should there be a body set up to monitor the testing?'

'That would be one way, but it would take time.'

Callum pondered.

'We need to press on, but we need to do the job properly.'

Setting up a quango would take at least three months. Wonderful.

David was nodding.

'And then we need to consider compensation schemes. And enforcement of restriction orders. We will have to make sure that all movement to and from affected farms is controlled – just like foot and mouth disease.'

'How are we going to deal with the restocking?'

This was the political nightmare, Callum knew. People would get upset about vast numbers of chickens being slaughtered and put into incinerators, but they would be livid at the fact that the limited numbers of stock left would command sky-high prices. The British liked their chickens. Particularly when they didn't cost very much.

'There's no way round it, Minister. We'll be able to encourage breeding programmes, and the market will adjust in time.'

'Yes, but I think it might be as well to start

identifying sources of new stock. If we found large-scale suppliers – not necessarily from the UK – that could help us over the initial period.'

David agreed.

'I suggest that you ask one of your assistants to start the search. We'll have to be discreet, of course. Then we might be able to purchase options and sell them on to the farmers in due course.'

'Yes, Minister.'

It would take a while to find the stock, and there would be the inevitable haggling over prices. That would delay matters, too.

'What is the notification level at the moment, David?'

'Two more. That's a total of twenty-two.'

'Any more threatening to sue?'

'Nothing at the moment.'

'I've checked with our legal department. Mrs Lander seems to have gone to ground. We've heard nothing since the documents were disclosed. I think that if we hear no more in the next three weeks, we can assume they'll not be pursuing anything. Then it's full steam ahead for us.'

David smiled. At last things were getting moving. He knew he had done the right thing.

After he had left the room, Callum Moncrieff rang the PM's office. He needed to see him, urgently.

Geri had returned to face a busy morning. First, the pre-arranged interview with Detective Sergeant Edgar and his lackey, Detective Constable

Lambert. It was on record. A tape was running. The senior officer started by reading her the caution.

They were using the boardroom for the interview. Roger and Pete had already spoken and Geri was last. The officers were waiting for her, various files spread out on the table in front of them. They had been talking as she entered, and then fell silent. Geri sat down on the other side of the table and waited for the questioning to begin.

DS Edgar started the interview.

'Mrs Lander, are you aware of the responsibilities of senior partners to ensure compliance with the Solicitors' Code of Practice?'

'Yes, I am.'

Lambert asked the next question.

'Can we just start with the partners' meetings? Do you recall being informed by Mr Davies that he was undertaking a lot of remortgaging work?'

She thought hard. He had said so, but it was an aside.

'Yes, I do recall it, but it was in the context of a discussion between us all about increasing the profit income...'

Edgar took up the attack. It seemed they were taking turns. His tone was different, though. A touch more sympathetic.

'Is it also right you had a complaint from one of the staff members that she was filling out inordinate numbers of application forms?'

They must have spoken to Gloria. Please let her have told them what Cefan was really like, Geri prayed.

'Yes. I actually went to see him about it.'

Briefly, she recounted her meeting with him to the officers.

'You also discovered later that he was using the same surveyor for the remortgages.'

Lambert had a sarcastic edge to his voice. He obviously thought she must have known what was going on.

'Yes, I did, but I knew that Cefan did a lot of work with this particular man. I didn't see any reason to suspect it.'

Edgar asked the next question.

'And is it right you were informed by Mr Davies's secretary at one point that she suspected something strange was going on?'

Geri realised suddenly how they had set this up. Lambert was just there to unnerve her. The dangerous questions were coming from Edgar. But he seemed sympathetic. It was so tempting just to roll over, tell him that she knew everything and was terribly sorry. In a moment, she understood why people confessed to things they hadn't done. She must not fall into that trap.

'Yes, it is right. But this was the Sunday before the Monday when you were called in. I tried to ring Cefan at home, but there was no answer. I wanted to discuss it, but thought I had no option other than to wait until Monday. I went to see him first thing in his office but he wasn't there. Then I was ... called away.'

'So you left matters.' Lambert's lip curled in disbelief. Geri tried to ignore it.

'Yes,' she said flatly. He'd never understand why her son was more important than a vague feeling of unease about Cefan.

'Mrs Lander, are you saying you had no idea of this fraud until it occurred?'

'Yes,' she stated firmly.

'Well, assuming that to be true...' the expression on Edgar's face seemed doubtful '...it would add up to a woeful lack of insight into the business of the firm.'

'Yes,' sighed Geri.

He was silent. She felt the need to go on, to justify herself.

'I've been dealing with the litigation cases – I do have to be out of the office rather a lot. At the time this was going on, I was involved in a High Court action and then had a County Court claim to deal with.'

'So you would agree that your management of the firm was lax?' Lambert again, putting in the boot.

'I suppose I would have to, yes.'

He nodded.

The interview continued. Her admission seemed to make no difference. They wanted to go through everything, seemingly three times over. By the end, Geri was exhausted.

Finally, the tape recorder was switched off. Edgar spoke again.

'Mrs Lander, we are preparing a file on prosecutions in this matter which will be forwarded to the CPS. I should also inform you that the Office for the Supervision of Solicitors has asked me to provide information to them.'

She nodded gravely. She'd been expecting a letter daily telling her she'd been struck off. It looked as if they were waiting to hear from the police. She left the boardroom, trying to look confident.

'Welcome back!' It was Jackie.

She had ticked off the last name on her list while Geri had been away. Her own statement had been safely received by the authorities – she had phoned to make sure. And Gloria really had come up trumps. She was tempted to tell Geri not to worry, that she'd done the best she possibly could. But it was sensible to keep quiet, all things considered.

'And how was the Spanish Inquisition? I was interviewed myself, you know. Told them what a bastard Cefan was and how straight you are.'

Geri smiled.

'OK, I think. And the holiday was so good – I can see everything in perspective now.'

She thought of Joanna's claim and dug out the pleading from her handbag.

'There's a bit of typing here – could you possibly get it ready for issue?' She handed over the rather grubby, handwritten sheets of paper. Jackie looked surprised.

'Of course. Don't you ever stop working?'

Then Jackie frowned a little, and shut the door.

'I need to mention something. While you were away, my boyfriend proposed.'

'Jackie, that's fantastic!'

Geri had always avoided getting embroiled in Jackie's private life. All she knew was that she had divorced years ago, but was seeing a teacher.

Jackie beamed.

'Well, yes, I'm delighted. Amazed too – I

thought he'd never pop the question.'

She looked away from Geri. 'But the thing is, he asked because he's been offered a headship in Yorkshire. He wants to go, and me to go with him.'

'Do you want to go?'

'Yes. It's my final chance, really. And I'm quite keen on the bloke. But with all your worries, I don't want to let you down.'

The final link of guilt tying her to the firm had gone.

'Honestly, Jackie, don't think about it at all. You won't be letting me down.'

The secretary beamed at her.

'Oh, I've forgotten to tell you – there's a partners' meeting in half an hour. You won't miss it because it's in your room. The police have rather taken over the boardroom.'

The partners' meeting had been arranged to discuss the future of the firm in the aftermath of the investigation.

Geri's two remaining partners came in together and sat down in chairs opposite her desk.

'What's the latest on the finances?' she asked.

'Could be worse, actually,' replied Roger. 'We've had about ten thousand in – slightly above the forecast – that's in addition to that thirty I mentioned the other day. The bank has replied setting out the new arrangement. We've also had a very tentative enquiry from Shaner's.'

Geri looked up. Shaner's were a leading union firm, specialising in personal injury work. They had taken much of the original Lander Ross union business when they had set up in the eighties.

Pete had more detail.

'They phoned me over the weekend. It's your work they're really interested in. I'm not sure that they want the commercial and private client stuff. Basically, they're worried that if Winchell Robins manage to take on all our clients long-term, they'll dominate the personal injury scene.'

'Well, at least something good might come out of the intervention,' said Geri.

'They'd heard about this claim of yours against the Ministry of Agriculture – I think Judge Butcher mentioned it to someone and the grapevine got hold of it. They wanted to know where you'd got the case from?'

Geri smiled.

'Actually, I'm just about to issue the claim. There was just enough to justify proceedings when we checked the Ministry's papers.'

Roger looked at her.

'What are the chances of success?'

'Difficult to say. It's cutting edge stuff – we don't know at this stage.'

'So you're taking a risk with firm time again?' He was politely insistent.

'I am, but we've got to take some chances now and then.'

Roger was not happy.

'Well, I have to say I am extremely concerned. We need to be pulling together now – getting this firm into some sort of shape. While the work is being done elsewhere, we need to sort out the billing and plan for the future – if we have one.

Frankly, Geri, the last thing we need is you flouncing around on some high-risk conditional fee case.'

Pete looked at the two of them and seemed to hesitate.

'I'm afraid I agree, Geri. We all need to get some money in, concentrate on that side of things. And if you lost the case it might make the firm look pretty stupid – I'm not sure what Shaner's would make of that.'

Geri looked at them both. They had clearly discussed this beforehand.

'But it's an important case, high profile – it's just what we need to generate some publicity.'

'But what if you lose?' asked Pete. 'I mean, wouldn't it be better to stall on the case for a while without committing too much time to it? Shaner's can always take on the risk if they take the firm over. And if the case is heard and lost, the firm's less attractive to them – they want it for themselves.'

'We need to be getting a wider base of work, Geri,' added Roger.

'Are you saying I don't have your support in running this case as anything other than a window-dressing operation?'

Roger looked at Pete.

'Put like that, then no, you don't.'

She looked at Pete. His expression was miserable as sin, but he was nodding at Roger's words. Geri was furious.

'In that case, I resign. With immediate effect. I'll send the case on to Sam Dyson at Shaner's if he's so interested. I'm obviously going to be struck off any day anyhow.'

Pete looked horrified.

'But, Geri, we're only trying to be reasonable. And if we're looking at selling the firm, we need to stick together. The last thing anyone will want to see is us separating.'

'If I can't do this case, I'm going. In fact, I want to go anyhow. It's just postponing the inevitable.'

'You can't go,' said Roger quietly.

'Why?'

'Because you've got to give six months' notice under the partnership deed.'

'But you can't enforce that – you know perfectly well you can't force me to work if I don't want to.'

Geri knew she was starting to sound like a teenager, but she just wanted to scream. She wanted out, she needed out, but they were insisting on her staying in.

'And think of this, Geri,' said Pete, 'if you go, the bank are all the more likely to call in the loan before we can get the money in. Then it's your house that's on the line.'

He was right. Damn, damn, damn. She wanted to butt her head against the wall.

Instead she sat back in her chair.

'OK. Let's all calm down, take some deep breaths and find a way out of this.'

They nodded.

'I need to stay on a while to let the finances improve. If I give my six months' notice now, that should leave plenty of time.'

Roger was smiling. Victory for him. But she wasn't going down without a fight.

'But while I'm here, I'm doing the Pascoe case. You can't stop me.'

Pete nodded reluctantly.

'Look, Geri, let's be sensible here. If you deal with it, but try to keep the hours down a little...'

She saw the sense of his words.

'OK. But I'm going to get as much done on it as I can before I leave.'

They parted shortly after that, agreeing to have another billing run. In reality they were getting ready for a sale of the firm. Bills, once sent out, would become firm assets – more tangible than work in progress. The more they billed, the more attractive they would look to a purchaser.

Geri walked down the corridor to Jackie's room. It was neat, tidy and almost humming with activity. Jeremy Gilbert was using her for the work coming from the Lander Ross files. But today Jackie was seated at her desk, typing out Geri's handwritten Particulars of Claim.

Geri sat down in one of the spare chairs at the end of the room.

'Jackie, do you know exactly when you want to leave?'

'Well, if it's OK by you, three weeks' time. Duncan wants to get settled in over the summer, before the new term starts.'

'Fine. Er, Jackie, I ought to mention that I'm leaving too.'

'You are?' She was clearly astonished.

'I couldn't tell you before I told the other partners.'

'But why are you going?'

'All sorts of reasons. Mainly because I want to.'

'How did the others take the news?'

'Not too well. They're insisting on the six months' notice. I haven't told them you're going, too – it may be they'll simply not replace you.'

'But how are you going to cope without someone to do the typing?'

'Two ways. First, we'll do as much as we can before you go. We can do the statement, sort out the medical evidence and so on. And then I'll just have to get by with a temp until I go.'

Jackie had produced the typed Particulars of Claim by three o'clock. Joanna had already delivered a brief report from the GP, Dougal Baines. Geri rushed the documents over to the Court to issue the claim before she lost her nerve. She stood in the queue at the desk as the issue clerk slowly worked her way down the line. By 3.45, the claim was official. Joanna Pascoe, suing as widow and executrice of the late Thomas Pascoe, versus Her Majesty's Minister for Agriculture. The Court would deal with service.

Geri took her copy home and put it at the top of Joanna's file. Then she loaded all the papers on the case into the back of the car and set off for home.

Joanna greeted her as she came in. They'd had no time for anything other than the basic niceties when she had arrived that morning.

'Congratulations. You are now a litigant! I issued the claim this morning.'

'Fantastic! Geri, I'm so pleased. And I hear that the holiday went well.' Joanna lowered her voice, 'I have to say, Rory looks much better on it.'

Geri smiled.

'It was really good, Joanna. Thanks so much for the cottage – it's lovely.'

'Yes. Ought to call it Millstone Cottage, really.' She laughed.

Geri paused. She'd been dreading breaking her decision to Joanna. But she had to do it soon. 'Joanna, Rory and I have been talking a lot – about his father, mainly. I've been spending too much time working – I've only just realised how much he's been needing me.'

'Ah.'

'I don't know, Joanna. I had an interview with the police... It made me realise what I've suspected all along – I'm not cut out for the management side of things. I'm very likely to be struck off anyhow because of Cefan's fraud. Even if I get reinstated, I don't think I can continue as I am now.'

'What do you mean?'

'To run a firm like ours these days, you have to be really efficient. Somebody needs to be around, keeping the organisation tight. I'm just never there – you can't be if you're in Court several days each week.'

'Could you cut down the Court work? Other solicitors must manage it somehow.'

'I could – and you're right, most solicitors use barristers much more than I do for the Court work. But that's the part of the job I really like. That's why I went into the profession.'

Joanna straightened her skirt as she sat down.

'So, if it were a straight choice between Court work and running the practice, what would it be?'

'Court work. Every time.'

'And you're quite sure the two are incompatible?'

'Yes. The only other solutions would be first, leave the administration to Roger or Pete. To some extent I suppose I've been doing that already, and you can see the mess it's caused.'

'You said solutions?'

'Yes. The other would be to try and run the firm better – take more of an interest in the administration. But, frankly, when I've just finished in Court, the last thing I need is to go back to the office and spend hours looking at figures. And then there's Rory ... that's the last thing he needs at the moment too.'

'Hmm. So what are you going to do? Give up completely?'

'Well, I nearly did, this morning. Roger and Pete were being so unbearable about ... well, about things generally. I tried to resign, but they reminded me I've got to give six months' notice.'

Joanna looked at her sharply.

'Do you really want to go?'

Geri sighed.

'When it comes to it, yes. But I don't know what I'd go to. I've no idea until we're out of this trouble with the mortgage fraud how the money side is going to be – whether I'd have enough money just to stop, completely.'

She thought of the bank's charge, looming over the house.

'Chances are there wouldn't be enough. And Rory is at school most of the time.'

'So what you need then, is a job with lots of Court work, no administration, and lots of free evenings. And a reasonable income.'

Geri smiled.

'And school holidays off. Now, that would be pretty good.'

Geri paused.

'The only trouble is, I don't think that there are jobs like that in existence.'

'If you want to do the Court side of things, can't you become a barrister?'

'I wanted to at University. But you need money to get started. You have to find a set of Chambers to take you on – that's very difficult these days. And then it takes time to get known, get a practice.'

'But that wouldn't happen with you – you're well known already.'

'True. And I could probably live off savings for a while. But the barristers I know seem to spend most of their lives travelling – Birmingham one day, Exeter the next. Rory would just be giving up one sort of absentee parent for another.'

'A part-time solicitor's job, then?'

'Possibly. But at the risk of sounding unbearably arrogant, nobody would believe that's what I wanted. They'd think it was some complicated plot to take over a firm. And besides, if you're a part-timer, you just end up with the bits and pieces nobody else in the firm wants. I don't really fancy that.'

'Perhaps the answer is to see what happens in the next six months? Sometimes, solutions do just emerge once the problem becomes clear.'

'Yes, you may well be right. But I will have to think about the future, cast around a bit.'

Joanna looked at her carefully.

'Do you want to deal with my case?'

'Yes, I do. But longer term ... it's a question of being torn. And there is another firm that's already heard about the claim and is interested – if need be, I can introduce them to you. Joanna, I hope you're not offended by my talking like this?'

Joanna smiled at her.

'It's just that you've become rather more than another client.'

The older woman looked at her and lightly touched her shoulder.

'No, you must make your own decisions in these things. Let's see how it goes. You're quite clearly the best woman for the job, but if you have to give up later, I'll just have to decide what to do then. Insh'allah.'

'What?'

'Whatever Allah wills.'

'Er, yes.'

'But when the time comes and someone makes you an offer, Geri, tell them what you want. It's only by saying how you want to work in the future that people will make an effort to fit around you. It's down to you to stick up for yourself, even if you feel a bit daft doing it.'

They celebrated with tea and biscuits. Rory came down from his room and Geri told him of her delayed resignation.

'Brilliant, Mum. I was a bit worried you'd change your mind once you got back.'

She shook her head.

'And we've started Joanna's claim.'

He smiled.

'Mum, do you want me to go back to school tomorrow?'

'Well, Mrs Davidson said that you could leave it if you wanted to – go back after the summer holidays.'

'I can be at home with you if you want, Rory,' said Joanna.

'Well, I've been thinking too. I want to go back. The longer I leave it, the more they'll go for me when I do return. And now I know all about ... well, what happened with Dad, there's nothing I'm frightened of.'

Geri wanted to hug him. She did.

'Are you sure?'

'Yes, I really am. And anyhow, there's only a few more weeks to the summer holidays. The really nasty boy Christopher – he'll probably have exam leave anyhow.'

'OK, I'll drop you off in the morning and have a word with Mrs Davidson.'

Chapter Nineteen

The next morning, Geri found a letter on the hall mat. It looked official and came from Leamington Spa.

Oh, dear.

Looked like this was the end of the road. She'd been warned she'd probably be struck off after the fraud.

She scanned the contents, looking for the key

words. Struck off, appeal procedure, that sort of thing.

The Office for the Supervision of Solicitors were still considering the question of disciplinary action against the partners of Lander Ross, it said. But they had carried out a preliminary enquiry and had had the benefit of a large number of letters of support for the firm – from members of the public and staff.

In addition, one of the firm's clients had taken the trouble to travel to their office to speak in support of Mrs Lander. In the circumstances, they would be striking off Cefan Davies, but the remaining partners could, for the time being, continue to practise. The intervention would be withdrawn.

There was a warning in the last paragraph, though. This was merely an interim decision and Geri was still the subject of an investigation into professional standards.

She couldn't believe it.

It couldn't be right. There must be a mistake. They must have missed out a 'not'.

She read the letter again. If they had mistyped it, there would have been no need to stop the intervention.

'Yes!' Geri punched the air. Letters of support, it had said. She wondered who had written. Clients could be so unpredictable. And staff, too... And who had travelled to see them?

She thought of Joanna, sitting politely but immovably in reception on the first day they'd met. The answer, now she thought of it, was obvious. God bless her.

Geri drove Rory to the school gates and walked in with him. One of his friends was just being dropped off and gave him a cheery wave. Rory seemed in a hurry to be off, so Geri let him join the other boy. She found Mrs Davidson in the classroom, marking some exercise books.

'Ah, Mrs Lander.'

'Mrs Davidson ... I thought I'd mention that Rory wants to come back to school today.'

'Excellent. Well, that really *is* good news. You must have done some sterling work with him.'

'Well, we did have a break together and talked through a lot of things. He knows about his father now, by the way.'

Mrs Davidson had been in on the secret.

'Very sensible, if I may say so. Well, I'll keep an eye open for him – tell him if he feels worried about a situation, he's to come straight to me, even in the staff room. I do think he's been very sensible in returning before the holidays start. Well done!'

Good grief. Approval from Mrs Davidson. Pigs would be flying next.

Next stop, the firm. Geri wondered if Jeremy Gilbert had heard yet that his services were no longer required. As she marched happily in through the door of Lander Ross & Co, she rather hoped he hadn't.

Tracey looked up, startled.

'Morning, Tracey. Is Mr Gilbert still in my room?'

'Yes...'

Geri swept past her.

'Time for you to go, Jeremy,' she said sweetly.

'I heard today that the intervention was at an end, but I needed to finalise a few things.'

He looked furtive.

'Take a few more of my clients over to your firm, you mean?'

'But, Mrs Lander...'

'Just go now, please. No excuses. Just go. And I want all my files returned by 5 p.m.'

'But some clients have decided that they would like to...'

'Return their files to me so that I can review your letters to them. Those files are my property and I'm going to look at them. And if I find that you've been touting for business, you're going to find yourself on the receiving end of a professional complaint. Do I make myself clear?'

It was good to be back in the driving seat again.

The Particulars of Claim had been sent the evening before by the Court. The document had been opened at the Ministry at 9.30 a.m. The legal executive who opened it had sent it straight up to the chief solicitor, and it was on the Minister's desk by 2 p.m.

Moncrieff was out of the building. A meeting with the Prime Minister, apparently. Just to be on the safe side, Geoffrey Atwell arranged a consultation for the afternoon with Gordon Hodder, QC. This was clearly going to be rather urgent.

At Number 10, the Prime Minister's windows

were wide open. The smell of newly mown grass drifted through into his office. He listened impassively as the Minister for Agriculture put his case.

'And so, you see, I do feel that in the circumstances, it would be a good moment for me to move on. If you were thinking of a reshuffle, a new Minister would probably want to start with a clean sheet.'

The Prime Minister nodded. Moncrieff had done well and it was reasonable for him to want to move up the ladder. He was popular – especially with the women voters – and phenomenally bright.

'Well, I will be reshuffling – probably in three months or so. I can say that I will give you very careful consideration for a post...'

He paused and smiled.

'...shall we say, a post which would make more demands on you?'

'Thank you, Prime Minister.'

Moncrieff turned his back and walked to the door. Just a little too confidently.

The PM had been in politics since he was seventeen. He knew very well that attack was far more likely to come from within than outside his government. After all, it had taken her own party to dislodge Thatcher.

He didn't trust Moncrieff. Far too good-looking. Men like that were so used to being accepted and trusted they learned to rely upon it.

If he was promoted, a bandwagon could start to roll. And the man had been making noises to get out of Agriculture for months. Perhaps he thought it was too quiet – not enough exposure before the rest of the party.

On the other hand, perhaps he was running from something. He was an inexperienced Minister. Perhaps he had committed some glorious cock-up which he wanted someone else to inherit. Well, it would all come out in the wash sooner or later. If something had gone wrong, the PM wanted a sackable politician to be holding the baby. Yes, come to think of it, a mistake would provide rather a good opportunity for action on his part.

Moncrieff would stay where he was.

Blissfully ignorant of the Prime Minister's thoughts, Callum strode back to the Ministry. It was a fine, warm day and he was in excellent spirits. He even gave a pound coin to a dosser, hoping that a photographer might have noticed and snapped a picture.

Back in the Ministry, he found the Particulars of Claim on his desk.

Shit!

He was on the phone to Atwell, the senior solicitor, in an instant.

'I want to see Hodder. Immediately.'

'Already arranged, sir. Six this evening.'

Geoffrey Atwell genuflected and thanked his patron saint.

'What the hell is this about? Didn't you give them the fucking report?'

'Yes, sir. All I can think is that it's nuisance litigation.'

'Nuisance? I'll give them fucking nuisance! I

want you up here now, Geoffrey.'

Poor Geoffrey Atwell spent the rest of the afternoon explaining the document trail to the Minister. How they had checked – Dr Vane himself had kindly assisted – and there was absolutely nothing to go on. How they really couldn't understand on what basis the claim had been filed.

By 6 o'clock, the Minister's temper had not improved.

Gordon Hodder was shown in.

'Hodder, they've fucking well started proceedings!'

Hodder realised this was not going to be the easiest of consultations. Mind you, after his principal's account of the last one, the clerk had negotiated two thousand for this meeting. He could take an awful lot of abuse for two grand. Hodder raised his hands in a gesture of resignation.

'Minister, sometimes, despite our best efforts, solicitors issue. There's nothing that can be done about it.'

'Rubbish!'

'Minister?'

'Absolute fucking crap!'

For a son of the church, swearing came remarkably easy to Moncrieff. He continued, face almost purple with fury.

'You are being paid a ridiculous fee to stop this case in its tracks. Then I find that they've started it anyhow.'

'But, Minister, if the solicitor takes it into her head to go to Court, there's nothing we can do.'

‘There must be! Are you telling me this woman can just go to Court with no case at all and we have to sit back and wait? This could be disastrous for the Department, Hodder.’

Gordon Hodder sat back in his chair and closed his eyes. Even Moncrieff fell silent in expectation. Finally, he spoke.

‘We could make an application to strike out.’

Moncrieff walked to the window and looked out for a moment.

‘Tell me more.’

‘If a claim is a real no-hoper – the words used are frivolous, vexatious or an abuse of process – we can apply to the Court for it to be stopped.’

‘How common is that?’

‘Well, it’s tried relatively frequently, but not always successfully. The Judge really has to be convinced that there is no issue to be heard.’

The Minister turned back towards the QC.

‘Is this sort of application made in open Court?’

‘No. In the Judge’s chambers.’

‘Then let’s do it. We’ve nothing to lose after all.’

‘I have to warn you, Minister, that we may not succeed. In fact, I would have to say that it is unlikely we would win. They only have to show a shred of a case to get by.’

‘But there’s a chance we might succeed?’

‘Yes. There’s always a chance.’

‘Then we have to try.’

Geoffrey Atwell breathed a sigh of relief. At least this would keep the Minister off the warpath for a while.

‘I’ll issue the application tomorrow.’

David Vane had actually finished early for once. He caught the 5.30 and was back at the cottage by 6.45. There were still several hours of daylight so he had plenty of time to do a little gardening. The roses were just coming into their second bloom, bursting into white florets around the pink walls of the cottage.

He opened the door to a mound of mail. He'd left, as always, long before the postman arrived and his first task on returning home was usually to go through the day's letters. There was the usual clutch of bills, unbeatable offers and notifications that he'd yet again won a prize draw.

At the bottom of the pile was an envelope covered in a familiar hand. His heart lurched as he saw it. Liz.

He opened it quickly, scanning the words, not really taking them in. She was sorry it had all got so bitter, she said, but her lawyer had told her not to give an inch. Perhaps he could visit them in New Zealand – she could find him a hotel if he wanted to stay a while, see the boys. They were fine, settling in nicely. Oh, and she ought to mention that she'd met someone, Andrew, and they were getting married.

David took the letter into the sitting room. He sat on the chintz-covered sofa which they'd chosen together as newly-weds. Somehow, he'd always nurtured the hope that one day she would return. Perhaps she'd tire of New Zealand as she'd tired of it before, and make the long trek back to the UK. If she did, perhaps they would get on a little better, even start again. At least he'd see the boys a little.

It wasn't going to happen now. She was happy, settled, in love again. He'd see the boys perhaps every two years or so. They'd look upon this Andrew as their father. He would be there for them: playing football in the garden, listening to carol concerts and taking them out on magical trips. David was just going to be a shadow in the background.

And the worst of it all was the fact that it was his own fault. He'd never listened to Liz. He'd wanted to do well at work, earn the family's bread and move up the ladder. So he'd left early in the morning and come home late at night, ignoring her cries for help.

And when she'd left, he made it even worse. He'd chosen an aggressive solicitor. Had thought she'd give in if she was pushed a little. But she hadn't. She'd fought for her children, knowing that she was right in wanting to have them. In the end, the hassle – his hassle – had driven her home to the other side of the world. If he'd just gone for a low-key, listening approach, she might have settled five miles away and he could have been getting ready at this moment to have the boys to stay for the weekend.

She hadn't been a demon mother at all – just someone forced to the wall by his stupidity. For an intelligent man, he was, he knew, pretty bloody stupid at times.

David took some writing paper and composed a reply. He was sorry too, he said. He'd thought a lot about what had happened, and deeply regretted it. She was a good mother and the boys would do well with her. He would like to visit before too long – perhaps she could send him some details of where he could stay.

Most painfully of all, he told her that he was glad she had found happiness and that he wished her well for the future.

It had hurt him to write, but he felt better for it. With a start, he realised he did genuinely want her to be happy. He had no idea how much a stamp to New Zealand cost and put the letter in his briefcase so that he could ask in the post office near work.

He walked down his garden to the vegetable patch at the bottom. The French beans were early this year and he picked a few for supper, along with some courgettes and tomatoes. He could curry them all up together for tea. It was deeply satisfying to be able to grow his own food. At times, he felt he would like to farm a little – perhaps start with a smallholding, all organic. But his life at the moment simply didn't allow that.

His thoughts turned to the antibiotic problem. It looked as though he was going to get a free rein in implementing his ideas. It wasn't going to be easy, but the Minister seemed to be with him at least. He needed to get a move on. David had a nasty feeling they were all sitting on a time bomb.

Chapter Twenty

The strike out application was posted to the Court and issued the following Monday. It reached Geri on Wednesday.

On the same day, Callum told David that he was going to have to call a temporary halt to the planned implementation.

'I'm afraid our Mrs Lander has taken it into her head to start proceedings anyhow.'

David was horrified.

'But why?'

'Think of it this way, David. We know her firm's in trouble. What they want is a nice difficult case with lots of hours to charge somebody for. They don't care if they win or lose. I'd hoped this wouldn't be the case, that she'd see sense, but clearly she's only interested in spinning things out.'

David looked at the Minister. He knew he had to rein himself in, keep rational, but his position was becoming untenable.

'So you are saying – saying seriously – that the entire scheme is going to grind to a halt because of this fucking woman?'

Moncrieff leaned closer to his civil servant.

'David, I was furious too. I called Hodder over immediately and gave him a bollocking. This can't be allowed to happen – we've got to get your programme underway as soon as we can.

He suggested a way of trying to strike out the claim before it goes any further. We're going to try that, give it our best shot.'

'And if it fails?'

Moncrieff looked him right in the eye.

'Then that bloody woman is going to stop us sorting out the industry. All for her stupid fucking fees. We've just got to stop her. It's down to us now.'

Geri sat in her office and read the application through carefully. They wanted the Court to throw out the claim because it was frivolous, vexatious and an abuse of process. In other words, she had no professional judgment whatsoever and was wasting everybody's time by pursuing a hopeless cause.

That was rather near the bone. Geri had always had a lurking doubt that perhaps she had just struck lucky at critical times. Perhaps she'd got her First because the exam contained the questions she had prepared best; perhaps she'd got the job at Lander Ross because Simon wanted a female solicitor; perhaps she'd done so well there because she'd married the senior partner. In her darkest moments, she wondered if the fact that the firm had slid downhill since Simon's death was simply evidence that she wasn't all she was made out to be.

But she could hardly throw in the towel now. If she was going to stick her neck out, she would have to expect this sort of response. And at least she had a week to get ready, and very little other work to do.

Benny Grimwood had found the property he wanted. A peaceful villa, it said, overlooking the sea. A snip at four hundred thousand. The international estate agents had sent him a file full of details and had recommended a Spanish lawyer. He would go out, install himself in a hotel and have a good look around the place. If he didn't like it, there would be plenty more.

But for now, the girl from the Health and Safety Executive was asking some rather stupid questions. He'd opted for the thick agrarian approach. No, he'd never had an accident with a silo before. No, he'd never really thought of how to check no one was in the silo before it was filled up. He did know it was dangerous, but had thought that Charlie would obey the formal warnings.

It seemed to be enough. Luckily no one had commented on the mobile phone lying at the bottom of the silo. He'd been quick to remove it after the police went. Didn't want anyone checking his bill, although frankly he didn't think the idea would have occurred to DC Morris in a million years.

'Well, we will be sending you a report. I'm afraid there will be some criticisms, Mr Grimwood.'

'Yes, I can understand that. I just wish I could put the clock back.'

She nodded briefly and was on her way. At least she wasn't threatening to close him down. Mind you, even that wouldn't be too much of a problem, given his immediate plans.

Another consignment would be due soon. Once the summer was over, there would be a vast pile of perinycin. He'd already started a few tentative negotiations with farmers who didn't know each other. Each thought he was getting the entirety of Benny's supply of the drug. Each, as a result, was willing to pay silly money.

It was looking very good indeed.

On the day of the strike out hearing, Geri was first at Court, her photocopied authorities arranged in a neat bundle. She had never been better prepared. Joanna had come with her – as the Plaintiff, it was her right, and Geri liked District Judges to see the people they were dealing with. She had a quaint notion that they found it harder to throw out a claim when the person concerned was sitting in front of them.

They were due on at 10 o'clock. Hodder arrived at 9.45 with his usual silent retinue.

'My dear girl!' he exclaimed.

D'Arby Colinder simply looked bored. He did at least manage to refrain from smoking.

'I do hope you aren't going to take this too personally. It's just that I felt it was time to put an end to this rather silly litigation,' Hodder intoned.

She wondered how he managed to be both ingratiating and offensive at the same time. It was almost a talent, really.

'Here are my authorities,' replied Geri, thrusting a bundle into his hand. He jumped back in mock astonishment.

'But, my good lady, I thought you didn't like to

trouble the Court with law? Far too much for your pretty head, I presumed.'

'Not at all. I just felt that perhaps you would have trouble keeping up. But don't worry, I'll go nice and slowly for you today. Just put your hand up if you don't understand, Gordon.'

He was momentarily silenced. Excellent. Fifteen love.

'Well, in that case, you'd better have my cases.'

Geri always wondered how important this robing room advocacy was. Most barristers seem quite addicted to it and argue the merits of their case loudly and vociferously long before the hearing actually starts. She thought that it was just a case of bolstering themselves up and getting into the right mood, but she knew there were those who swore by it as a psychological weapon. Plant the seed that they're not going to win into the other side's mind, and they start to think and act like losers. The Judge picks it up, thinks to himself that if the barrister thinks his own case isn't too hot it can't be, and rules accordingly.

They were called into the District Judge's room at 10 sharp. As she followed Hodder in, Geri saw to her horror that they had Deputy District Judge Benham. Lovely Judge Butcher must have gone back to his home Court in the Midlands.

Oh, shit, she thought.

Deputy District Judge Benham was a part-time member of the judiciary. He was also a partner in a firm specialising in Defendant litigation. He had worked for twenty years on the assumption that all Plaintiffs were whingeing scaremongers who either made up their symptoms entirely or at the very least malingered, hamming up their suffering for the benefit of the Court. Sitting as a part-time Judge had by no means caused a change of heart.

As a result, he awarded the lowest damages Geri had ever come across. She'd successfully appealed three of his awards – a fact that had done nothing to endear her to him. Like many of his judicial colleagues, Deputy District Judge Benham hated being appealed. It is like being corrected in front of the class at school, only a whole lot more vicious.

Unmarried because he was miserable rather than gay, he loathed women and had voted Tory all of his life. Geri stood for everything he detested and he let her know it every time she appeared in front of him.

And he loved to throw out cases. He imagined himself as a brave swordsman, cutting through the nuisance claims which were simply there to cause the maximum inconvenience to good upstanding Defendant companies. Geri thanked her lucky stars she had been able to prepare so well. Her only hope lay in relying so much on the law he would be worried that she would appeal him. Again.

He beamed a greeting at Hodder. Probably used him himself, thought Geri. They'd get on famously.

'Mr Hodder, may I welcome you to this Court. I have read the papers...'

It was a standard cue, telling the advocate he didn't have to plough through the history of the case, but could just move on to the real issues. It was almost always ignored. Advocates prepared their opening speeches with great care and attention and were as a rule damned if they were going to change them. Let the Judge listen. He'd probably misunderstood what he'd read, anyhow.

Hodder obviously agreed with this approach because he took the Judge inordinately slowly through the history of the case, pausing frequently to allow full notes to be kept of his words. Deputy District Judge Benham didn't seem to mind a bit. He was positively lapping it up. He even looked suitably disapproving when Hodder got to the bit about Judge Butcher ordering discovery.

When he'd finally churned through the history, he turned to Geri's Particulars of Claim. He'd clearly applied a fine-toothed comb to it and for a moment, she started to regret settling it late at night in the Devon cottage. There was the odd grammatical mistake. But Hodder grudgingly had to accept that although the document could have done with a little tidying up, it did plead a cause of action.

'And now, sir, I'll turn to the medical report, if I may?'

Hodder was starting to get into his stride. Pity it had taken him forty minutes to do so, thought Geri.

'As you'll be aware, under Order 6 rule 5(a) of the County Court rules, a medical report must be served with the Particulars of Claim. Well, sir, I would have to say that the document which was served could not possibly be regarded as a report. It simply recounts the death of the man concerned, and the fact that the author of the report believes that he died through eating contaminated meat.'

Hodder put the report down on to the table, as though it wasn't fit to be looked at any more. 'No evidence about the meat. No explanation of why the doctor thinks this might be so. And I note that the man concerned is just a GP – this is hardly the sort of area that an average GP is going to have any expertise in.'

Geri wanted to burst. But the cardinal rule was to shut up during speeches. She would have the right to reply. At this rate, probably after lunch with the Deputy nodding off.

'But that aside, I move on to the central thrust of my case, sir.'

Hodder changed his expression. Suddenly, he looked saddened, even disappointed that one in a linked profession should stoop so low. Alarmingly, the Judge's expression mirrored the QC's. This was never an encouraging sign.

'I'm afraid that this is a claim which is scandalous, frivolous and vexatious. It should never have been brought.'

Geri tried to keep her face impassive. She mustn't give away anything. She couldn't see Joanna, who was sitting behind her. Goodness only knew what she was making of all this. Good God, the Judge was nodding. And writing down every word the bloody man uttered. 'You see, sir, we have made extremely full discovery in this matter. Included in that discovery was a report.

Offered voluntarily, of course.'

He produced the report to the Judge and took him to the conclusions.

'This was prepared by an extremely eminent scientist with the Ministry, who explicitly states that he had inspected farms and found no evidence whatsoever of antibiotic abuse.'

Hodder turned to Geri, almost snarling.

'Yet still, despite all this evidence, my friend charges on and issues proceedings.'

He lowered his voice, almost conspiratorially.

'And it is quite clear that if this matter is brought to trial, however strong the Defendant's evidence is, the publicity will cause enormous damage to the meat industry. This, sir, is nothing more than nuisance litigation.'

He was finally building up to the grand finale. His voice was booming round the room, and a small roll of fat over his shirt collar was turning a virulent shade of red.

'And so, sir, I have to suggest that the only reasonable course is to strike this matter out. The harm of letting it proceed will be extraordinary and the claim has no prospect of success whatsoever.'

He finally stopped. Judge Benham looked to Geri as though to say, 'Top that, then.'

She had to get her best points in while he was still listening. She handed him her authorities.

'As you'll no doubt be aware, sir, there are a number of cases on this point. The approach of the higher Courts is consistent – it is not enough, with respect to my learned friend, to say that the claim stands little chance of success.'

The Judge looked up at her.

'But this stands no chance. What about that medical report?'

'There is also a report from a Professor Lebrun, sir.'

Geri produced it for the Judge. Her flourish was almost as good as Hodder's.

He frowned as he read it. She crossed her fingers under the table. Thank goodness she had Lebrun's report. He was keeping the show on the road.

'As you'll see, sir, the Professor cites evidence from various sources indicating that there is a problem with antibiotic abuse and comes to the conclusion that this is the most likely reason for Dr Pascoe's death.'

'But the Professor never went round the farms. Dr Vane did, and found nothing.'

Geri had to think extremely quickly. She didn't want to reveal her hand on the numbering inconsistencies. She wanted to save that for the trial, so that they wouldn't have a chance to put it right. But if that was the only way to get through today, she'd have to. She must make her mind up, and pretty quickly at that.

She made her decision. She'd keep her powder dry on the numbering for the time being and pray she had enough to get past the Judge on this application.

'That's a matter for the Trial Judge. He might come to the conclusion that he prefers Dr Vane's report, but there might be other factors which would make him prefer our evidence. I do say that it would be wrong as a matter of law, sir, for you to prefer one strand of expert evidence to another at this stage. You don't have the experts here, of course, so you can't compare their live testimony.'

He had to get the hint: find against me and I appeal you. And you'll never get a full-time judging job if you get appealed all the time, you miserable bastard. Simon always used to tell her that so much of advocacy consisted of the passing on of unspoken messages.

Judge Benham adjourned to consider matters. He told them he'd need at least two hours. It was obviously going to be tricky.

'Well done!' whispered Joanna as they left the Court.

They used up the intervening time as best they could, taking a light lunch in a tea shop near the Court and walking aimlessly around the rather downmarket shopping precinct nearby. The minutes crawled by and after what seemed more like two days, they were back in the Judge's Chambers, preparing to receive his judgment.

District Judges and their deputies are the real workhorses of the County Court. They may well deal with thirty cases in a day, any of which can throw up all sorts of hidden problems. Despite the workload, they sit on their own, with no clerk or usher with them. They have to give reasons for their judgments, but do not have tapes, like Circuit Judges, to record their words. As a result, appearing in a District Judge's Court calls for speedwriting skills that would grace many a secretary. The handwritten notes of each advocate would be the only record of the judgment. It was important to get it right, just in case one side wanted to appeal the ruling.

Geri was ready and waiting, notebook open and two pens placed neatly in front of her.

The Deputy began by reciting the history of the case – the fact that the claim arose from the death of Dr Thomas Pascoe, and, as pleaded, placed responsibility for the death on the Ministry of Agriculture for failing properly to control the use of antibiotics.

He started to put the knife in quite quickly.

'I have to say that this is a singularly unattractive claim. I have before me a report from Dr David Vane of the Defendants, which indicates that he made an exhaustive study of antibiotic use and found no problems whatsoever.'

He continued, with a sniff.

'The Plaintiff has obtained a report from a Professor Lebrun, upon which she seeks to rely. Professor Lebrun clearly takes the view that there is a problem with antibiotic abuse. Were I to be faced with the decision of which witness to prefer, I am sure that I would prefer Dr Vane, who is speaking from experience rather than theory.'

He stopped for a few moments. Geri felt the urge to cough. It was pure tension, would start as a tickle at the back of her throat at moments of stress. She'd try a discreet cough, but it would get worse. Before she knew it, she'd be gasping for breath. She had to get a grip on herself. She counted to ten and steadied her breathing.

Was he going to strike her out?

'However, I am not here to indicate which witness I prefer. I am aware of the authorities provided by Mrs Lander and know in particular that I may only strike out a claim if it stands no chance whatsoever of succeeding. In my view, we are perilously close to that point, but as expert evidence has been produced by the Plaintiff, I cannot go quite that far. As a result, I am duty bound to allow this claim to proceed to trial.'

Geri wanted to cheer. Thank goodness she had appealed him before! He must be terrified she'd do it again. Good. Serve him right. She turned to look at Joanna, who winked back.

The Judge had not quite finished, however. He was determined to place a sting firmly in the tail of his ruling.

'Mrs Lander, I have to indicate that I have concerns at your conduct in bringing such a weak case in this Court.'

She bridled at this.

'Well, sir, with respect, that's a matter for me.'

'With respect,' he hissed, 'it is a matter of concern to *me* if you are wasting the Court's time and that of the Ministry. Can you indicate to me whether you plan to call any witnesses other than the Plaintiff, this GP who prepared the report and Professor Lebrun?'

Geri had been put on the spot.

'Well, er...'

'Come on, surely you know?'

'There is a video of the late Dr Pascoe...'

'And what purpose will that serve?'

'To enable the Court to see the extent of this man's condition, sir.'

Hodder tried to intervene.

'With the greatest of respect to my friend...'

Keep your face still, thought Geri. 'With the greatest respect' is a standard insult. It means precisely the opposite to anyone who happens to be listening. The atmosphere in Court that afternoon was starting to get very respectful.

'...there is no evidential value to such a video. It is simply an attempt to introduce an emotional element into a weak case.'

'With the greatest of respect to my learned friend,' responded Geri, bitterly, 'it is a matter for the Plaintiff as to the evidence which she adduces. This Court is not in a position to prevent the Plaintiff putting evidence before the Trial Judge. That would be grossly irregular.'

Her voice was low and forceful. Even Benham looked intimidated.

'And my friend,' pressed Geri, 'has not even seen the video. It is unprofessional for him to comment before you on the value of evidence which he hasn't even looked at yet.'

She was on a roll now. Even Hodder looked chastened.

'Well, in that case, I won't rule on the video. But it seems as though the evidence is complete. Any more witnesses, Mrs Lander?'

'I can't rule out the fact that others may come forward.'

'Well, they'd better get their skates on. There's nothing to stop us moving on for trial swiftly, in my view. I don't want the Ministry to have to spend years defending this matter.'

Geri wasn't too disappointed by this. The case

probably wouldn't get any better with time, and she'd be able to wind it up before she left the firm with a bit of luck.

'I'm going to order that this is immediately transferred to the High Court, bundles of all evidence to be lodged and exchanged within forty-eight days and set down for a trial after six weeks. Time estimate?'

Crikey! That was pushing it a bit. Mind you, it would bother the Ministry more than her. Large bureaucracies always had trouble getting ready for a trial, in her experience.

'Two days?'

Both advocates nodded. Hodder was looking decidedly unhappy. The trial would probably coincide with his autumn holiday. What a pity.

'So ordered, in that case.'

Benham sniffed disdainfully. She had a nasty feeling that something else might be coming.

It was,

'Finally, Mrs Lander, I am putting you on notice at this point that should you not succeed at trial, the Court may wish to consider making a wasted costs order against you personally.'

Geri went pale.

'Sir!'

He waved his hand dismissively.

'You're not going to change my mind and now isn't the time to make representations. You can make those to the High Court should you lose. It's high time these nuisance claims stopped. If the only way to do it is to make you personally liable for the costs, then so be it. You've brought it upon yourself.'

Geri was in shock. She filed out of Court with Joanna and sat down in the waiting room. Her client took the chair next to her.

'What was all that about?' she whispered. Hodder was talking to his cronies on the other side of the room and she didn't want to be overheard.

Geri took a breath.

'A few years ago, the Courts got the power to make solicitors pay personally for costs wasted through their mistakes. Before they could only make costs orders against the clients, but that was sometimes unfair.'

Joanna looked perplexed and Geri carried on.

'Say, for example, the solicitor forgot to turn up for the trial and the whole thing had to be adjourned – that would be a good reason to make a wasted costs order.'

Joanna was nodding slowly.

'But here, they want to make it because they think we shouldn't be making the claim?'

'Basically, yes. The Judge is saying that we're wasting everybody's time. And if he's proved right, I may have to pay for that time personally.'

'But that's ludicrously unfair! We won't know until the end of the trial how much of a chance we stand.'

'Quite right. But he's just given me notice.'

'I can't have you taking this kind of risk. It's obscene – it could be tens of thousands.'

Geri smiled.

'I've got professional insurance which would cover most of it.' She declined to mention the ten thousand pound excess on her policy. 'And in any event, we can't be intimidated by these threats.'

She looked up at Joanna.

'That Judge is a Defendant hatchet man. He always takes their side and loathes me because I've appealed him in the past. He just wants to put the boot in. A High Court Judge wouldn't dream of making a wasted costs order, and it's him who would make the decision.'

She wished she was as confident as she sounded. But the decision was taken, and there was no point agonising over it. In any event, she was damned if she was going to back down now.

Hodder had been told to go straight to the Ministry after the hearing. He did as he was told, getting there just after 6.

'As expected, Minister, we didn't succeed. But I do have some good news...'

Moncrieff had been about to explode, but contained himself.

'...the Judge was most sympathetic to our plight. He ordered that Mrs Lander be put on notice that she may have to pay the costs personally if she loses. He felt that would be a more effective approach than actually striking the claim out.'

Hodder was not being totally generous with the truth, but at least the Minister looked reasonably happy. The QC gave him the rest of the good news.

'And he's made orders for a swift trial, so that we're not forced to spend months dealing with the claim. Get it over and done with as quickly as possible.'

The Minister had gone white. His voice, when he spoke, was so quiet they had to lean forward to hear him.

'Just how quick a trial?'

'First open date after six weeks. The High Court is being pretty efficient at the moment, so I'd say, the end of summer, early autumn.'

Hodder had been hoping for a quick drink with the Minister, but found himself dismissed within ten minutes. As he found his way out of the deserted building, Callum Moncrieff was already punching numbers into the telephone.

The Prime Minister had only that morning left on his summer holidays. He was not to be contacted and all enquiries were to be channelled through the Deputy PM. God only knew how far he was in on the reshuffle plans. Moncrieff didn't dare ask him where he stood.

He was going to have to deal with this himself.

David Vane had not heard about the result of the application. He was too busy. There was a steady trend of new superbug cases. Three workers from a chicken farm which had gone bankrupt had gone down with it, telling horrifying tales of being ordered to throw infected carcasses into black bags. The extent of their protection had been a pair of rubber gloves each.

It had been seven days before their symptoms had become serious enough to be noticed. He prayed that none of the infected chickens had found their way on to the food market. One of the farm hands, before he died, had confirmed they had been using perinycin, but that it had

had no effect.

David needed to put his plan into action. Damn this stupid solicitor! She was putting lives at risk.

Chapter Twenty-One

Geri had known that the fortnight or so of quiet, short days at work would not last. As soon as the ruling in the Pascoe case was made, she was plunged into a summer of increasingly desperate activity. It is the Plaintiff who has to keep the show on the road. It was now her duty to marshal the evidence and make sure that the case was ready for trial.

The case needed strengthening. Ideally, she would have sought more witnesses at her leisure. Now, though, with a trial date looming there was no time to lose. If she found anyone, she would need to get a statement and serve it pretty damn quick.

Usually, Geri could rely upon the publicity that any big case would generate. Now, though, she couldn't wait for the papers to come to her. Luckily, she had a few contacts on the national press. Now was going to be the time to put them to work for her. She picked up the phone.

Twenty minutes later, she moved to the next item on her list. She needed a new report from Dermot Lebrun. He had to comment on the Ministry's documentation, show up any scientific flaws. Geri rang the Porters Lodge at Trinity Hall. He was back from Geneva, but not in his rooms at the moment. They'd put a message on the board for him, they said.

The next day, Geri was delighted to see that several of the nationals had carried the antibiotic case story. One had even given it the splash treatment, with banner headlines screaming about deadly chickens. Her name was in all the reports, together with the firm details, so if there was anyone out there burning to give evidence, they shouldn't have too many problems finding her.

She tried Lebrun again. She needed a report very quickly. If he didn't return her call soon, she'd have to go and see him herself. Do a Joanna. Just turn up and refuse to go away until she got what she wanted.

With a sigh, she turned back to the file and started to sort out the documents for the trial bundle. All the documentary evidence would need to be in it – the reports of Dermot Lebrun and David Vane, and statements from any witnesses who were going to be used. Then they would need Dr Pascoe's health records, the medical report and Geri's drafted pleadings. All of these papers would need to be carefully paginated, photocopied and incorporated into six bundles – one each for the Judge, Geri, Hodder, the junior barrister for the Defence, the Ministry solicitor and one for keeping on the witness stand for use when the evidence was being given. This, although vital, was a thankless, time-consuming task.

Benny Grimwood saw the headlines when he was out shopping. He paused by the newspaper display at the supermarket and his pulse started to quicken. He took a paper out of the rack and read through the report quickly. Some bloody solicitor was trying to do something about superbugs. Thought they were down to antibiotic use.

Fucking hell! This was the last thing he needed, with that growing stockpile of perinycin in his barn. He bought a copy of every newspaper which carried the story, abandoned his shopping trip and drove straight home.

There he considered his options. There were three. First, he could abort the whole thing. Tell the farmers he couldn't get the drugs after all and they'd have to wait until the latest scare was over. The trouble was, he'd got rather used to the idea of taking his seven hundred and fifty grand and running to his place in the sun.

The heavier newspapers had clearly been to the Ministry. They were contesting the claim, had scientific evidence that it was a no-hoper. This solicitor was apparently some loose cannon firing off haphazardly. She'd been told that it was nuisance litigation and some Judge had threatened her about costs. There would be a hearing in the autumn. And there was some scandal about her firm making off with millions of pounds of someone else's money.

The second option was to get rid of the solicitor. He could do it, very easily. He'd killed dozens of people in his Army days, and felt nothing. Sometimes, lives just had to be extinguished and that was all there was to it. But he'd have to be very careful. He wanted to get out of the country, not spend twenty years in jail. They'd investigate the death of someone like this very carefully indeed. It would be risky.

No, he thought, I don't need to kill her yet. If she loses the case, I'll be OK for a while. Long enough to sell the drugs and move on.

He stared at the kitchen table, focusing on a stain that had been there since he was a kid. Yes, option three was the one to go for. Watch this case like a hawk and hope like hell it failed. If things started to look better for Mrs Lander, he could eliminate her then. That would give him a few months to sell the drugs off and get the hell out of the country. He'd get the trial date and sit quietly at the back. Hopefully, he could slide off into the shadows at the end, but if need be, he could deal with Mrs Lander before things got out of hand.

Pity in a way. She was rather a looker in the photos they'd printed in the papers. He smiled to himself. Well, this Mrs Lander would never know just how much it would serve her interests to lose this particular case.

That Friday Geri left work at 3, in time to collect Rory. Children were charging out of the school, and he eventually appeared, waving to one of his friends.

'Hi, Mum.'

His grin was enormous.

'End of term at last!'

'Yeah. There's a report somewhere in my bag.'

Geri tried to act cool. She could ruffle through the mess of his belongings later.

'Let's celebrate.'

'OK.' He grinned.

'McDonalds?'

'Brilliant.'

They made an odd couple in the glare of the local branch. He small and earnest in school uniform, and Geri in her work suit, trying to keep the sauce from dropping on her clothes.

'I'm glad I went back to school.'

'So am I.'

'And ... I was top in maths this year!'

'Brilliant. Well done!'

'And, Mum – Gary Street has asked me if I want to go and stay with him for a week. They're going to Yorkshire. He said that his mum would phone you. Can I go?'

'Do you want to?'

'Yes.'

'Well, OK. I'll have a chat with his mum. But what are you going to do for the rest of the holidays?' she asked.

'Dunno, really. Am I old enough to get a job? Washing up, stacking shelves...'

'I don't think so. But I can probably pay you a bit for some work on Joanna's case.'

'Brilliant! When do I start?'

'How about Monday?'

'Done!'

That evening, the phone rang just after supper. She'd changed into her weekend clothes and was just starting the washing up.

'Geri, it's Dermot.'

'Dermot! I've been leaving messages for you...'

It was good to hear his voice. She wondered what he was doing.

'Where are you?'

'I'm at the Angel.'

'The Angel where?'

'The Angel Islington. Can I pop round? I've got some information you may find interesting.'

Quickly, she gave him directions to the house. As she hung up, she told Rory that Dermot was on his way.

'Great, he seemed cool last time. But, Mum...'

Rory paused, surveying her.

'Don't you think it might be an idea to change?'

'He won't expect you to dress up, Rory.'

Her son looked sheepish.

'No, you. I mean, I don't like to be rude, but look...'

Geri ran her eyes downwards, taking in the worn man's jumper; the rather grubby khaki shorts and the plimsolls with a neat hole above each toe.

'Rory,' she sighed, 'it's not that sort of thing.'

'Oh, no? You should have seen how he was watching you when we were getting all those documents. All you had to do was stretch to get something off the shelf and...'

'Thank you, Rory,' she said, rather more sternly than she felt. 'But since it's so important to you, I might just find some clean clothes.'

With as much dignity as she could muster, Geri raced up the stairs to her room and flung open the wardrobe door. Really, this was too ridiculous for words. But then, Dermot was a professional witness and was taking the trouble to come all the way to see her ... but she couldn't put on her work clothes. She didn't want him to think she sat around at home at 8 on a Friday evening in a suit.

Her eyes settled on her white jeans. For once, they were spotless, and they certainly showed off her slim figure. She teamed them with a crisp blue poplin shirt. Dashing into the bathroom before she found some shoes, she ran a comb through her hair and sprayed some Fifth Avenue down her cleavage.

The doorbell rang just as she went back to the bedroom. Fearful that Rory might say something incriminating about her tarting herself up, she ran down the stairs and opened the door. Dermot stood in front of her, a bottle of Moët in his hand.

'Sorry I didn't ring back. Been a bit snowed under with marking and didn't check my message board. Felt the only thing I could do to make amends was come and apologise in person.'

Geri grinned and showed him into the kitchen. There were some champagne glasses at the back of one of the cupboards, and two of them were quickly filled. Rory opted for a coke.

'Now look, as of today I have some new evidence for you,' said Dermot.

'What?'

'I've got a graduate student who worked on a chicken farm last year and he told me they were using perinycin. He's called Ross Porter. Came to talk to me about it this morning.'

'Would he be a good witness?'

'Well, he's slightly student-ish, but I could lend him a suit and pay for a haircut. How about if I ask him to write down what he recalls, and e-mail it to you? Then you can do his statement without having to come up – although it's always nice to see you.'

He really was rather charming. If anything, a little too charming. If there was a girlfriend around, did she know what he was up to?

'Are you married?'

Trust Rory to voice something that was very close to Geri's thoughts.

Lebrun smiled.

'Good Lord, no.'

'Good. Do you know much about osmosis?'

Geri smiled at the sudden change of tack. She wouldn't have minded if Rory had dug a little deeper into the relationship question, maybe asked if Dermot had a current girlfriend...

The prizewinning Professor of Microbiology admitted he might know a little. Before he knew it, Rory's summer assignment was laid out in front of him.

'Have you eaten?' asked Geri.

'Well, I had a meal on the train, but I must admit, a sandwich would go down a treat,' Dermot laughed. Geri cut some doorstep slices of white bread and filled them with tuna mayonnaise.

'Wonderful!'

They giggled and had some more champagne. Eventually, at 10 o'clock, after several glasses and most of a bottle of Geri's wine, he stood up rather unsteadily.

'Geri, Rory, thank you – it's been a great evening.'

'Thank you for going to all the trouble of coming, Dermot.'

'I'm really glad I did.' He smiled, thinking to himself that solitary nights in his rooms weren't a patch on this. In the course of an evening, he had suddenly realised just how lonely he'd become. It had just crept up on him, really. He looked at his watch.

'I'm afraid I must go or I'll miss the last train back.'

'Stay here.'

He smiled at Rory, acknowledging the invitation.

'I'd love to, but ... well, I've got to see a student at eight, so I'd better get cracking now.'

Chapter Twenty-Two

David Vane needed to see the Minister. He was outside the office by 8.30 on an August Monday.

'Minister, I need to update you on some new developments...'

Callum was in expansive mood. He'd had a good weekend in Scotland forging a new relationship with a most obliging local businesswoman.

'There's been a new cluster from a farm in Suffolk. Three workers down with the superbug.

Looks like the chicken carcasses were burned, but we can't be sure. The owner's just walked out on the whole thing with his family. Daughters taken out of school, gone God knows where. So we're up to twenty-five deaths.'

'Christ!' Moncrieff breathed in deeply.

'We've got to get moving on the plan, Minister. Sod the case, there's going to be a huge outbreak if we don't do something. And it'll be your fault.'

Moncrieff stood up. He didn't like threats. Not unless he was making them.

'And what are you going to do then? Give in on this litigation, say you had found a problem but did nothing? Tell them you prepared a report for me saying there was no problem? I think it will be quite clear where the fault lies.'

'If you're saying...' David was rising to the bait.

'Now look, let's calm down. All I'm saying, David, is that we've got to see this through together. We agreed on a low key response...'

Cover up, more like, thought David.

'...and that is the right thing to do. We can't have a food scare – not like BSE. Perhaps there are a few carcasses out there, but we can minimise the risks without going belly up on this litigation. I can authorise a health campaign – cook all meat properly, that sort of thing. But if you think I'm going any further, you're in for a surprise.'

'But what about the long term?'

'We're going to have a trial date in the autumn, David. The moment that judgment is delivered, you and I will get to work. Then we'll sort out this whole mess.'

'Dermot, his evidence is wonderful! Exactly what we need.'

Geri waved the new statement at Lebrun. She'd come up to Cambridge to go through it with Ross Porter, who had signed and dated it. It could now be lodged with the other papers and put before the Court.

The Professor grinned. God, she thought, I need little excuse to come and see him. Mind you, he'd been pretty insistent that she visit.

'I thought it would help. Now, how about lunch?'

'I'd love to.'

'As it's sunny, how about the Backs?'

'That would be wonderful.'

He picked up a large wicker hamper and she followed him out of his room, then away from the college to the open space which bordered the river. It was a hot day, almost too warm for comfort.

'And now, lunch,' he said, opening the basket with a flourish. There was a bottle of champagne, two glasses, smoked salmon terrine, game pie and a vast salad.

'Dermot ... it's fantastic. I don't know what to say.'

'Then don't say anything at all,' he laughed, opening the champagne.

He sat opposite and filled their glasses. Geri took a sip.

'This is most definitely the life. I don't know why I stay in London sometimes.'

'Do you mean that?'

She frowned slightly.

'Yes, I do. I've been away with Rory for a bit and it's clarified so much for me. I've given in my notice at the firm.'

'What are you going to do?'

She smiled.

'For a bit, nothing. Spend some time with my son – I've never had the chance to do that, Dermot, not properly. And then, I'll just have to cast around, see if I can get some part-time work.'

She smiled at him.

'But what about you? Are you happy in what you do?'

He paused a moment.

'I thought about moving once but...'

He stopped.

'Tell me, Dermot.'

Quickly, he told her about Marie.

'So the long and short of it is I've been on my own for some time now.'

Geri wanted to do a somersault. He was perfectly available after all. She thought back to the first day they met, when they had sat by the river and she had surreptitiously looked at his left hand. Now, before she realised what she was doing, she reached over and took his hands in hers. These were strong, leathery, just as she'd imagined they'd be. Practical hands, reliable ones. She looked into his face. God, he was good-looking. Strong features, with dark blue eyes that held her gaze indefinitely...

She looked up to his face. He looked tense, worried.

'Geri, I'm way out of practice at this sort of thing, but since I've become involved in the case ... well...'

He paused for a moment, searching for the words.

But she had already been brought right back to reality. This was her star witness, for heaven's sake! In a High Court case which was coming on for hearing in a few months.

She frowned momentarily. He saw her expression and looked away.

'Dermot,' she said gently, 'we'd better keep things professional...'

She had been about to say 'for the time being', but he had already stood up, his face red, eyes fixed on the ground beside her.

'Yes. Of course. Think no more about it.'

With a start she realised how difficult that must have been. Her heart went out to him.

'Dermot – I meant, for the moment. I feel, well, something important for you, too.'

'Well, kind of you to let me down gently, I suppose. But don't worry, I'll stick to the straight and narrow from now on, rest assured.'

'Dermot...'

'No. I must have been stupid. It would be a crazy idea, anyhow.'

'What would?'

He bridled.

'Nothing at bloody all! Just take my evidence and go back to London. Once the case is over, I suppose I'll just be another on your list of useful contacts.'

Geri cursed herself.

'Dermot, it's not like that. But I've got to put the case first. If there was something going on and people found out, it would destroy your credibility.'

'Then put the bloody case first! At least I know where I stand in your scheme of things.'

He started to pack the hamper up, throwing in the plates. As they walked towards the college, he spoke again.

'Don't worry, the report will be in time and it'll say just what you need it to.'

'Dermot, for heaven's sake...'

'No, Geri. What do you women want these days anyhow? I bend over backwards to agree to Marie, who then tells me she wanted an old-fashioned man after all. Then I try to play it straight with you, and you calmly tell me not today, thank you, but perhaps when I fit in with your plans better... What do you all *want*?'

Geri glared at him.

'It's not a bloody case of fitting in. You've put me in an impossible position!'

'Well, I'm bloody sorry to be so inconvenient. From now on, I know exactly where I stand. It's just not worth the hassle anyhow.'

Geri blushed furiously.

'Well, if that's how you feel. I've tried to play things straight, too.'

He glared at her.

'Yes, that is how I bloody well feel. Now, I've got some proper work to do, if you'll excuse me?'

August got warmer and warmer. Both Pete and Roger had pre-booked holidays which their families insisted they took. Geri agreed, reminding them that the money was still coming in and they were on target for the bank. There had been no more rumblings from their manager – perhaps he was away too. There was, all in all, a lot to be said for summer.

She'd sent a brief note to Dermot, trying to apologise but stick up for herself at the same time. There was no reply.

Only Pete was around in the middle of the month when an ominously large envelope appeared from the Crown Prosecution Service. Geri had been expecting it and took it to her room.

There was sufficient evidence, they said, to prosecute. If Cefan Davies ever chose to return to England, he would be immediately arrested and charged with obtaining property by deception. There would be no criminal proceedings in relation to the remaining partners of Lander Ross & Co.

Geri smiled heavenwards, holding on to the letter as though it might disappear. Thank God she was not going to be prosecuted! Mind you, she still had to hear from the Office for the Supervision of Solicitors. She wondered whether they had heard from the CPS.

Well, that was one out of three. The CPS, the professional sanctions, and then the trial. She'd heard good luck came in threes.

They got the trial date a few days later. It would start in the second week of September, on a Tuesday. Geri wrote to Dermot once more, to confirm the fact that he and Ross Porter were required. Two days later, an updated report arrived with a formal note from Dermot. He had gone to town on David Vane's research methods, in particular the small number of farms used in the study. Geri had asked him not to refer to the numbering inconsistency so that she could surprise Dr Vane with it when he was giving his evidence.

Jackie had left and Geri had had a succession of temps since. They were perfectly good, but she missed her secretary. Somehow, it felt as though the firm wasn't hers any more.

Still, she could hardly say she was overworked. Usually, she was having to keep her other cases up and running while preparing for her Court hearings. Now, with very few clients, she could focus on Joanna's case. It was a rare luxury and she knew she was as prepared as she would ever be. She tried not to think too much about the wasted costs order threat.

At least she was making a fuss for Thomas Pascoe. The Ministry had replied with some elegantly spin-doctored statements implying she was some mad solicitor with a grudge against everyone. All that was needed was for everyone to cook their food properly and the public could rest safe in their beds at night.

Across town, Gordon Hodder, QC was having his final pre-trial consultation with the Minister. The preparations had been extremely time-consuming – none the less so for the fact that every minute of work was being recorded just in case they managed to get a wasted costs order against Geri. But they were ready, with statements lodged and witnesses warned.

On the subject of witnesses, Callum had thought carefully about David Vane. The man was with him wholeheartedly. He had maintained his fury at Geri throughout the summer and seemed to be positively chafing at the bit to get the trial over and done with.

But the Minister was worried. Dr Vane, he considered, had an awkward tendency to want to tell the truth. He had only agreed to provide damning evidence because he had believed the case was stopping the implementation of his plan. Once the trial was underway, though, that could no longer apply. Drastic action would have to be taken whether they won or lost.

And there had been all that effort over the summer to make sure people barbecued chickens properly. Even so, there had been another seven deaths from superbugs. Those three from the Suffolk farm, and another four from unidentified sources. Vane had been all over the country, trying to track down possible sources of contaminated meat.

The only thing that would hold him to his story would be fear. More precisely, fear that he would be shown up as someone who had falsified research. It was a powerful motive, but Callum Moncrieff wondered if it would be enough.

He turned to the QC and lowered his voice.

'I need to have a word about Dr Vane. He came to us from the academic world and has a bit of a tendency to ramble on. I'm not sure that he's going to be too convincing as a witness.'

Hodder looked surprised.

'He seemed fine at the pre-action discovery hearing.'

'Of course, but when it comes to scientific theory – he does rather take off. Of course we'll call him, but I was just wondering if it's ever possible to win a case without calling any evidence?'

Hodder paused to consider his reply.

'If you're the Defendant, yes. The Plaintiff has to prove his case and produce evidence. If that evidence is completely discredited, then he hasn't proved anything. If that happens, the Defence doesn't have to do anything.'

Callum Moncrieff considered this further.

'So, if we completely discredited what Mrs Lander was arguing – simply by cross-examining her witnesses – we could stop at that point?'

'Yes. It would be extremely difficult, though. You'd have to convince the Judge that her witnesses were speaking complete balderdash – find internal inconsistencies and so on. And if we took that route, we wouldn't be allowed to call our witnesses.'

'What else would discredit the Plaintiff's witnesses?'

'Evidence that they'd said exactly the opposite in another trial is always a good one. It's surprising how often they do. And anything about personalities, motives – someone with a chip on his shoulder, that sort of thing.'

Moncrieff sat back in his chair.

'In that case, we need to find out a little more

about their witnesses. I'm going to ask my staff to look at Professor Lebrun and this student character they've come up with a little more closely.' The Minister frowned.

'And I'm not sure that Mrs Lander hasn't a trick or two up her sleeve. I'm going to order some discreet surveillance of her office. And home, I think. Keep an eye on who's dropping in for tea. I wouldn't put it beyond her to spring a surprise witness on us.'

He looked thoughtful. Then he stood up and leaned towards the QC, his hands on the desk. Even Hodder felt intimidated.

'But what I want from you is her witnesses reduced to such shreds they can barely string two words together by the end of the cross-examination. You've got to make them look complete fools. Dangerous fools. Any less and you've failed. And if you fail – let's just say that your records will be flagged.'

Hodder had been applying for a seat on the High Court bench for five years. He knew exactly what the Minister meant.

Chapter Twenty-Three

Rory started back at school at the beginning of September. He seemed to have grown three inches over the summer and Geri had had to buy a completely new uniform for him. Still, he seemed happy to be going back. Joanna had to be at the trial so Rory was going to go home to a friend's house while it lasted. But Joanna would stay overnight with them, just in case Geri had to work.

By the day before the trial was due to start, Geri was ready. The bundles had been checked, double checked and finally lodged, and the witnesses had been given directions to the Court along with strict instructions to be there by 9.30.

Geri spent most of the day rehearsing her opening address. As lawyer for the Plaintiff, she had the right to open the case. This meant she could tell the Judge what the claim was all about, and why it was being brought. It was a powerful weapon which she wanted to use to the greatest possible effect. A good opening speech would be crucial.

Geri tried the options in the privacy of her room with the door shut. If the staff thought she was going mad, talking to herself, they didn't mention it. The speech would need to be powerful. That normally meant it would have to be short. Here, though, she would need to tell the Judge a little about Dermot Lebrun's findings. She tried summarising them, settled on an idea, and then moved on to the effects of perinycin abuse.

'This will affect every one of us, My Lord. The Plaintiff's case is that the government should have, and must start exercising better control over antibiotic use. The current system is dangerous, outmoded and open to large-scale abuse by meat producers.'

Yes, that would be the closing line. That should

put Hodder firmly on the defensive.

The letter from the Office for the Supervision of Solicitors arrived in the afternoon post. Geri took it into her room and shut the door.

It was a long letter. They were concerned, it said, at the lack of management structure in the firm and made some fairly caustic comments about Geri's control over it. She flipped through, reading as quickly as she could. Cefan's fraud was explained in detail. It was brilliantly simple. He had approached three regular clients of his, all companies which had mortgaged their premises on variable rate deals.

He had written to them suggesting that they allow him to shop around for some of the fixed rate arrangements that were then available. Each had agreed and had deposited its deeds with the firm.

He had obviously cooked something up with the surveyor. Usually, they provided a vital safety net. Any bank which is lending money will want a surveyor's valuation on a property. Most owners will only want to pay once for this and will quickly raise the alarm if multiple surveys are carried out.

Only here, the surveyor had been in on it and had only charged each company once. He was on all the lenders' lists of acceptable valuers and Cefan had used him each time. As a result, he had been able to prepare six valuations on each factory. For good measure, he had also overvalued each building, making the deal look even more attractive to the lenders.

After that, it had all been quite simple. The valuations had been sent and eighteen lenders had agreed to forward money in return for charges over three pieces of land. Each was completely unaware of the others. The money – two and a half million pounds – had been sent to the firm's client account. From there, it had in one transaction been moved on to a numbered account in Liechtenstein. That account was now empty and Cefan and his surveyor had been missing ever since.

It was recommended that Cefan be struck off the roll of Solicitors, the letter said. Geri was to be criticised for her lack of effective management over the firm but in the circumstances was not considered to be guilty of any wrongdoing or involvement in fraud.

They had given careful consideration to the question of whether disciplinary action should be taken against her, it said. They had been impressed by a large number of unsolicited testimonials as to her good character. Further, they accepted that the evidence pointed to a clever fraud, carried out by a partner who had taken careful steps to ensure his colleagues would remain unaware of his plans. In the circumstances, they proposed to exercise their discretion not to take disciplinary action, but they trusted that the partners, and in particular, the senior partner, would learn from this episode.

In other words, Geri was off the hook.

She breathed a long, low sigh of relief. Two out of three. It had to be an omen. She was going to win Joanna's case.

Pete, too, had received a copy of the report. He brought it into Geri's room at about the same time as she finished reading hers.

'Looks like we're in the clear.'

He sounded relieved.

'Yes. We can really move on now. There are some decisions that need to be made about our future,' said Geri.

He looked awkward.

'Geri, I've been thinking a lot on holiday. Bridget and the kids – they rely on me... I've had an offer from Partridge's. I wasn't going to accept it, but I really think I ought to.'

She looked at him. He quite clearly felt dreadful about it.

'It's OK, Pete. Looks like poor old Roger is going to be on his own once my six months is up.'

'I don't want to do it, but – well, you know.'

'Yes, believe me, I do.'

'I think we'd better tell Roger as soon as he's back.'

On the morning of the trial, Geri was at the High Court far too early. Passing through the security desks, she found her way down to the lady advocates' robing room.

The ladies' robing room is a haven of sense in the Royal Courts of Justice. It may be hidden away in the basement, but as soon as the door is opened, the atmosphere is one of quiet support. There is always a cup of coffee on the boil, and for once ample distribution of mirrors, seats and desks. Inside, all is quiet – totally different from the charged atmosphere of the usual male-dominated robing room, where the usual testosterone-fuelled tactics rule. Geri was grateful for this opportunity to avoid Hodder and his entourage.

She had her notebook in her bag. For at least the seventeenth time, she checked it was there. It contained her opening speech, along with page references for every single piece of evidence that she wanted to use. As always, it was there purely as a safety net. She knew every line of her opening remarks and every page reference by heart.

Waiting here was not helping much. With a sigh, she put on her solicitor's robe and went up the stairs to the main lobby.

The Royal Courts of Justice were built in the Victorian era when justice was considered to demand Gothic arches and vaulted roofs. The main entrance is almost cathedral-like – the only difference being that the floor here is made of an elaborate mosaic pattern. Geri had heard that staff at the Court used it as a set of badminton courts in the evenings.

The building is home to the High Court and Court of Appeal. In fact, there are over a hundred Court rooms. The original Victorian ones are high-ceilinged with wooden pews and the Judge sitting apparently half a mile away. Bar students are taught how to project their voices into the furthermost corners of the architecture.

A modern extension, the Queen's Building, has been tacked on to the Royal Courts. This is a good example of the utilitarian approach to justice adopted in the 1970s. Then high-vaulted ceilings gave way to something looking more like an office suite. Instead of mosaic, there is dirty stone on the floor decorated with ground-in cigarette ash. Two lifts serve the building – one of which breaks down so frequently that those in the know avoid using it.

Geri was in one of the older-style Courts. She looked up the list kept in the centre of the entrance hall to find out which Judge she had.

Excellent. Sutton-Jones. Plenty of experience, a very safe pair of hands, and fair. Not particularly regarded as a Plaintiff's Judge, but not a Defendant's either. He would be a fair tribunal, at least.

With a clitter-clatter of heels, Joanna approached, smiling nervously.

'Ready?' she asked.

'Ready as I'll ever be.'

They walked up the stairs and negotiated a long dark corridor to get to the Court. Once in, Geri gave her name to the usher and settled herself into her place. She had a lectern to use – something which she never had in the County Court. She always found it a godsend, particularly in Courts where the lighting was gloomy.

Benny Grimwood paused outside the Court and checked the list on the small board beside the door. Yes, it would be in here. Quietly and unobtrusively, he made his way up to the public gallery and settled himself down. He had a small notebook ready. Anyone looking might think he was a mature student, or perhaps a reporter who didn't want to go in the press stall.

Before long, the door crashed open and Hodder came into the room with his team. He settled himself on the opposite side of the Court in the row in front of Geri. QCs can sit nearest the Judge and have their own special row of seats. If there are no QCs in the case, the row is respectfully left empty.

Strictly speaking, solicitors should only occupy the third row back. The second is reserved for barristers. But Geri was not going to start running her case from the back of the Court. She'd have enough difficulty making herself heard as it was.

So she placed herself in the second row. D'Arby Colinder glared at her and took up position on the same seat but much further along. He and Hodder were in wigs and gowns. Not for the first time, Geri wondered how much of a difference the outfits really made. Did she look as though she wasn't a proper lawyer without a wig?

She watched David Vane being shown to a seat. Geri recognised him from the discovery hearing and avoided looking at him. She watched the door, though, for the arrival of Dermot Lebrun and his student. Both appeared in a few moments, slightly flustered after a late arrival from Cambridge.

Dermot looked pale. He nodded quickly to Geri before assuming his place in the Court. He smiled a greeting to David Vane. It was their battle as much as anyone else's but scientists like to think they are a little more civilised than lawyers about these things.

The Judge entered promptly and everyone stood up. He sat, they sat and he looked at Geri.

'May it please Your Lordship...'

And she was off. She ran through the history, emphasising the factors that Dermot Lebrun would be mentioning in his report – Tom Pascoe's good health before he ate the meat, the sudden onset of symptoms, the discovery of a superbug. Then she focused on chicken farming and the endemic use of antibiotics. All that was in dispute, she told the Judge, was whether a particular antibiotic, perinycin, was being regularly used on British farms. The temptation was there, as it was so effective, she told him. And she had evidence that it *was* being used.

The Judge was listening attentively, noting what she said from time to time. She'd expected some resistance, but was pleased at the reception she was getting so far. He seemed to be taking it seriously, at least.

She'd managed to keep the speech short and powerful. The Judge would have read the papers and she'd have been telling him nothing new, simply putting the claim into context. Geri called Joanna first. Her evidence would be confined to fact, and would be uncontroversial.

'Mrs Pascoe, please.'

Joanna was good. She answered the questions with dignity and composure, telling the Court Tom had told her he'd microwaved some chicken korma while she'd been out. That night, he'd developed stomach cramps. By morning, he was no better. He'd been unable to work, had taken some medication. But he developed a fever and became unable to eat. After two days they'd taken him into the hospital.

'They told me that he would be OK – they'd put him on a drug called perinycin which would kill whatever bug he had. But he just got worse. He started to turn yellow and they realised his liver was failing. Then they realised he had a superbug and that the perinycin couldn't deal with it.'

She paused.

'So they moved him into a ward a long way away from the rest of the patients so that he couldn't infect them. He had to be barrier nursed and I wasn't allowed to touch him. He had a TV in his room and that was it. He was just waiting to die and I couldn't do a thing about it.'

Joanna took a deep breath. She was fighting to compose herself. The Judge was looking at her, clearly concerned. She dismissed his suggestion that they adjourn for a few moments.

'Nobody could do anything. He was a GP – he knew what was happening. First, the infection went into his blood and he got septicaemia. Then his spleen and pancreas. They kept his liver going for a while but eventually it went. There was no point in transplanting because the infection was everywhere in his body. He just had to lie there and wait, getting thinner and thinner, in more and more pain. Eventually, he went into a coma.'

Joanna paused for a moment. Her voice fell but the Court was absolutely still.

'He died three days later. He weighed six stone.'

'Thank you, Mrs Pascoe,' said Geri softly.

They didn't bother to cross-examine. They didn't need to. Nobody could question the fact that Joanna's husband had died. To cross-examine would have seemed to be harassing a bereaved middle-class woman. Judges weren't too keen on that. So Hodder sat quiet, trying very hard to look sympathetic.

The Judge was obviously quite taken with Joanna. She was genuine, factual and sensible. All the qualities for an ideal witness.

Geri had the video played next. They'd not objected to it in the end, had backed down. Even Hodder looked ashamed by the end. David Vane looked at his feet. The Judge seemed extremely moved and adjourned for a few minutes after it had finished.

Tom's former partner, Dougal Baines, was next to take the stand. He took the oath and glared across at Hodder. Geri had used him simply to provide the medical report required by the rules. It had been brief and to the point. She got him to confirm the fact that he had written the report and then sat down.

Hodder got to his feet.

'Doctor, you've formed the view, expressed in your report, that this death was due to the ingestion of chicken which had been fed perinycin?'

'Yes.' The doctor was far too aggressive. Spoiling for a fight.

'Did you sample the chicken?'

'No, of course not, how could I?'

'So you have no evidence at all on that point.'

'But it was obvious – that was the thing he ate before the illness started.'

'How do you know that?'

'He told me so.'

'But you didn't see it.'

The doctor was becoming exasperated.

'Of course I didn't but he'd have no reason to lie to me.'

'You were in no way involved in his care at the hospital.'

'No.'

'So you do not have first-hand experience of the condition he was suffering from?'

'No, but I've seen the records.'

'So, if we can summarise, you make two assertions in your report.'

Hodder was clearly warming up as this went on.

'First, you say that his illness was caused by catching this bug from a chicken?'

'Yes.'

'And you have no evidence other than what Dr Pascoe thought.'

Hodder didn't bother to wait for an answer, he was enjoying this so much.

'And then you surmise that the reason the chicken had the superbug was because it had been fed perinycin.'

'But it can't have developed a superbug any other way!'

'An assertion you make without even knowing where the bird in question came from, let alone the feeding and antibiotic regime at its farm.'

Baines raised his voice. He was almost shouting.

'But it's the only way, I tell you!'

He didn't need to go any further. The GP looked like a fool. He had been neutralised. Hodder hoped that word of this would find its way back to the Minister pretty quickly. He was standing by, ready to come to Court if things were looking good. If the case were thrown out, he would be on the TV screens condemning the actions of Mrs Lander. If, God forbid, it went the other way, he wouldn't be seen for dust.

Hodder sat down, his point well made. Geri decided not to re-examine, but move on to her most important witness.

'Professor Lebrun, please.'

She looked around the Court as he walked towards the witness box. There was a perceptible stir as everyone sat up and prepared to take careful note. David Vane, she noted, looked particularly interested in what Dermot Lebrun had to say.

He took the oath and she went through the routine questions for any expert – his qualifications, job, research publications and books. Experts are the only witnesses allowed to give opinions in Court and their special knowledge has to be proved before any of their evidence is given.

Dermot Lebrun recited an impressive list of publications and two books which he had written on microbiology. He was dressed, thank goodness, in a conservative grey suit and tie. Sutton-Jones was smiling benignly at him and listening hard to what he had to say.

The Judge had already read his report. Geri

just needed to ask a few questions to reinforce the basic message. Prompted by her, he started with the facts of Tom Pascoe's illness and death, and reviewed the medical and microbiological evidence.

'And if I can take you to the conclusion of your report, Professor Lebrun, could you explain your opinion as to the role of antibiotics in this man's death?'

The report set out his reasoning and there was no need to ask the question. But it always helped to ram home the central point from an expert's report.

'Certainly,' he answered, and turned to look at the Judge, sitting in his red robe, way above them at the front of the Court.

'The real answer lies in the way in which the illness developed. This was a previously healthy man who developed what seemed like food poisoning. He became ill enough to need hospital admission. The progress of the disease simply continued once he was in hospital and it quickly became clear that he had a multi-resistant organism. In my view, it must therefore have come from the initial food poisoning episode. Once that link is there, the only question is how the meat concerned could have been carrying such a bug? And in my view, the only way is by ingestion of antibiotics. Bugs cannot evolve resistance to perinycin unless they have been exposed to it.'

Geri took him through some of the research and made him explain in simple terms how resistance was acquired. He was by this stage well into his stride.

'Problems with antibiotic resistance really started to come to the fore in the 1980s. Penicillin was the first drug, of course, so that was the first in line for resistance and we started to find that certain bacteria, particularly those which occur in sexually transmitted diseases, were not affected by penicillin.'

He took a sip of water and continued.

'Until fairly recently, this wasn't such a problem as the hospitals kept perinycin back. Its use was highly restricted, and it was only prescribed if all else failed. But this just bought a little time. Even so in the late 1980s, the first perinycin-resistant bug in England surfaced, and since then there have been sporadic outbreaks all over the world.'

The Judge was getting the point. He didn't wait for Geri to ask the next question. Always a good sign.

'So you are saying that when this last defence is completely breached, we will be back to the pre-antibiotic era?'

Lebrun nodded.

'Essentially, yes. There's always the possibility that we can invent a new super-antibiotic, but again, that's just buying time. There's some very interesting work on gene technology – inserting a code for non-resistance into the bug – but so far this isn't widely available.'

Geri decided to move on to the problems of species jumping. It was always better to deal with the controversial points of your evidence with your own witness rather than let the cross-examination reveal the potential problems.

'Professor Lebrun, if Dr Pascoe had caught this illness from the chicken, the bug would have had to have moved from a bird to a man, wouldn't it?'

'Yes. That is feasible, however. We can all recall, I'm sure, the arguments against BSE transfer between species. That's a different matter, of course, as we were talking about prions then, rather than bacteria, but the point was that illnesses can transfer. We may think we're completely different from other mammals, but in microbiological terms we're not.'

'Professor Lebrun, this is all very well, but might it be that the Ministry could not be expected to know that there is a problem?'

Dermot Lebrun looked directly at the Judge.

'I cannot believe that a responsible Ministry would be unaware, My Lord. There has been a wealth of scientific evidence about the emergence of these superbugs, and considerable anecdotal evidence that perinycin is being sold to farmers on the black market. I cannot believe the problem hasn't been identified.'

David Vane was transfixed. He'd heard of Dermot Lebrun, and had read some of his papers with interest. The man was absolutely right. The Judge seemed to be looking pretty impressed, too.

Geri finished on that high note. Gordon Hodder rose to cross-examine.

'Ever seen the inside of a police cell, Professor?'

Damn, thought Geri. They've been investigating him.

The room was completely quiet. Dermot Lebrun seemed momentarily shocked, and then

recovered his composure.
'Well, yes, some time ago.'
'For what, please?'
Lebrun was trying to avoid letting his voice drop, but he overcompensated and by now was almost shouting.
'I was arrested as a student. It was a fairly rough arrest and I hit back.'
'Why were you arrested?'
'I was at a demonstration.'
'In relation to what?'
Hodder knew the answers, clearly. But he was going to extract maximum leverage from them.
'Animal experimentation.'
'I see. And were you protesting in favour or against animal experimentation?'
'Against. But, look, this was over fifteen years ago.'
'Are you still against animal experimentation?'
That was an impossible question for a microbiologist.
'Not completely, but things have changed since then...'
Hodder didn't let him finish.
'What's changed is your mind, Professor.'
'To some extent, but not...'
'Let's see. You felt strongly enough at the time to lay out an officer, didn't you.'
Dermot nodded sheepishly.
'And then you changed your mind – to the extent that you now carry out such experimentation yourself.'
'Sometimes, one does have to modify certain views.'

'So you would not rule out the possibility that you might modify your views on multi-resistant organisms?'

'I really don't think that you can possibly...'

Hodder waved one hand dismissively.

'No doubt you feel as strongly as you did at that riot, Professor, but I shall move on.'

Geri wanted to hit her opponent. It was the lowest trick in the book, commenting on the evidence while not allowing the witness the chance to answer back. It was effective, though. Far too effective. She rose to her feet.

'If the witness might be allowed to answer the question...'

The Judge smiled at her.

'You may put questions in re-examination, Mrs Lander.'

Shit!

Hodder moved on to David Vane's report. Geri had told him not to worry about the inconsistencies in the farm numbering. She wanted to catch Dr Vane in the witness box, unprepared. All she needed was a comment from Lebrun that he must have found something, whatever the report seemed to be saying.

'You've read the report of Dr Vane, I take it?'

'Yes.'

'And you will note that he has carried out research into this area.'

'Yes.'

'And he has not found a single case of perinycin use.'

'I can't accept that.'

It was a dream of an answer for Hodder.

'Are you saying that this senior civil servant is lying? Making up spurious research?'

The trouble with Dermot, mused Geri, was that he was too honest. Lying would be an obvious explanation for the lack of results in the report, but it wouldn't occur to him that the Court would not find this too palatable. Thankfully, Dermot didn't go quite that far.

'I just think he didn't look hard enough.'

'He visited each farm, inspected their feed and drug cabinets and took blood samples. What more could he have done?'

'Visited more farms. Twenty-nine was a tiny sample.'

'How many more?'

Dermot was starting to get flustered. He wasn't a professional witness, hadn't had time to learn how to deal with this quick-fire approach. He hesitated. Bad move.

'Have you ever done research of this kind?'

Hodder was like a Jack Russell, yapping at the witness's feet.

'My work has been laboratory-based. I wouldn't have the power to visit farms and take samples.'

Hodder was moving in for the kill.

'So you've never undertaken work of this kind?'

'Not as such.'

'Yet still you find it in your heart to criticise someone who has.'

'You don't have to have done exactly the same piece of research to be qualified to comment...'

'In fact, you wouldn't even know how to take a blood sample, would you?'

'If you mean that I'm not a vet, that's true.'

'You're just criticising from an ivory tower, Professor.'

He spun out the last word to emphasise his point. Dermot Lebrun was starting to redden.

'No. I know what I'm talking about and so does Dr Vane. It's just that his research is completely at odds with what everyone who knows the slightest thing about this area expects. So I don't accept it.'

'So he's lying?'

'No, I don't think so. Just not being thorough enough.'

'Or you just might change your mind and decide he was right, Professor.'

Dermot was sounding peevish and annoyed. Hodder had clearly set out to portray him as some crackpot academic who changed his mind fortnightly and had no idea about anything at all. He was succeeding.

The damage done, Hodder sat down again and Geri stood up to re-examine. The trouble was, Lebrun was shattered, and looked it. He couldn't take the cues from her questions, and simply reiterated what he had said before. By lunchtime, his evidence was over and the Judge sent them away until 2.30 as he had an urgent case to interpose.

The Court emptied quickly. Before long, David Vane was alone in the empty stalls. What he had seen had just confirmed all his misgivings about the Court system. Lebrun had been badly mauled by that brute Hodder. The professor had been absolutely right, but no one cared about that. They were too concerned with point scoring. It was all a game to the lawyers.

But David knew he was hemmed in. Circumstances had placed him on the other side of the dispute – in different territory, with a different perspective on the truth.

He shook himself. He couldn't soft talk himself into some pseudo-philosophical nonsense about the nature of truth. It was really quite simple. If he stuck by his interim report, he was going to have to lie. He was going to have to go into that witness box and swear he'd obtained completely different research results. Bugger his motives, he would be standing in a Court of Law telling lies.

He'd told those lies to avoid all this Court nonsense. But here he was, about to be the Ministry's star witness.

With a start, David realised he had ended up being far more involved in the cover up than anyone else. Callum Moncrieff, if he wanted to cover his tracks, would simply point to the report and say he had relied upon what David had told him. Stories about false reports wouldn't stick – who would believe that of a scientist? And David knew that if he came up with the truth – that he had edited his information to produce a false result – then he would carry the can in the resultant scandal. He would lose his job and someone else who might not stand up to Moncrieff would be put in his place to avoid the implementation plan. That was the worst of all possible outcomes.

He had to get some fresh air, take a break from the stultifying atmosphere. He left the building and walked in a straight line, skirting the edge of the Temple, until he found himself by the river. Funny, he'd never realised that the Courts were so close to the Thames.

It was good to be there, watching the river traffic ply its way up and down. He could think much more clearly here. He knew that he needed to plan, get a strategy worked out before he had to give evidence. It took him fifteen minutes to do so.

He would not – could not – admit to lying about his research. But if he was asked, he would say that his report had been interim and that he agreed with the Professor that he needed to look at more farms. He might even concede that perhaps the Ministry should have looked at this earlier, and on a larger scale. That would be fair. He'd be walking a bit of a tightrope, but it was better than telling an outright lie. And it would leave him in control of the implementation plan, at least.

Moncrieff wouldn't like it if he softened his line on the evidence. Well, he could go to hell.

Benny Grimwood had left the Court only long enough to buy a sandwich. He returned quickly, went through the security screen, and took up a suitable place on a seat beneath one of the gothic arches just beyond the entrance. There he sat quietly. To anyone passing, he looked like a solicitor's clerk surreptitiously munching a sandwich. In fact, he was monitoring matters in front of him very closely indeed. After half an hour, he knew the system and had worked out his plan.

It looked as though he wouldn't need it. He'd sat quietly at the back of the public gallery that morning, just like any vaguely interested member of the public with nothing better to do. It had been rather encouraging. Any fool could see that the claim was in deep trouble. Even so, it paid to be ready, just in case.

Chapter Twenty-Four

Joanna needed to visit the Ladies' room and Geri had therefore left the Court alone. As she walked down the long dark corridor, she felt someone looming up behind her. She looked back. 'Dermot ... sorry they gave you a bit of a mauling. Don't worry. Now you've finished your evidence, I can talk to you.'

He frowned.

'I had no idea it would be that bold, Geri. I didn't think it would get so personal.'

He paused for a moment.

'I'm sorry about what I said in Cambridge. You were absolutely right to say what you did. God, if anything had happened and they'd got on to it, I would have been a laughing stock in there.'

They stopped walking and turned towards each other.

'Come to lunch... I'm just going to find Joanna.'

Geri never ate at the Court cafeteria. It was always overfull with witnesses, barristers, solicitors, and quite impossible to think in. There was a small place off Fleet Street that she liked to use. She, Joanna and Dermot found seats at the back.

'It's not going well, is it?'

Joanna was clearly concerned. Her hand trembled slightly as she ate her salad.

Dermot was furious with himself.

'I should have realised what Hodder was going to do. It's all my bloody fault.'

Geri tried to reassure him.

'I didn't expect him to go for you like that. I thought he'd concentrate on pushing his own witness rather than going all out for you. It could be counterproductive if Vane accepts some of your criticisms.'

Joanna looked at Geri.

'Where do we go from here?'

'We have the student, Ross, then it's over to them. The Defence.'

'At least the Press are there.'

'But if the case goes against us, there'll be nothing to report. An unsuccessful case was brought in which there was no evidence...'

Joanna took a sip of her tea, grimaced and then smiled.

'Perhaps Dr Vane will come up with something. You never know.'

'Don't bank on it.'

'But, Geri, I can see him from my seat. He's not happy. Not at all. He was twitching about all over the place when Professor Lebrun was speaking. And did you see how he didn't leave Court at the end? It wouldn't surprise me if there's something up, you know.'

Geri looked up. It didn't look good at the moment, but you never knew. She wondered about David Vane. Everything she knew about him indicated he was bright, motivated and effective. He must know something more.

They were back in Court for 2.30. David watched as Geri stood up. She scanned the Court, checking that her next witness was in the room and ready. As she looked, he noticed that her eyes rested on him for a few moments. What did she see there? It was a most peculiar expression. She seemed quizzical, probing. Not for the first time, he felt extremely uncomfortable. He was not looking forward to her questions.

'I'll call Ross Porter, please.'

The student climbed the steps to the witness box. He was wearing a dark suit which was a little too large for him.

Dermot had offered to lend him something and it showed. But actually it made rather a good impression – a young man who was doing his best to show respect for the Court. He was sworn in and gave his name and address.

'Now, Mr Porter, in your statement you talk about spending some time at a farm last year?'

'Yes. I'm a microbiology student and got a summer job working on a chicken farm.'

'Can you tell us a little about it?'

'Yes. It was a factory farm in Sussex, housing around two thousand birds.'

The student gave the address of the farm to the Court.

David sat up. He had visited that farm in the spring. Thank God the student hadn't been there then. If he'd identified him as having visited...

'...and I went back over Easter as they were a little short-staffed.'

Oh, shit! He must have been there during David's visit.

He shrank back in his seat. He was in the gloom at the back of the Court. He hadn't seen the student outside. Please God, he hadn't been recognised.

The solicitor was moving on.

'Can you tell me about antibiotic use on the farm?'

'Yes. I was responsible for feeding in the mornings. We were told to add some scoops of antibiotic to the mix.'

'Are you aware of the type of antibiotic?'

'Yes. It was perinycin.'

Geri paused to let the words sink in. Then, slowly, 'How do you know?'

'There was one occasion when I unwrapped the delivery. It was in tins, clearly labelled.'

'Did you know what perinycin was?'

'Yes, from my studies. I knew it was a last-resort antibiotic.'

'Did you ask the farmer why he was using it?'

There was a short, bitter laugh.

'No. If you asked questions, you were fired. And although I thought it was unwise to be using the drug, I didn't know anything about whether it was allowed on farms or not.'

David's hands were running with sweat. Was she going to ask him if the farm had been visited by the Ministry? She hadn't so far. She was probably saving it up for last.

Geri was pausing, looking as though she was trying to formulate another question. She was going to make the connection any second now.

The silence had become oppressive by now. Someone in the public gallery coughed. A frown of irritation crossed Geri's face and the question escaped her. She sat down.

Hodder stood up.

'Were you ever aware of a visit from the Ministry of Agriculture?'

David's heart must have stopped beating. The question he'd been dreading, put in blissful ignorance by his own side.

Porter was taking his time. David sat stock still, not wanting to move in case the witness saw him and remembered.

'Well...'

This was it.

'...I do remember there was a visit from an official.'

Shit!

'But I wasn't on duty at the time. It was my day off. I think it was something to do with the books, so it must have been the tax people.'

'Not from the Ministry?'

'Not so far as I was aware.'

David let out a long, slow breath.

Hodder would never know how close he had come to disaster.

He was continuing.

'And tell me, Mr Porter, you no longer work at the farm, do you?'

'No.'
'Is it right you were dismissed?'
'I was.'
'For fiddling your hours?'
'No. *I* was fiddled. They said I'd worked thirty-eight when I'd done forty-seven. When I complained, they sacked me.'
'That's nonsense, isn't it? You'd had a warning once before for overstating your hours.'
The witness blushed.
'There had been one occasion, yes, but...'
'And you were caught out again.'
'If you like, yes, but all the staff were doing it.'
'Don't try to justify yourself, Mr Porter. And so you've got a grudge against the farm now.'
'No. It was just a holiday job, you know.'
'So you admit you lied to the farm about your hours? Twice.'
'Yes, I suppose I do.'
'And you're lying today.'
'No, I'm not.'
'Who is your supervisor?'
'Professor Lebrun.'
'Is he marking your dissertation this year?'
'Yes.'
'So you want him on your side.'
'If you're saying that I'm doing this to get a good mark...'
'Well, you said it. The idea has obviously occurred to you.'
Hodder was dangling the poor student on the end of a line.
'How did you come to be involved in this case?'
'The Professor asked if any of us had noticed

antibiotic abuse. Said he was working on a legal case. So I said yes.'

Hodder was moving in for the kill.

'So the Professor wanted information. You had a grudge against the farm and supplied it, knowing it to be false.'

'That's not true!'

Hodder smiled at the Judge.

'No more questions.'

Mr Justice Sutton-Jones looked down at Geri.

'I take it that's your case, Mrs Lander?'

'Yes, My Lord.'

At least there was Dr Vane. She would just have to cross-examine him well. Once those missing numbers were put to him, it would be all right. He wouldn't be expecting to be caught out like that. Everything would depend on him.

Hodder stood up. All eyes turned to him.

'In the circumstances, My Lord, I do not propose to call evidence. I will make my submissions now.'

Chapter Twenty-Five

Geri had walked right into the trap.

Of course Dr Vane knew more. And they knew it, too. So they weren't going to call him. So she'd never be able to ask him those questions. Her last lifeline had been ripped away from her.

She wanted to scream. It was brilliant, and so obvious now. Nobody had disputed the fact that

Dr Vane had visited the farms in question. Lebrun had said that Dr Vane wasn't lying. No wonder they'd wanted to tie him down on that. So they didn't have to prove the report – it was already accepted. All that was in dispute was comment on it.

Hodder was into his submissions. The Professor's evidence had been woefully inadequate, bearing the hallmarks of an academic with no experience of the real world. He had been reduced to trawling his students for information and had finally found one with a grudge against his former employers. They accepted that the Ministry had investigated and had found nothing. He reminded the Judge that the case had come perilously close to being struck out before and that it had been brought on for a swift trial.

His Lordship was nodding.

'Mr Hodder, is it right that a warning was given to Mrs Lander in relation to the costs of this litigation?'

'It is, My Lord.'

The Judge turned to her.

'Mrs Lander, I'm aware that you're under some pressure in relation to costs. I have to indicate that I am giving consideration to this factor, as well as to the question of liability. I would be grateful if you would make submissions in due course as to why a wasted costs order should not be made. If you fail on liability, of course.'

His expression made it quite clear that she would.

He had turned, completely. It's an unpleasant

feeling, to start off with a friendly, fair judge and to end up with one making all sorts of threats. She wondered when she had lost him. Probably half way through Dermot's testimony.

Geri glanced at the Court clock. Five o'clock, nearly. Play for time.

'My Lord, these are important submissions and...'

'And you want some time, I suppose? Well, Mrs Lander, I'm going to give you every opportunity to prepare your comments. Ten-thirty tomorrow.'

He rose and was gone. Even Hodder seemed embarrassed by such a sympathetic response. He left quickly, muttering about a consultation at 5.

Geri watched Dr Vane picking up his things. She looked at his face. He seemed stunned, unsure whether he was expected to stay or go.

He didn't know, she thought to herself.

After a few moments, Vane left, leaving Geri, Joanna and Dermot alone in the Courtroom. There was a muddle of conflicting thoughts running through Geri's mind. She tried to control her racing brain.

'There must be a reason why they didn't call him,' muttered Dermot.

Geri nodded. Something didn't fit. And as for not telling him...

She tried to steady herself, force herself to think logically. Why would they take such a risk? The answer could only be that they felt it was dangerous. Had he done some work since the report and found antibiotic abuse? Or was he going to admit that he had already found problems and had edited his findings?

She would never know. Perhaps she didn't want to know. She just wanted to walk away from this building, this job, this world of dusty pedantry.

But the thought was irritating her. Dr Vane knew something important. They were worried about him.

'I've got to find him.'

'Can you do that?' asked Joanna.

'He's not being called by them. There's no property in a witness, although I'll have to be careful what I say.'

She had to get to him. Quickly.

But where would he have gone? She gathered up her files and left the Court, running down the staircase.

He wasn't in the entrance hall. Must have gone home.

Where was his home? She'd heard before where he was from. Somehow, she knew it. It was just a case of getting the information out of her brain.

She trawled through her memory. That pre-action discovery hearing when he'd been late. Hodder had said that his train was coming from where? Damn. She couldn't remember.

She put herself back in the Courtroom that day. She'd been concentrating on her submissions, hadn't really been listening. Fast forward. Dr Vane had arrived. The District Judge had made some comment. No, he'd made it before, when Hodder said Vine would be late. Hodder hadn't got some reference. Something to do with fairytales, goodies, baddies ... witches.

Witchfinder General! Matthew Hopkins. Manningtree. Dr Vane had been delayed that day coming from Manningtree in Essex. If he was going home on the train, that meant Liverpool Street station.

'I've got to get to Liverpool Street. As fast as I can!'

Things continued to look distinctly encouraging to Grimwood. Mrs Lander was clearly in rather a tricky situation. Served the silly cow right! She'd never know, though, how lucky she was to lose this one. Shame, really.

The stockpile was almost ready now. Two more deliveries and he could be away. Mrs Lander's case looked like it was going down the plughole, so he'd have a clear run at selling the lot. They'd clamp down in the end, but not soon enough to stop him making his fortune.

Still, he'd come back tomorrow to see this thing out. It could be quite interesting.

It was 5.20. Every taxi in London seemed to be full. As she stood in Fleet Street waving uselessly at the passing cabs, Geri spotted a red bus coming towards her. Liverpool Street, it said. It stopped at a traffic light and she jumped on at the back. She'd litigated against the open platform buses in the past, saying they were dangerous. She was never more grateful than she was now for their continued existence.

The bus ground noisily towards Liverpool Street. She had no idea whether he would even be catching a train, let alone what time it would leave. For all she knew, he could be staying in London overnight. But then, if he came to

London every day for work, he'd be unlikely to stay in a hotel just because he was in Court. And he'd come by train on the day of the discovery hearing. It had to be worth a try.

It was 5.50. The bus finally stopped at the side of the station and Geri hurried off and down the escalator leading into the station concourse. She'd never been to Liverpool Street before. It was shiny, smart, and thronged with people. Not a hope in hell of spotting her man.

There was an enormous blue departures board above the concourse. She scanned it. There must have been twenty trains listed. Stansted, Southend, Cambridge. Norwich, 6 p.m. Stopping at Manningtree. Platform 8.

She found the platform and moved forwards towards the gate. Damn! No ticket. She didn't want a fare evasion conviction in addition to all her other problems. The ticket office was on the other side of the station. She raced across, her shoes slipping on the shiny floor.

She stood impatiently in the queue. 5.56.

'Where to please?'

'Er, Manningtree.'

She paid and ran back across the building. They were just closing the gate and she was the last one through. She hurtled up to the train and jumped into the open door to the first-class carriages.

Geri stopped for a moment in the carriage end to catch her breath. There was a toilet nearby and she went into it. She looked a complete state. Her face was red, some mascara seeping down on to her cheek. Her shirt had come up above her waist top and was hanging out. She had the unpleasant feeling that she was sweating.

Geri did the best she could to tidy herself up. She had no idea how long it would take to get to Manningtree. She didn't even know if Dr Vane was on the train. There might have been an earlier departure, he might have gone somewhere else.

She walked the length of the train. It was long, twelve carriages, one of which was cast in gloom as the lighting wasn't working. It was crowded and she tried to look closely at all the faces. Some obviously thought her mad and instinctively moved away, shifting their eyes when they met her look.

He wasn't there. Damn! The train was going through Chelmsford. One last try in the opposite direction. She could get a better look at those facing the engine.

As she walked back through the third carriage, she saw him. He was in an outside seat in the darkened carriage. His eyes met hers and he looked away, shocked.

'Dr Vane, can we have a word?'

The other commuters were clearly listening in. He reddened.

'But I'm on a train.'

Talk about the obvious. Still, must try to be pleasant, she told herself.

'Yes, I know, but I need to talk.'

The others probably thought she was a spurned lover.

'Are you allowed to talk to me like this?' He clearly had no idea whether she was.

'Yes. You're not a witness any more so I'm

allowed to talk to you.'

'But surely you have to go through the Ministry?'

Geri was exasperated.

'The Ministry isn't here. I am, and I just want to ask you about your report.'

'But there are people around.'

'Then let's go up to the end.'

He shifted in his seat, embarrassed. Everyone was listening in. He shrugged, and then nodded. She led him to the end – at least it was deserted.

They took up position, leaning against the sides, bracing themselves against the jolts of the train. Geri spoke first.

'You're not giving evidence. Do you know why?'

'Like the barrister said, there's no need.'

Geri shook her head.

'No, I don't think so. I think they're frightened you might say something.'

He rallied.

'I don't know what they think. I'm not running the case. I'm just a scientist.'

He glared at her.

'I just want to get back to my work. I don't get paid a bloody fortune to sit around in Court like you do.'

Geri bridled.

'I'm not getting a penny if we lose this.'

'So you're just like an American ambulance chaser then? Makes it even worse.'

'Let's not get into that. I just want to know if there have been any new developments – have you done some work since the research which has changed your findings?'

'No, I bloody well haven't. Look if this is all...'

'You haven't looked too happy during the hearing. In fact, at one point...'

'I'm not too happy a person. Particularly now. There's nothing more I can say.'

'What about this?'

Geri showed him her copy of the report, turned to the appendix.

'Your numbers are out of synch. Were there more farms that you left out?'

She was spot on.

Even in the dimness of the train, she could see she was right. His face changed instantaneously. From defensive, he went to wounded.

'No.'

He was a bad liar. A terrible liar. Which probably meant he was an honest man. No wonder they weren't calling him.

She had to speak loudly to be heard above the train. Her voice was going hoarse.

'I know you found something on those farms you left out. That's a matter for your conscience. Even if I lose my case, do you think that the truth will never come out? Of course it will – and when it does, you'll be right in the firing line. Your Minister will have long moved on and who do you think will get the blame?'

Vane looked at her blankly.

'If you've finished, I need to get back to my papers. You can't be allowed to harass me like this.'

There was no point. He wasn't going to come over.

'OK. I'm going to go.'

She ripped off the cover page of his report and scribbled on it.

'This is my address and phone number. If you change your mind, let me know.'

'I won't.'

He took it at least, seemed to read it and went back through the automatic door to his seat. She saw him throw the piece of paper on to the floor.

Damn.

Geri walked up the train to find a seat. She hadn't even started to prepare her submissions yet. After ten minutes or so, the train slowed down and the intercom told them they were at Manningtree.

She left the train and crossed under the track through a damp pedestrian tunnel. It was still light and she could see fields behind the station. Then she was aware of footsteps behind her as she came up the steps. She heard Dr Vane's voice.

'Can I ask one thing?'

'Please do.'

'What did the Judge mean when he said something about wasted costs?'

Geri took a breath as she got to the top of the steps and turned towards him.

'Your lawyers think I'm wasting everyone's time in this case. So, if I lose, the Judge may well order me to pay everyone's costs.'

He looked shocked.

'How much will that be?'

'With Hodder, the bill will be over a hundred thousand.'

'Jesus!'

'My insurance will pay some, but there's a ten thousand pound excess. And I might get struck off if I've acted improperly in bringing the case.'

'And were you saying that you won't get paid if you lose?'

'In a word, yes.'

At least he looked guilty.

'Well, I'm sorry about that. But it doesn't change anything.'

'No, well, there it is.'

Geri hoped her contempt for him was clear. A train was coming into the station. Liverpool Street, said the announcer. She wasn't going to talk him round.

'If you don't mind...'

'You're going back again?'

'Unless you've got any other ideas?'

He looked so surprised she wanted to laugh. The train rolled in and she jumped on. He didn't wait. She'd rather hoped he might have jumped on after her and pursued her back to London in a crazy reversal of what she'd done. She sat for a few moments. The train, though, was almost empty. It would have taken only minutes for him to find her. He was going to stick to his guns.

She found her notebook and tried to prepare some submissions, but whatever she wrote looked trite and obvious. She was in big trouble. She could explain herself only by reference to what was in Dr Vane's head. That information, she now knew, was inaccessible to her.

Chapter Twenty-Six

Geri sat back in her seat and thought through the options. She would lose. There would be a costs order against her. Her partners would disown her, especially as they hadn't wanted her to do the work in the first place. They might even say she was doing the case without the authority of the firm and that the insurance didn't cover it. Then God knew what would happen. She'd have to pay it herself. Sell the house – if the bank hadn't taken it first. David Vane would probably complain to Hodder about her approach and she would be reported for witness intimidation.

So much for the golden touch, she thought to herself.

She climbed off the train at Liverpool Street and caught the tube home. By the time she was back, she was completely exhausted. It was nearly 9 and she just wanted to go to bed.

Joanna was in the kitchen. Rory was in his pyjamas, watching the TV. Dermot had arranged to stay at the Oxford and Cambridge club.

Joanna had kept a meal warm for Geri. She ladled out the last of the casserole from the pot and added a few new potatoes.

'I take it things aren't looking good?'

Geri took her through the train ride, ending with the plea to David Vane.

'Pity,' said Joanna, 'I really had him down as

someone who might spring some surprises in his evidence.'

'He's not going to get the chance.'

Joanna sat down rather heavily on a chair. She looked almost as tired as Geri.

'Did they say anything more about the costs against you?'

Geri didn't want to upset Joanna. There was no point in telling her.

'Not really. They'll decide that point at the same time as the judgment is given.'

Joanna looked at her quizzically.

'Look, I feel awful about this. If you are made to pay – I'm going to repay you somehow.' The older woman's eyes were damp.

'I've been so grateful to you for taking this on. You have made a fuss – Tom would have been so proud. But if you end up having to pay for it, well, that's just not right. Especially when it's all a cover up by that bloody Ministry.'

'Joanna, that's kind, but it's me that's taken the decisions. My insurance will pay. There's no point in worrying.'

Geri looked at the clock.

'It's getting on. I'd better get ready for to-morrow.'

'Yes. If you want to do some work, I'll sort out the washing up.'

'Thanks, Joanna.'

Geri felt a bit better after a meal. She'd not noticed how hungry she was. Even then, thoughts about condemned solicitors and hearty meals lurked uncomfortably in her mind.

She sketched out some submissions in response

to Hodder. She decided to concentrate on his failure to call David Vane. She couldn't say what she suspected, but she could focus on the fear point – what were the Ministry doing apparently abandoning a witness? It was a reasonable point, but the Judge would probably tell her they didn't need one as she hadn't proved her case. Game, set and match.

Damn Hodder and his bloody trap. He'd had to spring it because there was something wrong with his case. He was obviously frightened of Dr Vane's evidence. But he was going to succeed.

She sat up until midnight. Joanna and Rory had long since turned in. Wearily, Geri climbed the stairs to her room, wondering what Simon would do at a moment like this. He wouldn't have got himself into such a mess, was the obvious answer.

Sleep took a long time to come. Eventually, Geri drifted off into a dream where the costs order had been made and she couldn't pay because the bank had taken the house. So they had thrown her into prison and there was this terrible banging, which just went on and on.

She sat up in bed. The banging didn't stop. Someone was at the door. Some nutter probably. She tiptoed into Rory's room and looked out of his window. She could see a shape outside the door. One person.

She hurried downstairs, picking up her dressing gown from the bathroom en route. Carefully, leaving the security chain on, she opened the door.

It was David Vane.

She loosened the chain and opened the door.

He was grinning like an extremely daft cat. She couldn't believe it. Had to blink several times. 'Good, I got the right house – I'd chucked away that bit of paper. At least the memory's not playing me up.'

'Come in.'

She shut the door behind him, conscious that she hadn't pulled her dressing gown tight. As a result, her lace nightie was looking all too transparent. Quickly, Geri covered herself up.

'Sorry to wake you, but I've been doing some thinking.'

She led him into the kitchen and put the kettle on. He sat at the table.

'I got home and had a look at the newspaper. There's some rumour that that shit Moncrieff wants out of Agriculture. He's walking away from it.'

She brought the coffee over and sat down.

'From what, exactly?'

David looked at her and smiled gently.

'You've rumbled me. I did look at many more firms, and found perinycin being used.'

Geri was startled.

'But why...'

'I wrote a report, setting out the problem and recommending the solution.'

'Which was?'

'Large-scale testing – every single chicken farm in the country. One infected chicken to mean slaughter of all stock on the farm and restriction of movement of humans and animals from the infected area.'

Geri sucked her cheeks in.

'Phew!'

'Yes. Well, I'd just done the report and then your claim came along. Moncrieff made it clear we couldn't do anything while there was litigation. If I redated the report, then we could put it into action after you'd gone off the scene.'

'But I didn't.'

'So I'd said I had no evidence, and was stuck with it. Then I had to write an edited report, missing out the affected farms.'

'So what about your plan?'

'Moncrieff was obviously just using this case as an excuse. He wanted out so it didn't blemish his career. And he needed time – just a few months. What a bastard!'

Geri paused. There was a sound from the stairs, and Rory padded into the kitchen.

'Mum? What's going on?'

'Rory – this man is Dr Vane. He's in the case and he's come to tell me about some things I didn't know.'

'Oh, fine,' said Rory, as though it happened every day of the week.

'Will you give evidence for us?' asked Geri.

David Vane looked at her.

'Yes. If it's not too late.'

'I need a statement. We'll need to type something out now, produce it to the Court.'

'I'll start up the PC, Mum. You can borrow that.'

'Good idea. Do you want to crash out in my bed, Rory?'

He looked reluctant.

'I'll never sleep. And you're useless at typing.

Why don't you let me do it for you?'

She smiled reluctantly.

'OK – but we'll have to be as quick as we can.'

They went up to Rory's room and he started up the PC.

Joanna, hearing the noise, appeared on the landing.

'I thought I heard something ... good Lord!' she exclaimed as she saw David.

'No, only me.' He grinned.

'Right, let's begin the statement. Can we start with your research?'

He started to talk and Rory started to type. Joanna sat listening, astonishment all over her face. They had done a couple of pages when there was a knock at the door.

'This is getting ridiculous,' said Geri.

She opened it to be confronted by two police officers.

'Mrs Geri Lander?'

'Yes.'

'Dr Vane with you, is he?'

'Well...'

The officers were already past her. She followed them up the stairs.

They went into Rory's room. David was sitting beside the PC.

'Dr Vane?'

'Yes.'

'You are being arrested under the Official Secrets Act.'

Geri was quick to speak.

'What the hell do you think...'

'We have reason to believe that a breach of the

Act has occurred, madam.'

He went through David's rights.

'Stand up, please.'

David was amazed. He did as ordered. Handcuffs were placed around his wrists.

'This is ridiculous,' protested Geri.

'No, madam. This man has been arrested. We'll have a print out, please, of what's on that machine.'

'No, you bloody well won't!'

'Then in that case we'll have to do it ourselves.'

He moved towards the machine and pressed the P button. The sheet obediently came out, with the half-finished statement on it.

'Now, we'll be taking you with us,' the officer told David.

They took him down the stairs. Outside, there was a police car, siren and flash thankfully off.

'David – I'll tell the Court, get you out. I'm sorry this...'

'Not now, madam.'

He was bundled into the car.

On the other side of London, Callum Moncrieff was also awake. He spoke rapidly into the phone. Thank God he had arranged the surveillance of that bloody woman's house and office.

There had been a clear breach of the Act. They were to interview the man, charge him and refuse police bail. Then he made another phone call to Geoffrey. The Public Interest Immunity Certificate was to be ready by 9 a.m. that morning for signature. And he wanted to see Hodder at 7 a.m.

Chapter Twenty-Seven

Geri was at the High Court by 10. She hadn't slept since David Vane had appeared on her doorstep. She looked terrible. She hadn't had a chance to wash her hair, which had become greasy overnight. There were bags appearing below her eyes.

Dermot was waiting outside the Courtroom. Geri's heart went out to him. After the grilling yesterday, he must have wanted to stay away. She drew him to one side.

'Watch and see what happens – no time to tell you now, but something rather interesting happened in the night!'

Hodder was late into Court. She went to tell him the nature of her application.

'Just make it,' he hissed.

It seemed that he had not had a very peaceful night either. He was rapidly reading some faxed sheets of paper which a clerk had brought to him.

Geri knew what she had to do. As the Judge was brought in, she rose to her feet. He was expecting her to make submissions about the case.

'Mrs Lander.'

'My Lord, since last night there have been certain developments.'

'I see.'

'My Lord, I was contacted last night by Dr Vane, who carried out the research on behalf of the Defendants. Your Lordship may recall that the defendants had decided not to call Dr Vane?'

'Yes.'

'Dr Vane has indicated to me that the account of his research set out in the report is not accurate and that he wishes to give evidence for us.'

Right at the back of the public gallery, Grimwood felt his blood run cold.

Hodder was on his feet in an instant.

'My Lord, I must protest. I was contacted earlier this morning to be told that Dr Vane had been arrested under the Official Secrets Act. It seems that he was found in Mrs Lander's bedroom with her in the early hours of this morning. I would have to protest in the strongest possible terms about Mrs Lander's continuing to act in the circumstances.'

Even Dermot looked shocked. Geri blushed deepest red. There was a sharp prod in the back. It was Joanna.

'Call me. I was there.'

'My Lord, I resent most strongly the imputations cast by my learned friend.'

The prodding continued.

'I will call Mrs Pascoe.'

Bemused, the Judge sat back and allowed Joanna to be sworn in.

'I was there last night.'

She was at her outraged best, her matronly bosom clearly heaving under its Jacques Vert blouse.

'And what that – that man – says is quite wrong. Dr Vane turned up to say that there had been a cover up at the Ministry and he no longer felt he could go along with it. Mrs Lander and myself were trying to prepare a statement in her son's bedroom when the police arrived.'

'Her son's room?' asked the Judge, clearly worried where all this was going.

'Yes, he has a computer, word processing thing. We were typing out the statement. It is absolutely ridiculous to suggest that there was any funny business going on.'

Joanna stared directly at Hodder. She wants a good argument with him, thought Geri. The older woman looked rather disappointed when Hodder refused to cross-examine her. He simply confined himself to the observation that Dr Vane had put himself in an impossible position and could hardly be regarded as a reliable witness.

The Judge looked down at Geri.

'So what is it you seek, Mrs Lander?'

Geri was ready.

'Two things, My Lord. First, an adjournment until tomorrow to allow me to take a statement. Second...'

'Bail for your new witness, presumably,' said the Judge.

'Yes.'

'Granted. But I will review the position tomorrow at the end of his evidence. I have to say, Mrs Lander, I am concerned at this development. He'd better have a good explanation for his conduct.'

'Yes, My Lord. I'm afraid that I have no idea which police station he is in.'

'Can you assist, Mr Hodder?'

He looked disappointed. They could have wasted several hours of Geri's time by making her ring round every station.

'Tottenham Court Road, My Lord.'

The Court adjourned and Geri waited for the bail certificate. She caught the tube to Tottenham Court Road where the prisoner was waiting for her.

'My heroine,' he grinned as he was brought out.

On the way back, he settled back into his seat.

'I must say, it's nice to be free again. And just in case I get arrested again, I've got to tell you something now. You may have rumbled me on the research results, but you've no idea of the rest.'

He spent the journey explaining his discovery to her.

Grimwood thanked his lucky stars that he had come along for the second day. It just showed, you had to be ready.

He'd formulated his plan of action the previous lunchtime as he sat in the entrance hall. The only change he needed to make to it was that now there were going to be two deaths rather than one.

He'd really thought that such drastic action would be unnecessary. But now it was, and that was all there was to it. It was a simple choice – either he was ruined, with an unsaleable pile of antibiotics on which he'd spent his life savings, or he was going to make a fortune and a new life for himself.

He couldn't help feeling the old surge of

excitement once again. Charlie's death had been straightforward. This little campaign had needed planning and he could only carry it off by using his skills to their limit. He was confident enough. The element of surprise was so often effective.

He was quietly confident. Just two people stood between him and his goal.

Tomorrow they would both be dead.

'Professor Lebrun, I'm delighted to meet you.'

Dermot and David shook hands over Geri's kitchen table. Together with her, Joanna and Rory, they shared a quick sandwich and retired to Rory's room. Geri got the PC working, found the file (stored by Rory under the name 'pigs' – obviously saved after David had gone) and typed while David dictated the rest of his statement. With a small smile, he signed and dated it.

'I'd better disappear, now, in the light of what that shit Hodder was trying to imply,' said David.

Geri grinned in agreement.

'Don't forget to bring a copy of your original report tomorrow, will you?'

'OK – perhaps if we can meet up outside so we can go in together?'

'Sure – on the steps outside at 9.30.'

He was away, striding quickly down the street.

Chapter Twenty-Eight

Geri had retired to bed, exhausted, at 8 o'clock. By the morning she was feeling on top of the world. Dermot had gone back to the club after a shared meal in the company of Rory and Joanna.

The four adults met up, as planned, at the steps to the Court at 9.30. David Vane was waiting, looking nervous but grimly determined.

'I've run off a copy of the original report – it was on my PC at home. I'll get it out of the case when we get into the building.'

'Thanks, David.'

Geri smiled at him. She'd asked for a copy yesterday and he'd agreed. She felt a stab of sympathy for him. His career would probably be ruined because of this. She hoped she'd have had the guts to do what he had done if the tables were turned.

Together, they turned towards the main doors and went through. There was the inevitable queue as people waited to go through the security screen. Geri, Dermot and David opted for the right-hand queue and the three of them placed their briefcases on the rollers so that they could go through the X-ray machine. Joanna had for some reason charged on ahead, and was already through on the other side.

The queue was moving slowly and a man stood behind David. He was a little too close, and Geri saw David inch forward, away from him. Just an everyday incident, one that happened a million times a day in a crowded city. She turned her head towards the security guard.

Everything seemed to happen in slow motion after that. The guard looked up and behind her, shock on his face. Then she felt herself pushed forward violently, so hard that she fell, her head striking the edge of the scanning machine that she had been going to walk through. She felt an enormous weight fall on top of her, and heard Dermot shout.

Dazed, she realised that David Vane was lying on top of her, his bulk holding her down. She could feel something warm trickling over her neck. Then she heard a scream from Joanna.

They lifted him from her then. She moved a hand across her neck and looked at it. Blood.

Geri screamed. At that moment, Dermot came running back into the entrance, and pulled her to him.

'Geri, for God's sake, are you OK? I tried to catch him, but he lost me in the crowd.'

Then he saw David Vane's body on the floor. Blood was seeping through the back of his jacket, leaving a dark stain around his shoulder. A security guard was kneeling beside him, while another was speaking urgently into a phone.

Geri knelt down beside David. She was trembling so hard that she felt she was going to faint. 'Is there a pulse?' she asked, feeling for his wrist. Damn, she couldn't quite grab it. She had no control over her hands. Finally, she had her thumb over his pulse.

She could feel something but it was irregular, stopping for long periods. She looked at Dermot. He was with the security guard, trying to stem the flow of blood. He looked towards her.

'I saw it all. The man behind him just came in. I saw a knife – really thin. He must have had it up his sleeve. He pushed it into David's back, and he went down.'

Geri gasped.

'Then he went for you. You were in front, he could barely reach you. Your back was turned and...'

'Was it you who pushed me?'

'Yes.'

Geri hesitated. Then she burst into tears.

'You've just saved my life, then.'

She felt her legs collapse from under her for the second time that day. Suddenly she was aware of strong arms around her. She wept into Dermot's broad chest, her body shaking convulsively. He held her tight, whispering words into her ear. They were gentle words, soft and soothing, and she clung to him, never wanting to let go.

Around them, ambulancemen suddenly swarmed, bending down to David Vane, setting up drips, searching for pulses and gently moving him on to a stretcher.

They were ushered into a first aid room where a matronly lady whistled up some strong tea. Someone brought the three briefcases in. They'd gone through the X-ray machine and had been sitting unclaimed at the other end. All the time, Dermot refused to let go of Geri's hand. She didn't want him to. It was a rock in a world that had suddenly gone completely mad.

Suddenly, she stood up.

'The Court!'

Dermot spoke soothingly.

'Bugger the case, Geri. No one will expect it to go on today, not after what's happened.'

'But you don't understand – if it was the bloody government getting at David ... it's fucking outrageous!'

She tore her hand away and strode off towards the Court.

As she entered, Hodder and his coterie were standing in a small group, shock registering on their faces.

'Mrs Lander, are you all right? We've heard the most awful things about what went on earlier...'

Hodder actually looked worried. She was about to respond when the Judge's clerk came into the Court.

'His Lordship has been told what has happened. He's asked if Mrs Lander and Mr Hodder could go through into his private Chambers.'

They followed the clerk through the doors and into a world of deep carpets and ancient-looking oil paintings. A door had been left ajar and the clerk showed them in.

Mr Justice Sutton-Jones was seated at a desk.

'Mrs Lander, I heard that you had been involved. I must say it's beyond the call of duty to come up to Court. You may well need medical attention.'

Geri smiled wanly.

'That's OK, My Lord. I wasn't hurt.'

Sutton-Jones looked at her.

'Terrible shock for all of us. I've just been talking to the security guard. You may owe your life to Professor Lebrun.'

'Yes, I think I do.'

'Now, I think the best way forward would be to leave things for today, don't you? You can't be expected to appear after what you've been through?'

The phone on the Judge's desk rang shrilly. Everyone jumped, including Sutton-Jones.

He listened to the voice, and said, 'I see.' Gently, he replaced the phone.

'Mrs Lander, I'm very sorry. Dr Vane died on his way to hospital.'

There was utter silence in the room. Hodder's face was white and he was looking at the floor. Geri spoke. She tried to sound firm, but her voice was too loud.

'I want to go on. Now.'

'But Mrs Lander, no one will mind...'

'I've got to finish this. Sooner rather than later, My Lord.'

Sutton-Jones smiled.

'Mrs Lander, may I say that I'm deeply impressed with your actions this morning.'

'Thank you, My Lord. But I really do want to go on.'

'Mr Hodder?'

'If Mrs Lander can go on, it ill behoves me to stand in her way. But I will need a few minutes, My Lord, there is a matter which I need to discuss before we continue.'

'Very well then.'

Geri coughed.

'I have a statement from Dr Vane. In the circumstances, I'll be relying upon it.'

'Of course, Mrs Lander. I see it's signed and dated, so I take it there'll be no objection from Mr Hodder?'

He looked uneasy.

'As I said, I do need to discuss matters, My Lord.'

'Very well.'

Moncrieff cursed as Hodder gave him the news over the phone.

'Shit! Why the hell did someone have to do that?'

'No idea. But it leaves us in a somewhat delicate position...'

'Well, we have to fight on. It's still rubbish, the whole claim.'

'Minister, I'm thinking of the certificate.'

'What about it? You recommended it and I signed it. Dr Vane's evidence will be blocked on the grounds of public interest immunity.'

'Minister, given what's happened, it may not look too good.'

'Bugger that!'

'Minister, I really think I ought to read the statement to you.'

He read it from start to finish. It took ten minutes. At the end, there was silence.

Hodder spoke first.

'You see, Minister, if there is an attempt to stop this statement being used, it will surface somehow. Mrs Lander has it in her possession and I'm sure she will use it, even if we get our PII certificate.'

'But it sinks us.'

'Yes, that could be said to be true.'

'So you're saying we just roll over and die on this?'

'I could make some observations against it and still oppose the claim.'

'Well, you'd better bloody well do it, then.'

Dermot had followed Geri, and waited in the Courtroom while she went through to see the Judge. He had grabbed the three briefcases and taken them with him.

As he waited, he looked at David Vane's case. It was standard Ministry issue, unlocked. Dermot wondered who he should take it to. It must belong to someone now but it didn't feel right to give it to the Ministry.

The original report. Geri had said Vane was bringing it.

The rest of the Ministry lawyers were huddled on the other side of the Courtroom. Dermot carefully picked up Vane's briefcase and carried it out into the gloom. He took a seat just down the corridor outside the Courtroom.

Feeling extremely uncomfortable, he opened the case and looked inside. It was empty, save for some papers. He took them out. There it was, the final, vital piece in their jigsaw of evidence.

'Report into emergence of Salmonella TO2 in British chicken farms.'

Dermot scanned it.

The Court door opened, and Geri came out.

'Geri,' he called down the corridor, 'I think you may need this.'

Chapter Twenty-Nine

'My Lord, I'm grateful for the adjournment. Your Lordship will be aware of the incidents this morning. I have a statement from Dr Vane which complies with the provisions of the Civil Evidence Act.'

Geri handed the original up to the Judge, and gave a copy to Hodder. With a glance to the press who immediately looked ready to start scribbling, she started to read. She went through it slowly and loudly, her voice reverberating off the Victorian panels.

The case had started with a voice from the grave. And it was ending with one.

David Vane's statement started off with his new discovery: Salmonella TO2, a new organism, spawned by the over-use of antibiotics. It had grown with a resistance to perinycin. It had probably been around for some time, but kept in check by the multitude of other bugs inhabiting any piece of flesh. But they had been wiped out by constant use of perinycin. Salmonella TO2, with its resistance, had had all the space it wanted to multiply and spread. And, lethally, it could cross the species barrier. Anyone who ate infected meat was at risk from the superbug.

The victims had taken infected meat into their bodies and the superbug had taken over the new host. There was a recognised pattern of intestinal problems and internal haemorrhaging. The next stage saw the infection of the blood, and the steady spread of the superbug to the main organs of the body. If the patient was lucky, the heart went first and they died quickly. If he was not, the other organs – liver, kidneys, pancreas – failed one by one and the victim died a slow, painful death.

They'd known there was a problem long before he discovered Salmonella TO2. But they'd acted too late.

A notification system had been put in place and regular updates provided to the Minister of Agriculture, Mr Callum Moncrieff. David Vane had seen the Minister on an almost daily basis and had recommended urgent action including a mass slaughter of all chickens together with a compensation scheme.

He detailed his researches – all those farm visits, and finding perinycin on so many. Urgent action was desperately needed to prevent catastrophe.

Geri paused at that stage to allow the press sitting at the back of the Court to catch up. As she looked at the statement in her hand, the words seemed to recede a little and merge into each other. Then they spun and formed themselves into an elegant vortex.

She put the statement down and pinched her hand hard. Everything came back into focus. Her head was starting to throb. Pretending to push her hair out of her eyes, she felt her brow and was alarmed to feel a large bump. The Judge was still writing.

Geri carried on reading, her voice a little unsteady. Dr Vane was dealing with his reports now. The suggestion from Mr Moncrieff that he redate the first report and his decision to go along with it. Then Moncrieff's asking him to produce a fraudulent report.

At that, there was an audible gasp from behind. Geri grinned to herself. This was going to end a promising Ministerial career. Served him bloody well right! She reached up to her forehead. She couldn't be sure, but the lump seemed bigger.

Geri turned back to the statement, reading as quickly as she could now. Everyone was struggling to keep up. David Vane dealt with the summer, the extra deaths.

He then set out what he knew about Tom Pascoe. He had received notification. This was definitely a superbug death, and the most likely explanation was that he had eaten infected meat. If they'd acted when the problem was first recognised, Tom would be alive today.

And then, in the last section, he produced the forecasts for the disease spread. These had been prepared with the aid of epidemiological research. The worst case scenario, if the disease got a real grip, was quite terrifying. Once enough people caught the superbug, cross-infections would start up as those infected passed the disease on to those closest to them. Once that started to happen, the medical services would be unable to cope.

By that stage the death toll would climb rapidly. Civil unrest would follow. People would be terrified of their friends, family and neighbours.

They would try to establish disease-free areas, barring entry to strangers, just like they had in the 'flu epidemic of the 1920s. People who developed symptoms would be left to die. The hospitals would be full up; only a few brave souls would dare to nurse them.

Cemeteries and crematoriums would be overwhelmed. A state of emergency would have to be declared and bodies burned in mass incinerators. And the bug would spread, of course. It would make rapid progress through the world, leaving a wake of death and chaos.

There would be simply nothing anyone could do. There would be a frantic effort to find a new drug, of course, one that would knock out the superbug. And genetic engineering techniques would be pushed to their limit in a desperate attempt to gain control. But if these didn't work, then the superbug would be left to run its course. It would carry on killing until it ran out of new hosts.

The Minister had been prepared to run the risk of all of this by delaying the implementation plan.

'And this, My Lord, is a copy of the original report prepared by Dr Vane. Before he was encouraged to falsify it. It's just been found in his briefcase. Since the original appears to have been in the possession of the Defendant, I don't think they can object to our producing it. Your Lordship might like to compare it with the report produced for these proceedings.'

The original, taken from Vane's briefcase, was handed up to the Judge. He read it through carefully, taking his pen to highlight certain passages.

'Mrs Lander, in one of the schedules of the changed report, some of the numbering appears out of synch.'

'My Lord, yes. I had intended to ask more about that in cross-examination.'

His Lordship frowned.

'And, of course, the fact that Dr Vane did not give evidence prevented you from adopting that approach.'

'Yes, My Lord.'

He glared at Hodder. So much for clever tactics, thought the QC.

There was silence.

'And that, My Lord, completes my case.'

With relief, Geri sat down. The dizziness had returned and she struggled to focus her eyes.

The Judge smiled thinly.

'Mr Hodder, if you wish, you can address me again. Mrs Lander, I don't need to hear from you.'

The words that every advocate yearns to hear. It means, you've won. The Judge doesn't need to hear your argument because he agrees with it totally. Thank God, she muttered to herself.

Hodder was clearly having a bad day. He struggled to his feet and made a few submissions about being ambushed by the unfortunate circumstances. His Lordship had to bear in mind that the witness couldn't be cross-examined and attach little weight to the statement. Sutton-Jones heard him politely and took no notes.

It was 3 o'clock. He would give his judgment

now, he said.

Then he blasted into the actions of Callum Moncrieff. Duplicitous, improper. Applying pressure to expert civil servants. Failing in his duties. The condemnations flowed from the Judge. The fact that he had such a mild manner made it even more damning.

Half an hour later, it was all over.

Joanna Pascoe had won her case. Damages would be assessed at a later date but the Ministry was one hundred percent liable. The government had caused the death of her husband. Dr Vane was to be applauded for having the courage to admit his wrongdoing. His death was an appalling tragedy.

Geri turned round in her seat.

Joanna was grinning from ear to ear.

'Told you it would be easy!' she whispered.

'Now, Mrs Lander, I take it that you're applying for costs...'

The Judge was looking at her. Of course, now they'd won, the Ministry would have to pay for both sides. She got to her feet to make the formal application.

Damn, that dizziness again. Her head felt as though an arrow had pierced the skin, just above the temple.

Geri lost her balance and swayed. Oh my God, she thought, how embarrassing. And then everything went very black indeed.

Chapter Thirty

And then, it was all rather white. Geri opened her eyes, and then shut them again as pain shot through her head. She lay for a moment, trying to gather her wits about her. She was lying down in a bed. There was an antiseptic smell.

Therefore, she thought to herself, I am in hospital.

'Mrs Lander?'

It was an unfamiliar voice, but gentle and rather pleasant.

This time, she opened her eyes gingerly. No stab of pain now.

A nurse was bending over her bed, looking at her. She smiled at Geri.

'I thought you were waking up. How do you feel?'

'Fine. Well, bit of a headache...'

'I'm not surprised. They brought you in yesterday with the most enormous bump on your forehead. Got us all quite worried about a sub-dural, it did. But you've had all the tests and things look fine, thank goodness.'

'Did you say yesterday?'

'Yes. You came in at about four-thirty. You'd been in Court and collapsed. Do you remember?'

It all seemed rather fuzzy, but she could remember something. She'd won ... yes, she'd definitely won.

'What time is it now?'

'It's just after six in the evening.'

Geri tried to sit up but the pain in her temple returned.

'You mean, I've been out for over a day and a night?'

'Certainly have. And I've got three people outside who have sat there waiting. Couldn't get rid of them, even through the night.'

'Who?'

'Your son, a lady called Joanna. And a man, says he's not your husband or partner but he was the one who pushed you over. He's been confessing to things all night long so far as I can understand but it turns out that he saved your life.'

'Can they come in?' smiled Geri.

The door opened and three very tired-looking individuals came into the room. Joanna and Dermot stayed back for a moment while Rory rushed over to Geri.

'Mum – you're OK. We've been so worried.'

'I'm just fine, but I've no idea what happened.'

Dermot and Joanna took up places to either side of the bed.

Joanna started.

'You had just won, and the Judge said something about costs. And then you keeled over.'

'Oh my God, how embarrassing.'

'Sutton-Jones just rang a buzzer, said he was awarding you costs. Then it all went a bit crazy. You came here in an ambulance. They scanned you – thought you might have a haemorrhage, but then decided you had a nasty bruise but should be OK.'

'We've been so worried, Geri.'

It was Dermot. He looked utterly exhausted. He felt for her hand on the blanket. Geri squeezed it.

'Mum, Jo and I said we'd get some flowers when you came round – and I need something to eat. We'll be back in a moment.'

Rory and Joanna left the room.

'I thought I'd killed you when they started talking about head injuries. I really did. I started telling them it was all my fault.'

Geri laughed, then stopped as the pain came back.

'I had no idea what they must have been thinking – luckily Joanna told them what had happened at Court. Then they saw the papers this morning.'

'We're in the papers?'

'Yes, I'll be keeping them. It all carried on happening after you conked out. Moncrieff resigned, a new man appointed saying that he'll start David's plan today. And they arrested someone at the airport – they think it's the man who got David. Turns out that he's a grain merchant. It wouldn't surprise me if he's been selling a bit of perinycin on the side.'

'Good grief,' said Geri.

'I'm just glad you're OK.'

'How long have I got to spend here?'

'A few days, until you're up and moving. And then you can go home if you're going to be properly looked after.'

He looked at her closely.

'In fact, I was going to volunteer for that job myself.'

He was still holding her hand, smiling down at her.

Geri grinned back.

'But you can't – you've got to work...'

'It's only for a week or so. I can clear it for a while. And, for God's sake, shut up about work for once.'

She smiled again.

'Thanks, Dermot.'

He bent down and whispered in her ear.

'But don't go thinking my intentions are totally honourable.'

She really couldn't resist it any longer. Despite herself, the fact that she was in hospital and had a head which felt like grizzly bears were rampaging around inside it, she kissed him gently on the cheek.

'I don't want honourable intentions any more.'

He blushed, and then recovered himself.

'Thank God for that.'

Gently, Geri eased herself back on to the pillow, trying to keep her head steady as he continued. 'But seriously, Geri, I've been thinking a lot – too much really – about this and I've decided to say what I think.'

'Which is?'

'Which is that I'm completely, totally, utterly mad about you. When you keeled over in that Court, I just thought, well, you know...'

He looked at the floor before continuing.

'Anyhow, what it comes down to is this. I want to court you. I know it sounds ridiculously old-fashioned, but I'd like to start from the beginning. Take you out, buy you meals, generally look after you. And you can say I'm a total neanderthal and that women like you don't need to be pampered and you'd be absolutely right but that's just how I feel and it's only fair I say so.' He had been speaking like an express train, eyes still fixed on the floor. But there was a vulnerable tone in his voice which made Geri want to reach out to him.

My God, she thought, he's never spoken like this to anyone. I'd put money on it.

'Look at me, Dermot.'

He looked up slowly. His eyes were red, she saw.

'I would love to be courted by you. I don't care if it's old-fashioned, it sounds pretty good to me.'

A slow grin started around the edges of his mouth and gradually worked its way up his features until his entire face resembled a Cheshire cat on Prozac.

'Fantastic! Oh, you'll kill me for not mentioning this earlier, but Jo said to tell you there was a message on your ansaphone from Roger last night. Shaner's put in a bid for the firm immediately after the hearing. Winchell Robins did just the same and the pair of them are pushing the price up into the stratosphere.'

Geri breathed out gently.

'Looks like I may be able to take a bit of a break, then.'

'All the better for me to pamper you. But look, the nurse is going to do something dreadful to me – she said five minutes only and not to stress you out. And I'm sure you'd like to see Rory and Jo. I'll be back as soon as I'm allowed.'

Gently, he kissed her cheek.

'Here's to the future, Geri. I can't wait, you know.'

She nodded back and grinned as he moved towards the door.

'Nor me, Dermot.'

The publishers hope that this book has given you enjoyable reading. Large Print Books are especially designed to be as easy to see and hold as possible. If you wish a complete list of our books please ask at your local library or write directly to: